Before she moved to writing full-time, Pernille (pronounced Pernilla) Hughes studied Film & Literature at university. After graduating she went into advertising and later on to market Natural History films before working in Children's television, which meant living in actual Teletubbyland for a while! From 2011–2015, she was a regular contributor for the *Sunday Times* column 'Confessions of a Tourist'.

Pernille lives in Buckinghamshire and while the kids are at school she scoffs cake and writes stories in order to maintain a shred of sanity.

pernillehughes.com

twitter.com/pernillehughes
facebook.com/pernillehughesauthor
instagram.com/pernillehughes

TEN YEARS

PERNILLE HUGHES

One More Chapter
a division of HarperCollins*Publishers*
1 London Bridge Street
London SE1 9GF
www.harpercollins.co.uk

HarperCollins*Publishers*
1st Floor, Watermarque Building, Ringsend Road
Dublin 4, Ireland

This paperback edition 2022
1
First published in Great Britain
by HarperCollins*Publishers* 2022

A catalogue record of this book is available from the British Library

ISBN: 978-0-00-847842-1

Printed and bound in the UK using 100% Renewable Electricity
by CPI Group (UK) Ltd

To Lisa and Bjørn Knappe
for giving me my love of books
and
to Charlotte Ledger
for this one
xx

Prologue

Statistics said that people who met their life mate at university would do so on the middle day of the middle term in the middle year. As a statistician, Ally knew this was no mystical phenomenon. It was simply the median. You were as likely to meet The One – if you met them at all – on the first day of the first term or the last day of the last term. The median was just the middle of the range. So while meeting Charlie on the middle day of the middle term of the middle year struck her as a neat quirk, she didn't try to romanticise it. Statistics weren't historically good with romance.

Love at First Sight was also a theoretical myth. Love at First Sight really only became so if it lasted. Otherwise it was more Lust at First Sight which had petered out. Even so, meeting Charlie was a moment she couldn't explain, either by statistics or by science. It was more than an animal attraction. It was a consuming need to be with him and the deepest of connections. She'd researched high and low and could find no statistic for Love at First Sight, its One in Something chance. As a statistician, Ally wanted to acknowledge that what she and Charlie had was that One. There *always* had to be that One. There was that One in Something for so many things in life. And in this case, the statistic was in her favour.

The cancer that developed in her pancreas had a One in Thirteen survival rate.

Much as she wished for it, in this case, Ally wasn't The One.

2011

Ally had planned everything.

Even so, Charlie wished he wasn't there. At her end of the pew, Ally's best friend Becca looked like she wanted to run. Or vomit. Perhaps both. And given the choice, Charlie would have preferred to curl up foetus-style under the seat – though at six foot four and being broad-shouldered, the fit would have been snug. However, as everything looked so perfectly planned and beautifully executed, there was little or no room for bizarre behaviour.

It was all just as Ally had arranged it: the abundance of potted pink hydrangeas decorating St Raphael's Church that the guests would be offered to take home as a memento; the projected montage with happy photos of her gorgeous face and the "Ally's Faves" playlist. Her coffin was of simple pale wickerwork, with more hydrangea blooms laid lengthwise down the middle. The little Order of Service booklet placed in the pews had a delightful image of her on the front, the perfect reminder of her huge grin, freckled tawny skin and dark brown corkscrew curls when she'd still had them. It contained the least dreary hymns she'd been able to find plus Hanson's "MmmBop" to finish, because "If you can't laugh at the end, when can you?"

Looking behind him, Charlie had a quick scan of the church. His mother was sitting two rows behind and mouthed, "Are you all right?" She kept asking him that.

Of course he wasn't bloody all right. He'd lost the love of his life.

Next to her sat his best friend Ollie and Ollie's girlfriend, Shrinidhi. Shrin was already ugly crying and things hadn't even started. Two rows further back and on the other side of the aisle sat his dad, at a safe distance from his mother. He gave Charlie a brisk nod, which would be the sum total of his emotional support, no doubt. Sending weak smiles to other people he recognised, Charlie turned back, pleased with the numbers. Ally, who was the best person in the world, deserved the best of turnouts.

Ally's mum Valerie sat in the front pew between him and Ally's best friend, Becca. Tired and drawn, yet serene. She mustered small smiles and nods to the arriving mourners who came to offer their condolences with light touches to her shoulder. Becca was holding her hand, with her other placed protectively on top of both. Neither of them spoke. They knew each other so well, they didn't need to.

Charlie looked towards the coffin, the large lump he'd got on entering the church instantly re-forming in his throat. He reminded himself that it wasn't his fiancée in there, just a body – a beautiful body and one he'd hung onto for a long while after she'd gone – but now just a body, nonetheless.

He glanced back at Becca. She looked as wrecked as he felt inside, but he'd at least managed a hairbrush and an iron. They'd barely nodded a Hello to one another, then performed their customary begrudged greeting, where he'd said "White" and she'd responded with "Lister", and that was it. Surname terms was their norm. Despite both loving Ally, they weren't friends. They'd clashed from the start when they met at uni and Becca didn't subscribe to forgiving and forgetting. Today, thankfully, they had Valerie between them as a buffer. This would not be an appropriate venue for one of their spats. His gaze flicked instinctively towards the coffin – Ally would have rolled her eyes at the thought of them bickering here.

Valerie rose and went to speak to the vicar, leaving them alone in the pew. Becca's eyes followed Valerie as she passed the coffin on its bier at the top of the nave. That basket, bathed in the shaft of light from the tall glass windows, the dust motes dancing around it like dots of magic, held his future, his dreams, his everything. They were supposed to be getting married, travelling and having adventures he'd write about and one day starting a family. Now, he no longer had much idea of who he was, what he was supposed to do or how to even begin working it all out.

Somewhere in the back of his head, a desire to vanish was brewing. It had started germinating when the newspaper had asked when he was coming back to work. The compassion of Compassionate Leave had an end date, apparently. He'd thought then about his job and his ambitions, but without Ally to share things with, what was the point? How many times in these last two weeks had he just wanted to get on a plane and go, somewhere, *any*where, away from this life and the future that wasn't going to be?

Perhaps sensing his stare, Becca turned slowly to look at him, her jaw set. She didn't crack out a smile for him. Instead she gave him the bug eye and mouthed *What?* He looked away. She had to be feeling the same. She'd lost her best friend too. She'd been Ally's shadow since childhood and loved her as much as Charlie and Valerie. But she'd made it patently clear to him, over the five years he'd known her, that she didn't want his friendship or support. These last months with Ally had perhaps brought them closer together, but only if you considered the Grand Canyon to be narrow. After today there'd be no reason for them ever to speak to each other again. Their paths didn't cross professionally, seldom socially, and as a rare point of commonality between them, neither of them believed in sending Christmas cards. His gaze returned to the coffin. Ally had loved sending Christmas cards. She had them written and ready for posting on December 1st. She got a thrill from hers being the first card received. Yet another thing, of the million things, he'd miss about her.

The service began with the organ playing "Who Wants to Live Forever?" It had been one of Ally's favourites. It had made her cry when he'd taken her to see the Royal Philharmonic play Queen's greatest hits at the Royal Albert Hall. It took a couple of moments for him to notice the organist was playing out of key. Just the odd note here and there, but enough to jar. Becca must have heard it too, and gave voice to his own thoughts, as she breathed out a withering "Fuck sake." His bubble of laughter came from nowhere and without warning and he only just managed to keep it from escaping. He saw Becca's eye flick in his direction, and her lips purse together, not in disapproval, but in an effort to suppress her own laugh. Another bum note made her grip her side and clamp her hand over her mouth, which upped his amusement a notch and he was suddenly at risk of being indecorous. The following wrong note made her snort and he was just about to lose it completely when Valerie appeared at the end of the pew. He ducked his head and did his best to regain the solemnity.

Sneaking a glance at Becca, he saw her take a deep breath and suspected she was experiencing the same. She turned to look at him and he knew for sure they were both remembering what it was like to laugh. It had been a long while.

The vicar did his best to sound upbeat when thanking them all for coming and talking about Ally, but it was white noise to Charlie. He mouthed the words to the first verse of the hymn, not feeling he had it in him to sing. Apparently most of the congregation felt the same; the combined effort was on the weedy side of thin. After a truly pathetic chorus, he stepped up and engaged his vocal cords, simply to support Valerie, who was ploughing through the verses, keen to fulfil Ally's wishes, in spite of having the singing talent of deflating bagpipes.

Charlie felt a small nudge to his ribs. The church had fallen silent. With a start he understood it was time for his reading. He took his place at the lectern, sliding his fingertips over the piece of paper on it.

It was a poem. Not a long one but well known, though not particularly to him. He'd planned to practise it at home, but had never quite been able to. And now he really wished he had. He looked at the expectant faces in front of him and regretted having hidden from it. Becca was looking at him with a stony face. That wasn't helping either. Taking a long deep breath he started, but his voice came out clumsy. He increased his volume, but the timbre didn't sound right. He was simply reading the lines, not giving them meaning. Charlie tried to give himself more time, tried to think about the words, and therein lay his downfall. Suddenly his mind made the connections between the words and the coffin, the emotions and the moment, and he was filled with such an overwhelming bolt of distress that his mouth seemed to swell within and no words came. He felt the shift of discomfort in the room as people noticed, but it didn't make any difference. The words weren't coming, although the tears now did. Instinctively he wiped his nose on the back of his hand, trying to pull this together, to regain some composure and fulfil his hope of doing Ally proud. But not today. Today he was immobile, like those first days after she'd gone.

Fingertips took the paper he was now clutching. He heard someone draw a breath and the poem resume from where he'd left off, the reader doing him the kindness of not repeating his poor first efforts. The poem came to an end and he felt a hand on his arm, guiding him back to the front pew, where he sat dumbly, shocked in many ways: that he'd bombed so badly, that Becca had helped him out, that she'd sailed through it, that she'd been able to look past herself to see he needed it. Slowly, he turned his head to look at her, to give her a nod of thanks, but on the other side of Valerie, Becca sat in the exact same pose as before, resolutely facing forward, her perfectly straight nose tilted slightly upward, her posture sagging as if she was broken.

He didn't even attempt the next hymn. As it ended Becca stood and walked back to the lectern. She morphed as she walked, from the slumped figure in the pew to an upright being, head held high, a steely defiant look on her face as she turned to face the congregation.

She extracted a couple of sheets of paper from her pocket, plucking away a scrunched tissue which had got stuck to them. She scanned the words, as if trying to work out where to start, and his nervousness grew. Would she break, like he did?

"Allyson Rose Walker," Becca started, her voice holding its own and repeating its journey of the room, "…"

Nothing followed. Just silence. She looked at the congregation and then back at her pages. "Bollocks," she said to herself, but the acoustics carried it. She folded the papers back up and shoved them roughly into her pocket.

"I'm supposed to stand up here and tell you all what a good person Ally Walker was." She appeared truly appalled by the task. "Well, I'm not going to do that." Charlie's eyes narrowed. "She wasn't good." He felt his fingers curl into two fists. "Ally Walker was the Best." The entire congregation, and probably St Raphael himself, breathed a collective sigh of relief. Becca stepped to the side of the lectern, but left one hand on it, as if it was keeping her grounded or perhaps tethered. "Ally Walker was my best friend and the very best of friends. I wrote a eulogy listing all of her qualities and there were many, but the bottom line is, she was the very best of people. The world is poorer for having lost her, not just for the potential she isn't able to fulfil and the benefit we all would have had of it, but also for the exemplary kindness and loyalty she exuded.

"I always thought it was in wedding speeches that people said someone was the best thing to ever happen to them, but here we are. Ally was the best thing to ever happen to me. No one else will ever come close. My friend, my rock, my cheerleader. She kicked my arse when I needed it and when I needed love she gave it in spades, freely and enthusiastically, because she saw me in a way no one ever could or ever will.

"We met when we were ten. She was new and nerdy, I was the class bully, hurting others before they could hurt me." Becca spoke factually and without remorse. "By all definitions she should have been easy prey; she was scrawny, had milk-bottle lensed glasses and knew no one. But before I could make my move, she made hers. Walker and White, we were placed together at the back of the room and there she made me her friend. I really didn't have much choice about it, which is Ally's way. She imposed her friendship on me before I really got a word in, and I quickly recognised its value and that I wouldn't be without it."

Glancing behind him, Charlie could see everyone was enthralled. This adoration and part confession from Becca was both heartwarming and heartbreaking.

"But now I *am* without it, and it takes my breath away every time I let myself come close to thinking about her. I feel like I've been widowed. I feel I've lost a limb. I've lost the person who saw the good in me, and I can't see how that will happen again. But we go on, because we must and because it's what she would have wanted, and even if it's with only half the joy it would have been with her here, that's what we'll do. And while I might hate life without her, I'll take solace in having known her. We are all fu—" she looked at Valerie and corrected herself, "*very* lucky for having known her."

She took a couple of steps towards the coffin and laid her hand flat on the top. Charlie saw her lips move, but now Becca didn't want the rest of them to hear. She dug something out of a pocket and laid it on the top. Small, bright red and knobbly, it looked like … it looked like a Haribo gummy bear. Then Becca's shoulders visibly sank and she returned to the pew. But she didn't sit. Instead, she bent to give Valerie a kiss on the cheek, before murmuring, "I'll be in the pub." And then she walked defiantly down the aisle.

There was a stunned silence, until the slam of the oak door jolted everyone from their stasis. The vicar hurried to bring things back to the Order of Service. Charlie dared a side glance at Valerie, to see whether she was upset, but her eyes were suddenly bright and she wore a small smile, pride almost. He didn't know what to think. Becca had been a tower of strength up there, angry but composed, and she'd spoken without prompts and straight from the heart. He was begrudgingly impressed, and just that bit more humiliated for his own effort.

Perhaps Valerie knew what he was thinking as she leaned into him and said, "You both did well, Charlie. No one here is in any doubt of the effect Ally had on people now. You made her mark for her."

Why, then, did he feel he'd let everyone down?

Charlie couldn't make a decision. He needed a drink, unlike he'd ever needed one before, but equally, saying farewell to Ally's coffin had almost sent him over the edge, so he also wanted to be somewhere far away from people. He didn't want to stand in the pub, receiving condolences, or trying to "celebrate" Ally with fond stories. He appreciated that wakes were supposed to be for good memories and moving people on, but frankly, he didn't want to move on. He wanted to wallow in his grief and be left alone. This was, by far, superseding the day his parents had told him they were getting divorced.

He stood, shoulders hanging, in front of the old Victorian building. It was the pub they'd spent many hours in, either with friends or just the two of them for a relaxed drink. Or not so relaxed if she'd invited Becca along, for what would always be more red wine than was wise.

He slid his hand into his pocket, his fingers seeking out a coin. It was an old habit he'd re-adopted recently; letting the coin make decisions for him. It made things easier; drowning out the noise, cutting the anxiety of choosing incorrectly. He extracted a ten-pence piece. Heads, he stayed; tails, he went home.

In a well-practised move, he flipped it off his thumb into the air, then snatched it back as it began its descent, to clench it in his fist. He didn't slam it onto the back of his other hand. That was for amateurs. It was a flourished move, honed to impress girls as a teen, and one that allowed him to keep one hand free.

"Won't you walk me in, Charlie?" Valerie asked, sliding her hand under his elbow, before he could unfurl his fingers. She carried one of the hydrangeas under her other arm. She looked up at him, with a gaze so open and kind, it was a done deal. He slid the coin back into his pocket. They had a mutual understanding. Neither wanted to go in, but both knew they had to. Charlie decided he'd see her in, find a spot in a corner and stay for just as long as he could get away with. He had a firm date with a large bottle of whisky at home.

Stepping in, they were met with light murmurs and some laughter, but not much. He quietly got Valerie a gin and tonic while enduring several squeezed shoulders and pats on the back. Nobody really knew what to say, because what was there to say? Ally *hadn't* had a good innings, she hadn't got to a ripe old age. He'd planned for her to have "a good life", but she hadn't got to have it, had she? He wanted to snarl at the platitudes, but they were only trying to be kind and cover their own discomfort.

Valerie had found some friends and so having placed her glass on the table, Charlie took his pint of pale ale and, seeking somewhere to hide, aimed for the far corner with its high-backed bench which made for a secluded nook. Unfortunately, having rounded it to the point of no return, he saw it was already taken. Becca, wedged uncomfortably into the corner like a spooked cat, looked up at him with a scowl. The crumbed plate in front of her told him she'd already hit the buffet.

"The carrot cake is good, but the Battenberg sucks." Ally had talked Charlie through making sure there was money from her account left behind the bar and the buffet being exclusively of cake. She'd always appreciated cake.

It was a dilemma. Not the cake thing, the sitting thing. Now he'd reached this point, turning around and walking away would appear very rude, and sitting down with her ranked up there with poking his own eyes out. But then again, that was perhaps the theme of the entire day. He considered the throng back in the open part of the bar and then the surly woman in front of him. Which was the lesser evil for the duration of this pint, after which he'd be gone? His fingers twitched to flip the coin for it.

"Whatcha gonna do, Lister? Stick or run?" Given the three glasses in front of her, two drained, he suspected she'd necked a wine the moment she'd walked in. He knew she'd be snarky. Everything said Run, but a glance back into the room garnered him another formal nod from his dad, and so he sat. He probably also had some gratitude to express, unenthusiastic about it as he might be. Being in debt to Becca did not sit well.

There was a long moment of silence, neither of them wanting to start the conversation, but eventually the awkwardness of not speaking outweighed their reluctance to interact. Becca relaxed from her braced stance, but the curve of her posture still made her look like a used black sweet wrapper, twisted and discarded.

"New suit?" she asked. It was, as it happened. Best suit he'd ever owned, decent dark fabric and a dark shirt to match.

"Ally picked it." She'd asked him not to bother with a black tie, because she liked that tuft of hair at his clavicle. It was a hot day, so the open collar was a blessing, but he wasn't feeling any less strangled. "Wanted everything covered. You know what she's like." He paused. "*Was*. Was like."

Becca nodded. She did know. She'd also know Ally had sorted it, ahead of the day, so he wouldn't have to worry about it in his grief.

"She completely failed to audition that organist, though, didn't she?" Becca said, her mouth pulling up slightly to the side.

His barked laugh was spontaneous and a relief, venting some of the pent-up feelings. Becca leaned her head back against the wood, allowed the laughter to rise, and some colour came back to her face. Only, the laughter didn't last, and as it dissipated the scowl returned, as if she'd just remembered where they were, why they were there and who she now found herself with. It wiped the smile off Charlie's face.

"That was summarily shit, wasn't it?" she said and

followed it with a sigh, like life was a series of disappointments.

His face hardened. "I think it was beautiful. I think it was just what she planned and what she wanted."

"You know what I meant," she snapped. He did. He'd just not been able to overcome the chance to make her look bad. Neither of them liked to miss an opportunity. It was their way, bringing the worst out in each other. Dropping his head, he shook it. He was better than this. He shouldn't take this out on her, she was hurting too.

"Granted, it just topped the list of bad moments in my life." He took a sip of the beer and then another longer one. Looking up, he saw she'd fixed him with a sneer.

"Cos so many bad things have happened to you." Becca rolled her eyes.

His jaw dropped. Not only was her timing shit to pick a fight, but who was she to judge whether he'd had tough times?

She crossed her arms. "Come on then, tell me about all the bad things." Charlie was aware that on paper she had a point: he'd walked easily into his journalism job while Becca was still trying to make it as an actor; he'd inherited the flat he lived in with Ally, while Becca ... well, Becca appeared to have a more nomadic existence. He decided to ignore her.

But she wouldn't let it lie. "What's been so bad, other than Mummy and Daddy deciding being apart was better for you?"

"The divorce was still shit," he said, through gritted teeth.

"Sure," she nodded and took a large mouthful of the wine, "must have been much harder having two parents fighting over you than fighting *not* to have you. Tragic."

"Shut up, Becca," he growled. "Only you could make

17

divorce a competition. I'm sure it was awful for both of us." She'd always been bitter about her childhood, but this, right now, was just plain shitty. He took a deep steadying breath. "Let's just sit here quietly and remember Ally, and how she preferred us to get along, and then when I've finished this pint I'll be going. I only came over to be nice. I didn't think you should be alone today, and I thought Ally would want me to sit with you."

For a moment it looked like she could agree to the truce. Heaven knew they'd negotiated the last year with plenty of that, neither of them wanting to upset Ally, both of them working together to minimise the amount of time their paths crossed. But apparently Becca was spoiling for a fight right now, fuelled either by the wine or the grief, though most likely both.

She leaned in and said, "Bullshit. You came over here as you wanted to be away from everyone. I know because I did the same. Only, I got here when it was empty and you didn't. Unlike me, however, you're too polite to turn around and walk away – or else I'm the lesser evil." She stood up and scoped the bar, her head pausing roughly level with his dad. "Yeps," she said, sitting again, but she wasn't done yet. "And probably, you feel a bit beholden to me for saving you back there in the church and felt you should sit. But don't tell me it was for Ally's sake." Apparently done with her theorising, she cocked her head at him. "Am I right or am I right?"

In the time he'd known her, there had been many occasions when he'd wanted to slap her. He wasn't a violent person, he knew it was wrong, but Becca made it very hard to remember that sometimes. And right now, the urge was almost overwhelming. She was mean. Obviously, it also irked beyond measure that she could read him like a book. That she was so smug about it was the least surprising thing in the package.

He didn't need this. He wasn't beholden or obliged to her in any way. And he didn't care if she was just lashing out, *everyone* was hurting.

"Fuck you," he said, leaning forward so his voice didn't carry over the back of her bench. He could feel his face heating and the vein at his temple throbbing. Then he downed the remainder of his pint, thankful for his university speed-drinking training. He stood, trying to control his breathing and composure. "And fuck this. I'm done and if I'm not mistaken, that's us done too. I can't think of any reason why we'll need to talk again, which, frankly, suits me fine." He'd say goodbye to Valerie and then he was out of there. She'd understand. He threw Becca a glare and saw she was regarding him with a tiny smirk. God, she knew how to rile him.

"Silver linings then, eh?" she said, glibly.

Charlie put his hands on the table and leaned in really close, their noses almost touching. "There isn't a single lining to be had from Ally dying," he said, his teeth gritted again, "and you know it." He saw a flash of shame cross her face, but he didn't wait around. He tossed her a "Have a nice life" – because he couldn't shake his manners even when he desperately wanted to – and left the pub, the area and presumably that entire chapter of his life.

2012

B ecca stepped out onto the stage, the lights blinding her to what lay beyond. This was second nature to her, she'd done it so many times. There might be two people watching, perhaps eighty, she couldn't tell, but she saw it as part of the test. She always hoped it was eighty; the more people to see her perform the better. It was all she'd ever wanted, to entertain them, impress them, make them love her.

Taking her spot, she took a breath to begin.

"STOP!"

What? She hadn't even started.

"Becca! What are you doing here?" Becca shielded her eyes from the spotlight.

"Alan?"

She heard stomping and the face of one of London's most established casting agents appeared out of the gloom, at the edge of the stage. She'd auditioned for him so often, she recognised his particular brand of "STOP!"

"Why's Marcia sent you to this?" He appeared irritated, but Becca knew he was fond of her. She had that wearing effect.

Um, well, actually, Marcia *hadn't*. Marcia had gone for a wee, as she always did mid-meeting to make it appear she'd given Becca more time than she actually had, during which Becca had snapped a photo of the audition planner on Marcia's desk. Becca told herself she was saving her agent some work.

"I've prepared a whole soliloquy, Alan. Please?"

His face softened. "Becca, you're completely wrong for the role."

"Why?" she asked and straightened herself out. "I could totally be a Tina."

"*Tiny*. Her name is Tiny." He gave her a pointed look to the top of her head, which was high up from his perspective and also because Becca was very tall.

Becca held onto her enthusiasm. "What if it's an ironic nickname? Like Aussies call gingers 'Blue'." Sometimes she felt film producers could do with an alternative take, a fresh idea. She had fresh ideas in abundance and she liked to share.

"It's a retelling of Thumbelina. You're more Celtic Amazon in my listings than thumb-size elfin girl. Can you see my issue?"

Becca pursed her lips, trying very very hard to find another angle to pitch him, but admittedly she was pushing it.

"Any roles requiring taller people?" she tried, wishing she'd tied her red hair back, now that "big impact" was the wrong approach. "For perspective? Pick taller surrounding roles and you might not need someone as small as you thought?"

He rolled his eyes at her, but his irritation was gone. He understood what the jobs meant to actors. He spent most of his days disappointing people.

"Good to see you, but can you fuck off now? You're wasting my time and I haven't got much as it is."

Becca nodded. She understood. "See you soon, Alan," she said and departed the stage, passing a minuscule girl as Alan shouted "NEXT!" behind her.

Walking along the pavement towards her crappy café job (the café was crappy, the job was tenable), Becca gave herself a little pep talk, in lieu of Ally not being there to do it. It had been about her height today, not her acting. On the positive side, she'd learned another piece she could use another day. She was quite pragmatic at times, and she generally believed nothing went to waste, which fuelled her tenacity. Or maybe it was stubbornness, maybe it was that...

Becca's pepping floundered at the thought of Ally. It was nearly a year since her death. Having had little experience of grief, Becca had assumed it was a short-term contained event, but no, apparently not. Loss was a much longer affair, sometimes a constant feeling of something being missing, or forgetting you couldn't just pick up the phone for a natter. Or else it sprang on you and punched you in the face when you thought you were doing all right. Somehow though, you were just supposed to carry on with life, hoping this new normal would become bearable. Unless you were Charlie, of course, and then you just fucked off to the Americas on some kind of gap year. Valerie had called her a month after the funeral, asking whether she might know where he was. *As if.* His parents were worried, evidently. He'd locked up the flat and left the country without a word. Then a postcard from Bogotá had appeared on Valerie's birthday and the panic was over. Becca thought it must be nice to be able to bugger off travelling. She couldn't even remember what a holiday looked like.

Approaching the café, she took a moment to finish the

coffee she'd bought before the audition and to check her emails for any new casting calls. Jean, her boss at the café, got pissy if her phone was visible.

The cup hit the concrete, losing its top and final dregs, splashing her purple Docs, but Becca didn't move.

An email sat in her inbox, the first line of its contents visible. Resisting the temptation to throw the phone far away, she wildly searched the street for some hidden camera or trace of who was pranking her. It wasn't fear of looking stupid causing her panic, but a deep-seated knowledge that someone somewhere knew how to strike her where it would hurt most.

The subject line read simply: *Task for Becca*.

The sender was *allysonrwalker87@gmail.com*

The first line had the hair rising on her neck.

Darling Becca,

Don't freak out, it's me, Ally. Sorry if this is a bit of a shock. It's been almost a year and I'm hoping this is something you can bear now. I have something to ask of you and something to remind you of.

Becca stumbled a couple of steps backwards, gaining a shop window for support and giving herself a chance to regulate her breathing. Then there was swearing. WTF was this?

Reminders first! If I could have stayed, seen out our old age together, terrorising the Saga cruises, you know I would have. But this thing, it was simply bigger than me, Becs. Some things are just bigger than us. If I could have stayed, I would have continued to tell you how brilliant you are, and how loved you are – by me, and how loved you should be – by you. If I could have stayed I would have harangued you to care about yourself, as you are completely worth it, Becca, even if you don't believe it. If I could have stayed I would have harassed you to Make It Happen.

Becca only realised the tears were running down her face when she snorted in recognition. Ally would have done exactly that. *Make It Happen* was her mantra. There wasn't much in life Ally didn't believe you could make happen if you put your mind to it.

I hope you're OK, Becs. I've had a blast knowing you. I hope when you think of me you think about the fun stuff from when we were together, not the sadness of me not being around. If the tables were turned, I'd be feeling broken without you, half of me would have dropped away. Chances are you feel the same.

She did. She *so* did. The pain of it and reading the words now made her slide down the window to sit huddled on the ground, one arm wrapped around herself.

So, my request: Becca, will you visit my mum on the anniversary of my dying? I don't know exactly when that'll be, but it'll be soon. I can feel it. But please see Mum. She'll be alone otherwise, and I'd rather she wasn't.

Have you ever considered what you'd say to your best friend, if you got a chance to pop back for a moment after you'd gone? There are so many 'Do you remember…?'s – but I doubt you've forgotten a thing, and I have little advice to offer you – I barely got started. So I'm sticking with the basics, in the hope you'll learn them and never ever doubt them, because these are the things I want you to know:

You are brilliant, Becs, don't ever forget it – you can have your dreams, you deserve to be successful, you deserve to be happy, but you'll have to Make It Happen.

And above all else: I love you, Becca. Don't ever forget that either.

A x

Becca reread it, then hung her head and sobbed.

It *sounded* like Ally. Whoever had written this knew exactly how she would have written it. But how?

And then it struck her. *Charlie.* Fucking Charlie! Only he could have done this. She raced over the words again, gathering the tone, the sense of hearing Ally's voice in her ears escalating with every sentence. By the end, she was shaking. If she wasn't so utterly furious, she'd have been impressed with his mimicry. It was so spot on. Arsehole. Why would he do this? The anniversary of her death was next week. He must know she'd be taking it hard. Becca expected Charlie to find it hard himself, but to pull a stunt like this was downright shitty. Not least because they'd finally had the opportunity to exit each other's lives. It had suited them both. Why drag things back up?

She called him a fucker several times, as she hunted around her contacts for his number. There was an outside chance she hadn't deleted it – she was prone to contact culls when she'd had a drink too many – and right now she had a large and sharp piece of her mind to give him.

The sudden sound of her ringtone made her jump. She'd reject the call and dial Charlie and tell him what an absolute piece of crap he was for doing this. It wasn't funny, it was vile and cruel. Yes, he'd always been a cocky arse, but she wouldn't have thought him capable of this. However, she'd learned across her life that there was nothing as disappointing as People, and everyone had a capacity to crap on you.

She didn't recognise the number, but it didn't matter. Whoever was ringing could do one. With a quick "Come on, fuck off!" she declined the call. It started again. She declined it. A WhatsApp pinged in.

PICK UP, WHITE!

It was Charlie. She *knew* it. Utter shitgibbon.

The ringtone started again. Answering it, she barely had the phone to her ear before she started, "You total wan—"

But she was met with a rant from the other end. "Becca! You complete bitch. What is wrong with you? Haven't you got enough going on in your own miserable life? You've always been a cow, but this? This is the worst." Becca couldn't remember ever hearing Charlie shout. He was more of a growly kind of person. So this, well, it shocked her into silence and it took a moment for her to rally her own anger. She scrabbled to stand up, needing her full height and lung capacity.

"Hey! Dickhead! I'm not the arsehole here." Various pedestrians turned to stare, but she didn't care. "I don't know what the hell you think you're playing at, but this email gag is sick. Who the fuck does that? Sending an email from a dead best friend. Ally would be horrified."

"What? Me?" he butted in, raging.

"Yes, of course *you*. I've a good mind to tell Valerie, so she knows what a monster you are." She almost said Ally had dodged a bullet not getting to marry him, but then remembered Ally had died, so the point was lost.

"Stop shouting at me. I didn't send you any bloody email!" he snapped at her. "You sent one to *me*. And I tell you what, this is primary school shit now, suggesting *I* did it when it was you. I don't even have your email address. Did you think this would be a lark when you were pissed or something? It isn't funny. It's twisted."

Was it possible he didn't have her email address? She supposed so. They always texted when they were arranging who was seeing Ally in those last months. The ping of his updates or shift confirmations had been one of the few dependable things during that time. After Ally had died, their absence had added to the silence of Becca's devastation.

"This is bollocks," she said, crossly. "I didn't send you anything. We said our goodbyes at the funeral. I wouldn't take the time or energy to piss about emailing you."

"And you think I would?"

"My email supposedly comes from Ally. It's written like her, and who else could do that other than you and me, and I can assure you I've better things to do with my time than write emails to myself, you loon."

She heard him puff out at the other end of the call. "I don't understand," he said, quieter now, and she wasn't sure it was meant for her.

"You really think it comes from someone else?" she asked.

"I *know* it isn't me, and you insist it isn't you. I'd hazard a guess Valerie's had other shit going on, and she's not the pranky type."

"Do you think," she could hardly believe it, but had to suggest it, "do you think it might really be Ally? That she's sent us an email from beyond the grave?"

"A ghostly email?" he asked, less angry now, but still tense. Becca drew a relieved breath, pleased he was thinking along the same lines, that she wasn't going mad. "Don't be an idiot," he said bluntly. "Of course it's bloody not. But Ally was totally capable of scheduling an email ahead of time."

Becca felt her head getting hot.

"Is that even a thing?" she asked, crossly.

"Yeah, it's just scheduled sending. Basic Gmail tool. You can schedule them years in advance."

"Holy shit." Becca couldn't decide whether it was brilliant or creepy. But if it meant it was genuine, she'd overlook it. "Why the fuck hasn't she written before?" The notion burst out of her before she had a chance to filter it.

"Guess what? I don't know. I wasn't exactly expecting this. I don't know how I feel about it. But that's probably why she didn't schedule anything before. She'd have known we'd need some time to grieve and recoup."

Becca was going to need a lot longer than that. She still felt like she'd lost a chunk of her heart. There was something she liked about the way he said "we" though. Not because she and Charlie would ever be classed as a "we" – *ew* – but it suggested she wasn't alone in this. She'd learned to take the small comforts where she could.

"Have you recouped?" she asked, her anger subsiding.

"Not even close." He was calming too.

"Me neither."

"So. Valerie. You'll go, right? I'm assuming that's what your email was about." He was sounding officious, like he wanted to wrap this up now. Well, that suited her fine, but she didn't like his bossy tone. He had no boss rights over her. *She* was the boss of her. She'd been telling herself that for years. And her email was about so much more than just visiting Valerie. Not that she intended sharing any of it with him.

"Of course I'll go! Valerie's been like a mum to me," she said, searching around for a pen in her bag, a tragically scuffed vintage Anya Hindmarch she'd found in a charity shop. Finding one, she scribbled *Visit Valerie* on the front of an unopened bill. She underlined it, hoping the emphasis would make it override her instinctive plan to wallow under her duvet that day.

"I land back at Heathrow that morning, so all being well I'll manage to see her, but connections from here can be crappy."

"Where's there?"

"Honduras."

She wasn't sure about the exact geography, but she guessed it was far away.

"Well, don't bust a gut. I'll be there for Valerie either way," she said primly, pushing away her guilt for not having visited Valerie in a year. She'd *seen* her – Valerie liked to come and try each new café she started at – but Becca had avoided going to the house. She'd been busy with shifts and auditions, and a single call-back, and … well, the details didn't spring to mind right now, but she'd definitely been busy.

Charlie talking again pulled her back into the now.

"So this definitely isn't you pissing about?" He didn't sound sure.

"Jeez. You really do think badly of me. Pulling something like this would be the lowest. Thanks a bunch, dickhead."

"Two points here, BJ," he said, deliberately out to annoy her now with the nickname she hated. "One, you just accused me of the same thing and two, let's be honest, you've pushed me to think badly of you since we first met."

Well, the feeling was mutual – particularly since the day he'd spotted her post in their shared student house, addressed to Becca-Jayne White, and seen the mileage in her initials.

She drew a breath to respond, but there was a click at the end of the line and then nothing. He'd hung up on her! How fucking rude was that? Arsehole. She banged her phone in her hand several times in frustration. She'd call him back, that's what she'd do, but then stalled with her finger over the call button. Honduras sounded expensively long distance away. She flung her phone down in her bag, deciding she didn't care enough about him to spend the money she didn't have on him, and set off grumbling and swearing for work.

Valerie had seen Becca in her full teenage grunge state, so the bar was low, but Becca still dug out a clean, clean*ish*, T-shirt from her washing mountain for her visit. She spent the bus journey scratching some dried unknown substance away from the weave of her jeans. It earned her a grimace from a woman across the aisle. Becca responded by pulling a face. The woman minded her own business after that.

Knocking on Valerie's door, she felt unusually twitchy. As a kid she would have gone around the back and let herself in with a shout for Ally, but that seemed closed to her now. Now it felt correct to knock politely and wait.

"Becca, darling," Valerie said with a genuine smile upon opening the door. "So good to see you, come in." If Valerie was cross at Becca, for not having visited before, then she was a better actor than Becca. Or else it was simply kindness, which was not a trait Becca thought she'd been gifted genetically.

It wasn't until she was in the full lock of Valerie's embrace that Becca realised just how much she missed it. Both Ally and her mother had always been tactile, and while Becca had initially shunned it because she wasn't used to it, over time she'd fallen to the pleasure of it. The world had been far colder this past year, and Becca let herself lean into the hug.

Valerie led her into the front room. The familiar scent of the house hit her, a delicate fusion of their washing powder, fabric conditioner and Shake 'n' Vac carpet freshener. Becca had bought the same products, trying to conjure hints of Ally in her rented room, but never managed the same blend. Enveloped in it now, it was as if she'd never been away, and Ally was still somewhere in the house. Her eyes flitted towards the ceiling, expecting to hear Ally shout she'd be down in a sec, followed by the thumping of feet on the stairs. No shout came, nor footfall, but the scent alone was enough to make Becca sway.

"Are you eating properly? You're looking as skinny as last

year." They'd all lost weight in Ally's last months. Appetites had waned.

"Ah, you know, Valerie – skinny is what directors want. I'm fine." Her belly disagreed loudly. Skinny was what her finances dictated, too. Her money seemed to evaporate travelling to auditions.

The room hadn't changed much since she'd last been there, except for a large photograph of Ally and a rose quartz urn on the mantelpiece. Putting the two together came as a punch to her gut. That was her best friend up there.

"I talk to her every day," said Valerie, spotting Becca's gaze. She didn't sound remotely embarrassed. "I hear her answers in my head. We have lovely chats." Becca said nothing. If Valerie thought she could hear her daughter, if it helped her grieve, then who was Becca to point out it was barmy nonsense? Besides, Becca was there today at the behest of a posthumous email, so maybe she wasn't one to talk.

"Tell me how you've been, darling." Valerie patted the seat next to her on the sofa then poured them each a cup of tea. Sitting, Becca spotted the table was laid for three. Clearly, Charlie hadn't made it, and frankly she was glad. Being in a room with Ally's ashes was hard enough; doing it under his scrutiny would have been worse.

Sinking back into the sofa, her teacup resting on her belly, Becca was definitely glad it was only the two of them. Valerie wouldn't mind if she slobbed a bit. She'd spent hours slobbing on this sofa in her time.

A toilet flushed from beyond the hallway, and Becca's eyes skittered from Valerie to the doorway, in time for it to fill with Charlie's large frame. He had an uncanny knack for having a presence in a room before he even made it over the threshold. He paused when he saw her, his smile for Valerie faltering, then took the third place at the coffee table, selecting a floral tub chair.

"White," he said, formally. There was no notion of a hug or anything like that. "I didn't hear you arrive."

"You must have been really straining in there," she said, taking a sip of the tea.

Valerie asked him about his travels and he detailed how he'd landed in Argentina, and travelled up through the neighbouring lands to Colombia before making his way through Central America. Becca had googled Honduras after his call, not because she cared where he was, purely for curiosity's sake. She now knew Honduras had the accolade of being the planet's murder capital, closely contested by several of the other countries he'd just mentioned.

She studied him from behind her default slightly-bored game-face. He looked like shit. Granted, not as shit as at the funeral where he was properly wrung out like a gnarly dishcloth, but still gaunt. His cheekbones were more defined than they should be by her reckoning, and his shave hadn't happened for some days. Somehow, he still managed to look ashen under the suntanned skin. His eyes were tired, but he was doing his best to appear perky. It made her think this was his norm, the faking. He obviously didn't trust the Honduran barbers, his dark brown hair being overdue a cut. However, in spite of his current state, Becca conceded he was still a good-looking bloke. If you liked that sort of thing. Which she didn't.

"And, you, Becca? Tell us what you're up to," Valerie said, drawing her into the conversation. Becca swung her head back towards Valerie in case Charlie thought she was checking him out. It had been an assessment, not a check-out.

"Still working shifts at the café and auditions. I did get a call-back on a couple of things. I'm waiting for one of them."

Valerie looked excited for her. She'd always been a superb listener and enthusiast, no matter how lame the occasion. She'd come to every school event to support them, virtually adopting Becca for school assemblies and sports days. She'd quickly spotted there was no one there for Becca.

"Good for you. Tenacity will get you through. Fingers crossed for the one you're waiting on." Valerie waved crossed fingers at her. "I won't ask too much about it, don't want to jinx things." Becca had used that line for many years, more often because she'd already known she hadn't got the gig, and didn't want to talk about it.

"Anything we'll have heard of?" Charlie asked, not at all bothered about jinxing things.

"It's new. So no," she said, which was untrue, but curtailed the questions. A silence fell then and she caved to its awkwardness. "I did have a film role recently actually – a short, but the lead." She didn't want any pity for the disappointing state of her working life. She managed that well enough by herself, thank you.

"How exciting," gushed Valerie, perking up again. "What was it?"

"I performed as an animal. Really got into its psyche. It was very impactful, apparently."

"Like in *Cats*?"

"Similar." She nodded and took another bite of her cake. She'd been a polar bear in an escape drill at London Zoo. It *was* filmed, and her method performance had gone viral on the internet. Unfortunately, no one would ever know it was her inside the bear costume, taunting the zoo staff, flinging the furniture, scaring the fake visitors and finally giving a beautiful, heart-rending descent to the ground, as the effect of the imaginary tranquilliser dart took effect.

"What's it called?" asked Charlie, looking unconvinced. "I'll check it out at the cinema."

"It's not out yet," she said briskly, "and they're still wrangling over the title." She shrugged at him in a "What can you do?" way.

"And in the meantime the waitressing job is valuable too, isn't it?" Valerie trilled. "I imagine you meet all sorts of people who'll inform your character acting, and also you're doing an important service bringing them coffee."

"I suppose," Becca said, sullenly. She only thought of it as bringing in the rent and getting her out of bed each day – although some days, not even that.

Valerie suddenly looked around, confused. "I forgot the cucumber sandwiches."

"I'll go," said Charlie, rising. Valerie stayed him with a hand on his knee.

"No. You've travelled so far. Have a rest." She wandered out, leaving them alone, watching each other. They'd have to do small talk now.

"You made it then," he said. How dumb was that?

"Obviously," she said, taking an exaggerated slurp of her tea. She did it to irritate him. It was habitual. Any needly thing she could do to put him on edge. Best to get in there first, she found – he gave as good as he got. "Can't get much past you."

He gave her an unimpressed stare. "You haven't changed."

"It's only been a year. What were you expecting?"

"Hardly expecting, just hoping."

Knob. This was the Charlie she was used to – not the broken shell of last year. He'd stood taller again, too, when he'd walked through the door. Perhaps going away had been for the best.

"And I know why *my* shirt's wrinkled, what's your excuse? You might have made an effort."

He was admonishing her. He could stuff that. She shrugged at him and rolled her eyes for good measure.

"Maybe it's called Fashion, grandad," she said. He wasn't convinced. It was an original Katherine Hamnett she'd found in Oxfam, with USE A CONDOM emblazoned across it, which, while sound advice, was, on reflection, not necessarily right for the occasion. At least it was clean. *Ish.*

"Have you seen her urn is behind you?" Becca blurted out in a loud whisper. It had been in her eye-line all the time and she needed to share.

He gave her a steely look. "Of course I've seen."

Unfazed, she gave him the bug-eye. "On the mantelpiece though…"

He leaned in and said quietly – not wanting to partake in the stage whispering – "She didn't want to be buried, remember?"

Hmm. Becca didn't remember. She'd point-blank refused to discuss the post-death part with Ally. It hadn't occurred to her that Charlie had been willing.

"If it makes Valerie happy, what does it matter? Didn't

matter to Ally, other than she didn't want worms going through her."

Becca gave a proper shudder now. *Ew*. The twinge at the side of Charlie's mouth said grossing her out amused him. She turned away from him then. It was too soon for jokes. So much of it was still raw.

Valerie appeared from the hallway, a plate of sandwiches in her hand. "Now then, Becca, are there any nice men around for you at the moment?"

Charlie's mouth spread to a wider grin as he settled back into his chair and drank his tea. He was only missing the popcorn.

When she and Ally had lounged around here as teens this would have been a regular question from Valerie, an opportunity to snigger about boys and discuss crushes. Valerie wouldn't be intense about it, it was just fun chatter. Right now though, not so much. Valerie seemed to have forgotten Girl Code. Not asking about boys in front of a boy was definitely carved in stone somewhere. Surely it was a basic law, like the first rule of *Fight Club*, along with "Don't sleep with a friend's BF", "Don't sleep with a friend's ex" and "Don't sleep with a friend's dad". Becca might be quite louche in some ways, but she knew her Girl Code.

"Well, I … um," she began.

"Yes, *Becca*, how *are* things on the man front?" Charlie contributed, and she was inclined to pelt her cucumber sarnie at him. He was enjoying watching her squirm. And then it dawned on her: she needn't squirm. She was a grown-arsed woman, who had relationships, admittedly very brief ones sometimes, but she was absolutely capable of attracting a man and she should own it. Sitting up straight she spoke to Valerie, soundly ignoring Smug-face on the other side of the table.

"Well, *actually* Valerie, I've been seeing a decent guy for the last two months."

Valerie's face went up a rung on the ladder of Pleased. God, Becca loved this woman. Becca vowed there and then to *Be More Valerie*, not bearing grudges against anyone … OK, *mostly* anyone. Becca flicked Charlie a quick look. He wasn't looking so smug now. Ha! He'd clearly wanted her to be as single and sad as he was.

"Tell us about him," Valerie urged.

"Yes, *do*," concurred Charlie, his blue eyes vaguely mocking her under their black lashes.

"Well … it's still quite new…"

"Two months, dear, that's not so new." Valerie was trying to be reassuring.

"And a record, surely?" Charlie added. He leaned across and snaffled another couple of sandwiches and a scone. He was almost close enough for Becca to punch him in the ear. Almost, but not quite.

"Come on then," Valerie said, excited, "dish the goss." It sounded so wrong coming from the older woman, but Ally would have said the exact same thing, so Becca didn't feel she could decline.

"Well, his name's Milton. Milt. He's American."

"Oh, exciting, and what does he do over here?"

"He lives over *there*." She sensed Charlie raising an eyebrow at that. "So I only see him when he's here on business."

"Another actor?" Valerie asked.

"Businessman," she tried, keen to get off the subject. They'd met at an exhibition where she'd been working as a stand hostess one weekend and he was the client. She only spent dinners and nights with him. No real strings, it was just easy. She swung her head towards Charlie, a question about the state of his love life on the tip of her tongue to divert the conversation, then chewed it right back, remembering. It was *Charlie*. And Charlie belonged to Ally. There would surely never be anyone else. And rightly so.

She turned back to Valerie, who was waiting for more intel. "He's nice," Becca managed. "He's a considered sort of guy. Not one for partying all the time." Valerie would think it a good thing. "I think you'd like him, Valerie, he's a calming influence on me." Now, having regrouped, she turned to Charlie and said, "Tell us more about the travelling. No one knew where you'd gone," deftly changing the subject before she blabbed that Milton and Valerie had lots in common, particularly age and greying hair. She didn't want Charlie's judgey looks. Milt really *was* a decent guy, charming, respectful and, as it happened, generous. He liked her company, she made him laugh, he desired her.

Becca imagined Charlie's parents had given him hell for disappearing, which pleased her. And filled her with envy; of him having parents who cared or even noticed he'd gone and also of his financial ability to spontaneously buy a ticket and go. What she wouldn't have given for that in the past year…

Judging by the way he was squirming in his seat, Becca suspected Charlie didn't want quizzing on his travels, but he'd not been amenable when she didn't want to talk about Milton, so…

"Knowing something about the countries you mentioned," she said, "I'd say you have a penchant for picking the most dangerous ones." If he could be Big Brother-y at her, then right back at him.

"*All* countries have crime, Becca." He said it like she was an imbecile, which got her hackles right up.

"Not all countries make the Top Five lists for murder stats, Charlie." She mimicked his tone perfectly. "You could choose to avoid them."

"I can look after myself," he said, giving her a bored stare, as if it was a Man thing.

"Where d'you stay?"

"Wherever the road took me. Wherever I found a bed. I swapped labour for lodgings in some places." This was totally not his usual MO. Ally's Charlie liked a plan. Ally devised great itineraries for their trips and Charlie followed them, always happy for the decisions to be taken out of his hands.

Valerie's expression said she admired his bravery and ingenuity.

Becca looked at him shrewdly. This was out of character, both for Charlie and any sane tourist. She'd put money on his risking these countries because he felt he had nothing to lose. Becca's intention to annoy him was replaced by dismay. Ally's death had made Charlie reckless.

"Of course, I could stay here and get people coffee," he sniped, "if you're worried about my safety." She'd clearly riled him, but his tone cast off her sudden sympathy for him. She didn't want him thinking she worried about him. Heaven forbid.

"Your safety's your own concern," she said with a

withering look. "And come down and take a shift sometime. You'll see waitressing can be pretty dicey. There's plenty worth documenting on the assault front." Not a day went by where her arse didn't get patted or pinched. She'd lost three jobs already from accidentally yet accurately pouring things on the perpetrators' crotches.

He reached for the last scone, but she swiped it before he got there. She didn't need to look at him; he'd know her smile, as she nodded along to what Valerie was saying, was for him. She made a meal of each mouthful, enjoying the light seethe emanating from him. It was childish, yes, but he had it coming.

"Now then, children," Valerie said with a tone of fond admonishment, "let's be kind to each other." Both Becca and Charlie busied themselves with their food, Charlie taking the last slice of coffee walnut cake, which Becca suspected was a dig at her. Not being a nut fan, she wasn't bothered. Despite his fondness for cake, he was looking lean, she noted, his forearms toned, giving credence to his labouring-for-board story.

Valerie got up. "I have something for you."

She moved to the mantelpiece, and for a brief moment Becca feared she was going to converse with Ally. Becca had acted lots of shit in her time, but there was no way she could muster fake conversation with the quartz pot, not even for Valerie. There were limits to her skills. She watched Valerie pause and run her fingertips across the lid. It was something she did with people too, a tactile motion as much greeting as comfort. Becca had seen her run her fingertips across Ally's back hundreds of times, neither of them aware that she was doing it, but a silent dialogue happening between them all the same. It caused a lump in Becca's throat; for all of Valerie's chirpiness, Becca saw how much she must miss her daughter. It had always been just the two of them.

Becca looked about the room again, seeing it both exactly as she remembered it, but now also as a space missing a vital component part. Ally had moved out as a student and then lived with Charlie, but she constantly popped home to see Valerie. Her absence, even a year on, was palpable.

Valerie drew something out from behind the urn, and returned to her seat. She placed an object and an envelope on the table. Becca and Charlie stared at them.

It was a small bulbous bottle, made of opaque red glass, with a cork stopper. The shadowing showed there was a substance inside it, something powdery rather than liquid.

They waited. Valerie looked at them both, expectantly. Charlie glanced at Becca. She gave him a small shrug.

"It's some of Ally's ashes," Valerie prompted. Becca held her breath. She was only just getting her head around Ally being on the mantelpiece; her now being on the coffee table, was pushing Becca's comfort zone boundaries.

"OK," Charlie said, slowly. It wasn't much of an encouragement, but it was enough for Valerie.

"I thought she'd talked to you about this, Charlie. About Snowdon?"

Charlie's brow was furrowed and then released a little as something dawned.

"We talked about it, it was the one we had left to do, but she got too ill." He suddenly looked so sad that Valerie was moved to squeeze his knee.

"Yes, I know, but she wants you to take her, anyway."

Valerie pointed to the bottle. "She wants you to take her ashes up there."

Becca's eyes were wide. There was quite a bit to unpack here, not least Valerie's referring to Ally in the present tense.

"Um ... Valerie ... how do you know this?"

Valerie gave her an incredulous but kind look. "She told me."

Becca looked from Charlie to the urn and back. "Do you mean recently?"

Valerie laughed. "No, darling, of course not. I've not lost my senses. We discussed it in her last days." Valerie turned to Charlie, "She wants you to take her up Snowdon and scatter these ashes there."

Becca supposed it was plausible. Ally and Charlie had been into this hiking thing, wanting to scale all three peaks of the UK mainland: Ben Nevis, Snowdon and Scafell Pike. They'd even camped, much to Becca's confusion. Surely there were warm B&Bs with full toileting facilities around those places? "Ah right," she said, popping the last of her scone into her mouth. "Over to you then, Charlie."

"Oh, it's you too," Valerie said, smiling back to her. "The letter's for both of you, for afterwards."

Becca just averted a full choke. "Me? Why me? I wasn't part of their walking fetish." Ally had once – and once only – asked whether she'd like to join them on their hiking nonsense, inexplicably thinking Becca might have any interest in summiting a mountain. It had been a discombobulating moment where Becca had questioned whether her best friend really knew her at all. Charlie had been blatantly relieved when Becca had given her a clear "Fuck no!", keen for there to be no doubt in the matter or a repeat of the offer. Becca absolutely couldn't see why she was being dragged into this now.

Valerie chuckled at Becca's appalled face. "Don't be mardy at *me*. I didn't make the rules."

What rules? Becca had not signed up for any game. How were there rules? Her jaw flapped up and down as she cobbled together her thoughts and censored half the words.

"She just wanted to get to the top and be scattered there?" Charlie asked, ignoring Becca's agitation. That "just" was for her benefit, like she was making a fuss over nothing. Git.

"That's right."

He looked at Becca, his expression hardly the epitome of delight, but determined nonetheless. "My new job starts next week. I only have Saturday free. We'll travel up early Saturday, walk for the day and come home Sunday morning."

"I have work," Becca said, annoyed he was commandeering her time.

"Change your shift." He was brooking little argument here.

"How d'you know it isn't an acting job?"

"It isn't," he said, "or you would have mentioned it earlier." Dammit.

Valerie slid the bottle over to Charlie for safe keeping.

Becca slid her eyes to the clock on the wall. She was stuffed on this, and about to have a miserable weekend to boot. Much as she loved Valerie, Becca sensed she'd come to the end of her own goodwill. Unlike Ally, it was a limited commodity in Becca's genetic make-up and she was spent.

She made her excuses and got up to leave. Charlie stayed put.

"I'll text you the details," he said.

"I know," she answered miserably. She made it a couple of steps to the door and then turned with a thought. "I'm working on Sunday morning and I don't want to stay over." She didn't have the cash for a B&B or the capacity to spend so long with him.

"Fine," agreed Charlie with a sigh, like he was granting her the earth. "Up and down in a day."

Having hugged Valerie, Becca quickly made her way up the garden path, leaving them to discuss his new job, whatever it was he'd been able to skip straight into. *Again.* She wasn't hanging about to find out. Her eyes were beginning to sting and her nose to twitch. She needed to be away. The lounge with all its memories, the familiar smell, the mantelpiece with the urn, and everything pointing to Ally, was too much. She thought she'd got more used to it over the last year. Apparently not. The overwhelming need to get under her duvet fuelled her on her way, as she took deep breaths to keep herself steady along with a chant of *Don't Cry, Don't Cry.* And she didn't want to walk up a bloody mountain either, especially not with Charlie, all the while carrying a bit of Ally with them.

That letter though…

She managed the bus and even the speed-walking back to the shit-pad she lived in. But seeing her front door, peeling grey nightmare that it was, came as such a relief, she had to grab onto a railing spike as she bent over and let out the first huge sob.

"White? White! Wake up, we're here." Charlie's mardy voice was a cruel awakening, but then it wasn't for the first time that morning. The halting of his VW Golf as they parked jolted her out of her sleep. Becca cranked open a single eye to survey the situation. *Ugh.* Countryside. "Thanks for the navigation and company," he muttered, getting out of the car and pouring himself a cup of something hot from the thermos. She found herself coveting his thermos. What was this trip doing to her already? A *thermos*, for fuck's sake. She was only twenty-six, not a geriatric.

Opening the car door, Becca tumbled out, having got groggily caught up in her duvet. It was wrapped around her in the seat like a snuggly cocoon. Charlie had thought she was joking when she'd emerged from her doorway at 5 a.m. That she was still in her PJs and wrapped in her duvet like a walking hotdog seemed sensible to her. She'd been asleep again, face smooshed against the window, before they'd made it to the end of her street.

Becca wiped a dribble of drool from the side of her mouth and took a proper look about. The car park was full, the cars spewing out hiking types, with waterproof backpacks with water-bladder inserts and walking boots in various depressing colours. Becca had cobbled together what she considered suitable attire for the walk, a veritable buffet of charity shop finds: her red Tommy Hilfiger bucket hat, its hole fixed with an iron-on baby dragon patch; a Fjällräven turquoise backpack stuffed with Kendal mint cake and a bottle of pop; and apple-green Converse on her feet.

"Where's the loo? I need to change," she said. She'd tossed her jeans and jumper in the back as she'd got in. He nodded towards a small stone building that looked cold. "You could have woken me at the last services," she grumbled, but didn't stop for an answer. She needed a wee, and she wasn't awake enough for chitchat.

Walkers were a judgmental bunch, it seemed. Her PJs garnered quite the stares as she queued, but Becca was immune to sartorial judgment, especially from people wearing beige slacks.

Charlie looked her up and down when she got back to the car. She gave him the same assessment, and they both muttered "Bloody hell!" in unison.

"You look like a retiree," she said. He was wearing action slacks too, though thankfully in navy, with zips above the knee so he could remove the lower part according to the weather. He had a Gortex jacket and of course at his walking-booted feet sat the obligatory Karrimor rucksack, with the tell-tale water tube. Her heart sank with every item ticked off the list. Not only was she having to do this walk, but she was doing it with him, *and* with him dressed like this. Yes, he looked the part, yes, he had the good labels and yes, he had the physique to look like Bear Grylls' better-looking mate, but in Becca's book he was still dressed to distress.

"And *you* look like a walking jumble sale," he said, looking at her with concern. "If you needed kit, you should have said."

That caused her to look up. "What do you mean?" She was

dressed, wasn't she? She was wearing flats. What was his problem?

He looked towards the rear of the car and back, deliberating. "Ally's walking kit's in the boot. Your stuff isn't ideal. Use Ally's."

She was momentarily stunned. "First, we need to talk about you still having Ally's clothes, and in your car, but that'll keep," she said, having gathered herself. "Second, given the amount of naked women processing through your room before Ally, I'm alarmed you can't recognise when two of us are wildly different shapes. My legs are double the length of hers and my child-bearing hips would never fit in any of her trousers. D'you want me walking up a mountain, flies open, flashing my lack of underwear to all the descenders?" It thrilled her to see his face redden. *Of course* she had knickers on. Who scaled mountains commando? That had "cold ninny" written all over it.

"Have you got a waterproof at least?" he asked.

"Is it going to rain?"

"It isn't forecast."

"No need then, eh?" A pack-a-mac was the last thing she fancied spending her money on. She was waking up now and keen to get going. "Come on, Gok Wan, let's get this over with." She rummaged in her backpack for her mint cake. The Breakfast of Champions.

He didn't move, consternation written all over his face. "Can you wear her walking shoes, at least? Converse have holes in the sides, you'll get wet and cold feet in minutes."

Becca pulled her head back, surprised. "You worried about me?"

"Don't be deluded," he said, scowling. "I just don't want to suffer the whinging all the way up and back."

Becca considered it. If there was sheep poo or general mud, she didn't want her Chucks destroyed. "What size are they?"

Becca tried not to give too much thought to the "deadwoman's shoes" notion floating about in her head as she double-knotted the laces. Most of the clothes in her wardrobe, being second-hand, had probably belonged to now-dead people. But wearing something of Ally's was different, and she wasn't keen to examine it too deeply.

"So," he said, starting afresh, his chin tilting to one side, "do you want it at a steady pace and a swift climax, or a concentrated build to the peak?" He gave her a wolfish grin.

She raised her eyebrows at him, unimpressed.

"Sometimes, Lister, I just want it *fast*," she said, salaciously drawing out the "fast". His eyebrows rose. "Sometimes I just want it over as soon as possible. This is one of those times."

His cocky grin dissipated. Like she'd critiqued him. He stuffed his hands in his pockets, nodded to the track, and turned on his heel to join the hordes.

Becca exhaled crossly through her nose. She so didn't want to do this, but Ally wanted her to be part of the scattering thing. Not that she knew why. Possibly Ally hadn't wanted to be accused of favouritism, asking one of them to do this over the other – although Becca wouldn't have minded in this instance.

"Have you got the letter?" she checked. He kept walking.

Arse. With a quick "Fuck it", she employed her best teen-sulk trudge to catch up with him.

Walking alongside one another was awkward. Small talk. Three hours of small talk. Nightmare.

"Morning!" an older couple said, passing them on the gravel track.

"Morning!" Charlie responded. Becca gave him a side-eye.

"Who's that?"

"I don't know. Just walkers."

"Why d'you say hello?"

"It's what you do."

Becca's face contorted in confusion. "Why?" What earthly purpose could that have in the walking process? This was a mountain, for god's sake. She'd put money on Everest climbers not expending vital energy greeting randoms. Surely you just kept your head down and plodded miserably. Charlie gave her a shrug and then his mouth pulled up to one side.

"It's called being nice. You should try it some time. You might like it."

She ignored him. She was no more going to greet these people than she'd start chatting to strangers on the tube. And she didn't understand what all these people were doing up so early, anyway. They couldn't all have ashes to scatter.

"Bloody hell," Becca panted, taking a break after thirty minutes. The gravel had turned to jaggedy stones. There were crags around them, and a lake below, which was pretty, but she was focusing on not snapping her ankles on the uneven path.

She contemplated wrestling the car keys off him and making a dash back. The letter, though. Many people passed them by, chatting happily. A couple of children passed with their parents, laughing at something, tempting her to trip one of them up. Little show-offs. "What is this for?" she whined. "Why do people do this?"

"It's walking. It's exercise. It's being with nature," Charlie reeled off like it was basics. He took a swig of his water, killing time as opposed to needing it. He hadn't even broken a sweat. A passing sheep bleated at her. It could do one, too.

"It's bloody awful," she countered in the same tone. "I can see nature outside my bedroom window." Moss on brick counted as nature. It was green. "I could do an exercise thing off YouTube if I was that way inclined." Which she wasn't, but she understood the principle. "I see it's walking, but it's going nowhere."

"It isn't. We're heading for the top," he said, pulling at her sleeve to set them off again. "If we keep stopping, we'll never make it down before sunset and we won't make it back to London before the wee hours. And I've got people to see in the morning. Nicer people. Actually, just nice people."

She ignored his diss. "It's not a destination with a purpose. It's a loop. Pointless." Charlie gave her a benign smile, like he knew differently.

"Come on, you whingebag, there's a café at the top. Best cup of tea you'll ever have. And it'll be on me, so you won't even have to pay for it." He rummaged in his pocket and held out a bag of Haribo gummy bears as an incentive. There was something about him remembering her tastes and having made provision for them that disconcerted her. Not sure what else to do, Becca snaffled a handful and marched past him, saying, "Hope you've brought lots."

He caught her up again in seconds, and with a change of subject. "So, who's this bloke of yours?"

"Aren't we supposed to do small talk?" Small talk suddenly seemed preferable.

"Aren't we beyond that?"

"Are we? Let's not pretend to be friends." She popped a red bear in her mouth. They'd been her and Ally's favourites.

"Well, three hours of small talk will be very boring."

"We could just walk in silence," she suggested.

"Beej, we—"

"Don't call me that."

"Sorry. BJ," he corrected, "we—"

"Do you want a punch?"

He sighed dramatically, which was normally her gig. "We might not be friends, as you've flagged, but we *are* acquaintances, however much you'd rather we weren't, and I know there's no way you can *not* talk for three hours."

"You don't want to be my acquaintance either," she pointed out. He'd made it sound like she was a bad person. She saw herself as a realist. They simply weren't supposed to be friends. They were just two people who had loved, in their respective ways, the same person. "You were quite happy to say 'Goodbye' and 'Have a nice life' at the funeral."

He turned his head to her. "You were being a mega-bitch."

She considered it for a moment. "It was a rough day."

"It was," he agreed, looking forward again and then after a brief silence, he made a small *huh* sound.

"What?"

"That was your moment to apologise. For being a bitch. At the funeral." He clearly felt the need to clarify which occasion.

"I was going with my emotions that day. That's what you're supposed to do. Let them out. And not apologise for it." She had a self-help app which told her so, although she only remembered the bits that appealed to her.

"Showing emotions, yes; being a dick, no."

"We'll just have to agree to disagree," she said blithely. "But that's our go-to, isn't it?" She wasn't really asking. "Got any more sweets?"

"Tell me about your American and you can have some more gummy bears." *Ugh*, he played dirty.

"What's it to you? You aren't interested in me or my life." She was getting out of breath again, so the words were coming out a bit raspy and brusque. The incline was steeper now, and they were zigzagging their way up bigger stones.

"True," he said with a nod, and she believed him. Generally, he'd been indifferent to what she did and with whom. He'd only talked about the here and now when she and he were around each other in Ally's presence. Otherwise, he did a very good version of uninterested. Which was fine by Becca, she'd grown up with that, both her parents being experts. "I'm not *interested* per se, more astonished and intrigued who'd sign up to you."

"Wow. Now who's being a mega-bitch?" It annoyed her how shocked that had come out.

"Just being honest, showing you my emotions," he said with a hint of snark and then added, "I'm not apologising for it."

Dickhead.

She was tempted to ignore him completely. Only, she really liked gummy bears, and bickering with Charlie made things go quicker. She'd looked up earlier and there was ages to the brow of the current hill and now, they were almost on it.

He pulled the gummy bear packet out of his pocket and extended it in her direction. She launched herself at it. Prepared, he held on when she tried to take it. Dammit.

As soon as three bears were in her mouth, the packet disappeared again. "The American, White."

Becca scowled at him, which was hard as her mouth was filling with saliva, the flavours doing their thing.

She took her own sweet time finishing them. "We already did this with Valerie. He's called Milt. He's a Yank, he works over here sometimes."

His curiosity was piqued, though. "How d'you meet?"

"None of your business."

"Ah, Tinder."

"No!"

"Pub?"

"I was working on an exhibition stand – handing out flyers – and he was over from the client's head office in the States and we got chatting." Charlie did not need to know he was older. It always gave people the wrong idea. She liked Milt's maturity. He didn't play silly games. She knew where she stood with him. That meant lots to her. "OK? He's nice. It's good. I'm happy. You don't need to know more."

"I think I *do*," Charlie insisted, enjoying this. "Ally would want me to find out what he's like. What are his intentions?"

"Fuck off," she spluttered and tried to walk ahead, but his legs were longer and stronger, and he was used to this stupid rocky ground, so he kept up, continuing his interrogation. Becca did a quick recce to see if there were any large sticks about she could whack him with.

"Just intrigued, like I said," he needled. He said she was a bitch, but god, he was annoying in his own right.

"*Astonished*, you said," she snapped, still stung. "You know, it *is* possible, on a planet of seven billion people, that someone would find me attractive and interesting company. Maybe I got lucky and found that *single* person. He's smart, he's got a good job, he finds me funny and a distraction from work. Suits me fine he isn't around all the time. It gives me time to be me. Feels like the perfect deal, not having someone in your space all the time. All right?" She hoped he got the message that the subject was now closed. Nosy arse. She looked ahead. God, the top couldn't come quick enough so she could do the scattering thing, read the letter, fight him for it, then come back down again and get home.

He took a breath to ask more, but she shut him down with a sterner "All right?"

They walked for a couple of minutes in a hostile silence, before she asked him, "Why have you still got Ally's stuff? And why are you driving about with it?"

She chucked him a glance. His face had clouded over. Although he'd seemed quite together at Valerie's – and frankly, who wouldn't after taking a year's holiday – perhaps he wasn't. Maybe he'd been a mess when he'd got home too. Had it been anyone else, Becca might have asked, "How are you doing?" But it wasn't, so she didn't. She wasn't sure she'd be able to keep a grip on herself if they started delving into feelings.

"I put it in the boot, because I suspected you wouldn't have the appropriate kit." He was being polite, skirting around her tight finances, but they both knew what he meant. He also looked appalled at her catching him doing her a kindness. The gummy bears didn't count, they were purely for coaxing.

"Okaaay," she said, deciding to let him off that one, "but why have you still got it at all?"

"I've been busy." He sounded snippy now.

"It's been a year."

"I've been away."

"Didn't Valerie offer? That time before the funeral." She had. Charlie had shaken his head, tight-jawed and red-eyed. Their entire flat was a weave of his and her things. Becca couldn't imagine unpicking all of that. But Ally's clothes? Couldn't those have gone?

"I've boxed it. Clothes, bags, shoes. It's all in the hallway. I just haven't got around to donating it." He sounded stiff about it. Like the boxing was a bad memory. And yet, he didn't seem able to move those boxes on, now he'd done it. He must walk past them every day. She supposed she should offer to take them to the charity shop. But she didn't fancy it much either. The image of Ally's things on the rails for random strangers to pick over was hard to swallow. However...

"You won't be getting these shoes back," she stated. She might keep them – shoes didn't grow on trees. "And her other things in the boot won't come home with you. That'll be a start and you'll see you can do it."

There was a momentary standoff as he digested her orders. Then he curtly nodded, after which they said no more about it, placing them in a truce with the probing questions. Instead they concentrated on the walking, which was turning out to be endless.

They hit a new rhythm; they trudged and Becca moaned. A lot. *What was the point of this? She had a stitch. Could they stop? There had better bloody be a pub at the top. Why was everyone so cheerful? Weirdos. Did he have any more sweets? Did they really need to get to the top? Ally wouldn't know. Being scattered midway was probably just as lovely. No really, didn't he have some more sweets?*

The summit was in sight, but Becca thought Charlie was joking when he now pointed out the curving ridge they'd be navigating to get up there. It looked properly dangerous.

He threw her an "It'll be fine," as he moved on, picking up his pace so he was just far enough ahead to keep an eye on her, but where people wouldn't assume they were together. The following sheep lent a calm ear to her swearing.

Becca cursed herself for not having packed her earphones. She could have done with some loud angry music to power her up there.

The path grew much steeper and Charlie allowed her to catch up, obviously aware of what lay ahead. The ground plateaued at the top of the ridge, but it was madly narrow with a steep drop to either side. Becca kept her eyes on his heels so as not to look Death in the eye. This was lunacy.

"Nearly there, BJ," he coached, far enough ahead so she couldn't lamp him.

Her heart was beating like the clappers, from exertion and fear. The summit wasn't too far off now, just another steep bit to go, so she paused at a gap between two crags to gain her breath for it. Looking out, she was treated to the view of the fields and lakes below and – "What the...?"

She sensed Charlie's shoulders slump.

"Lister!" He didn't turn. "Lister!" She found a spurt of energy, which carried her up to him in seconds. Looking him in the face and pointing over the crag, she saw his mouth was pulled in, braced. Oh! He'd been *expecting* this.

"What the fuck, Charlie, is that?" she asked.

He sighed. Deeply. "The Mountain Railway."

Becca's mouth opened and closed several times. It was a very rare occasion where she was speechless, or perhaps she couldn't decide which swear to fire out first.

"A train?"

"Yes."

"That goes from the bottom to the top?"

"Yes."

"With passenger people?"

"Yes."

Becca's posture transformed to something volcanic. "What are we doing this shit for, then? Why is my arse not on a seat in that?" She was livid. She raised her hands in the air with an exasperated *Ugh!*, missing his eye-roll and wincing smile to the other walkers.

"A train! A bleeding train! Why wouldn't you take or mention the train?" She was apoplectic.

"It wouldn't be in the spirit of things. Ally would have walked it."

"Ally said nothing about how to get up there, just to scatter her on Snowdon. There was no mention of the 'spirit of things'," she air-quoted and added an annoying voice for effect, which garnered her more stares from passing non-train-passengers, but she was beyond caring. "She would totally have expected me to take the train!"

Charlie thought for a moment. "You're right."

That took the wind out of her sails. She'd expected him to shrug and keep walking, leaving her to her hissy-fit. Which she was enjoying. Having a public hissy-fit in such a vast open space was a first for her. A huge stage and an audience. How pleasing.

"I am?" Her eyes narrowed, sensing a ruse.

"Ally would have expected you to take the train – had you bothered to do the homework and investigate your options – which Ally would also have known there was statistically very little chance of you doing." Now, with a grin, he shrugged and walked on. Knob.

Becca emitted a small shriek and chased after him up the rocks.

"Well, I think," she panted, wishing she hadn't chased so much, "given you hid the fact there was a train, or picked this route which was away from the train, that the least you can do is give me a piggy-back for the rest." Charlie had good, broad, reliable shoulders and Becca was sure he could manage it. She'd even put up with hanging onto his body, despite her non-contact rule. Not that there was anything *repulsive* about his body. Charlie was very well-regarded by the girls of her uni house, and she wasn't blind – she could appreciate his physical attributes as being on the finer side of things, but it was a simple point of law that she didn't go near her best friend's man.

He laughed and kept walking.

"No, really, I wasn't joking," she pointed out, still trying to keep up with him.

"And yet, it was ludicrously funny, BJ. Well done. Edinburgh Fringe next year?"

She'd love to go to the Fringe. But he was taking the piss, and she was still annoyed about the train, which was chuffing up towards the summit, the carriages filled with the happy faces of the people who couldn't be faffed with this walking malarkey either or hadn't been conned into it. She'd be giving them all filthy looks when they met at the top.

Becca muttered and chuntered the rest of the way, settling on a loop of her ripest swears which scared off the passing families and sent Charlie off ahead, with the promise of getting the teas in.

On the stony ground, knees pulled up in front of them, they sat sipping their tea. She had to admit it was the best tea she'd ever had, just as he'd promised. Not that she'd tell him, because she didn't like telling people they were right. That never set a good precedent. But he'd watched her face as she'd had the first mouthful, and she'd been unable to hold the poker face from the ecstasy, so he probably knew already.

The view was stunning; there were more mountains, but also, to her surprise, sea. She was aware of the shape of Wales and there being sea around three sides of it, but she hadn't listened much more than that in Geography. She hadn't known where Snowdon precisely was in Wales. But it was beautiful. Breathtakingly so. The sky was blue and so was the sea beyond. Charlie had said she was lucky: although it was a little windy, more often than not the summit was in the cloud, so this was a treat. She'd told him she'd expected nothing *but* blue skies, considering her efforts. The universe knew what she deserved.

They sat in almost companionable silence. This just had to be taken in. Sitting on top of a bit of the world, in the sweeter-smelling air, she felt small. In a good way. It made her issues feel small, the world seeming much much bigger than she normally thought of it. And despite all the people milling around them, racing up the last steps to the summit marker for selfies, there was a peace too. Ordinarily, she didn't like quiet, but this was a stillness she found both new and calming. Sipping more of her tea, Becca begrudgingly accepted why some people might put themselves through this walking crap now and again, why Ally and Charlie might have enjoyed sitting up here together, and possibly why Ally wanted Becca to experience it too. Right now, she was glad Ally had asked her.

Charlie pulled the glass bottle from his pocket. They'd already tapped it on the trig point at the top. It too looked tiny in the scheme of things. And yet, the value of the contents was huge. It brought a smile to Becca's face. Charlie held the glass up to the light, then moved it from one side to the other as if showing it the view.

"She'd have loved this," he said.

"Understandably," Becca conceded.

"She'd have loved you being here too."

"Well, let's face it, it would only have happened over my dead body, or as it turned out, hers." He swung to look at her, his brow scrunched up. She gave him a tart look. It was true, she wasn't going to take it back. And then he let out a laugh, deep and full. He'd always had a decent laugh, she thought. An honest laugh. He didn't bother if he didn't mean it. Not that she sought to entertain him at all, ever, but Becca always knew a joke, scene or quip worked if it got a laugh from him. Becca could always identify Charlie's laugh from the stage, when Ally had forced him along to Becca's student plays.

Charlie removed the bottle's stopper.

"How are you going to do it? The ashes aren't just going to fling out of there."

"I wasn't planning on *flinging* her." He sounded insulted.

"Pouring her in a heap feels wrong. And others might see. You aren't supposed to scatter ashes wherever you like. I looked it up." *There* was a Google wormhole she'd fallen into.

"Do you want me to make a hole in my trouser pocket and let her drop out as I walk, like in *The Great Escape*?"

"Hardly a dignified way of scattering her, is it? Sliding past your spuds. Grim."

"Look, whatever we do, as soon as the wind whips up she'll fly. And that's fine. I think that's what she wanted. So how about here, between us, we make a little pile of Ally? No one will know. And then we walk away and nature can do its thing."

She couldn't think of a better idea, and she liked the idea of them sitting on either side of her.

"We should wait though, until we go," he said. She was with him on this. She could imagine getting a faceful of ashes, if a gust hit them.

"Read the letter first then."

He pulled the envelope out of his pocket and began opening it with an air of slow reverence.

Becca plucked it out of his hands and tore it open. She'd climbed mountains for this. (OK, *one*, but still.)

Reading an email from Ally had been hard enough; seeing her handwriting, wobbly with weakness, was worse. Becca took several deep breaths to control the lump in her throat, cursing the walk up here for being so exhausting. She was not at her strongest for this sort of thing.

"Go on then," Charlie said.

"*My lovely loves,*" Becca started, and rubbed her eye with her palm. That was *so* Ally, refusing to put one of them in front of the other. "*If you're reading this, then you must be at the top of Snowdon.*" Becca tried to keep a grip on the tremor in her voice.

"Told you she intended us to do this at the top," Charlie interjected.

"Shh, Lister," she said, going on, "*in which case, Yay Becca! – look what you managed. And, bloody hell, Charlie – look what you got Becca to do! Some miracles can happen.*" Becca paused for a second. She didn't think a death note was the appropriate place for Ally to take the piss. Magnanimously, she put the gripe aside, wanting to know what Ally had to say. "*I'm so grateful you did it, I wanted to get there so badly.*" Becca felt a glow; they'd allowed her to fulfil her wish. She would do anything for her bestie, then and now. She suspected Charlie felt the same.

"*There were so many things I didn't get to do.*" Becca heard a small sniff from her side, but didn't stop and didn't look up, keen for Charlie to have his privacy and for her not to have to console him. They weren't in that place. "*Future things, of course; marriage, kids – but I see they simply weren't destined to be part of my story after all. But there are a few things, incidental experiences I'd hoped to get to, but didn't. Being unwell gives you lots of time to think about such things and distil them down to the most important few. My little bucket list."* Becca stopped. Ally never mentioned a bucket list to her. Not once. She would have moved heaven and earth to have taken Ally through it. "Did you know about this?"

"No." He was equally confounded.

Ally had listed five things. Becca scanned them, then showed Charlie. Snowdon, the top one, was struck through already.

"I understand that one," said Becca, pointing to one, "and that one."

"And I think I understand that one," he added, indicating another. "She never mentioned a list, though. Not to me."

Nor to her. Becca felt a moment of sadness, that perhaps she didn't know her friend as well as she'd thought, although it gave her an ounce of relief that Charlie didn't either.

"Maybe she came up with it at the end?"

"Maybe." That seemed an easier way to think about it.

Becca read on: *"I'd like to ask, if you have time, whether you would consider doing them for me, and take me along, like you did today? Mum will sort the ashes. I just need you to do the legwork, because, well, you know…"* Oh, they did. *"It would mean the world to me.*

"So this is it. No more letters or emails now, my loves, just my hope that you'll take me to my special places and let me live vicariously through you. Please say yes.

"Remember, I love you both – so so much.

"*Me xx.*"

They sat in stunned silence for some minutes, staring out at the vast scenery, before Charlie ventured, "Of course, it's a yes, right?"

"Of course."

"I mean, we'd do anything for her."

"Anything." Neither of them had shifted their gaze, and the conversation felt precarious. "Clearly," she added, given where they were sitting.

"Do you think," he asked carefully, "she meant do them *together*?" Becca could have been offended, but she was thinking the exact same thing.

"You mean maybe divvy them up?"

"Mmm-hh."

It felt like they were considering something of dubious ethics. Becca bounced the letter in front of her, her forearms resting on her tucked-up knees. She was debating it from all the angles, and every time, she came back to the same thing.

"She wrote the letter to both of us. To be read together," she decided, tucking a wisp of her hair back behind her ear as the breeze wafted it across her face. "I think – and it dismays me as much as it does you – it's implicit. I suspect doing it *together* is 'in the spirit of things'." Saying it like that made it sound like it was partly his fault. She could have sworn his head dropped a bit, at her side.

"Is there a time frame?"

"I read you everything there was. I guess we can take as long or short a time as we like." She turned to him then. "Let's be honest, while there are powerful arguments for getting them over and done with ASAP, neither of us are inclined to do this again soon, are we? I can't take that many weekends off either."

He didn't disagree with her. "What do you suggest, then?"

Becca thought about it. "Who else is there but us and Valerie to really remember her? As the years go by, she'll become just a name people remember now and again, or a face in the uni photos, who they'll try to place, and if they do remember, 'Whatever became of her?' will quickly move the conversation on because it was too sad." The thought of it made her heart ache. "She did so much for me. I want her memory honoured," she said quietly, "so, if you're up for it, we could do one of these each year?"

He mulled it over. She was pretty sure he was having the same struggle she was in terms of it being the pair of them, but she knew the principle was a goer.

"Deal," he said. Becca was relieved, not least because next year was a long way off. There was a moment of silence, neither of them knowing what to say or whether it required some sealing of the deal, but Charlie broke it. "Shall we start then? Scatter the first lot?"

They still needed a plan though, but sitting with the letter and the bottle, almost the three of them again, she'd had an idea.

"Do you remember the bark on the oak outside Senate House?" Becca asked, looking out again at the view. Outside the university administration building, there was a patch of grass they'd liked to sit out on between lectures. They'd leaned against the base of an ancient oak tree, Ally in the middle, which was always the way, keeping them all together and keeping Charlie and Becca apart. On the last night of uni, Ally had brought a penknife and carved their initials into the bark along with a heart. Becca had a photo of it and the three of them on her shelf. Actually, she'd bent Charlie's end of it back under in the frame so it was just her and Ally. But the bark was there.

"Sure." His hair hung long over his eyes, messy from the breeze, but she could see he understood.

"Let's do that." She picked up a pointy rock and carved a B into the ground. Then she etched a heart above and to the left, before handing him the stone. He scored out a C on his side and handed her the bottle. Becca snuck a brisk look around with the deftness of someone who wasn't unacquainted with shoplifting and poured the ashes out to make an A. The lightest particles flew with the wind almost immediately.

She heard a photo being taken and looked up to see Charlie sliding his phone away. She didn't know what to think of it. It wasn't a selfie moment, but then again, this was the last they'd see of these ashes…

"Send me that," she said gruffly, getting up and masking a sniff as she pocketed the bottle. She glanced at her watch and back towards the café. "Come on, we're outta here." Her tone was brusque and businesslike. Charlie sat for a while longer staring at the A on the ground. She saw his index finger stray towards the ashes, as if to brush the surface layer…

"Hey! Gotta go."

He whipped his hand away and pulled his backpack together. He kept his head down, unwilling to look at her or speak. Becca stalked back towards the visitor centre.

"It's this way, Becca," he said, pointing back the way they'd arrived, but she continued on.

"Yeah, no. I'm getting the train down. The one you didn't tell me about."

"You can't," he said, bewildered.

"Yeah, I *can*. I checked when I came out of the loos. If there's a space in it, I can have it."

"Ally wanted us to walk it."

"As mentioned before, Ally didn't specify, *as you well know*. And knowing Ally, she'd totally expect me to get the train down once I knew there was a train to take. I'm just following in the 'spirit of things'." She did the air-quote thing again for good measure and to set their interactions back on track. Things had got a bit … well, *amiable* … up there.

"You can't because the car is in Rhyd-Ddu."

She walked back up to him, tired of shouting. "Let's be honest here," she said. "You don't relish the idea of another three hours with me, listening to how much I hate the walking – and I *really* hate the walking – any more than I do. So I'm doing us both a favour taking the train and sitting in one of the hundred tea shops there's bound to be at the bottom, with cake and a strong cup of tea, until you come and get me."

His expression was a fight between outrage and relief. It was one she'd witnessed many times. The relief won out.

"Fine. I'll meet you in Llanberis. I'll call you when I get there."

She was already walking towards the train before he even finished.

Four hours later, she was back with her head against the car window, tummy full of bara brith, wrapped in her duvet, asleep as they drove south. They didn't speak again until they said their goodbyes at the kerb outside her house, a carrier bag of Ally's walking gear at her feet. Less angry than at the funeral last year, it was a simple "Bye then" and "Yeah". Charlie seemed eager to get on and perhaps a little cross with her. Not that she knew why. Maybe she'd snored? As his car moved down the street, Becca stood hotdogged in her duvet watching him, the midnight air – crisp, if dirtier-smelling – around her nose. The day had been long, emotional and disconcerting, given Ally's request. The letter sat warm in her pocket, Becca having purloined it with practised sleight of hand, thus avoiding any mountain-top wrestling.

Of course she'd see Ally's wishes through, even if it meant a day a year in Charlie's aggravating company for the next four. For Ally, Becca reckoned they could manage it; they'd meet, complete the task and depart again. Bish bash bosh. Simples. They were grown-ups, they could be reasonable, and they had a fairly accepted code of engagement. So really, how wrong could this go?

2013

There was something about a cold winter evening that Charlie enjoyed, the frigid air forcing him to be alert after the afternoon fug of the office. People passed, collars up, faces tucked into the comfort of their coats as they made their way towards the tube. Charlie liked the adventurousness of it, the being outside when sense and skin craved the warmth of home. He had a vague idea where the restaurant Ollie and Shrinidhi had booked for their engagement dinner was, but he hadn't searched for further detail, preferring a brief moment of detective work when he got there.

"Remind me how you know these guys," Liv said, taking Charlie's hand in hers. They walked along Dean Street, the Friday evening after-work crowds not spilling out onto the streets like they had the previous month. Dry-January was almost done. Another week and there'd be the usual buzz and milling about, murmurs of how much weight had been lost and how miserable it had been.

"I rented a room in Shrin's student house for a term during the second year of uni. My place had damp and needed sorting. Shrin's boyfriend Ollie and I have been close friends ever since."

"Brent's cousin?"

"The very same."

A week before he'd arrived back in the UK, Ollie had emailed, mentioning his cousin needing a researcher at his TV production company. Squirrelling himself away in a corner, thrashing Google for facts, had sounded perfect to Charlie. He had the experience from his journalism days and he could write notes pretty damn quick so Brent saw the potential. Liv worked for Brent, Charlie now worked for Liv, so it all slotted together nicely. And since the Christmas party where Liv had cornered him and suggested they work on an even closer basis, *they'd* slotted together nicely too.

Christmas had been rough the previous year. Nearly seven months on from Ally's death, he'd been five thousand miles from home and a mess. Christmas day he'd ended up in a Bogotá gutter, his cash stolen, and not yet able to feel the battering he'd taken, being numb still from all the aguardiente he'd drunk to get him through the day. He should have felt lucky to be alive, but he hadn't cared either way.

So, having been apprehensive about this Christmas, Liv's company had been a blessing. They'd only left her flat to go to work in the last six weeks. They were on first-name terms with the Just Eat man now – another reason getting out this evening felt like an adventure.

Charlie gave her hand a squeeze. He'd missed this: the holding hands, the arm slung around another body, the flirty looks. Losing Ally had shown him how he'd taken the smallest of touches for granted: the bump of bodies as they navigated the bathroom; the brush of her fingers across his back as she passed him at their breakfast bar. His skin craved even her slightest touches.

He hadn't exactly lived as a monk on his year away; there had been warm beds and soft bodies during his travels in the Americas, brief liaisons sought for quick-fix comfort, promising nothing. He'd needed them at the time, but they hadn't been meaningful or offered connection. His player days had ended with Ally, he knew that now. The companionship of another person was a tonic he hadn't been aware he needed before. Since he came back, he realised how easily solitude could become loneliness. Liv was reminding him now what meaningful comfort felt like and of the restorative powers of those everyday intimate touches.

"And they won't mind me coming along for their engagement dinner?" she asked.

Charlie pulled her in to plant a kiss on her temple. "They wanted you to come. They want to meet you. And of course they're nosy. They're lovely people, Liv." He felt his smile widen. He couldn't be happier for them. They were a Forever couple in his eyes. Two people who fitted perfectly. Like he had with Ally. Their forever just hadn't happened. He looked away and schooled his face, keen Liv wouldn't see any kind of wobble. He had yet to discuss Ally with her. Of course they'd had the "Why are you single?" discussion and he'd said he'd been travelling for the last year, which was true. He'd said he'd realised journalism wasn't for him and had taken a sabbatical year, which again was also factually correct, if not the true motivation. But Charlie figured talking about dead fiancées was the last thing to do in the fledgling moments of a new romance. That had disaster written all over it. So he'd swerved it. Only, now, he wasn't sure how to broach it. Maybe he wouldn't have to. He'd asked Shrin and Ollie not to mention it. Just for now.

Liv spotted the restaurant and as she made for the door, he impulsively spun her as if in a dance, then reeled her in and walked her backwards to the adjacent wall, where he eased himself against her.

Her eyes widened. He ducked his head to scoop a swift kiss from her.

"Stealing kisses?" she asked.

His eyes flicked to the door. "Survival provisions. I might not get to kiss you for a few hours."

Her smile spread. "Well then, if we're banking them, that one won't last long, will it?"

Charlie crinkled his nose, thinking. "Think we need to do better?"

She slid into his black peacoat, her arms wrapping around his waist. She gave him a slow bring-it-on nod.

There was lots he liked about Liv. She was a couple of years older and seemed to know what life was about. She knew what she wanted in the office, at home and, as it happened, in bed, and he found he enjoyed rising to meet her demands. She didn't play games, she spoke her mind. Bringing him a drink at the Christmas party, she'd set it down in front of him and said, "We should go out on a date," just like that, bold as. He'd liked it.

Perhaps it was the mood of the party, the throbbing beat from the dance floor, he wasn't sure, but his pulse increased as his eyes skipped between hers.

Accepting the drink, he took a sip. "Where will we go?" he asked, their eye contact locking.

She tilted her head. "Does it matter?"

"Nope," he said, not missing a beat. "You, me, what more do we need?"

He'd had a few drinks already. He'd thought he'd need

them to get him through the evening, but it turned out they'd put him in that magical realm of having all the slick answers, flirty without being letchy. And then there was that ego boost which came with knowing she liked him, the thrill of it giving extra shine to his eyes. He saw her respond to it too, her pupils dilating. The rest of the room faded into a haze as they conversed in short, loaded phrases, leaning in, knees brushing. Colleagues passed and said hello, but weren't invited into the conversation.

Finally, Liv had finished the remaining half of her drink in one, and said, "Let's go."

He hadn't needed asking twice. He'd pulled a coin from his pocket and flipping it, stated, "Heads, your place; tails, mine."

Other than visiting his parents over the Christmas days, he hadn't spent a night away from her since.

Matching her slow pace now, under the glow of the street light, Charlie's mouth glided back to hers, for a long deep kiss which would definitely set them up for the dinner and gave promises of what could happen later back at hers. There was an exhilaration to a new romance he wished could be bottled. The lightness, giddiness in fact, where things were fun and exciting, getting to know another personally, *intimately*, peeling off the layers with each encounter.

More than anything else, he was enjoying rediscovering old Charlie, *fun* Charlie, whom Ally had fallen in love with, who was good company to his mates. His facial muscles knew how to smile again, his endorphins had escaped some deep archive. Losing Ally had been losing half of himself. For months he couldn't work out who he even *was* without her. Moreover, the Charlie who'd been left behind was miserable, angry and lost.

He didn't like *that* Charlie, with his unshakable cloak of sadness. Charlie had desperately *missed* being himself. Now, having turned a corner on his travels and found a basic foundation to restart from, he felt he was emerging from his hibernation of gloom as Liv kindled the sparks.

Charlie touched his forehead to hers as they regained their breath. Not that he was one to compare, but Liv and Ally kissed similarly, keen to steer things, happy to stand their ground if challenged. It made for interesting kissing, a feisty dance between them, and one he liked.

Making it inside and upstairs, Charlie made the introductions between Liv, Ollie and Shrin. As he'd known they would, they welcomed Liv with wide smiles and looks of love towards him. All the while they stood with linked fingers, always happier when they were in contact. He'd missed that too.

"Sit next to me, Liv," Shrinidhi said, taking her seat on the banquette against the restaurant wall. They'd booked a long table for sixteen. Charlie had said many hellos walking in, knowing most of the faces from uni and pub nights. "I want to know all about how you got together with our Charlie."

"Told you, Liv," Charlie said, giving Shrin a stare, "*Nosy.*" Shrin stuck her tongue out at him.

"I enjoy hearing stories, that's all. Anything we can tease you with later. Call it 'intelligence gathering'."

"Well, I'll have the seat on the other side of her," he said, pointing to the space on the end, "then I can at least monitor the information flow." To Liv he said, "Shrin has a bank of embarrassing stories about me she likes to dish when she's had a few."

Liv raised an eyebrow. "You do embarrassing things?" She turned to Shrin and smiled. "He's always very serious in the office, so this I need to hear." Shrin linked arms with Liv, and gave Charlie a *Ha!* look. *Ah bugger*, he was in the crap now. He'd been known – during his uni days – to get lost when drunk. He'd turned up asleep in many unlikely places.

"Not a day goes by when I don't wish I'd picked more discreet friends," he told Liv, bracing himself. "I love them dearly, but they're a pair of blabbermouths."

"I work in PR, it's my actual job to disseminate information," Shrin said, unabashed.

"And I work in libel law, and none of it's illegal," Ollie said, mouth full of breadstick. Patience was not his forte, particularly with food.

Charlie took Liv's coat, and headed for the hatstand in the corner. On closer inspection there weren't any hooks left and he was left debating whether it was rude to rearrange other people's coats for more efficient hanging. Best not. He perched Liv's coat on top of numerous others. It slipped off. He tried again, then two other hooks, all to the same end. The garlic and grilled steak scents in the restaurant were calling his attention now and he was getting hungry. He flung both their coats over the top of the stand. The entire thing toppled over.

After some minutes of righting, rearranging and profuse apologising to the nearest diners, he had it all sorted, save for his and Liv's coats which he decided would be far better on the banquette with them.

He glanced back to Liv, in case she'd seen his hatstand altercation. Thankfully, she was facing the other way.

Bugger. It looked like someone had jumped into his seat.

He could see arms moving about, removing outerwear. Whatever the coat was, it looked like someone had skinned the cookie monster, petroleum blue and tufty.

Charlie headed back towards Liv. Who knew what Ollie had disclosed? Ollie's job required confidentiality, which conversely meant he was as watertight as a colander with any sensitive information outside of work. He simply didn't have the capacity to do both. This was an accepted fact amongst their friends, and equally, if you wanted to share news fast, Ollie was considered the go-to guy.

Reaching Ollie, he got a better look at who he was about to oust from his seat and faltered. The big mess of red hair had been unleashed from a crocheted beret, otherwise he'd have known immediately.

Charlie felt the blood drain from his face. This was the absolute worst. Becca sitting next to Liv was a shit-storm in the offing. She was already a law unto herself; he had an inkling of how she might take him seeing someone new and he didn't want her to be the one who landed the Ally information on Liv. *How* hadn't he twigged that, of course, Becca would be there? He could have headed this off, like he had with Shrin and Ollie. He could only imagine how wrong-footed Liv might feel, in front of strangers.

Moving quickly towards the end of the table, he acknowledged he should have tackled the subject with Liv earlier. *Damn damn damn.* Getting a better look at Becca now, her hair longer than last summer, her black-cat eyeliner and red lips bold as war paint, all Charlie could think was that Becca would absolutely take the opportunity for payback. Not for anything particular, but most likely for everything he'd done to bug her over the uni years, and Snowdon too. She was both petty and vindictive. She could bide her time with a grievance like a pro.

Liv caught his gaze. "Everything all right?" He wanted to shout *No*, but managed with a simple "Yeah yeah, all good."

Becca was rummaging in her huge tote, and popped a gift on the table along with a card with *Shrin + Ols* scrawled across it. It was wrapped in some kind of fabric. Her relaxed face tensed as she looked up and saw him standing above them.

"Lister," she said, with a curt nod. Clearly any goodwill from Snowdon had evaporated in the last six months.

"White."

All his alarm bells were telling him to shield Liv from the hurricane sitting to her right. He looked down at the empty wooden chair. Wisdom told him there was no chance he was getting Becca's bum off the padded banquette. She already looked soundly sunk into it. Bracing himself, Charlie sat.

Ignoring him, Becca handed her gift to Shrin. "Ollie, this is for the pair of you, but we all know Shrin does the unwrapping." Shrin beamed. Becca gave Liv a friendly smile and said, "I've never known anyone like her with unwrapping. Have you seen the sheer bliss she gets from even opening a crisp packet?"

Liv shook her head.

"Pure joy," Becca said. "It's delightful."

Charlie relaxed slightly. She seemed to be on agreeable form this evening.

Shrin gave a little squeal and showed Ollie a photo frame she'd uncovered from what turned out to be a souvenir tea towel from their uni. Ollie studied the photo. "Is that...?"

"Sure is," said Becca. "Took me fucking hours to find. I wish I'd had a camera phone back then." Shrin showed Liv, who had absolutely no idea of the grainy photo's significance. Shrin and Ollie, with questionable hairstyles, sat in what looked like a student kitchen. "First time you brought him back to halls for the night, Shrin. The pre-shag nerves are written all over his face."

"It must be the first photo of us," Shrin said, getting teary, not that this was unusual. Just as she got joy from surprises, she was a complete sap with anything emotional.

"That's what I thought," said Becca. She sat with a small smile, but Charlie could see the response pleased her. He wished he'd spent longer on what to get them than the bottle of Bollinger he'd plopped in front of Ollie earlier. He should at least have wrapped it and given Shrin a hit of her unwrapping-drug.

Liv winked at him across the table. He decided it would be no good for him to sit there tensed the entire evening. Perhaps he could keep the conversation going and away from anything Ally-related all night. He felt a bead of sweat at his temple.

"How's work, Becca?" he started, but with such gusto that Becca seemed faintly alarmed.

"You all right, Lister?"

"Sorry, yes. Just thought you might have some new stories."

Becca paused, then deadpanned, "Glad my working life can be entertaining for you."

"Tell him about the *A&E* gig," Ollie cut in. "I love this one."

Charlie looked at her, enquiring. He knew the hospital drama, but didn't watch it.

"Oh, it was just a one-off."

He found himself genuinely pleased for her. "*A&E* though? TV. That's great."

She shrugged. "It was just two days' filming and I doubt it's a recurring role."

"Tell him the role, Becca," Ollie insisted, his grin enormous.

"Shrin, your fiancé is a malicious perv," said Becca, but with good humour. She turned to Charlie and with a straight face said, "I'm 'Patient with stuck Kinder egg'."

Liv got it before Charlie and couldn't mask her snort. Ollie's roar of laughter turned heads across the room.

"Seriously," Shrin said, "it's had Ollie tickled since you told us. He keeps sniggering around the flat and I know that's what he's thinking of."

Becca's face became serious. "It's based on an actual case. I researched the role thoroughly. Woman wanted to propose to her bloke, popped the ring inside the inner egg, resealed the chocolate and foil wrap and hid the whole thing in her ninny, and then neither the daft bint nor her bloke could get the thing out. Totally true."

Charlie didn't know what to make of it. Becca's air of being a professional made it impossible to know whether she would tolerate any piss-taking today, and he was desperate to. However, he knew how hard it was for her to land jobs and so mocking this one felt harsh.

"Anyway," said Becca, taking a swig of her red wine and waving the hilarity off, "easiest work, lying on my back with my legs in stirrups." The table laughed, and Becca laughed with them. She thrived on their being entertained by her stories, even if she was the clown here. But having just witnessed her watching Shrinidhi's joy at unwrapping her gift, Charlie could see the thrill of this didn't quite reach Becca's eyes.

"Your turn, Ollie," Becca said. "I want to hear about the proposal."

Ollie's face glowed with pride.

"I properly surprised her. She blubbed like a little girl."

"I did not!" Shrin exclaimed. "Well, maybe just a little bit."

Becca scoffed. Shrin would have been a mess. "And you had no idea?"

Ollie's fiancée looked at him with adoration. "Not a clue. He was like a stealthy spy." She gave him a smutty smile which suggested this was a game they'd continued after. Then she turned to the girls and behind a hand whispered loudly, "It was an impromptu trip to Paris and he was insisting on seeing the Eiffel Tower right before dinner *and* that I had to wear my best dress, and when we got there he kept trying to shoo the other tourists away." She turned back, with a smirk. "I was clueless anything was afoot. Wasn't I, my James Bond?" She waggled her eyebrows at him, making Ollie blush.

"Well played, Ols," congratulated Charlie, keen to support his best friend. "Romance is clearly alive and well. Were you nervous?"

"Me?" Ollie scoffed, indignant. Then his expression softened, "Totally cacking it. But also trying hard not to blurt it out all the way there. Mate, it was like holding in a fart on a first date." All the guys at the table seemed to nod at that one.

At the lull in the laughter Becca turned to Charlie.

"Weren't you starting a new job when I last saw you?"

"I was. I'm a researcher, for a TV company."

Becca's chin lifted. "TV? Got any roles for me?" Always hustling. Charlie had to give her credit for seizing the moment. Ally had trained her well.

"Not unless you've recently become a Bedouin. Or are looking to join the Yakuza. Then it might be a journey for us to follow."

He watched as she weighed it up, and it made him laugh. She was actually thinking how she might make it happen.

"Maybe another time," she settled with herself, banking the information for future use. "Do you work with Shrin, Liv?" she asked, politely drawing Liv into the conversation.

Liv swallowed her mouthful of wine, "No. We met about two minutes before you arrived."

Becca gave her a confused look. Then she sussed it. "Oh, you know Ollie?"

"Not that either," Liv said with a smile. "I'm here with Charlie." She leaned in conspiratorially, "I snuck in under the 'plus-one' card."

It was only because he knew Becca's face that Charlie caught the fractional freeze. "Oh." She gave Charlie a tilted look. "I didn't know Charlie had a plus one." Charlie returned to a full-body clench.

"We're quite new," he said, as if it explained and settled everything. Liv shot a glance between the two of them, but didn't speak. "Liv and I work together."

Becca turned back to Liv. "How interesting," she said, sweetly. "An office romance."

"An office Christmas party romance, no less," Liv filled in. "But one that's still going after the beer goggles have dissipated." Liv gave Charlie a private look which was both affectionate and flirty. It wasn't lost on Becca.

"So, you're Charlie's boss?" Becca said. It wasn't really a question.

"Ah, more of a line manager than boss. And only because I've been doing it longer, I suspect. He'll whizz up the career path soon enough."

Charlie was trying to second-guess Becca. He couldn't predict where her mind went – she might suggest Liv was taking advantage of her senior position, for all he knew. He was praying she'd behave this evening, although he had scant past evidence on which to base any such hope. In the end he chose to have faith in Becca's loyalty to Shrin and Ollie. For all her flaws, she had always been unbudgingly loyal. She wouldn't spoil their night.

Ollie asked about the programmes they were working on, and where they would take them. Liv got to travel with the crews; Charlie was wishing he could too, soon. Detailing things to Ollie, swapping the narrative with Liv across their stories, Charlie couldn't avoid feeling the eyes watching him from across the table. To others it looked like Becca was following the conversation, but he knew he was being scrutinised.

The starters arrived, Shrin and Ollie having set the menu for the evening. A beautiful plate of mixed antipasti. Becca wolfed hers in a matter of minutes. Charlie had never known her not to scoff a meal as if it might be her last. Ally had said as a young kid she'd been forgotten at times, and as an adult she didn't have the steadiest of incomes. Charlie suspected she chose café jobs to supplement her acting work as much for the leftovers as for the flexible shifts.

"So, Becca," Liv said, between mouthfuls, "do you know Charlie through Ollie?"

Becca gave him a long look. "Actually, I've known him longer than Ollie has. We shared a wall for a term in second-year uni." Liv nodded her on. "So," Becca continued, "Ally was studying abroad for autumn term, and the housing office moved Charlie into her vacant room while they fixed something in his." Liv looked down the table, reminding herself of the names.

"Who's Ally?"

A light silence settled as Shrinidhi and Ollie both paused their conversations. Liv looked about to see what it was she'd said. Becca looked at Charlie and tilted her head in question.

"So, um, Ally isn't here tonight," he explained, "because she died a couple of years ago." Becca's brow drew in. OK, so maybe it wasn't quite two years ago, but he'd made himself stop noting the days, weeks, months, because it hurt too much. Not knowing exactly numbed things.

"Oh," said Liv, understanding. "I'm so sorry you lost your friend."

They all nodded and Shrinidhi made a blunt-headed effort to change the subject by telling everyone the main course would be posh fish-fingers and chips, as Ollie was still ten at heart.

"And how was he as a house-mate?" Liv asked Becca, perhaps thinking she was moving the conversation on from Ally, but so not.

Charlie braced. This was where she'd lay everything on the line.

"Ally was my best friend," she clarified, "and…" She paused, giving Charlie a look. Here it came. His not having told Liv about Ally earlier and not having claimed her as his girlfriend just now was about to bite him in the arse.

"… I was very grumpy about her leaving me for a term in Munich, so I wasn't perhaps best disposed to be welcoming," Becca said, "but, I can *definitively* say," she continued, leaning in, "I hated sharing that wall with him. He was so noisy. His guests too." Liv gave him a mock-shocked look, because everyone considered him a placid guy at work. "Honestly, Liv, I was glad to see the back of him." Liv laughed, Shrin and Ollie laughed. Charlie forced himself to grin, but he knew Becca wasn't fooling. Like a court jester, Becca was rather good at being truthful under the guise of comedy.

"And also, as soon as he introduced himself," she continued, hamming it up, "I knew we were sworn enemies." She made it sound like some mafia vendetta. Charlie rolled his eyes and sank in his seat, ready for what was coming.

"Why?" asked Liv, intrigued as much as enjoying his being harangued. She didn't think Becca was serious.

"Turns out, we'd sort of met the previous term. I performed in a play, an experimental piece, but good—"

"It was dire," Charlie interjected, but Becca had the floor.

"Not everyone was intellectual enough to understand it," she explained to Liv.

"Not unless they were stoned," he tried, to no one in particular.

He hadn't wanted to do the theatre reviews. He'd fancied

himself as an investigative journo, but the student newspaper's editor had put him on the Arts pages, which, by Charlie's estimation, had involved wasting his evenings watching nonsensical self-indulgent tosh.

"It was thought-provoking," Becca insisted. It had definitely provoked him.

"It was shite." He'd written the five-hundred-word review in the bus shelter waiting for his bus home, the words spilling out of him with the angry speed of someone who'd just spaffed two hours when they had an essay deadline looming.

"And he trashed it in his review. It was vicious." Becca did a masterful job of looking pained.

Everyone looked at him.

"It really *was* shite," he tried weakly, then remembered he was entitled to his opinion and decent journalists stood by their words. Yes, it had been salty, but it was a well-written, valid review. He sat up again in his chair.

"Becca, it was a fair review. The play was rubbish and you know it. But I actually praised you in it. You were the *only* bit I praised, so I don't see why you've held it against me for years. I said you were good."

Becca leaned in. "You said, and I quote, '*White, who already displays a commendable sense of humour for agreeing to writhe on the floor in nothing but a bikini and green paint for the play's duration, has a clear talent for comedy.*'"

Charlie flung his hands out to everyone. "There, you see? I was nice to Becca. That's not vicious. I was nice!" Why did he feel like a condemned man pleading his innocence?

Becca's eyes narrowed. "It was a tragedy, Charlie," she said, her gritted teeth suggesting that no, she still wasn't past it. "There wasn't any comedy in it."

Ah.

Swinging back to Liv, Becca instantly dropped her maligned stance, and said chirpily, "See why I wasn't chuffed to share a wall?"

Deflating again in his chair, Charlie experienced a state of confusion: his discomfort at being deemed a poor house-mate in his new girlfriend's eyes, melded with the relief of Becca not having thrown him under the bus.

Sitting through further stories of his student blunders, Charlie finished his main course and looked for the loos. He was bursting for a wee but reluctant to leave Liv alone with Becca. Could he make it through the trio of desserts Shrin was gushing about? Finally, he reasoned if he was quick he'd limit the risk, *plus* Becca hadn't dobbed him in so far.

He'd never peed so fast. Racing back out of the swing door, he came to an abrupt halt. Becca stood leaning against the wall opposite, arms folded. The Ladies' toilets were downstairs. She was there for him.

"Are you lost?" he asked, instinct telling him to take the attacking position. He pointed to the Men's sign. "Or are you waiting for trade?"

She pulled her mouth flat and with an unimpressed nod said, "Sex worker gags, now? Classy." Argh, he was being a dick, but she brought it out in him, and he knew he was on the back foot. He wanted to keep walking, but it would do him no good to back down from her.

"What can I do for you, BJ?" he crossed his arms, mirroring

hers. She probably was entitled to say her piece, given she'd not stuck it to him in there.

"Don't call me that," she snarled, scowling. Her eyes bounced between his, trying to fathom him out. "Didn't take you long, did it, replacing her?"

"It's two years—" he started.

"Not even. A year and a half. I've read men don't wait long, but seriously?"

"This is new, *recent*, so who knows where it will lead? But even so, I can't help the timing."

"You have choices, Lister. You could have said, 'No one for five years.'"

"Five years?" Her thinking she had rules for him to follow suddenly made him angry. "You have no idea," he spat out. "I've been lonely, so bloody lonely. And Ally wanted me to be happy, so when Liv asked me out, I said yes, all right? Because I like her, because I'm ready and because I don't need your effing permission."

Becca's eyes had grown narrower with each of his words. She took a clear step forward, but he stood his ground.

"Ask yourself this, Charlie," she said, using his name for once, but it wasn't any friendlier. "If you're so *effing* ready, why haven't you told her about Ally? Why haven't you been open with her, when you're bringing her to meet Ally's old mates? Hmm? Not so fucking ready, are you?"

Charlie said nothing. He was seething with indignation at her taking him to task, but fighting the annoyance of her being right. He had absolutely avoided the conversation.

But Becca was still going. "I thought you and I were the ones Ally could count on, the ones to remember her, but here we are, only eighteen months on and you're already brushing her under the carpet."

Charlie leaned in now, straining not to raise his voice. Their noses were just a centimetre apart, anger radiating off them both.

"I am *not* brushing her under the carpet," he bit out. "We just haven't got to the past relationships chat yet. Which, also, is none of your business. It's my *life*, and I have a right to live it, because the last two years—"

"Eighteen months!" she tried but he was having none of it.

"In the last *years* I've been a shell, properly broken, and I want myself back. I don't owe you any explanations for that and I certainly don't owe you any apologies for wanting to live my life."

Their staring match was interrupted by a low cough. They both turned to see Liv standing at the end of the corridor watching them. He abruptly leaned away from Becca, keen to put some distance between their faces, but neither of them took a step back. Old habits died hard.

Liv walked closer.

"Look, I'm new to this group, I imagine there's loads of history going on here, but I've no time for bullshit or games, so let's cut to the chase. Have you two got something going on?" She looked at Charlie. "I'd just rather know and I'll leave you to it."

The "Ha!" that exploded from Charlie's mouth was pure impulse. Liv looked shocked and he had to qualify it, so she didn't think he was laughing at her. "Honestly Liv, the concept of that is truly laughable. Becca and I are the least likely coupling. Ever." He took her hand and rubbed his thumb over her knuckles. "You've nothing to worry about there. I promise."

Liv studied his face but said nothing. To Charlie's relief she didn't remove her hand. She turned to Becca, her eyebrows rising, ready for Becca to contradict him.

Becca gave her a deadpan look, but one which Charlie knew held respect. Becca was a straight-talker herself.

"You have absolutely nothing to worry about there, as he said," Becca reiterated, which surprised him. He hadn't counted on her support. "Hand on heart, your boyfriend is the biggest dickhead I know." She raised her eyes to him and shot him a look of utter contempt, before walking past Liv back to the table.

"Want to tell me what that was about?" Liv asked, letting go of his hand and stepping away. She leaned against the wall with her arms folded, like she had all the time in the world for confessions.

Hands on his hips, Charlie dropped his head with a shake. Running Liv through Becca's agenda of grievances wasn't something he fancied doing, and updating Liv on who Ally really was wasn't something he wanted to do outside a toilet in a restaurant miles from their homes. Damn. This would be so much easier if she already knew, but that would, of course, have meant having had the nuts to have the conversation earlier. Choosing the route of least immediate conflict, Charlie postponed it again. He'd sort things later...

"Becca's unpredictable at the best of times, not least when she's been drinking. She gets all beefed up on the attention the others give her and her stories, and then all that energy has to go somewhere, most often at me." Yes, he was trashing Becca for his own benefit, but this was a damage limitation exercise and his choices were sparse. "We didn't get on at uni, and it's like she feels she needs to keep the feud going." Liv said nothing. He felt the back of his neck get hot. He hated being put on the spot.

Liv considered it then held out a hand to him. "I don't know her, Charlie, so I'll take your word for it. Come on, there's dessert to be had, and then you can take me home and show me you aren't a dickhead." He felt an accord had been met, but that she wasn't completely sold. There'd be ground to make up there. But that was OK. He had some ideas to take her mind off it.

Ollie gave them a smutty "Oi oi!" as they emerged from the corridor, which sounded ridiculous from a posh boy like him.

Liv gave him a very polite and smiley "Fuck off, Ollie," which Charlie appreciated, as did the rest of the table.

It wasn't until Liv sat back down without having to shuffle past her that Charlie realised Becca, along with her enormous bag and muppet-skin coat, had gone.

As he took the spot next to Liv, he'd have been lying if he'd said he wasn't relieved, but somewhere in the back of his mind there was a nagging sense Becca was right. God, how he hated that...

Saturday 27th July
Lower Regent Street, London

"Explain this one to me, please," Charlie said, looking about the vintage double-decker bus. With its chintzy decor and peonies strung everywhere, the Gin Bus looked like a country tearoom on steroids. And wheels. Ally had definitely never mentioned anything like this to him. A quick sweep of the top deck – and his ears – told him he was one of only two guys on the bus.

Becca had been about as effusive to see him emerge from the crowd of tourists in Trafalgar Square as she had been about the pigeons milling around her feet, threatening to peck or crap on her black dolly shoes, but now she had an air of excitement about her as she read through the floral menu card. Every so often their knees knocked together, but there wasn't much he could do about that. The fixed formica table was slim and their legs were long. Charlie half expected Becca to gripe about the knee knocking, but she didn't, and he'd already decided to try making this bearable, casting off the unshed annoyance over January. He would come at this afresh. They were another half year older, he reasoned. They must be able to get through a couple of hours in each other's company without falling out. And this bus was so cheery, anything else would surely be impossible.

Clearly knowing what this task was about, Becca was appropriately dressed. Her navy blue tea-dress with its white spots had that vintage cut about it. She'd done something with her hair, which made her look sort of vintage too. Victory rolls, were they called? It suited her. Had it been Ally, he would have complimented her as soon as the thought crossed his mind. Given it was Becca, he kept his comment to himself, not wanting a lecture on patriarchal viewpoint, objectification and definitions of femininity, but sat back instead and enjoyed her looking smiley for once. It was better than the "wretched" of two years ago, the "tired and mardy" of the previous year, and the "spitting bricks" of the engagement party. Instead, he pulled the new glass bottle, orange this time, from his pocket and placed it on the table. With the sun passing through the window, he could just see the shade of the ashes within.

"She made me tell her," Becca started, like that explained anything. "The deets were supposed to be secret, but I gave in when I thought she could still overcome the cancer. It seemed like something she could hold on for." Becca scanned the deck with a wistful gaze. She was right, of course. Ally would have adored everything about this: the dresses, the low tones of the 1940s playlist and the decor, which no doubt would have inspired an immediate make-over of their flat. "It was going to be part of her hen-do," Becca said carefully. Never having experienced it before, it took him a moment to realise she was being considerate of his feelings.

He felt a tightness in his throat. A city tour on a vintage bus, with high tea and gin, was the perfect choice. Little things like this, things Ally liked, were easily forgotten. Much as he wanted to hold onto all his memories of her, as time passed, the smaller intangible things were like water running between his fingers.

"Good call, White," he said, "she really would have loved this."

The compliment made Becca smile. She had a good smile. It properly filled her face and lit her hazel eyes. And when you got a full one – which admittedly had been rare in his case because she generally reserved a scowl for him – you immediately felt good yourself. That had to be a gift.

The bus had started its tour up Lower Regent Street and a waiter appeared with a pretty three-tiered stand of finger sandwiches, cupcakes and macarons. He could have wolfed the lot, and judging by the way Becca was scoping the tower of food, so could she.

She leaned across the table and whispered, "Do you think they'll do seconds?" The waiter was back before he could answer, with the first of their gins, an Earl Grey Martini, served in pretty teacups.

He raised his cup with a "To Ally" and they clinked. She knocked it back at such a speed, it suggested she wasn't as relaxed about this as she was letting on. Which was understandable. He was having his own issues. Little memories of the plans for the wedding-that-never-was kept popping into his head. Tucked away in a mental box for the last two years, they were suddenly surfacing, reminding him of Ally's ever-evolving wedding mood board and its ideas, which brought such joy to her face. He did his best now to reseal the lid on that box.

He finished his gin, hoping for a Dutch courage kick. He was planning to tell Becca about moving in with Liv. Liv wasn't a woman to waste time and he liked how she steered things. Her empowerment and confidence were a turn-on. It had worked for him and Ally too. Now, he and Liv had been dating for months and they had plans. Looking about the bus, now knowing its significance and considering Becca's good mood, Charlie decided he was going to need more gin.

Becca noted his empty cup and seemed pleased. "Liking the attitude, Lister. You might have made a decent hen." She finished her own and looked about for the next. Oh crap, this might get messy.

"So how shall we do this? The scattering?"

Both their eyes went to the window. Charlie envisaged Ally's ashes flying behind the bus, like a Red Arrows vapour trail.

"Not sensible," Becca chided. "That'll just give us ash-covered, angry tourists."

"There!" he suddenly said, pointing out of the window. Rather than sailing gracefully past London's sights, the stop–start of mid-city traffic had them approaching Piccadilly Circus at a snail's pace, and a catatonic snail at that.

Becca looked in the direction he was pointing.

"In the middle of a flash mob?" A cluster of girls were dancing in formation outside Lillywhites.

"No. *Eros*. The statue."

He was already out of his seat, scooping up the bottle as he went. This was perfect. Eros *was* Romance.

"Lister, wait," Becca said, "let's discuss—"

But he wasn't listening. He'd had this idea and he wanted to go with it, spurred on by something he couldn't quite fathom. "Charlie!" Heads from other tables turned as he vanished down the stairs.

Moments later he was dodging through the traffic to honks from the stationary drivers. Reaching the pavement, he looked back to see Becca's alarmed face pressed up against the glass.

Reaching the base of the monument, Charlie pounded up the nine steps only to realise his memory of it had been false. In his head, he'd remembered it as a working fountain, but in fact there was just a thin moat of murky rainwater in the base. Not something he fancied tipping Ally into.

"Charlie!" Bloody hell, she had a voice like a foghorn when she fancied it. Becca's mouth was crammed up against the small window in the large pane. Her voice actually overrode the traffic and the flash-mob music. Turning, he saw the hold-up had only been for the lights, and now the traffic was moving freely, including their bus, which was turning its nose towards Leicester Square.

He looked back at the statue, suddenly incapable of a decision, having been so sure before.

"Charlie!!" she shouted again. A tourist knocked him and it jolted him into following her command. Clutching the bottle in his fist, he started speed walking towards the bus, not wanting to make more of a scene than he already had. The bus sped up, and he picked up his pace to a trot.

A pack of language-school kids blocked his path and Charlie was tempted to step into the road to avoid them. A bike courier almost took his eyebrows off, leaving him with swearwords ringing in his ears.

"*Mi Scusi, escusez moi, disculpa, entschuldigung,*" he shouted as he mashed his way through the students, the bus getting ahead of him now.

Making it to the other side, Charlie saw Becca standing on the bus's boarding platform, shouting him on. The pavement was still littered with people, checking maps, drinking slushies, or simply dawdling in his way. Charlie broke into a sprint, telling himself this was what all those gym sessions had been for.

More honking indicated his time was up and with a last burst of energy, he reached the bus. Only it seemed to speed up. Becca held onto the bus pole and stretched her hand out to him. He grabbed it and leaped. Her pulling him on board and his momentum brought both of them crashing against the wall of the bus.

"What the fuck was that?" Becca asked into his chest. His one hand still held hers between them; the other, holding the bottle, was braced against the wall above her head, having broken their backward flight.

The panting lasted a couple of moments. This was embarrassing.

"I ... umm ..." He stopped and pulled away, realising he was breathing into her hair. Becca stayed perfectly still against the scarlet metal wall.

"Excuse me, sir! Please stay on the bus, or we'll ask you to leave." The angry waiter shooed them crossly back up the stairs.

"Sorry," he mumbled to them, "I dropped something." He vaguely waved the bottle at the waiter, as Becca dragged him to their seats.

She left him to regain his breath, first smoothing down her dress and then simply staring at him. Just as the other diners were doing.

"Talk me through that?" She seemed a bit pissed about his going rogue.

"I just thought *Eros* was a romantic place to scatter her." He couldn't explain better than that.

She mulled it. Then appeared to let him off.

"Did you do it?"

He shook his head. "The water in it was gross."

Becca nodded. "And, of course, you know that it isn't actually *Eros*. It's *Anteros*, his brother. Not the romantic one."

Oh. Well, so no, he hadn't known that.

"Really?"

"Yep. Really." She leaned in, like she had a secret and whispered, "I know all sorts of stuff. Who'd have thought it, right? If you'd waited to discuss it, I could have saved you all that panting."

He was *not* panting. Merely regaining his breath at a fast pace.

Thankfully, and wisely, the table came with a jug of water, and he drained his water glass twice in quick succession.

"So, what are we going to do?" He placed the ashes bottle on the table between them.

"Have another drink. We'll think of something."

The waiter arrived, giving Charlie a disapproving look. He placed a teapot and fresh cups between them and snippily informed them it was a Bramble.

"I'll be mother," Becca said primly and poured.

Charlie felt the need to distract from his failure.

"So how's your Yank?" he asked. He'd not got around to asking in January.

"Back in the States," she said with a huff, "and in his wife." She took a moment to brush something off the plastic seating, muttering "Arsehole" under her breath. "And no, I didn't know he was married. I have rules about that kind of thing."

"Anyone new?" he ventured.

"Nope," she said, "I'm still in the AMAB phase."

"AMAB?"

"All men are bastards."

He simply gave her a nod. It seemed safest.

"How's Liz?" Becca asked, reciprocating politely.

"*Liv*."

"Yes, exactly. Liv."

"She's good."

Becca tilted her head and nodded to the bottle.

"I assume you've told her about Ally now." It wasn't really a question.

"Sure, sure," he said, picking up and studying the menu card again.

"Lister." Becca sounded like his primary school teacher. "Have you told her about Ally?"

"She knows about Ally. We talked about her at Shrin and Ollie's do."

Becca's brow furrowed. "No, you made out she was just a friend who died, and whose room you'd rented. You didn't mention she was the love of your life—"

"Because that's exactly what you tell a new girlfriend," he pointed out, sarcastically.

She ignored him. "Or that you lived with her, or that you were getting married. Those are facts any partner should know."

"Yes, of course."

"But you haven't told her."

"The right time hasn't come up."

"What about all the photos at your place?"

"I took them down," he admitted, "they were too hard." He

had them still, of course he did, but it had become impossible to navigate his home with all the visual reminders of his loss.

The flat, the space they'd loved so much, had become unendurable to him in the weeks after her death. There wasn't a single thing she hadn't bought, arranged or simply touched. His hand in a coat pocket would find a shopping list with her handwriting, or post would arrive in her name. He'd never realised how many words ended with -*ally* and whether he was reading them or writing them, they punched him in the heart each time. It was endless and relentless. The toothpaste was the last straw. The tube had run out and binning the old one which she'd squeezed in her hand, and starting a new one, which she never would, had seen him sliding down the bathroom wall in tears. Every reminder of her hurt, but starting new things without her gutted him. He was trapped. There was no way to go, other than *away*. And so he'd removed himself. He'd packed a rucksack, headed for the airport and picked the first plane he found to South America. Now he was back, he could face things better, but staying at Liv's offered more than one advantage.

Becca paused in her rant.

"I don't know Liv, but having recently discovered a boyfriend was lying, I'm telling you, you need to sort this."

"I'm not lying to her, I just haven't laid it all out there yet," he snapped. "And why do you care?"

She frowned hard at him. "Don't you think there's an element of hypocrisy for us to sit here, celebrating Ally, honouring her bucket list at the same time as brushing her under the carpet?"

"I said before, I'm *not* brushing her under the carpet," he said crossly. He thought of Ally often, but he tried to do it with some element of control. The fear of landing back in that dark place gave him no other choice.

She gave him a *whatever* shrug.

"What's Liv doing today?"

"Running. She and her cousin like doing marathons."

Becca pulled a face. He could agree with her there.

"And where does she think you are?"

"She knows I'm out," he said defensively.

Becca sat back with her arms crossed, and a wicked glint in her eye.

"She thinks I'm shopping. Which I totally will be later."

"Such a fibber, Charlie Lister," she concluded, giving her head a slow shake.

He wouldn't win this and he knew it. "Look, what shall we do with the ashes?" he diverted.

Becca tilted her head back and stared at the pink flower-strung ceiling.

"I like the idea of her staying here on the bus, pootling around the city, having a good time with all the future guests."

"A never-ending hen-do?"

Becca smiled. "Exactly. How best to do it?"

Looking about, he considered options. Not the floor, she'd be stamped on or swept away.

"We could slide her down the crease in our seats," he suggested. "She'd be safe in there."

She didn't look convinced. "I don't want her under anyone's bum. It could be farty."

An idea suddenly hit her, and she spun around and up onto

her knees in her seat to peer down the back of it. Like his, it backed onto the next seat.

"The seats would have originally all been facing forward," she mumbled to herself, leaning to look in the gap between the back-to-back seats. "Ha! I thought so."

"What?" he asked.

"Where's the place to put cigarette ashes, Charlie?" So thrilled with her own brilliance, she was actually using his name. It was both disconcerting and infectious.

"The bin?" He'd never smoked.

"Almost. An ashtray. Look in the gap." She pointed to the back of his seat and in seconds he'd contorted himself to be peering in through the gap. A small grill-fronted metal box was mounted to the back of one seat.

"Perfect," said Charlie. If they could get the ashes in there, Ally could enjoy the partying for many years. "How did you know?"

"Misspent youth," she said, sounding slightly wistful.

"Everything OK?" The concerned voice came from above them. The waiter was giving them a suspicious eye. Charlie winched himself up to sitting. "Yes, absolutely. We're checking out the amazing way you've converted the bus."

The waiter nodded like they were a pair of loons and left.

Becca looked about, then with a determined air, slid the bottle towards him.

They were passing along Victoria Embankment, and she got up to look out of the window further up the bus. "Gather round, everyone," she announced loudly to the entire top deck, "we're passing Cleopatra's Needle, a gift from Egypt, erected here in 1878." Nobody seemed confused by this random tourguidery. She was speaking with such authority, they didn't question it and the gin was absolutely helping. Turning, she addressed the tables on either side of theirs, "And you." She waved them across, her tone brooking no argument. "Come and see." They meekly scrambled to look out of the window. Becca gave Charlie an urgent "Go on then" look and, chivvying everyone, took their focus back outside, telling them about the red granite obelisk.

Charlie swung into action, unstoppering the bottle, then, sliding to the end of his seat like he was joining everyone, slid his arm back between the seat frames. It took him a moment to locate the ashtray and tip the ashes out.

Becca gave him a checking glance, just as the other male passenger turned for his drink, but catching his chin with her hand, she fixed his eye and asked, "Do you know what's buried beneath it?"

He stuttered a quick "No."

"Under the needle," Becca announced to the entire top deck, "is a time capsule, with many items, including a box of cigars, the bible, newspapers, a map of London, a portrait of Queen Victoria and twelve photos of the best-looking women in England. See, my friends, every day is a school day!" Becca concluded her tour with a flourish. She slipped back into her seat and holding his eye, poured the remaining dregs of Bramble from the teapot.

"How did you know all that?" He didn't even try to keep the admiration from his voice.

"Oh, I was a tour guide for a bit. Didn't work out. The fake Beefeater outfit they insisted I wear had a teeny tiny skirt which garnered a well-publicised 'Cease and Desist' letter from the Tower, plus I didn't always stick to the script or, in fact, the truth." With a shrug, she popped the last morsel of a blue macaron in her mouth.

She took a quick peek at the floor beneath them. "Nice job, no spillage. She'll be safe there for years, don't you think?" She held her glass up in another toast. "Working partners."

This toast gave him pause. It felt like a truce and he wasn't sure he trusted it. She tilted her head, but her expression wasn't goading.

"Working partners," he agreed, feeling like he was stepping off some precipice.

They settled back into their seats and, business done, let the jolly mood of the bus envelop them, as they demolished the cake tiers, rating each sweet component as they went. Charlie championed the sandwiches, and Becca wasn't convinced about macarons.

Having been brought up in a family where you learned to make the most of ceasefires, Charlie grabbed his moment for the discussion he'd been running in his head for the last week.

"So, how's your house?"

She dropped her head back with an exaggerated groan. "This one is an utter shithole. And winter is coming," she added, dramatically.

"It's July." It was also 28 degrees outside and glorious sunshine.

"Which means I've only just thawed out from last winter, and you cannot deny," she slurred slightly and wiggled her finger at him, "that winter *is* coming."

She had a point, and her expression said he couldn't have moved her on it, anyway. "Same place as last year?"

"God no," said Becca, accepting the next gin – strawberry rhubarb gin fizzes, served in crystal tumblers – from the waiter. "That was rooms ago. There's been…" she counted in her head, "are we including sofa surfing?" she continued counting, "three since then. All awful, all scumbag landlords. One suggested an alternative payment arrangement, involving role play. The lettings agents are getting cheekier with what they palm off as a 'room'. Before this current one I slept on a mattress in a recess, with a curtain for a fourth wall." She spoke about it with a blasé tone, but he could tell it had left its scars.

"And the one you saw had mice, but the landlord wouldn't sort it or give us a cat. I'd wake up to mice playing across my bed. Little fuckers kept crapping on the duvet." Charlie felt a pang of guilt; he'd always had nice places to live. *More* than his share when his parents split, and he'd had a newly decorated room in each new house. Then he'd inherited his uncle's place, a ground-floor flat in a Georgian conversion with a small courtyard garden in a blossomy street.

"Well, here's the thing," he said, trying to keep a grip of his tone, but faintly aware the gin had made it sort of wavey. "I'm moving out of the flat and I wondered whether you might want it?" He gave her a small smile, but felt a big glow. His offering her this would have delighted Ally. She was all about helping people, although sometimes he'd had to point out they weren't asking for any. That didn't dissuade her though. Still, right now, he understood the thrill she'd got from it.

Becca opened her mouth in shock and then let rip to an enormous honking laugh.

"Do you think I'm living in shitholes for larks? You think

I'm considering creepy landlords for the frisson?" She was incredulous.

Confused, his sense of benevolence deflated. Then he got it.

"Oh, I didn't mean to *buy*. I meant to rent. We'd work out a mate's rates rent. Something that won't kill you and that'll cover my costs." That was clearly a different kettle of fish and her face relaxed. He could see her mind calculating the pros and cons, particularly the cons and where the catch was. "Look, it's a win/win. You get somewhere decent to stay, I get a tenant I know, without the faff of some wide-boy letting agent who's going to fleece me for every call and ignore yours if he can, plus charge a princely percentage every month."

She nodded. "I've dated him, I think."

"Quite. So what do you think?"

This was where he figured she'd ask why he was moving out and she'd kick off. But apparently Becca focused on the "what" rather than the "wherefores".

"How soon?"

"As soon as you can get out of your contract."

Her brow creased. She was still looking for the catch.

"And you'd be the landlord, right?"

"Yes."

"And I'll have the same rights as any random tenant?" Despite being on a gin bus, surrounded by twee cakes and peonies, this now felt like quite the business meeting.

"Absolutely, although obviously I'd be expecting you to look after it a million times better than some random, because *Ally*." She nodded, understanding. Her expression was so solemn, he suspected she took it as a vow.

"And you won't be able to kick me out on a whim?"

He shook his head. "And I won't be able to walk in without an invitation, just to catch you kitless." That scenario regularly happened to Liv when the film crew were staying in less salubrious places and he only said it to lighten the moment, but immediately realised it had come out creepy. He quickly raised his hands in surrender to her appalled expression. "It was a joke, Becca. A shit one, I see that, but I wouldn't. You have my word I'll never set foot inside unless invited." He brought his hands back down to the table. One hand hit his teaspoon which pinged to the floor. He bent down to retrieve it, which was tricky due to his size and the space. "And besides," he carried on, stuck under the formica, "it's not like I haven't seen you kitless already." Again, the words were out before he could filter them. Bloody gin. He froze in the silence. Unfortunately, remaining where he was wasn't practical.

He rose back up to an icy glare. Ah crap. It was a dumb thing to have said, but it had always hung there between them, like fly paper waiting for them to venture near.

He put down the teaspoon, resolute. "Look, the bad jokes are down to the gin. Sorry. But don't you think it's time we talked about this?"

"No." She looked out of the window, her mardy face scaring a toddler on a passing double decker.

"It's been years."

"No." Her eyes were firmly fixed on the outside of the bus.

The gin was egging him on. He'd fancied having this conversation for a long time. She wasn't the only one who enjoyed needling the other.

"Don't you think elephants in the room need addressing?"

"There is no elephant, there is no room. Move on." She drained the last of the gin fizz.

"Right," he said, absolutely not about to move on. "See, the way you're acting says there's definitely an elephant."

"The point of the elephant," Becca hissed as she leaned in towards him, possibly to intimidate, which she totally didn't with her spotty frock, "is not to talk about the elephant. I don't want to talk about it."

"Becca. We slept together. It happened. Life moved on, why can't we laugh about it?"

"Because it meant *nothing*."

"So it didn't happen?" He couldn't help his smile.

She looked peeved. "There are things in your life, *many many* things I'm sure, you aren't proud of. And imagine my disappointment when, in thinking I could just forget about that night, seeing as you'd moved out, you appear again ... with my best friend."

He didn't get it. "But as far as I'm aware you weren't interested in me."

The horror on her face was a picture.

"Oh. My. God." She placed both hands flat on the table. "Let's just get something one hundred per cent crystal clear. I was never *ever* interested in you. I've never felt jealous of Ally for being with you." She actually shuddered at the thought. It didn't sting. He felt exactly the same. "The disappointment was that she'd fallen for *you*. I didn't want her to be another notch on your bedpost."

"She wasn't."

"No, as it turned out, she wasn't, but I didn't know that then, did I?"

A waiter passed and Becca grabbed their forearm.

"Can I have another round, please?"

"Sorry, I've served all the included drinks," said the waiter.

"Oh, I'll pay," said Becca, pulling some cash out of her little vintage bag.

"Which of the cocktails would you like?"

Becca pulled an incredulous face. "Uh, all of them."

Charlie gave the waiter an apologetic look, then ordered the same, because he didn't want her drinking alone.

Reassured support was on its way, Becca was ready to engage. "She was my best friend, Charlie," she said, like he was an idiot. "I would rather die than see her hurt." It was true of course, and he knew it. Becca's loyalty to Ally was unimpeachable. "You seemed exactly like the kind of guy to hurt her. I'd seen your track record the previous term, remember? I was one of those notches on your bedpost."

"I wasn't that bad," he tried.

"Ha! Your room should've had a revolving door. And the noise they made! Flipping inconsiderate."

"I think they found me very considerate." He smirked.

"To the rest of us, you arse."

"Not my fault I could show them a good time." He paused, then added, "Didn't hear much noise coming from your room that term."

"Fuck off. I just have some awareness of my neighbours."

"Not so much when it was you though, eh?" he asked, cocking his head at her. OK, maybe he was pushing it. "Anyway," he said, keen to change the angle, "this isn't about them. This is about us."

"There is no us," she snapped. "*You* know it, *Ally* knew it –

because she knew exactly what had happened as soon as it had happened. After that I didn't – *and don't* – see the need to delve into it."

"Ally thought it was funny."

"Yeah well, she could have an odd sense of humour sometimes." Becca didn't appear charmed at the memory. "Thankfully, she had my emails bitching about you from both before and after, clearly expressing how I felt about you. She definitely didn't feel threatened." That explained quite a lot. He'd once thought he'd have a fight on his hands to convince Ally he didn't harbour feelings for her best friend. But in fact, the two of them were so loved up, so fast, it had only taken Ally to raise the subject early on to get any idea of that nixed. They'd always been open and honest with each other. Ally had displayed no mistrust or jealousy, trusting their loyalty to her implicitly. Her teasing Becca about it said as much.

As Becca said, it had meant nothing. The girls he'd seen generally hadn't. He'd just been having a fun time and so had they – that was what uni was about, wasn't it? Moving away from home had offered him freedom.

Which brought him back to Becca.

"*You* jumped me, Beej. I didn't seduce you."

Her face turned a vivid shade of puce. "I don't recall much about what happened." Then she added tartly, "That's how good it was."

"You had a good time. Twice."

"One night. Only counts as once."

"That's not how it works."

She wafted the point away with her hand.

Becca defiantly stuck things out for a while, stubbornly

staring at the London Eye as they passed. But he could hear the cogs angrily turning as she weighed things up. Then, with a cross huff, she eventually caved. "It was a *game*. Tilly, Mags and I had a 'Kiss, Snog, Shag' competition running for the term. Ally was following the scores from Munich, so knew all about it. Maggie and I stood at a draw, and you may not have noticed, but I am quite competitive." He nearly laughed at the understatement. She chewed the inside of her cheek. "Term was ending, we were all wasted after our Christmas dinner. You were leaving for good and I saw an opportunity. And you weren't really much effort."

No, he probably hadn't been.

She shrugged. "I'm not proud of it, but that's what it was. And don't get all moral about it. Most of the sports teams had some variation on the go. Ally knew exactly what it had been because I emailed her the next morning. Even later, when I suggested she shouldn't date you because you were Mr Not-Serious—"

"Hang on—"

"You *were*, Charlie. You and your lame 'Heads, your place; tails, my place' coin gimmick. I can't believe so many found that cute."

"That line was a winner," he said, smirking again. She rolled her eyes at him.

"Ally knew it had just been a competition shag. Nothing more, nothing less." She sighed, running a finger around the rim of her empty tumbler. The relief on her face as the waiter brought the extra drinks was enormous. She knocked back the Bramble straight off.

Charlie leisurely sat back and threaded his fingers together across his stomach. Her being so bothered by this piqued his interest. "Still doesn't explain why you hated me for it."

"I didn't *hate* you," she said, then gave him an arch look. "That would require something more than indifference." Ouch. She dropped her expression to something verging on bored. He might have let it get to him, if he hadn't remembered she was an actor. Also, they'd been playing this game for years, both of them taking little swipes at each other, not letting their guard down – unless in times of grief, of course.

"So making an effort with your best friend's boyfriend isn't a normal thing to do?" The bonhomie of the afternoon had vanished, but he had the chance to tackle something which had intrigued him for years. Women, of all ages, normally found him charming, but not Becca. Not that he was trying to charm her, of course, he was just curious.

"What for?" Becca countered with a laugh that felt forced. She was properly uncomfortable, he could see it in her eyes. "Three's a crowd, right? I think I did us all a favour by keeping clear of you two. Friendships get strained when the friend becomes a third wheel. Makes things really awkward."

Charlie laughed.

"What?" Becca appeared genuinely confused.

"Becca," it was like explaining to a child, "the way you behaved – the avoiding, the sniping, the general disdain – it was absolutely a strain. How could you not see that?"

"That wasn't to do with being a gooseberry. I just thought you were a twat." She took a sip of the martini and pointed out, "We had form before we even met, remember?"

Charlie slumped dramatically. "That? Still? Let it go, woman. It was a shit play and a fair review."

"I disagree."

He rolled his eyes. "As ever."

She sipped her martini again to end the conversation, but he needed to set something straight and maybe get a revenge dig in.

"All this time you've assumed it mattered more to me than it did to you," he said. "Younger Charlie wouldn't have cared, a shag being a shag, after all." He took a pointed swig of his own drink.

Younger Charlie had had nothing like a relationship on his radar – his newfound freedom having gone straight to his groin. Which probably added to the smack in the head he'd felt when he'd met Ally. Meeting Ally had been everything when he'd been expecting nothing.

Taking it on the chin, Becca nodded curtly.

"So there you go, Lister. We have discussed it. Now we need never mention it again." Apparently, she deemed the subject now closed, and finished the martini to reiterate the point.

"Oh, I don't know. Things like this are much better out in the open." His smile was sharkish. Before it had just been an awkward piece of knowledge between them. Now it was an actual thing he could tease her with. It felt like a win. He didn't care she was embarrassed to have slept with him. Young Charlie had enjoyed it, and if honest, he'd done exactly what she'd accused him of – added a notch to his bedpost. Recognising this, older Charlie cut her some slack.

"Come on, cheer up. It turned out for the best, didn't it?" She gave him a quizzical look. He explained, "Imagine if we'd made more of it? Dated. It would have been over as soon as I met Ally. My dumping you would have skyrocketed your 'indifference'." He air-quoted it because the gin was making him more dramatic and he was pleased how her eyes widened in response. But he'd seen how Becca had dealt with blokes who'd crossed her. That last guy was lucky he was back in the States.

Becca had stilled at his words. Then she suddenly busied herself meticulously brushing crumbs off the table, into her hand and onto her plate. "Right." She looked up then, her eyes looking noticeably bright, her mouth tight-lipped. "I'm so glad we were and are on the same page."

Something was off. This felt too … straightforward and painless. And her tone was eerily not hers, like a demonically possessed child in a horror film. Though dulled by the gins, his internal alarm started warming up.

"Maybe we *should've* had this chat a long time ago," she said, but sounding snippy, as opposed to relieved.

He gave her a "You think?" look. Their animosity was totally down to her, by his estimation.

Looking out of the window, Charlie saw they were nearly back where they'd started. They both had the final cocktail to finish. He started sipping at his, but watched Becca over the rim, as there was clearly something bothering her. She was twitchy and her lips pursed as she mulled whatever it was.

Suddenly she knocked back the entirety of her pink gin fizz.

"Actually, maybe you owe me an apology for that night," she said, her voice hard. Past the slur, he detected that edge to her tone, which from experience told him to brace.

"What?" Hadn't they just agreed it was what it was, and neither party was damaged from it? "An apology for what?"

She sent him a death stare. "Oh, so you think it's fine to fuck a girl with no care?" She sounded haughty and outraged. The next table was on their feet to leave, but suddenly stilled and heads turned. He raised an eyebrow at them and they scurried on down the stairs.

"Piss off. You came on to me. You just said it was a game." This was mad. She couldn't turn everything on its head simply to have a go at him.

"You needn't have responded to my advances. Apparently, I didn't *matter*. That's cold."

Charlie was indignant. "There was nothing cold going on there. You were up for it," Becca's jaw dropped, but he stopped her retort by holding up his hand and continuing his point, "and so was I."

"If you'd been a decent guy, you'd have said no, that we could date first."

"What decade are you living in? I saw a liberated woman, wanting sex and not being afraid to ask – which was a turn-on, and given the purring I was hearing from you, there was consent from start to finish. And you *did* finish. *Twice*." He wanted that noted too. "Do not put this on me. It was honourable sex. If—"

"Honourable sex?" she blustered. "What the fuck is that?" Their waiter appeared at the stairs, looked between them, then made a hasty retreat.

"You know what I mean. *You* virtually threw me on the bed and there were condoms. Plural. Neither of us should have any shame about it."

Her angry face begged to differ. God, she was baffling. If he hadn't witnessed her random vacillations a million times before, he would have been astounded.

"Becca!" he snapped, having had enough. "What do you want from me? One minute you want me to forget it ever happened, the next you want some blame taken – not that you even remember it, allegedly. But either way it doesn't matter. It just happened, like you say. Which Ally understood. So no harm done. It all came good."

She stood up and grabbed her bag. Here we go, he thought, it always came to this. He'd seen Becca storm out of places so many times. When would she grow up?

"I'll get you a cab," he said, gruffly.

"I don't need anything from you," she hissed.

"I'm not offering you anything. For *my* sake I want to see you tipped into a cab that will take just you safely home. Then I needn't give you another thought for the next year until we have the outrageous fun of doing this all over again." The thought nearly broke him.

Stomping out of the bus and hailing a cab was executed in mardy silence, underpinned by sour scowls from Becca. He opened the door for her and the last look she shot him was as if he'd goosed her as she'd got in. Which he definitely hadn't.

He didn't understand what had sent her ballistic like that. He was right – picking Ally over her *would* have damaged the girls' friendship, maybe irrevocably. Couldn't she see that? Or maybe it was something else that had narked her. Who bloody knew?

As the cab pulled away, he tried to think whether he'd said something wrong, but his memory was quite noodly already.

But she was always so touchy. *Women.* They were bewildering to him sometimes. He looked down the street as he considered which way he'd get home. *Nuts.* He had to buy some clothes. *No,* not an alibi. He genuinely needed new clothes. Or would at some point. He'd buy the first thing that fitted him in the first decent shop he passed.

A toss of a coin told him to go left. He didn't care if she thought it was a lame gimmick. He found it useful. Like right now, he didn't have mental space for further deliberating; his gin-addled brain was still trying to compute how it had spiralled to this and, more to the point, how they were going to get through this bucket list.

2014

"Without putting too fine a point on it, Marcia," Becca said to her agent, eyeing the costume laid out on the green chesterfield sofa, "what the actual fuck?" The garments were offensive to her on so many levels.

"It's Princess Lia," Marcia said, attempting indignation.

"Leia. Her name is Leia." Becca's girl-crush on Carrie Fisher demanded accuracy.

Ignoring her, Marcia handed Becca the job spec, as if it was a done deal. They'd been here before, with Becca unimpressed with the role on offer. This was Marcia's usual way, a basic approach of "ignore and plough on".

"I am not wearing a bikini." The gold plastic bikini with the gauzy burgundy fabric between the legs was a hard limit.

"That's the costume. It was in the film." Marcia picked at the chipped shellac on her nails, either unwilling to look Becca in the eyes or uninterested in the conversation, Becca couldn't quite decide which.

"Leia had loads of costumes, several of them iconic and recognisable to fans. This one is just a wank-fest for the guys. No."

"This is the one the job involves. It's three days' work, lunch included, provided it's a Subway meal deal. The meal vouchers are in the envelope. Wear the costume, do the job, take the money."

That was very easy for Marcia to say, she'd be getting her fifteen per cent of the fee without taking most of her clothes off in Earl's Court to please film nerds in cosplay. Becca crossed her arms across her chest, protecting it from the offensive bikini. It wasn't even a good replica.

"Leia had black hair. I'm a red."

Marcia didn't look up, but paused her shellac picking to tilt one finger towards the costume. "The ear-bun wig is underneath." Crap.

"Still no. You need a model, not an actor." She was partly also self-conscious about what she'd look like in the outfit. She was not what magazines called "beach ready". She was more of a "couch ready" kind of girl and happy with it. "Ask Jessie." Her Australian agency mate had absolutely the right bod for that, and was a model first and foremost.

"Can't," snapped Marcia, already looking at new paperwork. "They want you to hand flyers out in character, and you know, Jessie has that speech problem."

"That's her *voice*," Becca admonished. Jessie had a broad Ozzie twang and was incapable of other accents.

Becca wondered, not for the first time, whether she'd ever have a better agent. At least one who listened to her, respected her and had her best interests at heart, rather than this.

"Plus I already asked Jessie," murmured Marcia. "She's booked for hospitality at the Victoria's Secret runway thing." Marcia waved the event away with a bored air, Becca guessing she hadn't made that booking.

Great. Second choice to one of London's least useful actors. She felt her life was about being second choice, or not even, most times.

"Why didn't you ask me first?" She knew it was a needy question, and one which without doubt wouldn't give her an answer she'd want, but it came out of her regardless. Like when she read reviews of shows she knew were bad. She'd hope they'd see her as the ruby in the dust.

"Because I knew you'd be a pain in the arse about the costume and I know the complaints I'll get after the show about your surly attitude."

Becca opened her mouth to protest, but figured Marcia probably had a point and closed it again. Not that she felt remorse. What were agents for if not to be the brunt of your moans? Becca considered it part of the fifteen per cent too.

"This is last Christmas all over again."

"Here we go," sighed Marcia and pulled a face, which was unattractive whilst still not a million miles from her normal visage. "You're being ridiculous, we're in July."

"Not what I meant and you know it. Remember the 'Christmas film'?" Becca did her spikiest finger-speechies to emphasise things. "The one 'set' in the shopping centre? That was 'just a weekend' too. With me in an elf suit."

"You looked good in it."

"Not the point, Marcia." She *had* actually rocked that elf suit, and at the very least it was warmer than that bikini would be, July or not. "You said it was a film role."

Marcia pointed her pen at Becca and said sternly, "There *was* filming. You can't deny that. I wouldn't have got you to sign all the release forms if there hadn't been." Marcia wasn't too hot on paperwork, unless it was her own contract.

But Becca had been with Marcia too long, and been screwed over too often by the roles Marcia found her, to be cowed. She leaned forward into the intimidation of the Bic biro, teeth bared: "Parents filming me guiding their snotty spoiled spawn onto Santa's lap does not constitute filming in the sense that I pay you for." Those forty-eight hours had culminated in two toddlers vomiting, and another creating a puddle of wee at her feet, which had rendered her velvet curly-toed elf slippers both damp and stinky for the rest of the day. And the crying. God, the crying. Apparently Santa scared the shit out of a lot of little children, despite the guy inside the outfit being genuinely lovely. Becca didn't know why parents put their toddlers through it.

"You can simply ask people not to film you at the Comic Con," Marcia snapped with a petulant shrug.

"Again, not the point I'm making and still no on that."

"Suit yourself," Marcia said, scribbling something on a page with such pressure and speed that the desk shifted. Becca knew this tactic. Her nan had done the same when she'd lived with her. She'd let young Becca think she'd won, then wait silently until Becca made some concession. Well, Marcia could think again.

"What else have you got for me?" Becca was hoping for some auditions.

"*De nada*," Marcia murmured. She seemed to consider the conversation over. So much for client care.

"Nothing at all?"

"Nothing suitable."

"Am I being punished now?"

Marcia looked up. "I'm a busy woman, Becca," she chided, although her computer was never on when Becca visited and the phone rarely rang. "I'm not your keeper, nor your disciplinarian. If you don't want the work, you don't want the work. It's money or no money and you're an adult and can make your own decisions. In the meantime I have nothing else you're suitable for, or else I'd have told you, because that's my job and I'm a professional." Marcia twirled her pen at the door. "Enjoy your weekend and I'll call you when something comes in." She dropped her gaze back to her notes, which if Becca wasn't mistaken was a crossword, leaving Becca dismissed in her chair, until she saw there was little else to do but go. If she'd learned anything about Marcia it was that she was hard as nails, regardless of whether you were a client or a customer, and while that might be great when she was fighting your corner, eventually it would come back to bite you in the bum if you crossed her.

───────────

As was more regular than not, Becca left Marcia's in a foul mood, stomping along the street, walking straight through a cluster of school kids. However, there was a glimmer of light to the rest of her morning. She had a café shift that afternoon, but before that she had shopping to do for three weekends' time. She was going to savour this, as it was kit she'd wanted to need for a very long time and finally Ally was making it happen. She'd met Valerie the previous week for tea and cake, where she'd delivered the next bottle of ashes. And Becca was beyond excited about it. Not the scattering of course, that still made her deeply sad, but this year Ally was fulfilling a promise; they'd be going to a festival. A proper tent-in-a-muddy-field, loud-music-that-could-be-heard-for-miles, with-dire-toilets-and-yummy-street-food festival, and Becca couldn't wait.

Her stomping brought her to a branch of Outdoor Adventure, not a shop she'd normally go near, because the walking gear on display gave her cold flashbacks to Snowdon and should have come with trigger warnings. However, today the window pulled her up short and for a moment she came to believe in love at first sight. There, on astro-turf, lounged the festival tent of her dreams and one she knew she had to own, or else she would feel bereft forever. The price card sat by its tempting door flap. It was ridiculously spendy, and while its gorgeousness no doubt justified the cost, Becca wisely saw that food and rent prioritised higher where her limited wages were concerned.

Becca walked away.

And then she came back.

She stroked the window while gazing at the tent with the saddest puppy dog eyes, but she knew the score and shook her head. "Sorry," she mouthed to the tent, praying it would understand.

She walked away.

And then she came back.

She leaned her forehead against the glass, hoping to commune with the tent so it truly knew how much she loved it.

Becca turned her head on the window and looked back towards Marcia's. *Ah shit.* She wrestled with her principles, the image of the bikini and her need for money. Her shoulders sagged. Principles were expensive, but so was festival kit. And work was work and beggars couldn't be choosers …

Becca sorted some music to fill the flat, then threw herself onto her sofa to crossly bang out a text rearranging her weekend shifts. The costume bag lay, lobbed, on the entrance hall floor. Text sent, she closed her eyes for a moment and dreamed about the tent which would soon be hers, for ever and ever. A text pinged back in and a one-eyed glance told her things were sorted on the work front, so she emitted a long sigh of relief – before remembering *why* she was rearranging shifts and drew it straight back in again. So, eating would be off the cards for the next few days before wearing that bikini, but hey, that would save money too.

Resigned, she allowed herself to relax into the sofa and think about the state of play. Dodgy jobs aside, life was feeling sorted on various fronts, and she wasn't used to that. One decent thing happening at any one time was usually her maximum quota. She surveyed the flat around her. It was the best thing in her life, no question. Not a day went by where she didn't pinch herself, like she was in a teen romance, as she wandered between the bedroom and the bathroom without fear of being leered at by some shady house-mate. She had a lounge, not just a closed door to one because the landlord had rented the space out as another bedroom instead. She had a kitchen that might be messy, but it was *her* mess; she knew what the dried-on substances were. The concept of having a space all to herself had blown her mind for several weeks after she moved in. Not having to listen to strains of other house-mates' shit music, not having to unclog other people's pubes from the drain, not having her food go missing when she'd spent the entire day looking forward to it, and subsequently no more having to leave PassAgg notes around the place to be ignored. Heaven.

There was a peace about the place she'd never quite imagined she would appreciate as much as she did. Even the light coming through the windows was better than the dingy light she'd always had from her alley-view windows. She'd never considered the peace or the light when hunting for accommodation. She'd always been desperate and on the brink of eviction. Sure, she could hear sounds from the homes around her, but it was a soft murmur or a calm beat as opposed to the deafening dirge of the *Kerrang* channel.

The flat felt safe. She didn't sleep with one ear open anymore in case a house-mate got too pissed to know which room was theirs, and so far the landlord had stuck to his word and not appeared unannounced, or *at all*.

And then there was Ally. She sensed her, not like a ghost or anything, and she wasn't prone to talking to her like Valerie, but Becca got an enormous sense of comfort being in a space Ally had inhabited. The walls were colours Ally had picked, the curtains too and the bench in the tiny courtyard garden. Soul-joy – that's what it brought her, something she wouldn't have got anywhere else. Much as she didn't want to give Charlie credit for anything, ever, this had been a complete win for her and a generous idea of his.

Charlie. She'd no idea how he'd take this next task. She'd picked a local festival in the Home Counties so the travel would be cheaper for her, and as something a little more genteel for him, whose previous festival experience was going to Reading the summer after finals and being stoned for the entire weekend due to Ollie inadvertently feeding him skunk flapjacks throughout. He'd fallen asleep wedged in a portaloo and been unable to move his shoulder for a week. He'd vowed off both flapjacks and festivals ever since.

Recognising she'd actively been kind towards him didn't sit well, but Becca traded it against him having done her a solid on the flat, so they were quits. She preferred things on an even keel with Charlie, all squared, without being indebted to him. She was the model tenant, prioritising the rent over all other expenses and religiously forwarding his mail to his production company address, fortnightly. And the rent itself said she wasn't indebted there either. She had it all balanced out in her head. Theirs was pretty much just a business relationship … plus the scattering thing.

Two glass bottles stood on the middle frame of the sash window, the summer light passing through them, casting circles of orange and red light across the wooden floor. Her thoughts passed to the previous year's task. Although not the same as Snowdon, the gin bus trip had been an endurance test of its own. She'd loved dressing up for it – a culmination of numerous vintage shop visits – and the tour itself, but why had he spoiled everything by dragging up the past? As she saw it, they could pitch up, do the tasks and part again without raking over things. She didn't understand this need for people to dig about in ancient history and past liaisons.

And as Charlie had so concisely, by which she meant bluntly, pointed out, he would have chosen Ally anyway.

Becca shifted in her seat. That was the bit she wasn't comfortable with, or rather her reaction to it. She'd gone off on one. It hadn't been her finest hour. Her skin was normally thicker than that. *Of course* he would have picked Ally. Anyone would. Becca knew she wasn't the person people picked over others. She was used to that. Her parents hadn't and the casting directors for the good roles didn't either. Being discarded or overlooked, rejected in general wasn't foreign to her and she'd survived it many many times. The gin had just got to her that day. Those little sandwiches were far too small to line her stomach. And those little macaron things? Useless.

Still, despite everything, Charlie had still been decent enough to send the tenancy details the following week. Which had been a blessing, as she'd been beating herself up about having arsed-up on that front. More than once she'd psyched herself to call him and grovel in order to bring the tenancy back to the table, but she'd chickened out. Then, finally, after a pebble-dashed toilet-bowl too many, she'd been at the end of her tether googling "best ways to murder flatmates" when miraculously he'd texted, tactfully not mentioning how things had left off last time, re-offering her the flat. She hadn't asked him where he was going. It wasn't any of her business, and experience had shown her if you asked too many questions, before you knew it, people talked themselves out of things. Shortly after, Kyle the letting agent had received a written middle-finger in a lengthy debrief on his portfolio standards and poor moral compass.

At some point she'd have to remember to thank Charlie. She was sure there might be a moment at the festival. Maybe when he was drunk and wouldn't remember the following day, she could say it, quickly, and then know it was done. There was another twinge in her belly. OK. Maybe she should do it when he was alert. He probably deserved a proper thank you. She could manage that. He was a decent guy. They just rubbed each other up the wrong way, and while she believed they could now be civil to each other for a day or two for as long as this bucket list lasted, she was in no doubt the fundamental wrong-rubbing would and could never change.

The doorbell rang.

"Oh" was all she could manage on opening the door. She really should put the chain on before she did that, but she enjoyed the flourish of opening her door grandly.

"Becca-Jayne," her mother said. She always made it sound like an admonishment, yet she'd been the one to name her. Becca did little to quell her groan. She faced a more wizened version of herself: as tall, as lanky, but with more white strands in the red hair. Stella's skin, though equally pale, had a sallow greyish tinge and carried more wrinkles. Becca made an immediate vow to scowl less and moisturise more.

Tilting her head to one side, Becca scrunched her brow. "Erm … aren't you … no, sorry, can't place you." She then reset her face to deadpan.

Stella gave her a thin smile. "Funny. You going to let me in?"

Becca gave her a quizzical look but stood firm. "No. Why?"

"Suit yourself." Stella didn't appear surprised.

"How did you find me? I didn't send you a moving card."

"I'm here about your nan. She told me where you live." Stella gave the frontage a quick flick of the eye. "Fancy." Becca got the distinct feeling Stella thought the place was too good for her daughter. Which Becca agreed with, but still.

"*My* nan. Not *your* mum?" Becca was used to this. Often when mums and daughters didn't get on, the daughter would get on with the grandmother instead. Not in this case. The three of them didn't get on in any direction amongst them. There were no alliances. Her nan would have instantly dished up Becca's address to get Stella off her back. Wilma was like that. "What about her?"

"The doctor called. She's got heart problems."

Oh. They might not get on, but Becca didn't wish ill on her. At least, nothing more than a stubbed toe when she was being a cow.

"When d'you last see her?" Stella asked, pulling a cigarette out of her bag and lighting it.

"I see her on a Thursday." Becca always dropped by on her way home from work, ostensibly to pick up any post, but also to check the old woman wasn't lying on the floor being eaten by her cat, Elvis. That cat didn't have a kind bone in its body and was undoubtedly the type to devour its dead owner without waiting for a bad whiff.

"You'll need to see her more often," Stella said, drawing on her B&H and exhaling a long plume very close to Becca's face.

"Or," Becca pointed out, "you could step up and see her more than your quarterly visit."

Stella gave her a withering look. "That doesn't work with my schedule."

"What schedule?" She did nails. In people's houses. She managed her own hours.

"I *do* work, you know, Becca-Jayne," she sneered, in the same tone she'd use when Becca asked her to take her anywhere as a kid.

"As do I."

"Not as much."

"How would you know?"

"You live nearer."

Becca had no idea, nor interest, where her mum currently lived. However, Becca didn't want this conversation lasting long. They sounded like a couple of squabbling teens, as they always had, most likely because Stella had never grown up from the sixteen she'd been when she'd had Becca. Stella was the poster girl for schools needing better sex ed.

"Fine," Becca sighed, "whatever. I'll look in on her an extra day then." Things had been easier when her nan had had a lodger. Becca had left a number on the pinboard in case of emergencies. It was an arrangement that suited everyone.

Stella smiled, satisfied. Becca wanted to point out it wasn't a victory, not when as Wilma's daughter she came out of it looking bad, but she saved her breath. Stella didn't care and Becca wanted her gone.

Seeing Stella always made her feel low and, dare she say it, *needy*. When she was younger she'd always imagined that *this* visit, *this* meet-up would be the one where she said, "Darling, I'm coming home," or "I'm here to get you." But it never happened and the subsequent disappointment was ingrained now. Having grown wise to her own feelings, Becca now armoured up as soon as she saw her mum. It didn't stop the hurt, but it showed less.

"You could have called. Saved yourself the journey," Becca pointed out. And then it dawned on her; her mum had come to see her in the flesh, when she didn't need to. Maybe she *should* ask her in, now she'd made the effort.

"I had a job in the next street," Stella said. "This way I save on call charges."

Right, of course. Becca cursed herself. When would she ever learn? So much for bloody armour.

"Well, best get up there soon," Stella said, moving away from the door. "It's been some days since the doc rang."

Becca was left speechless, rare in general, but not so much where Stella was concerned.

Slamming the door behind her, Becca leaned back on it, and let out a ream of swears, at her mother for being so awful, at having to rearrange things now to get to her nan's, but mainly at herself, for yet again letting herself think, for a second, that things would ever change, and her mum would like her.

"Impressive erection, Lister," Becca said as she watched Charlie diligently sort his tent. It was a small prism thing in a boring camouflage print. He'd clearly pitched it many many times, his movements were methodical and routine, working on autopilot as he stuck the pegs in the ground. She imagined he could do this in the dark or in high winds. Or possibly under gunfire. Shrinidhi had told her he'd been promoted to Assistant Producer and was travelling with the film crews now. The camouflage might even be a legitimate safety measure.

"So I'm told," he answered, without looking her way.

Becca had finished long before him and sat in the entrance to her beloved abode, madly pleased with the turquoise pop-up. It packed down to a flat circle, which admittedly was a pain to walk about with, but it was worth it for the theatrical flourish of conjuring a 3D tent from a 2D circle in a flash and a loud "Ta-dah!!!", even if his response had been an appalled "Fuck me..." The glow-in-the-dark smilies on it were the icing on the cake. No, so it wasn't effective camouflage, but this was the Chiltern Hills, not a war-zone.

Meeting at the station had been more formal.

"Good to see you, White," he'd said, but the look she'd given him said "Fibber." Things felt wary between them. Neither of them knew what to expect. They were tenant and landlord, they were Ally's bucket list allies, they were acquaintances who last saw each other a year ago and it hadn't ended well. They were both waiting to see the lie of the land.

Now, she took a moment to study him. She wasn't subtle about it; she'd known him for years and they'd been through a devastating loss together, so she had the right and possibly a duty of care. His face was less gaunt, like he'd started living again. The light stubble was a groomed weekend look as opposed to having given up on life. Satisfied so far, she looked him up and down.

"Going to a pub garden?" He was wearing navy cargo shorts and a loose white linen shirt, unbuttoned at the collar, with the sleeves rolled up.

"My festival wardrobe was pinching. I must have outgrown it." Becca ignored the suggestion that festivals were juvenile. While he'd recognise her well-used dungarees, she suspected her psychedelic T-shirt was threatening to bring him out in hives. The sun shone off her teal-varnished toenails which peeped out of her purple Birkenstocks, and her two plaits completed the look. "Your student wardrobe's longevity is impressive. It's like *vintage* vintage."

She stood to face him. "Charlie, I've waited years to come to a festival, and I am ridiculously excited. I'm wearing a cloak of ridiculous excitement in fact, so your digs will bounce off me. And for the record, I'm chuffed I can still fit my student wardrobe, so ha!" She gave him a beaming smile. "And you are Ally's stand-in, and I expect you to embrace the moment and live it for her."

She'd been counting the days to this. It had always been her and Ally's plan to come to a festival, but other events, money (by which she meant lack of) and death had got in the way. But what had Becca most thrilled was, given its inclusion on the bucket list, that it was important to Ally too.

Charlie, however, did not seem to be channelling the vibe.

"Relax. It'll be fun." She was simmering with excitement. "Don't worry, I'll look after you."

His "Great" didn't sound as confident, relieved or grateful as it might.

She checked her watch. "First bands should start soon. Anyone you're particularly wanting to see?"

"I haven't actually studied the line-up."

"Really?"

"I didn't think it really mattered," he said with a shrug.

"Why?"

"You picked it. That's fine by me." Though there was flattery in there, it bummed her out a bit that he wasn't as invested in this. He was just doing what he was told. Typical Charlie.

"What," he asked, looking at her midriff, "is *that*?"

Looking down, she couldn't work out what was suddenly amusing him. It seemed sensible to her. It had taken many charity shops to find one, but this was a gem: vintage Louis Vuitton.

"Blimey, Becca, the Eighties rang and want their bumbag back."

She sniffed at him. "It's practical." She unzipped it and showed its contents: her phone, some cash, a small suncream, Ally's bottle and some mini Haribo packets. "It's a Pinterest hack. One day, these'll be back in fashion."

He snorted. "Doubt it. And not while the bumbag/fanny-pack debacle still rages. And while you're wearing that and

141

sleeping in a ridiculous tent, you can't take the piss out of my clothes." Hmm, *she'd* be the judge of that.

Becca didn't care what he thought; she stroked the bumbag lightly to show it she cared and not to listen to the grumpy fashion-dunce.

A thought hit her. "Stay put. I'll be back," she said and sprinted off towards the merch stalls as quickly as falling over three sets of guy ropes would allow.

He was reading a book when Becca returned. She plucked it out of his hands and dropped her gift into them instead.

"Time to get with the programme, Lister." She rolled the legs of her dungarees further up to let her shins see the sun. "Honestly, this is perfect festival weather. I think Ally's got control of this."

Charlie assessed and processed her gift. It was a matching T-shirt to hers, a psychedelic rainbow tie-dye number and the least likely item for Charlie to wear, ever.

"Get it on. We have bands to watch." He didn't look happy, but more about the T-shirt than being bossed about. "You're welcome, by the way."

He muttered a "Thank you", but she suspected he didn't mean it. However, he did as he was told, removing his shirt in one move, pulling at the back of the neck. Her higher position gave her the full view of the breadth of his shoulders. She looked away, finding something else, *anything else*, but Charlie's bare skin to look at.

"It's the right size," he said, which was apparently the only good thing he could say about it.

Unless she was mistaken, he'd been working out. The arms on the T-shirt were just shy of being too tight for his biceps and he was garnering looks from girls at a nearby tent. He was trying really hard to look delighted with his gift, but was failing really badly. It didn't deter Becca at all.

Rummaging in her rucksack, she extracted a couple of beer bottles, which she swiftly uncapped with her teeth. She didn't bother to check his face for how he felt about *that*, simply handing him the first with a "Your starter for ten," and holding hers out for a clink. His resignation turned to something more like acceptance.

He clinked. They'd reached an accord, and they drank to it. (Him quicker than her, but if drink was what it took, then fine.)

She nodded towards the music in the distance. "Let's do this. We've a moshpit waiting and ashes to scatter."

Several hours later her arms were aching from being held aloft, her face was aching from smiling and her throat from singing at the top of her voice. Becca kept checking on Charlie, who was employing his rugby-song lungs for volume and was surprisingly enthusiastic about the Mexican waves.

The crowd shifted and the world's tallest man moved in front of her.

"Ah bollocks," she said under her breath and started scheming how to regain her view.

"Need a lift?" She felt his warm breath at her ear, and while she knew it was Charlie, it still surprised her having him so close. Not in a creepy way – they'd been jostled against each other frequently during the day already, but not so close to the sensitive skin at her ear.

She turned to him, wondering what he meant. He tapped his shoulder. There were many girls sitting on guys' shoulders around them, but this was her and he was him, so...

The next song started and she was sorely tempted. But no, there were boundaries to acknowledge. She smiled as she shook her head and mouthed, "It's OK."

The crowd was fully loosened up now after hours of drinking and dancing, and there was a concerted lean forward from the entire mass of bodies. His shoulder had been pressed against hers for a long while, when she felt him shift, pushing back against the crowd to stand behind her. Was he leaving? She turned to give him a questioning look. This would be a hellhole if he was claustrophobic. She hadn't thought to ask.

But he looked quite calm. "I'll stand here for a bit, keep this lot back," he said. It took her a moment to get it. Charlie was making himself a protective cage for her. She whipped her head back towards the stage while she worked out what she made of it. She wasn't used to people looking out for her. It was such a small thing he'd done, but it had her out of sorts and blinking back an itch in her eyes. She breathed deeply to stop this nonsense. It was just a shift in positions, woman, no big deal. The song ended and to accompany the cheer there was yet another forward surge within the crowd. Charlie's hands settled on her upper arms, as he steadied himself, the feeling and additional heat of his skin on her sun-warmed skin catching her entire focus. She braced herself to help him steady, working as a team, but kept her eyes firmly front and centre.

As the band played again, Becca found herself stuck between the strangest of rock and hard places: nose to spine with the guy in front, and also with Charlie in close contact with the entire length of her back. Had they been a couple his chin would have rested on her shoulder as his arms encircled her.

"Wouldn't you rather be able to see?" His shoulder-ride offer still stood. This time she grabbed it. The reduced contact of sitting on his shoulders in the open air was what she needed.

Within seconds he had her hoisted. Released from the crush of bodies and having settled onto the breadth of his shoulders, Becca took a moment to ascertain where to safely put her hands. Thereafter she kept her eyes on the stage, away from the head of clean wavy hair between her thighs as they bounced and sang with the band.

Becca felt on top of the world; the crowd was immense and she was above it all. Ally would have adored this. Had she been there, no doubt she'd have been up there on Charlie's shoulders hours ago. Becca felt she was doing it as much for Ally, and so allowed any worries she had about it being Charlie beneath her, his warm hands resting on her knees, to slide away.

The band knew how to whip the crowd into a frenzy, and Becca had both hands in the air: one splayed, almost in praise, the other holding the small yellow bottle aloft, making sure Ally got an excellent view. She'd uncorked it too, so Ally could hear the noise. Yeah, yeah, *bonkers*, she knew.

Her balance shifted. An unexpected surge in the crowd pushed Charlie forward, but her upper body swayed backwards. She windmilled her arms, but couldn't regain the balance and suddenly she was falling. Still moving forward, Charlie shifted his hands to get a better grip, but it dropped her further. Becca shut her eyes, mentally grappling for the falling exercises they'd done at uni, expecting her spine to hit the ground any second.

Only the impact didn't come. Instead, she felt hands on her back and suddenly she was travelling. Charlie tried to grip her legs, but the hands were too strong. Becca opened her eyes, looking up at the blue sky and started laughing. She was crowd surfing. All the hands were working as one and she felt completely safe.

"Becca!!" she heard Charlie shouting, but there was nothing she could do, and the laughter kept bubbling out of her at the wonder of it.

Moments later, she heard Charlie shout again, but how? The crowd were singing along with the band, and the noise should have drowned him out. Lifting her head to scan the melee, she saw him, coming closer, also starfished on his back, as the hands passed him along and towards her.

His face was a picture.

"This is amazing!" he shouted as they drew alongside one another. Becca stretched out her limbs to the biggest starfish she could, her fingertips touching his.

"Amazing!" she shouted right back, joy filling her face.

Only then she realised, somewhere along the way, perhaps in the falling, the jostling, or even the stretching, she'd let Ally's bottle go.

"Relax, White. It's fine." She'd told him about the bottle the moment their feet hit the ground at the edge of the crowd, holding out the cork stopper on her palm. She felt dreadful, but apparently nothing could shake his euphoria. "The ashes probably came out as they fell and the bottle will be pressed far into the soft ground so she'll be part of the field. I'm happy with that."

Looking back at the bouncing mass of bodies, she considered it. Ally would've loved being in there moshing. Like being a part of the gin bus now, Ally being part of the field and the annual festival was perhaps in the spirit of things too.

She felt a squeeze on her shoulder. "Really, Becca. It's fine." Reassured, she let the guilt go.

They browsed the stalls between the campsite and the bands, which homed the arts, crafts and food vendors. Her stomach rumbled at the cornucopia of scents: the mega-baltis of curry, the expansive pans of paella, the stacks of falafels, the baskets of doughnuts and cinnamon-dusted churros.

"Any preference?" he asked, clearly equally hungry.

"Hmmm, I'm stuck between Indian and falafel." It all smelled good to her.

Charlie pulled a coin out of his pocket, tossed it in the air and caught it. "Heads, Indian; tails, falafel." She rolled her eyes at his leaving it to chance.

Minutes later Charlie stood switching his steaming box of curry between his hands with Becca clutching a bag of three huge samosas, as they investigated the other stalls.

"Becca?" He realised she was eating, then waved a hand. "Doesn't matter."

"What?" she asked, mouth full and not caring. Exactly as she'd dreamed, this place encouraged you to abandon propriety.

His face coloured at whatever it was and he held up his curry box. "Let's eat."

She got the distinct impression he was backing out of something. He'd tell her eventually, she supposed, and she proceeded to scoff her samosas as she dragged him from one stall to the next. He followed, not remotely interested in any of the crafts, but decent enough to stick around and keep her company, while demolishing his food. She bought him a glow-stick necklace as a reward, garnering her a wrinkled nose, but also a smile.

Having bought a shit-tonne of crystals – because so many parts of her life could still do with healing – she suggested they venture back. They restocked their beer provisions from a pub stall en route.

Entering the campsite, Becca faced a sea of tents. She hadn't the foggiest idea which direction they'd come from hours ago. The light was gone now, and many tents across the field were glowing yellow from interior lamps.

"Bugger," said Charlie, none the wiser for where they should be heading.

It took thirty minutes of walking around in circles and falling over more sodding guy ropes for her to point triumphantly and shout "Smilies!" There, in the moonlight and gloamy glow of illuminated tents, was her amazing, life-saving, glow-in-the-dark, smiley-covered tent.

"Finally," he grumbled, and stomped past her. His party mood had waned somewhat.

"I think we deserve another beer now," she tried, not a little disappointed with his unspirited attitude in the face of adversity. She'd expected more from an adventurer.

"Where's…" Charlie looked about and scratched his head. "Are we still lost?"

"'S'up?" Becca asked.

"I—" he started again, befuddled, still looking around. "There can't be two of your tent."

Becca looked at her tent and smiled like a doting mother. "Of course it's mine."

He looked dismayed. "Then where the fuck is my tent?"

Becca looked behind him. There was a small, but very definitely empty, patch of grass. "Ahh, shit."

"Do people really steal other people's fucking tents?" He was in a mixed state of "shocked building to fuming". Becca was in a torn state of "shocked and put out" that someone had picked his dullard tent over hers.

"Camouflage failed," she noted.

"Not funny, Becca," he growled. She turned in the other direction under the guise of searching, but primarily to school her face. It *had* been funny.

Feeling responsible for this task, Becca knocked on a couple of neighbouring tents, but the inhabitants had seen nothing.

"Was there anything valuable in your bag?" He hadn't mentioned it, but they both knew it was gone. His face set further in anger, but then released. "Nothing irreplaceable. And we've done the ashes."

She shared his relief there. Telling Valerie that Ally had been stolen wasn't a conversation she fancied. And she liked

Charlie a little bit more at that moment, for Ally's ashes being his priority.

She looked out at the field beyond them. "Should we have a wander to see if they've pitched it somewhere?"

"Needle in a haystack, White," he said and while it struck her as quite defeatist of him, she was pleased too, because *definitely* needle in a haystack. "And it's dark, so y'know, not the best searching conditions."

"Especially with the camouflage," she mumbled.

"Piss off," he mumbled back, but without malice.

They trudged to Festival Security, who told them straight off they shouldn't expect to see either tent or bag again. There was, however, a spare sleeping bag they could loan him – the organisers provided a few for odd cases like this, though it was normally couples splitting up and needing alternative accommodation. They took it for granted Becca was offering him shelter in her tent.

Other than Charlie's grumpy thank you when Becca bought them more beer, neither of them spoke until they got back to the tent.

"So, um..." he began, looking uncomfortable and unhappily at her tent, the smilies grinning at him in welcome. "Can I... Would you mind if...?"

"Can you cope, sleeping in a tent this pretty?" He still appeared appalled, but they both knew he was a beggar rather than a chooser and Becca was destined to crow about it. Some opportunities couldn't be passed up.

"I could try, I suppose." He didn't sound as grateful as he might.

Charlie dropped to the ground, taking care not to spill his beer. He wasn't ready to give himself over to the tent yet.

It was a clear night, the stars twinkling above them in the Chiltern sky. "Hmm," she sighed, joining him, "you kind of forget there are stars behind the orange glow."

Charlie stretched out his legs and leaned back on his elbows for a full look. "You need to get out of the city more."

She wasn't arguing there; she'd kill for a holiday, somewhere warm, with sand and sea and stars.

"Know any?" she asked, nodding up above them, distracting herself from her lack of travel. One day she'd have money for far-flung trips.

"Big shopping trolley, little shopping trolley," Charlie pointed out, identifying parts of Ursa Major and Ursa Minor.

"Impressive," Becca murmured. "I only know the North Star," she added, looking at the bright star at the end of Ursa Minor.

"That's Ally's and my star," he sighed.

"Your star?" she asked. She hadn't heard this one.

"Whenever we were away from each other and could see that star, we knew the other could be looking at it too. Sort of like a shared point of focus." She got it. Sure, you could just pick up the phone and call, but sometimes it was nice having a reference point which linked you under the same sky. "And sometimes, towards the end, just as she was drifting off, it's where she'd whisper she was off to and would be."

Becca didn't know what to say.

"Where do you think she went, BJ?"

Becca thwacked him on the hip.

"Ooofff," he said, "what was that for?"

She ignored him. He knew.

"D'you think she's up there in the stars?" he asked again, the beer slowing his words.

Looking up, Becca felt the same calm as when she'd been on the top of Snowdon. The sky was so vast, she had a sense of how small she was. It pleased her. Another year had passed and while her life was far from perfect, with her grand plans far from fruition and being a best friend down, Becca took comfort in having weathered through. Life could be long or short, but it was wide as the sky and there would always be some path around the obstacles. She was beginning to believe that.

"I can't say for sure whether she's on your star, Charlie, but knowing Ally, if that was what she'd decided, she'll have done everything in her power to get there."

There were many times when Becca had arrived for the night shift to find Ally and Charlie sitting on the bench outside Valerie's. She'd be sat on his lap, a fleece beanie on her head, and he'd have them wrapped up in her duvet, keeping her warm, given she had no insulation left on her. They'd say they were just watching the stars. Becca now suspected they'd been forming a plan of where Charlie could find her.

It made her sigh. Ally had always been thinking about how to make it easier for them afterwards. She saved her own frustrations and anger for when she was alone with Valerie, and Valerie took it all, saw it as a mother's role and didn't complain, not once. It had all been so cruel, for all of them.

Becca felt herself getting angry, but quelled it. Not tonight. This was about celebrating Ally, not raging about the injustice of it all.

She felt his hand squeeze her shoulder in thanks for her belief, the warmth of it highlighting that the air had got chilly.

"Do you think it's time to go to sleep?"

He drained the dregs of his beer in assent.

"You know, of the two tents to go," she said, crouching and scooting inside, "it was probably best it was yours. Mine's roomier." She thought she heard a growl from outside the flaps. They opened again behind her and he crawled in. Kneeling at her feet, he looked about. She waited for that moment she saw on *Location, Location, Location*, when the unexpected homeliness wowed the buyers, but it didn't quite transpire.

"Top and tail?" he asked, all about the logistics. She couldn't detect his preference, but his feet weren't going anywhere near her face.

"Are you a snorer or a heavy breather?" He shook his head. "Then I vote we top and top. The sleeping bags will keep things decent, OK?"

He took a moment. She understood it. It would be the most intimate they'd been with each other in a very long time.

"I won't jump you, Lister."

Without skipping a beat, he said, "Wouldn't be the first—" before she stopped him with a swift punch to the arm.

"You're perfectly safe. You have my word." The roll of his eyes told her he didn't think that counted for much either, but he unfurled the borrowed sleeping bag towards her.

There was nothing more to do than strip down to their T-shirts and under-layers and get into the sleeping bags. The tent was small and they were tall, so the manoeuvres were ungainly. She shouldered him in the nose and he elbowed her in the boob, but both were suddenly too polite to complain. Before long they were lying in awkward silence, listening to the murmurings from the surrounding tents.

Charlie was lying on his back motionless, clearly used to this. Becca was regretting wanting the *full* festival experience and not selling everything she owned to afford a glamping yurt with a little cot bed instead. The ground was neither soft nor forgiving.

"Do you think about the ashes?" he asked softly. "You know, after we've released them?"

"Nope." She didn't want to think of them after. "I think about the spirit," she said, "being free. I think it went when she died. The body was just a shell, wasn't it? The nurse opened the window and her spirit went then."

"Do you really?" He didn't sound sure. But he also sounded like he'd thought about it plenty. "I stopped believing in any kind of God when she died. I couldn't believe He or She would take something so good away from us all. But I like the idea of the spirit flying away."

"It's about the only thing I remember from school physics," she said. "Energy is never lost, only transferred from one kind to another – so it makes sense, to me at least, that human energy can't truly be gone."

"And you believe that?" He sounded hopeful.

Becca sighed, tiredness creeping in at the edges, "I dunno, Charlie. But believing it is more bearable. It means she's still out there in some form that we might encounter again. Look at it, she's definitely a force of nature – she's got you here and me up Snowdon." Becca paused, then quietly asked, "What do you miss most about her?"

"Everything," he said simply. "Her smile, her laugh, her voice. The brown of her eyes, the feel of her hair, the smell of her skin. Her stats, her shouting at the TV if they got them wrong. Her snore, her awful singing, her difficulty with patience. Her kindness, her annoying insistence on seeing things from both points of view when sometimes I just wanted to her to agree with my gripe and sympathise. Her utter and complete optimism, even in the face of utter cancerous shitness. And I miss her love, her unquestionable, unconditional love, which came without demand. You?"

Oh. OK. Wow. Becca took a moment to think. "Well, she had this sweater I'd borrow now and again…"

He snorted. Then he knocked her with his hip for a proper answer.

"From a selfish point of view," she said, more seriously, "at first I missed her cheering me on, or her butt kickings, but now, as I'm forced to get on with it, I miss having her as counsel, her advice, discussing things with her, telling her how things have gone. I miss … I miss someone giving a crap about me. If you don't have someone like that, it makes it hard to care about yourself, you know?" She wondered whether he did know. He had two parents who'd dragged him through the courts to show how much they cared about him.

"And from a non-selfish point of view?" he prompted. They spoke in low tones, which was silly, as no one was listening in. But maybe this was about shared intimacies and anything above a whisper would be too exposing. Side by side in the darkness was easier than face to face in the glare of day.

"Well, obviously that's not my strong point, but I miss the space she filled in the world, watching her successes. I think about the adult she would've been, the wife she would've been to you and a mother maybe – sorry, I'm sure you think about these things too. She had so much to give and other than with us, she never got to make her mark." Becca sighed at the thought of it. "It's been three years now and like you say, it's still everything."

The subsequent silence was long and loaded, each of them lost in their thoughts. It wasn't uncomfortable – after all, their thinking was along the same path – but she wasn't used to this kind of thing, in this kind of proximity with him. Considering whether she should say more, it came down to whether she could be arsed, and she realised that, hard as it might be, it was always nice to discuss Ally when she saw him. Not *seeing* him per se, but the opportunity to share memories and sadness with someone who understood. So yes, she could be arsed. She opened her mouth with a question, but his snore beat her to it. He'd clearly lied about the snoring then.

―――――――――

Becca woke to footfall outside the tent. She didn't open her eyes yet, instead relishing the lovely warm softness surrounding her. It felt sturdy and safe, not her usual cold awakening. A small smile spread across her face as she nestled further into it, savouring the comfort. There was light outside, she could sense it, but it wasn't morning's full glare and she figured she could lie in, snuggled like this, for a while.

She must have snoozed off as the light was brighter on her eyelids when she became conscious again. She thought to look at her watch, but the sturdiness was weighing her down, making it difficult to move. Then she remembered where she was, who she was with and why, and realised the weight was Charlie's arm slung across her, as they spooned. It made her eyes go wide. A quick lift of her head verified they were each in their own sleeping bags. This spooning was simply human comfort, absolutely nothing more, but it needed to stop and she set about planning how to extricate herself without waking him.

The arm slid further around her, clamping tighter, as he rolled in towards her in his sleep and sighed. Becca lay frozen, trying to work out what to do, trying to calm her panicked heartbeat under his hand, admonishing herself for how pleasing this had all felt before she'd been properly awake.

She felt him twitch and she started counting in her head. It only took eight seconds for him to go through the same thought process she'd just had, and he immediately lifted his arm off her, faking a stretch to roll away.

It took her a further count of a hundred before he managed an overly cheery "Morning!", as if he'd just popped in with the post. Her reciprocal "Morning!" was equally exaggerated.

They packed their things in amicable peace, their small talk keeping strictly to the weather and train times. Charlie returned the sleeping bag, and brought back a couple of coffees for them. He arrived just in time to see her magic her tent away in four seconds flat. (Yes, of course she'd saved the moment until he'd returned.)

His brow was furrowed as he approached.

"What's up?" she asked, hoping he wouldn't go near the sleeping thing. He looked at her, then away, changing his mind. He'd been doing this yesterday too. Like he had something to say, but couldn't.

"Charlie?" She took a sip of her coffee and perused the neighbours so it wasn't too intense. One thing she knew about Charlie was he didn't like being put on the spot. Years of pressures from his parents had managed that. Ally had simply made decisions for them and he went along with them, happy that she was happy. It worked for them, so who was Becca to judge, but it seemed passive to her. That said, her childhood had been the complete opposite and her situation was hardly ideal; she didn't have any choice *but* to make her own decisions. She hadn't overplayed it when saying she'd missed Ally as a sounding board.

"My stuff wasn't handed in." He literally had the things he was wearing to travel home in. The glow-stick necklace, however, had mysteriously vanished.

"Need anything to get home?"

"Nah. 'S'fine," he said and patted his pocket, to what she assumed was his wallet and tickets. She finished clipping her rucksack together. That feeling of a meet-up ending was settling on them and for once it seemed they might take their leave amicably, rather than resenting each other. He was still keeping something from her though. Which was fine, he was entitled to his secrets. She wasn't about to start delving. She had all sorts of shit in her life she'd no intention of sharing with him. They weren't that kind of friends. She wasn't sure they ever would be. However, they seemed to have come to an unspoken accord this weekend, of living in the moment. They'd only talked about the festival and Ally – which was what the day was all about. He hadn't asked her to trawl through her crappy résumé for the year, she hadn't asked about his relationship. Given they were still on speaking terms, she'd say it was a winning formula.

After stopping at a porridge stall for breakfast, they trudged towards the shuttle bus. She could feel his unease. It was in stark contrast to last night's mood.

"Becca," he said as the bus stop came into view. It took her a moment to notice he wasn't walking. "Stop a sec. There's something I need to tell you."

She had a sense of foreboding. "Dish it, Charlie, you might even feel better," she said, resigned. Ally would've wanted her to listen if he had a problem.

Charlie took a deep breath and said, "I'm getting married."

The words sank in but they made little sense.

"What, like in a wedding?" she asked, dumbly.

He nodded.

"To another person?" She couldn't compute this properly.

He had the good grace not to laugh. This was definitely not a laughing moment. He'd taken all this time to build up to it, chickening out, only to dump it on her just before he scarpered. She was amazed he hadn't shouted it at her as his train pulled away.

"Well, yes. To Liv."

Becca was feeling quite wobbly.

"But … but it's only been three years." It bewildered her. Losing Ally still felt like yesterday to her. And he'd been wanting *forever* with Ally, so how could he…?

"But it *has* been three years," Charlie stated. "And life goes on, right?" He looked away. It sounded like he was repeating rehearsed words.

"*Only* three years," she repeated, anger growing in the pit of her stomach, because he didn't seem to get this.

Now he looked at her, right in the eye, "We've been living together for a year, it's not like it's a whirlwind."

Yes, so of course Becca knew he'd been living with her, but other than grabbing the opportunity to move into his flat, she hadn't given it much thought. Or rather she'd deliberately not given it much thought. In her head she'd portrayed them as house-mates, rather than life partners. *Marriage* though, that disrupted her deluded depiction of things.

"What about Ally's memory?"

"What about it?" His tone was defensive, defiant even. "I'll always miss her, but I'm still here and I deserve to be happy." She was about to let loose her immediate thought of *Not like that, you don't,* but the bus pulled up and they were instantly caught in a scrum.

Once on board, she attempted to burrow through the passengers, until she came to a crushed halt three people away from him. The flat tent at her side had made her "ballistic missile" approach less dynamic, but they were close enough for her to come at him with both barrels.

"Have you told Valerie?" She was livid and indignant now, not helped by being jostled. She'd bet he hadn't. He'd been such a wuss about telling *her,* she doubted he'd have had the nuts to tell Valerie. Becca's cross tone drew the attention of all the people between them, but she didn't care.

"Yes, I rang her." Oh.

"Broke her lovely heart, I bet." *Now,* she was angry for Valerie *and* Ally. Surrounding eyes flitted between the two of them.

"Actually," he snapped, "she took it well. Better than you. Said she wants me to be happy. That Ally would have wanted me to find love again." The audience's eyes turned back to her and she didn't feel like they were on her side now. The mention of love struck her.

"And *do* you?" she demanded.

"Do I what?" All the conviviality of the morning had vanished. His jaw was set, his eyes flashing.

"Love Liv?" Yes, she said "Liv" like she was an inanimate object and a shitty one at that. She knew it was unfair, but something had triggered in her. Who else was there to fight Ally's corner? The unsubtle onlookers should at least know there was more at play here. She turned to the nearest and said, "He was engaged to my best friend. Who *died*." The woman looked both appalled and embarrassed at being drawn into this. The woman behind her gave Charlie the stink-eye. Hurrah.

"Yes. *Of course* I love her," he hissed, aware he was losing the crowd. It gained him a nod of approval from the bloke next to him. Typical. Blokes – always sticking together. Bloody Patriarchy.

"As much as you loved Ally?"

Charlie glared at her. All eyes turned to him. He leaned in over a passenger to get closer to her, then realised he had his armpit in their face, excused himself and with his hip squeezed his way nearer. Nearer to hiss, "Stop it. There's no way I can please you on this." He gave an eavesdropper a filthy look, sending her gaze immediately to the floor. "If I say I love her as much as I did Ally, you'll be outraged anything could match. If anything less, then I've insulted her memory, and heaven forbid it could possibly be more."

Yes, all of that was true. Which surely underlined why he should stay away from matrimony, full stop.

"You slept in my tent last night!" she gasped, feeling complicit in something. She never knowingly got involved with married men. The woman Charlie had shamed suddenly felt vindicated, and shot him an evil look of her own. He immediately tried to explain.

"My tent was stolen. Nothing happened. We had a sleeping bag each. Perfectly respectable." Her raised eyebrow said she was reserving judgment. Neither woman was sure his fiancée would appreciate the distinction. Becca wondered where exactly Liv thought he was this weekend. Or with whom. And would Becca have offered him shelter, had she known? It was a moot point, she concluded, because had they had this conversation yesterday, they wouldn't have got to nightfall.

The bus halted and the doors pistoned open. The people between them seemed reluctant to follow the spill of the crowd, but eventually shifted. Alighting from the bus, Charlie bee-lined towards the trains, leaving Becca cross and muttering as she pulled on her rucksack while fighting the tent. The smilies seemed to be mocking her.

She speed-walked to catch him. "Seriously, why go to the faff of marriage?" She really meant the *sanctity*. She wanted that reserved for Ally.

"Because we *want* to," he retaliated, keeping his eyes on the station entrance. "We're well matched. We have lots in common. Being married helps when we film in dodgy places."

How practical.

"Whose idea was it?" Becca said, suspecting this was just another passive move from Charlie, simply going with what life – or Liv – threw at him.

"Well, she brought it up – but she beat me to it, that's all. I was absolutely planning it."

Bull. Shit. "And you're so confident this is the right thing to do that you chickened out of telling me until now."

He kept moving and his eyes rolled with him. "Because I didn't want this to happen before you'd had your festival experience. I knew you'd lose your shit. I was right."

Huh. She resented him being able to predict her. But then again, it probably confirmed he knew right from wrong and she was correct in her reaction. And she didn't appreciate the inference she was being unreasonable.

"I didn't 'lose my shit'," she said, pulling a face, over-mimicking his voice. "I'm dismayed on Ally's behalf."

Making it through the ticket hall and approaching his platform, Charlie looked down the line, possibly selling his soul for the train to come rolling in right that second. He was heading back to his dad's in Oxford, while she was London-bound. Then he faced her, his expression sad. "Ally wouldn't be dismayed, Becca. She told me to find someone else."

"She didn't mean it. It was a *test*. You failed." Becca couldn't pinpoint why she felt this so deeply. Yes, maybe one day, when he was a pensioner or something, he could find another pensioner for companionship, but this? It was too soon and too much.

"No, it wasn't," he said firmly, reining in his vexation. "She knew life would carry on. She loved me, like I loved her, and she didn't want me to be lonely."

"So, get some more mates to entertain you!" she snapped. Yeah, so her mates hadn't made her miss Ally any less, but "I didn't replace Ally with a new best mate. Ally wasn't a bloody hamster!" Becca's anger was more frustration now, at not being able to express herself better, at not being able to show him his incredible error.

Becca deflated. What did it matter? His mind was made up.

She shook her head and checked her watch. Their trains were about to arrive and she had to change platforms. Good. She didn't want to keep talking to him. He'd spoiled everything. She almost demanded the T-shirt back.

Becca pulled herself upright with a jiggle to adjust her rucksack, the tent flapping about. She felt a need to punch each of the smiley faces. "Well," she said with an air of conclusion, "congratulations." She tried to make it sound genuinely meant, but it wasn't.

Charlie hesitated, expecting some punchline or just a sucker punch. Becca simply stared at him until he gave her a guarded "Cheers."

Then she turned and walked away, casting a monotone "See you next year" back at him, not even sure there would be one. She didn't trust herself to say more now, stuck as she was on the WHAT THE FUCK? booming in her head.

She deliberately stomped loudly across the paving slabs like a tantrummy toddler. The train pulled up as she reached the platform and it felt like a blessing to throw herself onto the first seat. Only then was she willing to cast a glance towards him. His own train had pulled in and he was sitting watching her through the two panes of glass. He looked ... she didn't quite know ... *miserable?*

2015

"Heads up. Incoming," Ollie murmured. Charlie turned towards the opening glass doors. The congregation fell silent as the string quartet began to play Pachelbel's "Canon in D".

Though the veil blurred her face, Liv looked sensational as her father escorted her towards him. The cling of her designer dress showed her curves, but also her trimness. Her running hadn't been back-burnered like most things in the preparations for this day. Watching her now, Charlie knew, hand on heart, his imminent vows would be for ever, because there was no way in hell he was ever getting married again. The stress, the strops, the rage had been fucking awful. Considering Liv had been producing programmes for years, organising hordes of people for each project, she'd completely lost it on this one. She'd become a monster. No delegated task had been done well enough, quickly enough, or with enough acumen, communication or assurance. Winging it, like they were occasionally forced to when herding a crew, was out of the question, the very suggestion a crime against humanity. She was simultaneously acting in, directing and producing her own production, and while many offered to take jobs off her, she'd been having none of it. Charlie knew for a fact her entire family were feeling the same way he did. As they now reached Charlie at the end of the aisle, her father was visibly relieved to hand her over. Then he collected himself and shot his future son-in-law a look of guilty sympathy. Or was it outright pity? Yes, Charlie believed it might be.

Charlie was experiencing very mixed emotions. He loved her, of course he did. (As did her family, normally.) Getting married was the next step they'd agreed, and he'd done a brilliant job of proposing in precisely the way she'd described as her dream proposal, using the handy email of relevant links she'd sent him. But as if a buzzer had sounded after her acceptance, she'd become a wedding obsessive. No information request was answered satisfactorily, and Charlie was at a loss why she bothered asking his opinion when she already knew what she wanted.

And then he'd commented that he was happy with whatever she chose, and all hell had broken loose.

"You don't care about this wedding!" she'd shrieked, flinging a copy of *The Knot* across the room. She was not the flinging type and it had shocked him.

"That's not what I said. I just meant, if a detail is what you want, then I'm happy."

"Details? Is that how you see them? Trivial things?"

"Of course not." He tried to placate her, pulling her in to him. "All *I* need is you, me, the venue and an official to make it happen." Those were the facts and he thought she'd like the romance of it. "*Us*, Liv," he said, soothing her, "that's the important bit. The rest is just fluff, right?" He ducked his head to make eye contact with her and flash her his best smile. If he could get her into bed, he'd find other ways of soothing the stress off her. It had been a while, to be honest, and maybe that was part of the problem.

Liv's eyes widened and she pushed herself out of his

embrace. "Fluff? The biggest day of our lives, the start of our marriage, and you think it's fluff?"

He raised both his hands to slow her, "Whoa! My point was, we don't need to sweat the small stuff."

He didn't want a row about it, but it seemed to be escalating in front of him with everything he said.

She looked like she was about to cry, not weepy crying, but raging hacking crying of frustration. "This is a huge day for me. *Us*," she corrected. "Why isn't that how you see it?"

He was reluctant to give any answer now, unsure he'd get it right. Taking a deep breath, he considered his next words, while Liv breathed crossly, like a bull winding up to charge. He didn't recognise this woman.

"I want it to be the day you've always dreamed of, Liv. Your happiness is key for me. *That's* all I'd imagined: having a blissful bride." OK, this seemed to be going better. "It's not that I don't care, or think it isn't important, but I want you to have what you want. I'll be the luckiest man alive if you just meet me at the altar." *There*, he thought, that was better, wasn't it? Only, why was she looking dismayed now?

"Liv?"

"You said you didn't want a church."

He hadn't actually. Again, he was happy to go with the flow on the venue. He *had* said he wanted nothing uber-religious, but there were churches and there were churches, weren't there? One of those derelict ones filled with candles at dusk had sounded moody and atmospheric, but then it had changed numerous times, finally settling on a mahoosive glass orangery.

"No – I—"

"You said *altar*. That implies a church. Oh my God," she wailed, as if the world was ending, "the venue is wrong."

"I only meant 'up the front'," he said, at a loss, but she was leaving the room, waving him away. As the door slammed to their bedroom, he dropped onto the sofa, stunned. Was this what weddings did to people? Release them from all reason, nuance and understanding? His wedding with Ally was to have been a relaxed open-air do on a farm with glamping. They'd laughed when they'd envisaged it. Of course they'd never got to the point of bookings, deposits or invites. Perhaps that was the difference.

But here Liv was now, looking beautiful as the celebrant spoke. They had got here, and while not talking much in recent days, she hadn't called the whole thing off. He'd kept his head down, busying himself with everything requiring collection, transporting or sending. He couldn't think how else to show he was fully on board with her dreams. And yet, even now, as they exchanged vows, her brow looked pinched, in the same way it did when they started filming. It didn't normally last long, but despite all the controlled planning, the first moments of cameras rolling, the culmination of her work, were the moments where she braced herself. He wished she could relax and have faith. Faith in him and the congregation of their nearest and dearest (and Becca, who sat in the middle with Shrin). Even if all the plans fell apart, no one would care as long as the marriage happened.

So as he said the words "I do," Charlie absolutely meant them, as this *had* to be until death did them part; going through this again would definitely be the death of him.

"Dearly beloved," Ollie began and positively shone as he got his intended laugh from the many tables of guests, "my name's Ollie. I have the enormous honour of being Charlie's best friend and I'd like to thank you all for coming to my Best Man's day."

Charlie knew today was supposed to be about love for his bride, but looking at Ollie, Charlie felt his heart swell. They'd been friends for nine years now, and he was grateful for each of them. Ollie was a delightful mix of a baby Brian Blessed and a younger Gareth from *Four Weddings*. He was incredibly bright in some areas and a buffoon in others, and charmingly he recognised both, actually revelling in his mediocrity when it surfaced, rather than choosing to bluff. He was Mr Silver Lining and Mr Glass Half Full all in one, and Charlie couldn't think of anyone he'd rather have supporting him today. Choosing Ollie was a no-brainer. He'd seen enough best men stitch up their grooms and Ollie would *never* do that to him.

Charlie sat back to watch the show, lifting Liv's hand to kiss it lightly, weaving his fingers into hers as both hands rested back on the white damask tablecloth. This was better. She was relaxing at last. All it had taken was the main gig to be over and a shed-load of champagne during the photos.

"As some of you know," Ollie said, scanning the room, bringing everyone in, "this isn't the first time Charlie has asked me to be his best man, but I promise this isn't a recycled speech."

Ahh shit.

As Charlie's stomach plummeted into his arse area, he felt

his fingers squeeze tight. Very very tight. Keeping his smile plastered on, he glanced at Liv from the corner of his eye. She too hadn't dropped the facade, retaining a beatific expression he recognised as the one she used at work when she'd just been blindsided by a corrupt fixer and was about to kick him in the nuts. The vice-like grip on his fingers supported this assessment.

His eyes flicked to the rest of the room. All eyes were on Ollie. His charm and obvious joy at giving this speech had everyone transfixed.

"We are all beside ourselves that Charlie has found Liv, has found love again and someone to share his life with."

The schmaltzy collective "Aw" from the guests necessitated Charlie and Liv leaning in and sharing a kiss, which in turn, gained them a round of applause. It allowed Liv to look him deep in the eyes and demand, "What, Charlie, is he talking about?" without being overheard.

Charlie took a sip of his champagne, the sweat forming under his collar. Why hadn't he asked to look at the bloody speech? Why hadn't he asked Ollie not to mention Ally? Charlie knew, of course. He didn't want his friends knowing he hadn't had The Conversation. Now, he wanted to put his head in his hands, but currently one of them was turning white as the blood was crushed from it. He wasn't sure how this could get worse.

"I used to believe you only got one soul-mate in life," Ollie enthused on, "but clearly," he swung his arm towards them, "that isn't the case."

Ah yes, *there* it was.

Pain stabbed down his ankle as a stiletto heel, hidden by

the tablecloth, pressed firmly into it. He upped his smile in the hope no one would notice anything was amiss.

Charlie's ears went on a defensive shutdown, no longer receiving Ollie's words as anything more than white noise. What was he going to do?

Liv shuffled her seat closer so she could sit against him as they both watched Ollie at the far end of the table. Charlie took his chance to extricate his hand, concentrating on not wincing. He stretched the blood into his fingers behind her back, before wrapping his arm around her shoulder. Liv leaned in to whisper intimately to him, "Who *the fuck* is he talking about?"

She took a steady sip of his champagne. He faced a dilemma: keep schtum until later and let her come to the boil in the meantime, or head her fury off now with the facts, risking a top-table explosion. Trained from a young age to assess the incendiary potential of a situation, Charlie calculated the best path to damage limitation. After many months of work, he banked on her not spoiling the scene she'd striven to perfect.

Under the guise of whispering sweet nothings, he tenderly tucked a loose lock of her highly styled casual-style hair behind her ear and told her. "I was engaged to Ally, Shrin's friend whose uni room I rented. She died, remember?" He felt it important to remind her of that, partly in hope of a sympathy buffer but also to highlight there was no threat here. No scorned woman was about to burst in, hijacking things.

No one noticed Liv sliding her hand off the table, nor digging her nails into his thigh. At the guests' next "Aww" at Ollie's words, she turned further into him and growled "Tomorrow. Every detail. No omissions. No lies. Everything."

His relief was enormous. They still had a tomorrow, then. That was a start.

He kissed her on the temple and promised, with a deeply contrite "Everything."

———

The tables had been moved to the sides and the peony-festooned orangery now had a dance floor, although Charlie was standing safely on the sidelines.

"Need this?" Becca asked, offering him a pint of beer. Charlie immediately sank half of it, closing his eyes for the full impact, savouring it as a nod to normality.

"Thanks, White," he said. Dressed in a striking emerald green frock, she stood next to him, leaning on the bar, surveying the dancing guests. He'd already performed the first dance and it had gone splendidly. The six weeks of lessons for the choreographed routine had helped. He'd originally envisaged a leisurely shuffle in a steady circle for the duration of "Thinking Out Loud", murmuring lovely secret things to each other, but Liv wanted to surprise everyone with their "skillz". So, they'd just been a two-man flash-mob executing a high-energy jive, which had left everyone whooping and Charlie wheezing. Now, he watched his wife letting her hair down, razzing it up to "Love Shack" with her bridesmaids.

"Pleasure," Becca said. "I can be very generous at an open bar. And you looked like it would help."

"Bit of a busy day," he said, with a wan smile. Of the many many smiles of the day, this one didn't hurt his jaw.

"I *saw*," she said. "*Strictly* next?"

He took another long sip of the beer, watching Liv air-lasso her cousin Cara across the floor. She'd had plenty more champagne after Ollie's speech. And who could blame her for kicking back now? They only had "1 a.m.: Bed" left on the schedule, and that had "CHARLIE" assigned to it.

"Yeah, no. That's me done on the dancing front." Liv had signed them up for a regular swing-dance night when they returned from their honeymoon. He had two weeks to find an excuse or acquire some muscle damage.

"Looking forward to going away?" She swirled her cocktail in its glass, her eyes scoping the room, particularly the men.

"God yes!" Far away from all of this, and time to get Liv's mindset away from Planet Bride.

His outburst caught Becca's attention.

"Time to unwind required?"

"So much."

"Don't tell me…" she said, putting her index finger to her chin. "Hiking the Inca Trail?" She was making a concerted effort to be nice. It was somewhat disconcerting, but then it was probably basic etiquette to be nice to the groom.

"Ha! No." Man, the Inca Trail would have been a stonking trip to claim as a honeymoon. "Two weeks in Bali."

"Nice," Becca conceded politely and adjusted her guessing. "Two days by the pool then exploring the interior, *on foot*?"

If only. Charlie studied the floor briefly. "Actually, we agreed we just wanted to chill by the pool."

"The whole time?" she asked, amazed.

"Sure. That's what honeymoons are about," he said. "That's assuming we get out of bed for two weeks," he added, waggling his eyebrows at Becca, hoping it regained him a modicum of adventure.

"Ew. TMI, Lister."

A silence fell between them. This wasn't quite the future either of them had envisaged six years ago. A wedding yes, but a very different one and a different bride.

"She looks beautiful," Becca suddenly said.

"Yes, doesn't she," he agreed, as the bridesmaid posse gave a perfectly synchronised macarena in front of them. "I'm a very lucky guy."

"And you finally got around to telling her about Ally. About time. How did she take it?"

He considered lying, playing out some spiel of his having told her ages ago and Liv being chilled about it, but he was already exhausted.

"What you saw during the speech was how she took it. I'll have to let you know later how it landed."

Becca whistled. "Seriously, your conflict avoidance is spectacular," she said, with an impressed nod. "That said, the two of you could do well on the stage."

"Thanks," he muttered. He took it as praise coming from a professional. "How are the jobs going?" he asked, now they were on the subject.

Becca kept her eyes on the dance floor. "I landed a speaking role in a BBC show."

Charlie had just worked on a programme for the BBC. It hardly made them colleagues, but it was a point of commonality.

"That's great." It really was. Last he'd heard from Ollie, she and many of London's "resting" actors were schlepping through abandoned buildings at night dressed as the undead, chasing paying customers in Zombie Runs. "Which channel?"

"BBC Education." Not exactly the big time, but something reputable for the CV.

"Commendable."

Becca sighed. "It's a sex ed show and my role as narrator involves a sperm costume," she said, glumly. "Imagine that," she continued, turning to him and blatantly judging his coral-pink cravat, "keeping a straight face in a spunksuit."

Charlie caught her flat smile. When would she catch a break? He felt the need to cheer her up. "Shame they didn't tell you to 'cum as you are'."

For a moment she didn't speak and he tensed his abs for the impact. But then she stood tall and gave him the jazz hands. "That's showjizz, Lister."

He gave her the laugh she needed. "It's Lassiter-Lister now, actually."

Becca gave him the bug eye. "Really? *Really* really?"

"You can't give up your maiden name in our industry."

"Sure," she agreed, nodding, "but Lassiter-Lister?"

"It is what it is," he said, resigned. "You'll get used to it, BJ."

"Becca," she insisted. "Don't think I can't punch you on your wedding day. The photos have already been taken, the black eye won't be recorded."

Relaxing a little now, they both laughed. Liv's eyes connected with his at that exact moment, then slid to Becca beside him. Hmmm, frosty. He mouthed "I love you" at her and after a long beat, she mustered a smile and danced on with her womenfolk. And Ollie. Ollie, who was catching up on all the drinks now his speech had been deployed and his best man duties divested. He was launching a coup over the dance floor, manifesting his reign by performing *the sprinkler* at the guests bobbing at the sides, and rocking his broad groin almost to the beat.

"Ah feck..." Becca and Charlie both groaned. They'd seen this before. It never ended well. Ollie believed he was Travolta's love-child, generally combining both *Saturday Night Fever* and *Pulp Fiction* moves with enthusiastic abandon, which was all very well amongst friends, but not with people who didn't know him or appreciate he had zero rhythm. He'd never been able to clap in time or snap his fingers to a beat, yet still, he maintained he was a dance-floor deity. Soon he'd start challenging people to dance-offs.

"Shrin or Ollie?" Becca asked, necking the last of her Cosmopolitan.

He couldn't decide. It seemed unfair to send her out there.

He held out a clenched fist.

She did the same.

They lifted and dropped them three times, then chose their weapons.

"Dammit," grumbled Becca. "Fucking bloody scissors."

Charlie released his hand stone and gave her a small wave as he moved away to find Shrin. "Good luck, brave warrior."

"Coward," she muttered, as she straightened her dress, set her shoulders and headed off to tame the now break-dancing beast.

178

Shrinidhi was always in the middle of a crowd of women and the "Charlie's Friends" table was full of them.

Charlie put his hands on her shoulders, ducking down to her ear. "Emergency, Shrin."

She tipped her head back to look at him upside down. Her eyes weren't fully synchronised. When she saw who it was, they rolled.

"Nooo, not again."

"Not quite yet, but it's imminent." He stood back so she could right her head and slide out of her fabric-swaddled seat.

"Honestly, Charlie, when will he learn? My mother still sees a chiropractor from when he dipped her at our reception." She picked up the front of her maxi dress to allow for speed.

They stopped near the dance floor to survey the state of affairs. No one was wailing in pain as far as he could hear over the music, so that was something. The floor was crowded, so Ollie hadn't gone full dance-off yet.

Then, something was afoot. The dancing guests moved to the edges, and Ollie stood expectantly in the middle, looking pleased as spiked punch, hands on hips.

Shamefully late to the game, Charlie registered the song playing. Ally had had a *Dirty Dancing* fetish. He was trained.

"Come on, Becca," they lip-read Ollie shout over the strains of "Time of My Life". He gave a "bring it" gesture.

"Aw crap," Shrin whimpered.

Charlie's gaze cut to the other end of the floor, where Becca was looking about for support, and found only cheering and clapping in her face. She would know this was a bad idea, but attention and applause were her catnip. After all, this was the same Becca who'd once willingly writhed around on the drama studio floor in little more than green paint.

"Has he done this before?" Charlie asked, his concern increasing.

"Only with one of the rugby lads when you were travelling. He bust a rib breaking their fall."

Charlie remembered the broken rib, but Ollie had definitely told him it was a match injury.

"Plan?"

Shrin knew Becca well enough to see she was now a willing participant in this.

It turned out there was no time for a plan as Bill Medley and Jennifer Warnes hit the moment and on cue a streak of emerald green shot across the floor to cheers.

Becca launched herself.

Charlie held his breath.

Ollie caught her and held her aloft.

A laugh bubbled in Charlie's throat from relief and it erupted fully as her full skirt flew up to reveal very small orange lacy knickers, which gained her an additional roar from the crowd. His eyes skirted to Liv on the far side of the dance floor, beholding Becca's bum. He imagined this wasn't in keeping with the air of sophistication she'd been pursuing for their wedding.

The laugh wedged in his mouth as he saw Ollie, jubilant at having succeeded this time, listing backwards. He was too tipsy to gain better footing and everyone watched stunned, as Becca's graceful ascent, complete with outstretched arms, now became an equally graceful descent as she headed towards the floor.

The collective "Ooof" of the guests was louder than the soar of the music. Both Charlie and Shrin were already pushing through them.

Neither Becca nor Ollie were moving. Becca had her face turned to one side, lying prone on the floor, arms still outstretched. She was blinking however, so first indications were positive. Ollie was flat on his back, but his face was hidden by green silk and Becca's pelvis. His chest was rising up and down quickly, so again, basic stats were covered. Unlike Becca's bottom, which was not and had the crowd mesmerised.

Shrinidhi headed towards the lower part of the stricken entertainment, deftly correcting Becca's skirt, before checking her husband underneath, clearly an equal believer in Girl Code always coming first.

"White?" Charlie asked, on his knees, cheek flat to the floor in front of her spaced gaze. "You OK?"

"Mmm-hm," she managed.

"Are you winded?"

"Bit," she whispered.

She could talk. She could assess her status. Good signs.

Her body shifted as Shrin rolled Ollie out from under her.

"Lister," she rasped. He moved his head closer to hear better, just in case these were her last words. "Did anyone notice?"

Charlie looked up and around. Now Ollie was on his feet, and Charlie was managing Becca, the other guests were mingling. Not his bride and her bridesmaids though; they stood in a tribal cluster, watching his every move.

Returning to Becca, he sensed she was ruing being seduced by Ollie's antics. Her pride was on the line.

"You might just have got away with it, BJ."

A small smile spread across her face. "Thanks, Charlie." For once she seemed to appreciate his fibbing.

He helped her up, Becca keeping her eyes on the ground, and led her towards the patio doors.

"Is she OK?" Liv asked as they passed the bridal squad. She sounded snippy as opposed to sympathetic.

"Bit winded, a breath of fresh air should do it," he murmured. He leaned in and gave Liv a kiss. "Back soon for a dance." He hoped that would placate her, but the looks he was getting from the bridesmaids weren't encouraging.

A welcome change of air hit them as they reached the patio outside the orangery. A few guests stood in small groups chatting and drinking. Charlie wished he'd thought to bring a couple of drinks.

"Here, sit down," he said, guiding her to a chair. "Back in a sec," he said and hoofed back inside, to swiftly relieve a passing waiter of two glasses of champagne.

She gratefully took one when Charlie appeared in front of her again.

"Got your breath back?"

"Just. What was I thinking?"

"Quite," Charlie scolded. "You *know* what he's like."

She shook her head in mock shame. "I do. I should have known better."

He couldn't resist. "The call of the audience got you, you glory hound."

She moved to protest, but surrendered. "Yeah, probably. It played out better in my head."

Sitting down beside her, Charlie couldn't help but grin at the memory of it – now he knew she was OK, of course. He hadn't heard any ambulances coming for Ollie, so he assumed he was fine.

"Have I fucked up your reception?" Becca asked.

"Hell no! It was hysterical. Sorry, but it was. I'm sure the guests will remember our wedding now. That's fine by me."

"Will wifey be pissed with me?"

He was curious. "Do you care?"

"She's the bride. I'm sure she's put a shit-load of work into this. And no one wants to spoil the bride's day." He wasn't used to this Becca, concerned with the feelings of others. She really had been winded.

"She's used to quirks in a schedule, she'll be fine," he said, his tone more placid and confident than he felt. Given Liv's pre-wedding form, she might be spontaneously combusting in there. His eyes slid towards the door and the dance floor. Bodies were pulsing to "Gangnam Style", and on cue Liv ponied past, en troupe with her gang, arm waving in the air. He was quite glad to be outside.

"Is it true love?" he heard Becca ask bluntly.

"You're at my wedding reception, BJ," he answered, with an incredulous laugh. "Of course it's true love."

"I dunno, I've been to weddings where I swear they're in it for the gifts. But let's give you the benefit of the doubt, eh?" She was so charitable about it, he couldn't help but shake his head.

"Yes, it's true love. Liv and I *fit*."

"But is it the same as with Ally? The love?"

Her stare was defiant. He didn't think she wanted him to say yes. Her loyalty to Ally still raced in her veins.

He chose his words carefully. "Maybe you only get one of those in life, something that pure, so innocent." He instantly felt disloyal to Liv. "This is different. Still wonderful," he reiterated, keen for her to understand there was no chink in the armour to exploit here. And it *was* wonderful. It was a more mature relationship, with compromises made on both sides, whereas with Ally, having started so young, theirs was more of a shared path they grew with rather than stepped onto. He saw the same thing with Ollie and Shrin. Perhaps it just depended on how old you were when you met your partner, how established your own lives already were, and how much accommodation was required.

Either way, the answer seemed to satisfy Becca. He suspected she just wanted Ally safeguarded as unique in his heart.

The music from the orangery had shifted down a gear. After being "on" all day, Charlie welcomed the slower tempo. On a whim he stood and held out a hand to her.

She assessed it quizzically.

"Dance?" he prompted.

"Us?"

He looked about. Everyone else had gone in.

"Why not?"

She took a moment to process this and then stood, smoothed down her skirt, before placing her hand in his and the other on his shoulder.

It was the languid circular shuffle he'd imagined his first

dance would be. There was a respectable distance between them, and Becca's "Well, this is weird, Lister" probably wouldn't classify as a sweet nothing.

"Lassiter-Lister," she corrected herself, then shook her head. "Sorry, no, can't do it. Lasster?"

"No."

"Lissiter?"

"Still no."

She sighed. "It really is going to have to be Charlie now."

"Other people find it works."

Becca's pout was properly sulky and it made him laugh.

"And *is* it weird?" he asked. "The groom dancing with an invited guest?"

Becca studied his face. "I was going to ask you about that."

"About what?"

"Well, we didn't exactly end on the best of terms last year."

"Nothing new there," he interjected. She gave a quick nod.

"So I was wondering why you invited me."

Well now, *there* was an awkward question. He'd invited their entire student house. Leaving her out would have been obvious and inflammatory.

"We're old friends," he said, parroting what he'd told Liv.

"Bullshit," coughed Becca.

"OK, old *acquaintances*," he said, but paused. "No, we *are* friends, BJ. I don't think you can be lifelong acquaintances. At some point you cut the cord or you default to being friends. Tetchy ones, admittedly, in our case, but I would – *do* – class you as a friend. You *know* me. We laugh at the same things. You know my history, in some parts better than anyone else." He spun her out and back in, to make light of the sadder memory.

"And it turns out when you're putting together a wedding guest list, you pick the people you want standing on your side of the room supporting you, and in my case it was the people who, if the shit hit the fan, I reckon I could call for help."

She looked at him oddly. "You'd call me?" She looked touched.

"Well, maybe not *first*, but you know." He ducked his head. He didn't enjoy giving her ammo like this. "Tell me this then," he said, turning the tables. "Why d'you accept?" She wasn't averse to being there – she'd made an effort. The dress, the pretty eye-sparkle and her intricately braided hair said as much. "I could just have been inviting you for politeness's sake."

"Apart from me reckoning you needed more bodies on your side?" That was a fair point. He didn't have much family. Even so, Liv had questioned her being on the list, given Becca thought he was a dickhead. But Liv had invited a marathon mate, a guy who Charlie thought was an utter throbber, so things had got a bit tit-for-tatish and he'd dug his heels in. However, once they'd made a truce, each keeping their list as was, Charlie had been content with Becca being on there.

"Yes, apart from that. Thanks for filling a space."

"Well, I did umm and ahh," she said blithely, so he dipped her without warning as revenge. Unfazed, Becca neatly lifted a foot as she tipped. "And I have to warn you, I couldn't afford anything on your extensive wedding list."

"There were some less expensive things on there," he protested. That bloody list had been a bone of contention. He hated those things, they felt so presumptuous, but Liv had insisted it helped people, so he'd caved.

"I'm *not* buying you a chrome toilet brush set. I have standards."

Shit. That must have been added after. "Fair enough."

"When you get the 'Adopt a Donkey' voucher, you're welcome to call her Becca."

"Done," he said with a laugh. He wasn't sure Liv would see the funny side. "So tell me then, why d'you accept, if it wasn't to lavish me with four Egyptian towel bales or an essential cashmere throw?"

"Or a picnic set."

"That hadn't been taken?"

"Not as of this morning, no."

"Damn."

Becca sighed, relaxed, either from their amicable mood, or the champagne. "I guess I wanted to see you do it. And..."

She'd stopped and by the quiet tone of her voice, he knew it was something heartfelt. The glow of the exterior lights shadowed her face, but he could see a glint in her eye.

"And?" He sensed this was where she'd lodge her objection to the whole thing, but he'd rather they just had it out.

It took her a moment to form her words and look him in the eyes.

"I think I felt like an envoy too. I wanted to come in Ally's place, or bring her spirit with me, and to assure you she'd have wanted you to be happy. Maybe a blessing. Not that you need it, of course." She seemed unsure of herself for a second, but pushed on. "And while I couldn't ever have seen you with anyone else, I understand life can be long, and lonely, and from what I saw today, Liv seems to love you, so I know Ally would have been glad. That was it."

Wow. Right. Not what he'd been expecting. He felt his throat tighten as she mentioned Ally's blessing – which he knew he had, but suspected Becca needed to voice to accept it herself. Seeing her look away, her eyes blinking, he thought she was in a similar place too.

It meant more to him than he cared to tell her. He hoped he'd become a man Ally would have been proud of.

Having at first wandered aimlessly, recklessly through his South America trip, he'd slowly begun to pick himself back up off the floor, learning to live again by striving to be the man Ally would want him to be, resilient and positive. He'd grasped at life again because she couldn't. He'd pushed himself to engage with the countries he visited, imagining being there with her, and gradually unearthed traits of himself he recognised and ventured back into the light. Becca's blessing said he might just have managed it.

"Thank you," he managed and then spun her out, to reel her in again. The subject needed changing.

"Can you imagine our uni selves watching us now?" she said over-brightly.

"Well, they'd be appalled by the close proximity, obviously, and they wouldn't have thought much of the goodwill."

"They might be shouting at each other."

He released one hand to try out one of his new jive moves, passing her around his back and returning her to his front. It made her face flush. This Becca was enjoyable; relaxed and glowing. He always got the bitter and snarling version. But he'd seen her like this with Ally, when they were immersed in girl-talk, often forgetting he was there. "But look at us now," he said. "This is what therapists would call progress, don't you think?"

The tempo inside edged up a notch again. Ah, the Michael Bublé playlist had found its way to the forefront.

They fell into a companionable silence, both swaying to the music. His thoughts drifted back to how this could have been a different wedding, where he might have danced with Becca as chief bridesmaid, where Ally, dressed in white, would have been applauding them being so close without it being a brawl.

He closed his eyes and thought back to their plans. Ally had divvied up the tasks for their wedding early on. While she liked to organise things, she also liked surprises, so assigned elements of the day – the music, the groomsmen's outfits, the design of the wedding cake – to him, meaning he was both involved and contributing moments of delight for her. Perhaps it was tiredness from the long day, but he felt a wave of melancholy settle on him. Not because he regretted his marriage to Liv, more a low-level mourning for another life which hadn't played out, for the sheer joy Ally would have experienced and never did. His hand clenching a little harder around Becca's was a reflex, but one she returned. He suspected her own thoughts weren't a million miles away from his. And in that moment, he knew there was no one better to be dancing with, as he had such thoughts. Becca knew these things about him, understood them, more than anyone else, and she didn't need to say a thing.

"Having fun?" Liv stood with a couple of glasses of champagne, watching them. He and Becca had rather sunk into each other in their contemplation. Charlie had no idea how long she'd been there and he quickly tried to replay the scene as they stepped away from each other.

Becca turned toward Liv. The tension between the women caused him to hold his breath.

"I think Ollie's looking for you, Becca," Liv said with a smile which didn't reach her eyes. "The guests might find an encore amusing." The guests perhaps, Liv not so much, he suspected. Becca was being dismissed.

"Ha! Think I've learned my lesson there," Becca said, uncowed. She gave her ribcage a good-natured rub. The glasses in Liv's hands caught her eye. "Oh, you angel," she said, taking one and clinking Liv's glass. "Here's to your having many happy years together, you stunning bride, you." Then, picking up the beat, she sashayed back into the orangery, leaving Liv staring at Charlie, who was madly trying to work out how to play this, if he was still going to make it to the "Bed" part of the night's schedule.

Charlie's face held a teeth-clenched grimace. His lips were wide like an Aardman character and he was concentrating. Having done this before, knowing his timing, he pulled the green bottle from his jumpsuit, unstoppered it and let the ashes fly alongside him like a vapour trail as he hurtled towards the ground.

"Fly well, Ally," he wished her, then pulled his rip cord and watched as the cloud of ashes continued without him.

He floated his own way down to the landing site. The scatterings were never what he'd consider enjoyable, but his grimace today wasn't for the task. Today it was soundly, pissedly – yes, he was sure it was a word – directed at Becca, who hadn't bothered to bloody show up.

Pulling his parachute together to carry it back to the hangar, he swore many times and mainly at his own conflicting emotions. Doing the task solo was much easier, and yet he was seething that she hadn't come. *Fuck sake* – it was just one thing, once a year, for the friend who she'd loved above anyone. OK, so a skydive might not have been everyone's cup of tea, he got that. To his knowledge Becca hadn't skydived before – nor had Ally – but on the basis she'd suggested doing the tasks to honour Ally, he'd thought she'd put any wussy thoughts aside. Becca knew he'd done lots of jumps with the university parachuting club. He'd thought she'd trust him on the eight-minute jump's safety. But oh no, Miss White was being a diva as always.

He stomped across the airfield. He'd been looking forward to seeing Becca do this. His prediction was she'd have crapped herself. Her doing something out of her comfort zone offered him a certain pleasure. However, he'd also always enjoyed the thrill of a first-timer raving about their jump as they landed, remembering the fear, the rush and then the amazing stillness that followed. That said, Charlie was currently experiencing plenty of stillness of his own in his life – frosty stillness, having been in the doghouse since the weekend – and it wasn't so amazing.

Charlie was aware he'd played it badly with Liv. He couldn't quite see how he could have done it differently though, not without hurting her either way, and as always, he'd been doing everything possible to avoid an argument. So much for that strategy…

"Babe?" Liv's voice had come from the bedroom.

Charlie glanced up as Liv appeared, holding a garish piece of fabric. "Mmm?"

"What's this, babe?" she asked, smirking. He sensed he was about to be mocked. After a blistering post-wedding depression, "normal Liv" service had resumed. She could laugh again, cope with light teasing, and evidently give it back too. She unfurled the fabric which, to Charlie's dismay, was his festival T-shirt.

"You rummaging through my clothes?" he asked lightly, buying time.

"Just having a clear-out. I finished mine and thought I'd have a go at yours." It was a Sunday, and Liv didn't understand the meaning of lazy days. She'd already completed a 20K run and now this. In Charlie's opinion, Sundays should be about brunches and curling up together, reading the papers or watching films or even better, shagging like rabbits (albeit lazy ones).

He looked past her to the pile of clothes on the hallway floor. Most of it was his.

"It's a festival T-shirt," he said.

Liv laughed. "When have you ever been to a festival?" She said it like it was the most ridiculous thought ever.

"Back when I was young, I did, in fact, go to festivals." He kept it vague and returned to his book, hoping the subject would go away. He hadn't actually told Liv about his festival experience last year. She'd gone to Kerry to run the Killarney Marathon with her cousin, and he'd gone to visit his dad in Oxford. Which he *had* – for one of the nights, but not the other. Returning home, he'd had the T-shirt washed and hidden away, long before her key turned in the door. Right now, he was wishing he'd binned it. Or burned it.

Disappointed with his embarrassment levels, Liv gave it another assessment. "Charity shop it?"

He glanced at it over the top of his book. He should totally get rid. But it was out in the open now. "Umm, just shove it back in the wardrobe, maybe? Might need it for fancy dress one day." He gave her a smile. They'd never been to a fancy dress party yet. "But really far back, yeah? Don't want to open the door one morning and be blinded." There was obviously room in there for it, given how much of his other clothes she'd deemed expendable. "Do I have any clothes left? Not sure Brent'll be chuffed with me naked in the office."

She waggled her eyebrows at him, and for a second he

thought it might lead somewhere, but her phone rang, as it so often did, distracting her from smutty thoughts. Damn.

He went back to his reading, but she returned after ten minutes.

"Cara's in town next weekend. I said we'd meet up. You've nothing on, have you?"

He liked Liv's cousin, but he *did* have plans. He just hadn't broached them yet.

"Just on the Saturday," he murmured.

"What's that then?" she asked, making them a cup of tea.

He now wished he'd dropped it into conversation far earlier. But he hadn't wanted to rock the boat, and his internal conflict sensor said it would.

"Um, so I'm doing a bucket list thing." He tried to be blasé about it, like it was a regular occurrence, like it was something they'd talked about before …

She stopped stirring the tea, then said, "Remind me what that is again."

He didn't get to answer as she came and sat right in front of him on the coffee table, offering him his mug, looking very concerned. "Why are you doing your bucket list things, Charlie?"

"Oh, no," he said, suddenly understanding her worry. "It's not *mine*. It's someone else's," he ventured, knowing things could become precarious. "They didn't get to finish it and I said I'd do it." Was it too much to hope she wouldn't ask more questions? Deep down Charlie *knew* he was lying by omission, because that's what he'd grown up doing, trying not to upset either of his parents.

He watched her face as she considered which of his friends it might be and came up blank.

She deserved better. "It's Ally's bucket list," he confessed.

"Ally, your ex-fiancée?" she asked with a mix of shock, confusion and annoyance. They'd talked about Ally in the "Ollie's-speech debrief", a conversation which ran along congressional hearing lines, with Liv interrogating and Charlie squirming. They'd never spoken about her after that.

"Yes. We do a task each year and scatter some of her ashes." He felt relieved to tell the truth.

Her eyes widened. "Who's *we*?"

"Becca and I. Becca was Ally's best friend, remember?"

Liv gave a slow blink, her face setting to stone. "And what are these tasks?"

"Random things: walks, bus tours, skydiving in this case."

"Every year?"

"So far."

"When did you do it last year?" Feck. He'd painted himself into a corner.

"Becca handled the ashes last year. The weekend I saw Dad." Technically true, but he felt himself drop another rung on the ladder to hell. He didn't want to lie to his wife, but he didn't want to fight with her either.

"So, Becca can continue to do them from now on," Liv said, trying, and failing, to sound gentle about it. "You've got a new life now. Becca can do the best friend duties."

Charlie looked at Liv. She was normally the more adult and responsible of the two of them, and given his lying, rightly so, but now she appeared vulnerable and hurt. That wasn't his intention, he never wanted to hurt people. He'd never seen her insecure like this before, though. The bollocking he'd got after the wedding was about keeping secrets and her embarrassment that his friends all knew. She dismissed most suggestions of going out with them now.

He put his tea down, took hers and placed it on the table too, before holding her hands in his.

"Liv, Ally's gone." He stroked her skin with his thumb and looked her deeply in the eyes. "She's no threat to you. I promise. But I agreed to do this. The scattering and the tasks."

Liv looked at the floor, and pulling a hand from his, rubbed her brow.

"This is weird. All of it. Tasks, scatterings, like some bizarre ritual, doing it with Becca who made a scene at the reception. I don't see why you need to be part of it. Your secrecy tells me you know it's weird." A thought struck her. "Do Shrin and Ollie know you do this?"

He wanted to shield his friends, but he was determined to stop fibbing to her. "Yes."

"Great. Another team secret."

Charlie's inner klaxon, the one which had warned his younger self there was a hooley about to blow between his parents, was churning into action in his chest. It made him tense across his shoulders. He schooled his tone to be as amicable and reasonable as possible.

"I don't want to quarrel, I just want to do a decent thing for someone who died before their time."

Liv's face was a cocktail of emotions and "convinced" wasn't in the mix.

"But can't you see that by doing this, you're in a kind of

stasis? How can you move on? How can you put that part of your life behind you?"

Charlie was stunned. He'd never been aware of any problem there.

"But I *have* moved on, Liv. I met and married you. I love you." His last months in South America had pushed him forward in his life. He'd come back radically different from the Charlie who'd left. "How have I not moved on?"

Her eyes were glistening now, and she kept pressing her lips together. She was on the brink of tears and he couldn't understand why. Ally wasn't coming back. There was no threat.

"Because you're still accommodating her!"

Charlie was at a loss. "She was important to me. But she's gone. And *you* are important to me, and you're here and my wife. My future is with you, but I can't negate my past." He didn't see why he *should*, either.

He tried another tack. "Liv, think about your brother – your parents didn't halve their love for you when he arrived, they just loved *more*. It's the same. I have both you and Ally in my heart."

Her face froze. "Oh my God, you still *love* her?"

This wasn't coming out as he'd hoped. "No, I remember her, with love," he adjusted. "My point is, there's room for both of you."

A tear trickled down Liv's cheek. "I shouldn't have to share your heart with any other woman, Charlie." He tried to wipe it, but she slapped his hand aside and stood up, sending tea slopping from their mugs.

She looked so upset and it killed him. "Liv, please." But she shook her head and headed for the bedroom.

"Just do what you've got to do," she shouted angrily. "But for the record, you took a vow to forsake all others. So bloody much for that!"

Charlie sank back in the sofa and puffed out. That hadn't gone well and for the life of him he couldn't think how to fix it.

Now, Charlie went through the motions of debriefing the jump and small talk with the ground crew, while the other skydivers arrived back. The supervisor tried to give him a certificate, but his raised eyebrows put paid to that, he wasn't a rookie. He would have made Becca take hers of course, if she'd done the bloody jump. Suddenly he was seething again, which took him to his car and out of the airfield at a fair clip.

He fumed the entire hour's drive to her flat while he rehearsed his rant. And it needed rehearsing, not for smoothness of delivery, but to set limits for himself, so he didn't completely fly off the handle. He was winding himself up, and probably blowing it out of proportion, but this was out of order. He'd organised the entire thing and emailed her the details. It wasn't like she had a proper job that couldn't be rearranged, for fuck sake. At the very least, she could have called him.

Charlie slammed the car door behind him and stalked up the path, raising his hand angrily over his shoulder to activate the remote locking. He considered pressing the bell, but that felt too genteel for his mood, so he hammered on the door with his fist instead.

It went unanswered. Which made him even crosser. She thought she had something more important to do. More important than this, which he was in the shit for. He stuck his face against the lounge window and was sure he could see some light from the rear of the flat. Irritation hitting melting point, he poked the bell button, but was met with silence. Typical. How hard was it to change a bell battery? Hands on hips, he looked about, working out what to do next. Sense said he should walk away and calm the hell down before sending her a strongly worded email. She hadn't read a single text he'd sent her from the aerodrome and she hadn't picked up any of his calls nor returned his voice messages. His eyes fell to the lock and his mind to the bundle of keys in his pocket. He had a key to the door. He was the landlord, so he was within his rights. That said, Becca had some tenant's rights, plus he'd made her a promise.

Seeing as she was ignoring his communications, he squared it in his head that he'd just pop in and leave a note on the table. That way she'd know how hacked off he was with her. He slid the key into the lock ... and stopped. No. At best, it was passive aggressive, at worst it was creepy, a gross violation of her privacy. He leaned his head against the glass and pulled the key back out. He was angry. And disappointed. He found it easier to manage this day, scattering the ashes, when Becca was with him. Their bickering deflected any sadness. Not that he intended telling her that.

Huffing, he strode back down the path and rummaged in the car's glove compartment to find some paper and a pen. He scribbled that she'd missed the task on the back of an old envelope and punctuated it with many exclamation marks, which he regretted, it as it made him look like a teenager. He finished it with a *Call Me*, which he underlined hard enough to go through the paper, which felt more manly.

Back at the door, he crouched to pop it through the letterbox, keen to catch a glimpse beyond the door. That was totally legit. It allowed him to check the note didn't float in under a piece of furniture or something.

He'd been right about the light. Charlie could see a dim stripe under the bedroom door. He called her name. Nothing. Listening, there was nothing at all, which he also knew to be odd. At uni Becca always had music on in some form. Ally had said Becca hated the quiet; it reminded her of being left alone as a child. She slept with the radio on, just a low murmur but enough for her to feel better. It had annoyed him when they'd shared a wall.

Then, he heard something. It was a dull sound, a moan perhaps. He looked about to see if it was someone in the street, but there was no one. Unsure, he called again and at the lack of reply decided he was, probably, duty-bound to investigate. Just to support his decision, Charlie flipped a coin. Queen Elizabeth and her head gave him the royal approval to proceed.

He let himself into the flat and swiftly closed the door. His nostrils twitched. Something smelled wrong, something was iffy here.

"White?" he called, but still there was nothing. Now, he wondered whether there was something amiss, the hairs on the back of his neck beginning to rise. What if something bad had happened? He'd watched plenty of True Crime documentaries. He checked the air for flies, but couldn't see any.

Charlie approached the bedroom and braced himself, as every murder scene he'd ever viewed on TV morphed into an elegant montage in his head. At least there wasn't a sound track of foreboding cello music or the buzz of a bluebottle swarm within – although that could just mean they were still in the maggoty larva stage. He gave himself a mental slap and told himself to get a grip.

Hand on the doorknob, he took a breath and opened it. There, in the murky light, Becca's naked body lay splayed across the bed, her face deathly white, tendrils of her hair stuck to her cheeks. He felt the blood drain from his own. Oh God…

Her chest suddenly rose as she took a short jagged breath and with utter relief he breathed again. And immediately wished he hadn't. The room was thick with the rank odour of illness. That was a scent he'd already lived through once with Ally, and as those memories burst their banks, he fought to push them away.

"Becca?" he managed, still safe in the doorway, reluctant to go nearer unless invited. A small moan escaped her, but he wasn't sure it was intentional. He started asking her whether she was all right, but realised it was a moronic question. Instead, he turned on his heel and left the doorway, having seen enough.

The kitchen was dark and exactly the mess he'd expect from her. He could barely visualise the serene tidiness Ally had nurtured when it was theirs. Everything had been in its place and colour coordinated from tea towels to teapot. Unlike this permutation, where finding a clean glass felt like a game of hunt the thimble. He opted to wash a pint glass from the Everest of pending dish-washing, before refilling it, and adding a sachet of Dioralyte he found in a cupboard.

"Becca?" he asked, gently crouching beside her. She needed to know he was there, but he didn't want to scare her. There was no guarantee of how she'd react. Even on the brink of death, there was every chance she could lamp him. With a fingertip, he pushed a stiff wisp of sweat-stuck hair away from her forehead, then laid his hand on it to gauge her temperature. Obviously, she'd had a fever, but it must have broken now as her skin was merely hot as opposed to raging, and Becca was exhausted.

"Zarlie?" she murmured out of the side of her mouth. She neither lifted her head nor opened her eyes, the effort being beyond her. He smiled, relieved. Things had to be improving if she knew it was him. He tentatively tried to pull some of the sheet across her to cover her.

"I've got some water for you. Can you sit up to drink it?"

She groaned and told him to fuck off, although with none of her usual verve. Still, he took it as another good sign. He nipped back to the kitchen and after some rummaging found a straw. He didn't bother removing the plastic cock surrounding it. Charlie assumed she'd been on another hen-do, rather than it being a style choice.

Becca seemed grateful, in a barely conscious way, for the water. That she obeyed his command to drink was worrying in itself, but a compliant Becca was the dream ticket, as he surveyed her bed and body's devastation, planning how to proceed.

"I'm going to carry you to the shower. Do you think you can stand up in it?"

The weepy moan as she contemplated using her muscles again suggested not.

"OK," he said, sitting her up, against her whimpers, "I've got you."

The shower still had the flip-down seat he'd installed for Ally. She'd loved her showers and he'd made it possible for her to continue having them with the seat he'd found in a mobility shop. She'd sit for ages, enjoying the feel of the water falling on her. He used to sit on the lidded toilet just watching her, soaking up the bliss on her face, the discomfort soothed away for a moment.

Leaving Becca in the bedroom, he did a quick recce and cleaning job of the bathroom floor. The rest would have to wait. Then he prepped the biggest fluffiest towel he could find, before stripping down to just his boxers.

"Showertime, White," he said briskly, thinking that being matronly would be the way forward. It earned him another "Go away" and an added "Leave me to die." So dramatic. He almost rolled his eyes.

"Becca, I'm not asking you," he said, but dropped a little of the stern. "It'll make you feel so much better."

She groaned pathetically and then, sounding like a little girl, moaned, "I shat myself inside out, Charlie." She was beyond brazening it out, which would have been her usual MO. She was properly mortified, as any normal person would be. Charlie was secretly pleased to see there was a normal person under all that snark. *Who knew?*

"Happens to all of us at some point," he said, sliding his arms under her. "But no one has to know about it, right?"

She didn't resist him, instead letting her head loll onto his chest as he moved them.

Her nose wrinkled. "I don't smell so good," she murmured, more in statement than apology.

"Not gonna lie, you've smelled better." He navigated the doorway to the bathroom, the memories of doing the same with Ally cascading over him.

She turned her face further into his chest, in shame.

"It doesn't matter," he said, lightly. "Nothing I haven't experienced before."

He got into the shower, and turning the spray away from them, let it run until it was comfortably warm.

Becca was too weak to stand and remained leaning against him when he set her down. She slid her arms down from around his neck to circle his waist, but the burden of the weight was still very much on him.

For a moment he didn't know what to do with his hands. The skin on skin seemed too intimate in an already intimate moment. Instead he reached for a sponge, and squeezed her shower gel onto it. The floral scent had its work cut out.

"Hang on," he said, "I'll have you cleaned up in a jiffy." Charlie worked in silence and she seemed grateful for it, remaining clamped onto him, her eyes shut. He moved on to wash her hair, and the light groan of pleasure Becca emitted suggested he hadn't forgotten how to give a head massage, just as he used to for Ally.

Finally, he sat her on the seat, where she sagged against the shower wall, as if the last ten minutes had done for her. Rising, he considered the state of his boxers. Becca cracked open an eye.

"Looks like you've had an accident."

"Yeah," he mumbled, "ran into a bit of a shit show." She closed her eye again, but there was the faintest hint of a smile there. It was the most she had energy for. "What was it? Food poisoning?" He took the opportunity to turn his back, speed strip and clean up.

"Poisoning of some kind."

"Alcohol?"

"No," she said, sourly. "Drink's never done *that* to me." Weak as she was, she still had some pride apparently. "I had a job which involved lying face down in a pond. I'm guessing I ingested some stagnant grimness." He wrinkled his nose. With a towel secured safely around his waist, he grabbed the big fluffy one and wrapped her in it as gently as he could. Her light wince betrayed she was hiding the worst of it. Bloody hell, even at these depths she was stubborn.

"How you doing? Ready to move?" He wanted to get her warm and comfortable.

Her "Hmmm" suggested she was close to nodding off. He wanted to get her back into bed, but the entire bedroom needed sorting. "We're going for a change of scene on the sofa. All right?"

"Hmm"s were as much as she could manage, but he wasn't looking for more. Carrying her again, he moved them into the lounge, placed her on the sofa, and hoofed back into her bedroom for a fresh pair of pyjamas. Her old ones lay in a heap from where she'd torn them off in her fevered state.

Having prioritised opening the French doors, he

investigated her dresser where he found some very washed but soft-looking Snoopy PJs. He grabbed his jeans and pulled them on, then located the biggest T-shirt of hers he could find, as his own had not gone unscathed. It looked like a tight crop top on him. He'd just have to go without until he could get his kit through the wash along with hers.

Returning to the lounge, trying not to think about being topless, he dressed her and within minutes she was curled up under a blanket. "I'm going to sort your bed," he said. "Want the telly on?"

"No."

"Need food?"

"Ugh."

"Drink?"

"Water." Charlie waited. Becca jogged herself to manage a tired "Please."

After twenty minutes of cleaning, putting the wash on for every single thing she'd been in contact with and remaking her bed, he joined Becca on the sofa. He didn't ask permission, just waited for her to shuffle along. She gave him the smallest of spaces, and leaned against him for more warmth, despite him offering to turn the heating on. Her scowl said no.

"So this job, Becca? Lying face down in a pond?" Her skin was normal again now, if pale, the glisten of the fever sweat gone. She looked younger and vulnerable. Not in a scared way, more without defences and peaceful for it. He wasn't used to seeing her like that.

"Mmm. Corpse two of three. The actor playing the detective kept fucking up his lines, so it took hours of retakes.

Amateur. And all the while I get to lie there starkers in the bog."

"Seriously, there have to be Health and Safety issues there. You should complain." That gained him a snort. He guessed there were other actors lining up to be corpses.

"Job's finished now anyway. I did the body-on-morgue-slab shots last week. I can hold my breath and look lifeless for ages."

"When was the bog filming?" he asked.

"Hmm, yesterday? Wednesday."

It was Saturday. She'd been sick for days and she didn't know. He could have called her before the skydive to check she was coming. He could've been there when she was mid-fever if he'd bothered to check.

"Why didn't you call me?"

"When?"

"When you were ill?"

"Why?" She seemed surprised at the suggestion. "I'm seeing you on Saturday. Why are you here anyway?"

"Becca, it *is* Saturday."

It left her quiet for a moment. "I don't think I can do skydiving today, Charlie."

"I'm not here to take you skydiving. I already did it. Ally's floating about in the air."

A little V formed between her eyebrows. "Did you come here to tell me off for not coming?"

"No, of course not," he lied, his rage of earlier now a point of shame. He hadn't considered there being a legitimate reason – other than her having been bludgeoned to death – for her no-show. "I was worried something had happened to you, that some boyfriend had hurt you."

"Ah, come to check the wood floors aren't blood-stained," she said, nodding as if she'd have done the same.

"No. That's not true either. I'll admit I might have thought you'd bailed on the task."

"Me?" she asked. "Course not. I was totally there. Wouldn't have missed it for the world." There was no determination in her voice, and he couldn't tell whether it was down to tiredness or, in fact, not being the truth.

He felt her getting heavier against him and decided she should get some proper sleep. Without waiting for discussion, Charlie stood and lifted her, carrying her to bed. Pulling the fresh covers over her, he watched as her eyelids immediately slid together. He pushed a pile of clothes off the old armchair in the corner and dragged it closer. Ally had sulked over that chair, not being a fan. It having been his uncle's, it was one of the few times Charlie had stood his ground on the interior design. The crocheted blanket covering it would keep him warm while he kept watch. He wasn't going anywhere until she was back on her feet. Which meant he also had a call to make, one that had "touchpaper" written all over it.

Becca slept straight through until mid-Sunday morning. Charlie hardly slept at all. His call home had had his mind buzzing all night.

It was safe to say Liv was pissed with him.

Pissed he hadn't called earlier.

Pissed he hadn't arrived home already.

Pissed he wasn't there to see Cara.

Pissed he hadn't considered she'd worry.

Pissed he was so thoughtless.

He'd explained about Becca and she was royally pissed about that too, but initially tried to be reasonable about it. She hadn't completely exploded until he'd said he was staying the night.

"If Cara was ill, or Iz, Mel, Georgy or Sarah, *you'd* stay," he reasoned. "No question."

"Of cour—" Liv started but stopped. "This is different."

"How? She's a mate. She's ill and she's alone."

Liv remained silent. She let him do the maths.

"Her being female is irrelevant."

He heard her moving and a door closing behind her. "It isn't," she hissed.

"Liv," he said softly, "it's a human who needs help. That's all. Trust me, she can barely hold her head up, let alone think of seducing me."

"Why would you even say that?" Liv sounded almost vindicated in her worry.

Charlie was bewildered. "Have I ever given you reason not to trust me around other women?"

Silence. *What?* "Liv? *Really?*"

"No," she conceded sullenly. He thought not. The suggestion stung nonetheless. "Can't someone else help?"

"Shrin's in Sri Lanka with Ollie. Tilly just moved to Edinburgh. Maggie lives in Hove. I don't know anyone else to call." She said nothing. "I'll be back tomorrow, love," he said, gently but firmly now. This was a point of principle. "Once she's slept and I know she's OK, I'll be back. Send Cara my love and apologies." Silence again. His mum was good at those too. He knew they could be impenetrable and he was too tired now to fight. "Trust me, Liv. Please."

When she still wouldn't give him a response he sighed, told her he loved her and rang off, to sit staring at the phone.

Giving up on sleep around dawn, Charlie pottered about the kitchen and lounge, tidying, smiling when he discovered her hidden Haribo stashes and then cleaning, for want of something quiet to do. To finish, he added the green ashes bottle to the pair on the window frame.

It was strange being back. The furniture was the same, but the surface layer of post, books, discarded hoodies, strewn slippers was foreign to him. The walls were the same hotchpotch of colours. Becca could have changed them, he'd said she could. They weren't his choices anyway. Ally had had a penchant for redecorating when he was away and without any consultation. He didn't know whether it didn't occur to her he might not like that particular shade of orange or whether she was simply precluding any discussion of it. He'd once named the lounge's orange *Pale Puke* and she'd got stroppy. She'd ignored the hint though. The colour had stayed and he'd got used to it. That was the way they'd worked.

He was filling the kettle when he heard her move to the bathroom and minutes later she asked from the doorway, "Lister, is there something you need to tell me?"

"Eh?" he asked, turning with a tea for both of them.

"The Spice Girls?" she asked, nodding at his T-shirt. During the night he'd been forced to put her T-shirt back on, the flat being glacial. She still looked ashen, but the fact she'd walked in on her own showed she was rallying.

"Ah, no." He handed her a cup. "Biggest one I could find."

"That's a nightshirt and you make it look like something a teen would wear." Well, yes, the hem did skeeter around his midriff and the spread of his shoulders was threatening to split the seams. "You look ridiculous," she said and took a sip. A look of pure joy crossed her face as the sugar he'd added hit her.

"My top's still damp. Now you're sentient, I thought I'd cover up," he said, turning back to the toaster which he loaded with four slices.

"You're worried about my innocence?" They both snorted in unison.

"Hardly. More your eyes, White. I've been working out. My abs are blinding again." Back in the day, when he'd OD'ed on uni sports, he'd been rather proud of them. They'd become more of a party keg than a six pack since, but he'd started rowing with Ollie, and the joint gym membership Liv had got them for Christmas to get them wedding-ready was helping.

Becca opened her mouth, but thought better of it. She fiddled with an ornament on the sideboard. "I seem to remember sharing a shower with you, in my haze from yesterday. I survived that, so if you'd rather be without the top, I think I'll manage the blinding abs."

"Thank God." He pulled the top off and dropped it in front of the washer. He'd taken the liberty of turning the heating on, both to dry his clothes and, assuming his landlord's duties, to check it actually still worked.

The toast sprang up and he picked the slices out, muttering

"Feck!" as he burnt his fingers. "Let me know if your eyes start stinging," he said, making light of it. He gave Becca a quick grin. Her eyes snapped away from his back as he turned and she abruptly found the neat pile of bills on the side worth her focused consideration. After a moment she looked around the rest of the flat, taking in the other neat piles and general orderliness. "Did you tidy?"

He wasn't sure which way this would go. A normal person would be delighted, but this was Becca, so. "I needed something to do."

Becca looked quite uncomfortable as she took it all in. He shifted to show her that her kitchen worktop was in fact flat and quite roomy once you cleared it. She still said nothing, the look in her eyes somewhat like a deer in the headlights. He turned back to the worktop and finished buttering her toast, which he slid across the slim breakfast bar, and took a seat.

"Well," she said, approaching the toast, his abs and the high stool, "if it saved you from boredom, fine. Can't have that."

"Thanks," he said.

She was about to respond, but his phone pinged with a message. Reading it, he typed a quick reply and returned to his tea and toast, as if it never happened.

"Are you supposed to be somewhere?" she asked.

"Nothing that won't wait," he said. "I'm going to hang out here for a while, if that's all right." His tone wasn't really one of asking. His mind was set; you looked after sick people.

Becca seemed conflicted, her eyes dropping from his face, then immediately up again as her face suddenly found some pinkness, and then she looked away to the telly.

"Um, so I don't know whether I've watched *Frozen* enough

times," she said. "I don't feel I've properly mined the deeper themes."

Now Charlie's face looked conflicted, but he recovered it. "I checked the NHS website already, and the best thing for poisoning recovery is a Jason Bourne marathon."

She weighed it up, her eyes still scanning the room. It wasn't quite a makeover – shit, he wasn't a miracle worker – but it at least hinted at *manageable* again.

Becca picked up her breakfast and jerked her head for him to follow. She sorted a DVD at the player, then joined him on the sofa.

"Pierce Brosnan for me, Rene Russo for you," she divvied up, as *The Thomas Crown Affair* started on screen. He watched her face as she surrendered herself to the images, the relaxed gaze suggesting she'd watched it a million times. He settled in for what turned out to be a couple of hours of companionable viewing, as they swapped critiques, agreeing Russo was right up there in terms of #bumgoals, but arguing over Brosnan's Bond credentials.

As the credits rolled, Becca gave a small jolt. The gaps between her comments had lengthened and her breathing had steadily become heavier towards the end of the film, until Charlie had felt the full weight of her against his chest. Now as the film ended, she seemed to recognise where they were, and how they were positioned. With her eyes fixed on the screen, she said quietly, "Thanks, Charlie. For helping me out. For doing the jump and for coming to check on me." He felt guilty about letting her think that was his motive for coming, but he wasn't about to interrupt this momentous occasion.

"No problem," he said, then ventured, "It's what friends do."

She flicked her eyes up to him then and he figured he'd overstepped. She crimped her lips together considering it, then gave a so-tiny-it-almost-never-happened nod.

Then she stood. "I think I'm going to go back to bed. I'm good now, just tired." Looking up at her, he got it; she was either spent from the illness, or spent from being nice. Either way, she was letting him know, amicably, he should go.

Collecting his clothes, he headed for the door. "I'll … um … text you to see how you're doing."

"Sure," she said.

Charlie tilted his head for a moment thinking, then, deciding "nothing ventured, nothing gained", said, "Maybe we don't leave it a whole year before meeting up?" as he pulled his T-shirt on. He should arrange for Becca and Liv to get to know each other. He was sure it would help in the long run.

Her face gave nothing away. He was expecting a "Yeah, whatever" that would mean "Never going to happen", but instead, Becca gave him a nod and a "Maybe", which in Becca-speak was infinitely more possible. For the briefest of seconds he considered leaning in and giving her a kiss on the cheek, then realised he was way off base with that. "Look after yourself, Becca," he said, letting himself out.

The weather was glorious outside and Charlie felt it reflected his good fortune this weekend; he'd survived both the skydive and sick Becca with his limbs intact. And then he remembered the shitstorm he had brewing at home. He'd be spending the return journey rehearsing what to say to Liv.

There was an imminent fight he couldn't avoid. He'd already hidden all morning.

Walking to his car at less velocity than when he'd arrived, he took a moment to think about this year's take-away from the task. Scattering the ashes together in mid-air might have forced Becca to trust him a little, but perhaps he might have managed it himself without them flinging themselves out of a plane to do so.

2016

W alking towards her nan's house, Becca checked her phone for the hundredth time. She double-checked the ringer, so it wasn't on Silent. Still nothing. Dammit. She should be used to this, she should be much more chilled, but this time, it was so close she could taste it. She'd worked so hard for it and she wanted it so badly. So, so, so, where was the bleeding call?

She was down to the last two actors for the role which could properly launch her, at bloody last. It was a drama series called *StreetSmart* where "shady police detective Derek Street solves cases and climbs the career ladder by taking credit for the undercover work and deductions of savvy sex worker Kerry Smart." Becca figured she'd been screwed over enough in the past to bring something to the role. Against her better judgment and normal rules, she'd started imagining herself in Hair & Make-up for the role, and discussing the motivation behind Kerry's clothes choices with the costume department. The role made her heart race. Surely, after so many years and all the crappy jobs she'd taken, it was her turn now? Plus, it was her birthday. That had to count for something.

Thirty. Thirty had always sat in the distance as a defining beacon. Many actors felt the same; if you hadn't made it by then, it was time to pack it in; become a drama teacher or run those weekend franchises for the next generation of optimistic thespians. She didn't think she could do it. She'd spend every lesson telling them how hard it was and shattering their starry-eyed dreams. Becca didn't want to be that person.

The phone vibrated.

Her stomach knotted.

Counting to five, she turned it over.

Another WhatsApp from Shrin, a birthday GIF, the third today, making up for the fact she wasn't in the country to celebrate with her friend. Still, it was nice she was making the effort, whatever the time was in Sydney. Becca had barely seen anything of her recently. Shrin's rise through the corporate ranks was little short of stellar and having now reached the Big Three-Oh, Becca was feeling the acute sense of having got precisely nowhere in life. Being the entertainment at dinner parties had grown old. Her ongoing saga of shit jobs felt more like a tragedy than a comedy now. Nowadays her sum sense of achievement came from not dying in the stupid Spin class she'd joined, and that came with little glory when she'd spent the hour feeling miserable.

Marcia had made some comment about her weight, how you gained a permanent kilo with each new decade. Of course, that *had* to be nonsense. Ben too had a habit of making little remarks about her shape, about laying off the pies, and generally she'd ignored them in the eight months they'd been together, because her body was her own business, thanks very much. Besides, he didn't seem to have an issue when he was having sex with her. There he seemed to appreciate the softness, but over time the comments had chipped away at her. She'd tackled it with a "Fuck off with your criticisms" approach, but he'd simply laughed at her and told her she was being over-sensitive, though clearly he had some issue with her size to have thought about it.

Not that she was doing this spin thing for either of them, but Becca was questioning what state she wanted to be in, going into this new decade. She was even considering – mainly on a Sunday morning when her hangovers now hurt more than before – reducing her drinking. But not today.

Turning into her nan's street, she side-eyed her phone. If it wasn't for Shrin's message, she'd seriously think there was something wrong with the network. Becca checked the time on it. That was working too. Crap. She had a long afternoon in front of her. She always stopped in at Wilma's on her birthday. It was one of those win–wins in an unavoidable obligation. She'd be able to say she'd been, and there'd be a card with a tenner for her. She'd always save the cash and spend it in precisely one month's time, when it was Wilma's birthday and she was expected to pitch up with flowers.

Becca particularly missed Ally on her birthday. Not because she wasn't there to spoil her – although she totally would have done. Ally was queen of thoughtful gifts and surprising treats. She missed her company on the day, the excursions they'd make to a free exhibition, or a leisurely picnic. She missed their chats where Ally would make her go back over the past year and pick out the wins and the things she was grateful for. Becca always did this begrudgingly, because if you'd been moaning all year about not catching a break, then suddenly having a list of good things undermined one's case. Ally would also make her set some goals for the coming year. (And then reset them to achievable things. Apparently wishing for

Hollywood mega-stardom was setting yourself up for a fall. Better to have that as a bonus.)

This birthday felt stranger than the last five. It was twenty years since they'd met, which felt so long. It was five years that she'd been gone. This was a new decade, one which Ally would never experience or have any part of. Becca was making this endeavour alone, and utterly lonely it felt too.

She'd tried to explain it to Ben, when he'd called her a grump the previous evening. She'd hoped he'd understand, that it might be the opening into a deeper conversation about growing older and facing the future. But she'd been met with a "Yeah, sorry, I never knew her, did I?" and a "What's on telly?", putting paid to any further discussion. Maybe that's what you got, dating younger guys. The three years' difference sounded small, but could be cavernous. Still, he'd taken on the organising of her surprise party, and she had to give him credit for that.

Reaching the small end-of-terrace house, she was about to knock when the door opened. Her nan stood inside, righting the collar of the coat she'd clearly just put on.

"Becca-Jayne." It was more of a terse statement than a celebratory exclamation. Nothing new there.

"Nan," Becca countered. "You OK?" Becca rarely saw her out of her slippers, but those were definitely her sensible outdoor shoes.

"I'm off out. You're late."

"How can I be late? It's only just four. I always come at four."

"No, you come at three."

She had been coming at four o'clock for ever, as it was

when the Radio 4 drama finished. Anything earlier would garner an ignored knock.

"No," she said slowly, wondering whether the old woman was losing it. "I come at four."

Her nan appeared cross at being contradicted.

"Well, I'm going out."

"Where to?"

"Bingo."

"Who with?"

Her wrinkly skin coloured with a blush. "None of your business, nosy." Becca knew grandparents were supposed to be kind and welcoming, spoiling their grandchildren and ladling unconditional love on them. She'd come across the concept in books. Wilma, however, had always treated her like a bothersome lodger, having never got over being lumped with a nine-year-old without consultation.

"Nice. You should have said, I wouldn't have bothered coming." Had her nan really forgotten her birthday? She was the sole grandchild, there wasn't a list to remember.

"Well, I'm glad you did," Wilma said, with a sudden smile. "Saves me posting this." She picked a card off the hallway shelf. It was unstamped. "Happy birthday, then."

She shuffled forward, making Becca step back up the path. "Open it on the way home. I don't like the fuss of thank-yous." That would explain why Becca had had none from her in the past.

Her nan had her head down already, shooing her towards the pavement. A Ford Focus in hearing-aid beige pulled up, and the window descended.

"Giddy up, Willie! Time's a ticking!" shouted a gruff male

voice from within. Becca couldn't get a clear view of him, though she tried really hard. Nobody ever called her nan Willie.

"Perhaps you can call ahead from now on," Becca was told, as they left her on the pavement. She barely got a wave as the car pulled away and definitely no introduction, but clearly Willie was expecting future company.

Watching the car speed away, Becca absently opened the card. It wasn't even a birthday card, but the kind that came with a store token. Ten pounds to British Home Stores. Becca knew her mum always got Wilma a BHS voucher for her birthday – deeply sensible and infinitely appropriate, but still her mum's subtle dig that Wilma was old. Becca also knew the entire chain had gone bust the previous year. So not only had her nan ditched her on her birthday, she'd re-gifted her a defunct gift card, which now meant Becca was going to have to find the money to fund the next bunch of flowers. Bugger.

———————

Tony the landlord was clearly in on the "surprise" element. He didn't even give her a nod when she sashayed into the Nag's Head, just pointed absently to the ceiling. Ben had said to meet at their local. She imagined they'd go on to somewhere swanky from there. She fancied a night of cocktails. But as she climbed the stairs, it dawned on her he'd booked the function room. The "Private Event" sign confirmed her suspicions. And the crowd in the room were apparently also in on the "act like nothing is going on" thing, as they didn't give her any attention when she walked in and stood at the door, waiting for some kind of reaction.

Becca was looking fabulous. She'd spent bleeding ages on it too, face-masked in the bath all afternoon, with a large glass of wine, giving herself the full home-salon treatment. She'd selected a teal-coloured vintage 1930s dress, in honour of her new decade. Netflix had been nixed for some months to afford it. Her hair had a soft-wave Marlene Dietrich style to finish it all off.

"Babe." Her bumcheeks were suddenly squeezed, followed by a pair of arms sliding around her waist and a smoke-breathed kiss landing on her neck. "Looking good." He released her and moved around to face her. "Happy Birthday."

"Thanks, Ben." It was the first she'd heard from him all day, but she'd put it down to him being busy organising this. Besides, her brain had been focused on the audition call, which still hadn't come. It must really have gone to the wire. The producers must be scrutinising the audition recordings. She would have preferred the choice to be obvious (*her*, natch), but she'd settle for them giving the decision due and thorough consideration. No doubt she'd cross paths with Emilia, the other contender, at some point.

He waggled his empty bottle at her. "Want one while I'm there?"

She was rather thinking tonight warranted more than a beer. "Fizz, please." She'd start there and then cocktails... She looked at the landlord's eighteen-year-old son manning the bar. He had the brainpower to manage a rum and Coke, nothing more.

Looking about, she felt overdressed, but batted the thoughts away. She was the birthday girl; she was supposed to stand out, and her mates would appreciate the dress. Speaking of, why hadn't they ambushed her by now? The room was full of murmur and chat, not squeals. Obviously Shrin wasn't there, but looking about, she tried to pinpoint the dependable gaggle of Tilly, Maggie, and Maggie's girlfriend Nessa. She'd given Ben a list of their numbers and email addresses to help him along weeks ago.

"Have the girls arrived yet?" she asked, squeezing in next to him at the bar. He presented her with a coupe of fizz, which she had to admit was a sweet touch. She loved a coupe glass, it had an air of "party girl" about it, and now she was thirty she needed reminding. Becca took a sip as they moved further into the room and did a fine job of hiding her grimace. "What did you get me?"

He looked at the glass. "Babycham," he said, proud of himself. "Thought the retro kitsch thing went with your dress, and Tony had a job lot. The old birds love it, apparently." He realised what he'd said. "Not that you're an old bird," he backtracked. Rather than punch him, Becca decided she preferred having him on the back foot; he might pull out some stops later.

She hadn't envisaged her birthday being sponsored by Babycham. She swallowed her immediate comment, because new, older Becca was more tactful and thoughtful in her responses, and was trying to be more grateful for the small things – such as his trying to match her vintage dress which, for the record, was definitely not retro kitsch, but there was no point telling him so.

"Have you seen the girls?" she prompted him again.

He looked about. "There's loads of girls here." There were about seven, all other halves of his mates, who seemed to be the main contingent in the room. In fact, on conducting a full mental register, Becca could *only* see people she'd classify as *his* mates.

"*My* girls, Ben. Where are they?"

He glanced away, shiftily.

"Ben?" she insisted.

"Yeah … um…" He scanned the room. "Not sure they could make it." Becca felt a kick in her stomach. Disappointment. *And yet…* Her mates would normally never miss a birthday do, in fact they'd be early. The disappointment was replaced by something else. *Suspicion.*

"Did you call Tilly?" She didn't want to presume guilt before proof, but too late.

"She lives in Scotland."

"Her parents don't. She still comes home."

"Don't you think it was a bit of an ask?"

"She's one of my oldest friends."

"Still a big ask." Why was he making her feel like she was a demanding princess? It *was* a long way, and she would have kvetched at the ticket price, but Tilly had a good job, and like she said, came back to visit her Olds regularly. Not to mention Tilly loved a party.

"You didn't contact her, did you?" He glanced away. "Ben? Did you contact any of them?" *Ah shit.* She'd thought their "What's the plan?" WhatsApps had been part of the surprise ruse. She'd played along by saying she was going out with Ben. She'd honestly assumed they'd be there to pounce on her when she walked in. She'd got flowers from Tilly earlier and a box of Hotel Chocolat cocktail chocs through the post from Maggie and Nessa, but again, she'd believed it was a decoy thing. But no. They'd genuinely been asking, and she'd been coyly putting them off, thinking it was part of the game.

"Look, there's Mez!" Ben pointed to Meredith, sister of his mate Hadders and general hanger-on.

"She *actually* hates me," Becca snapped. "Why is she even here?" Last time she'd been out with the group, Meredith had told Becca it surprised her she and Ben were still together, that she couldn't quite picture them as a couple long term, no offence. Some times, like right now, Becca wondered whether she wasn't just trying to prove Meredith wrong.

"Because it's a party to celebrate your thirtieth. Other people put their differences aside to be nice sometimes."

"Don't be an arse, she isn't here to celebrate me. She's here for you."

"Me?"

"She fancies you."

"Nah, she's just Hadders' sister." He gave Becca a stern look. "She's always hung out with us."

"Wake up, Ben. Ask yourself why."

"You're being paranoid. You been drinking gin?"

She wanted to tell him to fuck off. But she was trying really hard to do the "older and more mature" thing. And not cry.

Dammit. She knew she should have organised this herself. A small dinner with just her mates, perhaps. *But* … she'd always been in love with the idea of a surprise party, of someone organising something purely for her, of feeling special in a roomful of people. He *had*, she had to concede, organised something for her, but on the lowest scale with least effort. And the room was more flashers than flash-mob, all of Ben's mates having admitted to sending dick-pics in their time. She wasn't feeling special at all. Hardly anyone had offered birthday wishes and she was pretty sure some had only come in to avoid the bar queue downstairs.

Ben suddenly had a mate who he urgently needed to see, and Becca found herself alone in the room of people. This essentially summed up the state of her life; partaking, but overlooked, even in the starring role. She considered necking as much drink as she could, as quickly as she could and simply crashing conversations, demanding birthday wishes and being obnoxious. It wouldn't be the first time. Instead, she wandered to the bar, bought herself a mini-bottle of prosecco, keeping her fingers safely clenched around the stem of the coupe glass. It was probably coming home with her. She deserved some prize for getting through this.

The small roof terrace off the function room was deserted, the cold keeping even the most desperate smokers in. The fresh air made a pleasant change from the scent of dozens of competing aftershaves layered over years of stale beer in the grotesque carpet. Becca leaned her forearms on the railings, surveying the splendour of the back alley's bins. The sky made for a better view and she focused on that instead, pretending she could see the stars through the orange light pollution of the city. Ally would have insisted she could see the North Star or some constellation as a distraction. That said, had Ally been alive, they wouldn't be here, doing this right now.

Becca sighed. She knew what Ally would have wanted her to do. She poured herself a glass of bubbles and took a breath.

"This year, I'm grateful for" – she stopped and checked whether anyone was watching. No, of course they weren't. She was only the birthday girl, alone, outside at her own party – "my friends, who would've been there if Ben wasn't a dickhead." She'd be texting them first thing to explain, not wanting them to think she'd excluded them. She raised her glass and drank to them. "My health." She always included that one, feeling obliged lest she appear to be taking it for granted, considering Ally's prognosis. She took another swig of the fizz. "Erm … the roles I've had this year." They were few and didn't really warrant individual mentions, but they got a drink. "Yesterday's audition," she suddenly remembered and her fingers automatically crossed themselves. That earned a refill of the glass. She scrounged around for more, knowing Ally would have prompted her on. "My home, my duvet, my clothes." Those were basics and were rightfully acknowledged, as some didn't have those things, but she felt she needed something more. "Oh, that time I was ill and Charlie helped me." It had popped into her head. Nearly a year ago, much of it had been a depleted blur, but she had an overwhelming sense of care from it, and a deep sense of gratitude for it. Charlie earned himself two long swigs. "Netflix, YouTube for the flash mobs and Haribo." She ended on those, as they were her staples in life now. The last of that glassful went down the hatch.

Someone opened the terrace door, the noise from the room interrupting her thinking. She hoped it was Ben looking for her, although anyone looking for her would have sufficed, but instead a stranger asked whether she had any drugs, then retreated back in. *Not* Ben then. She took a moment to consider why she was actually with him. Ah yes, because he'd chased her. He, at some level, desired her. Uncomfortable as she was to admit it, she craved having someone around her, giving her attention, even when the attention was shitty. "Shitty attention" beat "no attention". She'd learned that as a kid. When they rowed and he huffed off, slamming her door, it only took a couple of days before he appeared again as if it'd never happened. The sex – make-up sex or just regular garden variety – wasn't bad. She didn't add him to her gratitude list, though.

Gratitude covered, that left goals. Which was easy: to win her break-out role. She had three hundred and sixty-four days to do it. She'd decided "success by thirty" included the actual year of thirty. Anything else would be hasty, and she couldn't quite let go yet. Next year. Next year would be it. Sliding her hand to her phone, she hoped it would never come to that, because the *StreetSmart* role was hers for the taking. She'd lived that character yesterday, embodied it, breathed it. They *must* have noticed.

Her hand shuddered.

Of course the text would come now. She should have known. Ally and the universe wanted her to be grateful for what she already had before they allowed her the reward of good news. It gave her joy to feel her bestie was still watching over her.

Becca closed her eyes and moved the screen to her face, muttering "Please, please, please." This role could change everything for her, it would make all the years of slog worth it: the wasted hours of rehearsing pieces, only to be shot down; taking small, embarrassing jobs for the exposure, which regularly involved physical exposure; the constant poor pay, the constant uncertainty whether there'd be enough money for next month; seeing lesser actors get roles because they'd known the producer's son at uni; enduring Marcia; paying Marcia fifteen percent for the pleasure; watching her friends climb their career ladders and making light of their pity for her shitty shitty jobs.

Taking a breath, she opened her eyes.

Happy Birthday BJ!

Have a good one

She cursed it for not being the text she wanted. It was nice of Charlie to have remembered, though. They hadn't spoken since her full-body expulsion. Looking Charlie in the eye again required both time and courage. She typed a string of chirpy emojis to make it look like she was having a marvellous time, then wondered why she'd done that? She'd never felt the need to paper things over with Charlie. The smiley face, fizz glasses and streamer explosion were replaced with:

Thanks C

Frankly, 30 blows so far

Any tips?

His answer was instant, short, and made her smile.

Gin

She could buy into that.

She was about to slide the phone away but noticed some Twitter notifications. She paged through the birthday messages in her DMs, mainly from audition buddies and coffee shop colleagues, and then flicked to her timeline where a familiar face caught her eye. Emilia was virtually fellating a champagne bottle in the photo. The text filled in the details, and they came like a slap. Emilia had won the *StreetSmart* role. Becca checked her emails, her missed calls, her WhatsApp, her Insta messages, but there was nothing. The producers hadn't bothered to let her know.

It took everything she had not to slump down the wall and sit there like some dejected rag doll. There was nothing else for it; she'd have to get howling drunk. Ben could finish his birthday efforts by carrying her home.

She shook out three remaining drops of prosecco into her coupe. That glass might be her favourite thing of the entire day.

Raising it in a toast, she gave herself a "Happy Birthday me" and looked to the sky again. "Worst birthday ever, Ally. You aren't missing anything." What she wouldn't give to have her bestie here, even if it was just for a couple of minutes. Just long enough for a hug. That would do her.

Becca flung herself back inside, the warmth within making her aware of how cold it really was outside, especially in a flimsy nylon dress. Looking about, she couldn't see Ben. That was fine, she'd grab herself another drink and then do the rounds, claiming her birthday wishes and find him along the way.

Elbowing her way up to the bar, she waved the empty prosecco bottle at the barman. Looking about while she waited, she still couldn't see Ben. Maybe he was in the loos. Maybe he was on the other side of the room, hunting high and low for her. A door opened in the panelled wall at the end of the bar. Ben emerged, hands smoothing down his shirt, the small brass WC sign glinting in the lights as the door closed behind him. Well, that was fair enough – the guy had a right to pee, and the discrete single loo meant he could jump the queues downstairs. A new prosecco bottle was placed on the bar in front of her and having the barman's attention, she ordered a bottle of Bud "for my maaaaan". Now she had a plan to take her mind off this rubbish day, Becca was getting interesting ideas for later. She intended to show Ben what an old bird could do and blow his boyish mind. Turning to catch his eye, she saw the glint of the toilet sign for a second time. Meredith slid out, mirroring Ben in the way she smoothed down her clothes and walked in the opposite direction.

"Hey, babe. That for me?" Ben appeared at her side, face devoid of any guilt.

Her lusty plans draining from her veins, Becca handed him the beer. "Where've you been?"

"Ah, just went outside for some air," he answered and nodded towards the little terrace. Looking at him, Becca knew they were finished. She'd been where she'd been, she'd seen what she'd seen, and clearly Ben was a bare-faced liar. If there was something she also knew to be true, it was that at thirty, she was too old for this shit.

and turning to the red-faced girl at the bar, added, "Meredith, you're welcome to him." Then she held out her hand, splayed her fingers, dropping the mike to a sensationally pleasing thud, and armed with her prosecco bottle and coupe glass, left her own party. Perhaps it wasn't the most sophisticated response, but she reckoned she had a decade to work this maturity thing out.

Sunday 19th June
Clapham Common, London

"Get over it, Charlie, it was a brilliant idea," Becca insisted.

"Hard disagree." That was a more diplomatic response than his original "What the fuck, Becca?"

It was six thirty in the morning. Clapham Common was milling with riders, mostly on their singular bikes, and it had taken Charlie a moment from spotting her to register that their bike, their lovely hand-picked purple rental, was in fact a tandem.

"I'm not dragging you all the way from here to Brighton. I'm not your mule."

Becca looked outraged. "I don't need you to get me there, Lister. I *can* ride a bike, you know." She held his eye, not least to keep her eyes off his clothes; he was a symphony of tight cycling Lycra.

He raised an unconvinced eyebrow at her.

"Really?"

"*Really*. I've been in a Spin class since Christmas."

He scoffed. "This is fifty-four miles and there are hills."

"I know that. You seem convinced I'll be a burden to you. Maybe *you'll* be the burden, but do you hear me whinging? No. I'm about sharing the task." She waved her hand at the majestic bicycle. The rental shop had said it was a superb choice. *Lady Regina*, as they called her, had completed the London-to-Brighton bike ride twice already.

"Ally didn't mention doing this on a tandem," he insisted.

238

"It's in the spirit of things. Want me to steer?" Becca asked. Their group was about to start.

"No," he said. Grumpy.

She took the rear position, delighted to just pedal, and he wouldn't be able to see if she took a rest. They both mounted the bike as their fellow riders departed.

"Ready?" he asked.

"Sure," she said. "*Lady Regina* says she is too."

Neither moved. They didn't quite know what to do.

"OK. On three," he stated. The other riders were now streaming past them, and she heard grumbles from those behind them. "One, two, three!"

Becca had imagined them launching *Regina* off with an air of elegance. The reality was haphazard, with harried pushing, as if on scooters, then throwing themselves up onto their seats. Equally, she'd imagined they'd form a graceful streamlined entity, but *Regina* was over two metres long, so everything was wobbly and their trajectory was jagged, as he tackled the steering and she tried to get comfy on the seat.

"Stop fidgeting, BJ," he shouted. He didn't seem to find this easy. They seemed to be going backwards, as riders of all ages, some in fancy dress, shot past.

"Look," Becca exclaimed, "there's someone in a Little Mermaid costume." She pointed in the direction, but the suddenness of her movement took *Regina* by surprise and Charlie struggled to control the immediate and considerable wobble. The tandem veered, and Becca didn't know which way to lean to compensate. Apparently, she picked the wrong way, as there was a bump and a clang followed by an "Argh!"

The two St John's Ambulance first aiders said this was the

fifth time they'd manned the event, and Charlie was the earliest casualty they'd ever had. He didn't appear cheered by the accolade.

Becca stood with the unscathed *Regina*, as they butterflied the minor cut he'd taken to his cheek. The shrub he'd steered into had been quite spikey. His arm had sustained scratches, but from his fuming, Becca suspected his pride had suffered most.

They restarted in silence, and fifteen minutes in, he still hadn't spoken to her. The tense atmosphere forced them both to focus on the bike, their balance and working together (albeit begrudgingly) as the traffic made for a very stop–start beginning.

"That's enough moping now, Charlie," Becca eventually said, as the road cleared a little and they were moving along more smoothly. "Admit it, this is fun. *Lady Regina* goes like a dream."

"I am not calling her *Lady Regina*," he snapped. "It's an inanimate object."

She sighed. Boys were so emotionally stifled with vehicles. Becca let it go. She was working hard on the maturity thing, meaning she'd had a word with herself about not deliberately winding him up today. She needed him if they were to reach Brighton, and she was already visualising the chips they'd have when they got there.

"Any idea why Ally wanted to do this one?" The British Heart Foundation organised the annual ride, so it didn't relate to her cancer.

He remained silent while they negotiated a turn which

required more concentration than she'd imagined. The street being full of other riders complicated matters further.

Back on the straight, heading out of the built-up streets towards leafier suburbs, he finally deigned to answer her.

"She mentioned going to Brighton, and I wasn't that bothered. I always convinced her to go somewhere further afield, to walk a hill or something. I guess she wanted to go more than I knew." He sounded regretful now. Becca didn't want to make him sad. Today was about honouring Ally, celebrating her. Ally would have loved them doing it on a tandem. She would never have believed the two of them could have got to the point where they could do that. Only, his currently being super-pissy with her perhaps indicated they hadn't got to any such point. Becca felt her face get warm. After last year's incident she'd thought they'd put some of their animosity behind them. Not that she cared. Of course not. If it was spiky he wanted, then that was fine with her, she could dish that up too. It wasn't like this friendship had to last for ever and after today all the tasks were done, so they could go back to their original plan of never seeing each other again, if he insisted. She paid her rent by standing order, she could simply be a line in his bank statement. Fine by her. She felt a weird ache in her chest, but put it down to a high stitch, and dropping her head, ploughed on with the pedalling.

"Do we actually know where we're going? Or am I just following the crowd?" he asked, a mardy edge to his voice at the first fuel stop, ten miles in.

"Follow the others, or else there'll be marshals pointing the way. Relax, Charlie, it's a professionally organised event, been going for years," she answered, trying to keep the snip out of her own voice, but couldn't help but add, "Don't worry, you won't have to make any decisions at any point."

"What's that supposed to mean?"

"Nothing."

"Clearly it does." He sounded cross. This wasn't how today had played out in her head. She'd genuinely imagined a fun day, but here they were, only a little way into what would take hours, and it was as if they'd set themselves back years.

Becca took a deep breath, deciding to play nice. "I didn't mean anything. I know you like to throw a coin for choices, and given how little the Lycra leaves to the imagination, unless it's in your mouth or up your bum, I know there's no coin on you." OK, so her version of nice was an acquired taste. And probably not his, as, getting back on *Regina*, he ignored her for the next while.

Her bottom ached. There were no two ways about it; *Lady Regina*'s seats weren't built for the bonier derrieres and Becca was regretting not having invested in a pair of super-padded undershorts. They'd reminded her too much of Tena pants.

As the melee of cyclists spread out across the route, the silence between them became even more painful. Having taken on the organising role for this year, Becca knew she should attempt to get this back on track. But there was something amiss with him. He'd been snappy and snarky with her before, but his basic demeanour had never been sour to start with.

And given last year, she didn't think it was down to being in her company.

"Are you all right?" she tried carefully, then screwed it up by adding, "You aren't usually this moody. You can't still be grouching about *Regina*."

All it garnered her was an "I'm fine."

She sighed. They were only fifteen miles in. This could be a very hard ride, if she didn't sort things.

"How's work?"

He took a moment to consider it, but when he answered, "Pretty shit," she reckoned he'd been pondering whether or not to lie. She was rather pleased he hadn't, even if the answer wasn't great. "I'm looking for something new."

He didn't sound like he wanted to elaborate, but that had never put Becca off.

"Why's it shit? I thought you were hoofing up the production ladder."

"Yeah, well, it's time to leave Brent's. Time to try somewhere new."

"Oh, right. Getting anywhere with that?"

"Not much." He was being very tight-lipped.

"Are you interviewing?"

"Not yet. Not much coming up."

Something was definitely off.

"Have you actually interviewed for a job before?"

Unlike her, he'd never had to scrap for employment, so she wasn't at all surprised he wasn't enjoying the process. Plus, it involved him making choices. That coin of his must be exhausted.

"No." And they were back to silence. So much for conversation.

They passed under the M25 and were now properly in the countryside, with leafy lanes and fields. They boosted her resolve and she tried again.

"Did I miss Liv at the start line?" Being honest, she hadn't looked for her, and he'd turned up late, so there hadn't been time for pleasantries, not that they'd been forthcoming after the *Regina* reveal.

"No." Granted, it had been stupid o'clock. Becca wouldn't have been up herself, given the choice. Getting out of London before the traffic and any heat racked up was a sensible plan, though.

"Well, I'm sure she'll be there waving as we cross the finishing line," she said. If she'd had a partner, she'd have forced them to be there with beers for them, then insisted on a foot massage on the entire train-trip home. As it was, she was staying at Maggie's place in Hove, having been promised a night out in the Brighton bars and hoping her self-inflicted man-hiatus could come to a spectacular end. Celibacy sucked.

"Yeah, actually, she won't," Charlie said, his voice now sounding resigned to her conversation rather than cross. "We've separated."

Becca wasn't often lost for words, but for the next few miles and a mean climb she truly was. What could she say? She'd managed the standard "I'm sorry to hear that," but obviously her mind filled with *all* the questions thereafter, and while he was somewhat in a hostage situation, it seemed unfair and possibly foolhardy bombarding him with them when he was steering. She still had things to achieve in life. Her Bafta wouldn't win itself.

Conversely, the studious not-talking-about-it transformed them into a cycling machine, perfectly tuned to *Lady Regina* and the need to lean in synch when a bend necessitated it. Powering on in this determined fashion, getting pumped by overtaking other riders or staying ahead of others – "We are *not* being overtaken by someone on a Raleigh Chopper, BJ!" – time and miles passed quickly. Becca spurred herself on through Surrey with an internal mantra of *my bum hurts, my bum hurts, my bum hurts* to a point of almost trance-like haze, visualising slumping on the grass at the midway checkpoint, until they pulled up into Turners Hill village, where food and a brass band awaited them.

Becca left him to wrestle *Regina* to the ground, as she gathered food and bottles of water. Not walking like John Wayne took effort, as did keeping the gurn of pain off her face.

"Shift over." He'd ditched his helmet next to hers on the ground and lay with his head on *Regina's* front saddle, his eyes shut, perhaps hoping she wouldn't try any conversation, but he was on a loser there. He sat up, allowing her some room, and tore into his bacon roll.

"If you were that hungry, Charlie, you should have said. I had snacks with me." She patted her trusty bumbag.

"I didn't want to acknowledge that thing," he said. She assumed he meant it fondly.

"I've got sun lotion and Ally too, and gummy bears, obviously."

"Obviously," he said through a mouthful.

They regained their breaths and sorted the fuel

replenishment. Becca gave her bottom a discreet massage by shifting about on the ground, getting the blood moving about again in her nether regions. The seats at Spin class were far more forgiving.

Charlie lay back in the sun, eyes closed again, while she finished. Becca watched his face, not least because Lycra cycling shorts were no friend to the male body in her book; no mystique left there whatsoever. The butterflies on his cut were doing their job, so she felt better about that. His face was resting, but she wouldn't have considered it peaceful. It was more the rest of a face which had been tense for too long and knew it was merely taking respite. Something about it pained her.

"So, what's going on, Charlie?"

His chest rose, then released deeply. His eyes stayed shut.

"We called it a day about two months ago." She hadn't heard. She hadn't seen Shrin or Ollie recently, or perhaps the pair were having a go at discretion.

"I'm sorry."

He opened one eye at her. "Really?" he drawled.

She was a bit shocked.

"Yes, of course. The end of a marriage is sad."

"You didn't like her."

"I didn't *know* her. I didn't get the chance. But you loved her, so, it's sad. For which I can express sympathy." In her head she sounded very grown up. She hoped he noticed.

He mulled it and then closed the eye again.

"Can't you fix it? Go to Relate or something?"

"Nope," he said glibly. "She doesn't want me, her mind's

made up." There was a hint of bitterness there, but he clearly wasn't fighting things.

"What went wrong?" It had been such a short marriage.

"I'm an indecisive, dishonest, secretive dickhead, apparently," he said.

She was taken aback. But then again... "I could have told her that," Becca said, unable to help herself. "Could have saved you a packet on that wedding." Thankfully his mouth pulled up in a smile and she continued scoffing her free orange slices.

"She was tired of running our relationship. *I* thought I was giving her everything she wanted." Becca tilted her head, thinking. Surely by the time they'd got married Liv had been aware Charlie's constant compliance was down to decision-making phobia. It had suited Ally fine, she'd assumed Liv had liked it too.

Now Charlie seemed ready to talk. "And owing to my following all her plans and the apparent frustrations it provoked, she was compelled into a fling with Brent on a shoot which has now turned out to be the partnership she should have had, meaning she's moved out of our place, into his. Work is lots of fun, as you'd imagine, hence the search for alternative employment." Wow. Right.

"How d'you find out?" Becca wasn't above a spot of gossip.

"Nothing salacious," he said, and Becca thought *Meh*. "Liv's a straight talker and simply told me what was going on, and that she wanted a divorce, although her view seems to be I drove her to it."

"Oh."

"Quite. How's *your* life, White?"

"For once, not as shit as yours," she said. "But only just. Still no acting career, I'm months off giving up, a weapons-grade wankpuffin cheated on me and now I'm frightened you need your flat back." The notion of him moving back had only just struck her, but the fear it brought almost took her breath away. She loved that flat, and imagining being back out there amid the horror houses made her place a hand on the ground to quell the panic attack.

"Relax Beej, you're safe. I'm buying her out of the flat. The location's decent, plus the rowing club, a.k.a. the sole source of my social life, is nearby."

Was it OK to get up and yell "Thank Fuck for that!" when someone else was lamenting their imminent divorce? No, probably not. She restrained herself.

He sat up and looked at her. "It's a bit shit all round, isn't it?" His smile was small, but she sensed he appreciated the solidarity. Well, if her shit state of life could give him a boost, at least something good could come of it.

"Welcome to my world!" she said and got up. If they didn't get going again soon, she'd never get her bum back on the torturous saddle at all.

While it took them a moment to find their equilibrium again, *Regina* was easier to get started this time. His not being in a scowling hunch was helpful. He'd offered her the front for this stint, but she'd declined. He'd had a point about her getting distracted by the sights, and the countryside kept catching her eye. Oh God, she really was getting older if countryside was of interest.

"So, I guess we're both at a metaphorical crossroads," he said, as they found a decent pace.

"I guess," she said. He waited. "I mean, I'm thirty now and the acting success hasn't happened, so I should probably ditch that dream."

"Why?" he demanded.

His response surprised her. She'd expected him to agree with her. Her school careers adviser would have done; she'd never been on board with Becca's acting plan.

"Well, you might not have noticed, but the industry favours youth. Older bints don't get a look-in, other than in serial dramas, and I've already been in *Holby City* in four different bit-parts in the last eight years. The American market's not going to pick me for anything, and I can't be arsed with being inside costumes anymore. I peaked at the spunksuit."

"Why are you always waiting for them to pick you?" he asked, indicating right for a turn. She took a moment to concentrate on the manoeuvre.

"That's actually how the job works, Charlie," she said, trying to curb her sarcasm. "You audition. They pick. I've yet to find a boyfriend who writes me a film."

"Why d'you need a boyfriend to do that? You can do it. That's my point. Write your own role," he said, his tone brisk and no-nonsense.

"I don't have the money to go on a film course, Moneybags."

"People wrote scripts before courses existed, Beej." She gave him a light jab to the kidney, but not enough to prompt a swerve. "There's enough free info on the internet to teach yourself screenwriting basics. And I wasn't thinking of a film. Maybe a series or something."

He sounded serious, but with that naïve sense that everything was possible. "Maybe you can do that on your side of the industry, but…"

"But nothing. I'm no actor, but I suspect you're already trained to think in terms of scenes, structure and dramatic effect."

It struck her that he believed she could do something like this, and she couldn't think where the foundation for that came from.

"I don't have any ideas." She'd written nothing of her own since her degree, and she wasn't good at the social commentary they'd wanted. "And I'm crap at serious stuff."

"Becca!" He sounded quite exasperated. "Who said anything about being serious? You're funny. You've *always* been funny. You were funny in that awful thing I reviewed—"

"Don't go there."

"You were, though. You make *me* laugh. Even when you're being a cow, you've always made me laugh."

That was true.

"And you don't need a new idea. You've got your life experience to write about. That's what I would do. A comedy."

"You'd write your life as a comedy?" He'd been through some rough years recently. It might be a hard sell.

"Not *mine*, no. But I do wonder whether there's mileage in my trip to the Americas after Ally died. Some kind of travelogue or something." He sounded shy about it. "Or whatever. But think of all the stories you've told people about your jobs."

"My pathetic jobs?" She dined out on her stories amongst friends; she didn't particularly like hearing them considered as TV comedy fodder.

"Don't get offended. Think about it. You've slaved for years trying to get your career going, and you've done plenty of jobs you weren't chuffed about. But what if," he rang *Regina*'s bell at a couple of oldies meandering into the road, "what if it's all been leading you to a script, one where you can both tell and act in your stories?"

"So people can laugh at me?" Friends was one thing, the public was another.

"No, they aren't laughing at *you*, but at the circumstances, and in recognition. People have shit jobs in all industries, and while they assume acting is a glory career, they'll relate to the less-than-brilliant jobs you've had."

He let her mull it over as they pushed on towards Brighton. She wanted to protest, to tell him to stop judging her jobs, but perhaps he had a point. Maybe he was right about the relatability too. There was comedy in everything, like family, or education, or an office. Ultimately, acting was still just a job.

"What do you think?" he asked.

"You really think I could write something like that?"

"I can't think of anyone who's better placed to do it. You've shed-loads of material."

"All right, Lister, no need to rub it in," she said mildly, still not comfortable laying out her failures for larks, but also having a disturbing feeling that he might be onto something. "I could go all-in and call it *It's All About Me!*"

"Perfect," he agreed with a laugh. "You can do this, BJ. You're tenacious. Having seen you squirming on stage in green paint and pants, I know the depths you'll stoop to for attention." The jab to his kidney was harder this time. "Oi! All right, White. You can do this, and more importantly you *need* to do this. Stop waiting for the universe to drop something in your lap and take control of your destiny. What was it a wise woman always used to harp on about?"

"Make it happen!" Becca chimed, in a perfect Ally voice.

Charlie's head pulled up. "How do you do that?"

"What, voices?"

"No, *Ally's* voice. I know you can do voices, but how d'you still remember hers?" His voice was graver, as if ashamed.

"You don't?"

His head shook, but he kept his eyes facing forwards.

"I'd saved some of her old voicemails. I listen to them now and again."

He said nothing. He clearly didn't have that option and she supposed she should offer him a listen, but she wanted to keep some things as hers.

"And what about *you* making it happen?" she said, turning the tables. It was all right for him to dish the advice, suggesting she expected the universe to gift her things, but he'd had things easy. "You've come this far in life with everything being given to you or taken care of." OK, so it came out sharper than she'd intended, but it had been a chip on her shoulder, like for ever.

"I don't think that's quite fair," he said, his hackles rising.

"It kind of *is*," she cut in. "Jobs appear in front of you and because they'll *do*, you take them. And your women make decisions for you which you're happy to follow. And in the event of having to make the decisions, you rely on the coin."

"I thought you thought the coin was a lame gimmick."

He was deflecting, and she knew it.

"Maybe at uni with the women, but you aren't the only observant one, Charlie; you don't like decisions. And here you are, needing to make some. You can't be a passive sloth forever."

Was that a growl coming from him? Yes, she believed it might have been. "You know I'm right and I'm guessing it came from your childhood – no, please don't bore me with the details – but you've been passive at best or ruled by the flip of a coin otherwise, and frankly, you're too old for that now." She heard him muttering under his breath. "Ha, not so much fun when the boot's on the other foot, is it, having the mirror held up to you?"

"Being *dragged*, more like," he grouched.

"Charlie," she said, "do you really think I'm being unfair? Perhaps you're right that I've spent years waiting to be picked and I should change it up. You're probably the only person who can say that to me. But I'm probably the only person who can say this to you too, because I've known you so long."

His silence said she was right, and it pushed her on.

"If you could do anything now, what would it be?"

He still didn't respond, and she wondered whether he was going to give her the silent treatment again. They had the steep horror of Ditchling Beacon to climb yet, and she'd need someone to swear with.

"I'd like to present," he said finally, as if testing the words aloud for the first time. "Something travel-based, showing countries beyond the tourist resorts."

"That sounds doable, doesn't it? You've travelled, and you've got production experience." It made sense to her, and being in the realms of "make it happen", she wanted him to believe it was attainable. "You could totally do that, you just need a USP, something to differentiate you from the likes of that Levinson Woods bloke."

"Levison Wood."

"Exactly. Levison. People like those shows. He's interesting and easy on the eye. And your face isn't awful." She reached down and extracted her water bottle from the bottle cage to take a swig. She couldn't have done *that* six hours ago.

"Thanks very much."

"You're welcome," she said smiling, as much for helping his mood as at enjoying the water cooling her. The gradient was steadily increasing and her legs were smarting, though not enough to distract from the bum ache. She'd need a cushion at Maggie's.

"So, we need to find your slant," she said. They were maintaining a decent pace despite the rising hill, and she was enjoying being officious.

He didn't offer anything, which stumped her bossy mode. "Come on, Charlie, think."

"Actually, I do have a slant. But you'll take the piss, so I'll keep it to myself."

She made a loud sound, like a quiz show's "Incorrect" klaxon. "We have no secrets, Lister."

"We have plenty, White," he countered.

"Fine," she said, "but you should dish this one, given we're mapping out careers."

"Is that what we're doing? I thought you were suggesting I've had it easy."

"I'm not suggesting that. That was more of a statement," she said honestly. "But we *are* looking at alleviating this stasis you find yourself in."

"Like you are too," he said, defensive again.

"Sure, like me. And misery loves company, right? So perhaps being stuck together today on *Regina* was a blessing."

She often wondered whether Ally was steering things from afar.

Charlie exhaled. "OK. My slant is navigating countries by the toss of a coin. Land at the airport, then follow the coin's decision."

It suited him down to a tee. Becca could see it immediately. "That's perfect; Passive Adventuring. And can I suggest naming your production company Tosser Productions?"

His snort of laughter pleased her.

"And yours would be Harridan Productions." It had a certain ring to it.

She wanted to discuss it further, but the sheer effort of the cycling nixed that. The gradient had suddenly increased and Becca began regretting her tandem choice. With a single bike, she could have dismounted like some other riders. They had until 7 p.m. to finish, and she wasn't too proud to walk.

But Charlie apparently had other ideas for Ditchling Beacon.

"Please, Charlie," she gasped, her quads screaming at her.

"I'll drop us another gear. Come on, Beej, we can do this."

"Noo, I can't," she moaned.

"I believe in you," he called, channelling some fitness guru, and she wanted to slap him, but she needed her hands to pull on the handle bars to get any traction.

"Other people are walking," she managed through gritted teeth.

"That," he said, sounding challenged too, "would not be in the spirit of things," which reminded Becca why she intensely disliked him at times.

The view out over Brighton, the fields and the sea from the top of the Beacon, was majestic, and no doubt Becca would have appreciated it more had she not been feeling the need to vomit from her exertions.

"Come on, it's all downhill from here," Charlie called, sounding far too gleeful at her misery. Git.

They still had seven miles to go, but the thrill of the salty wind in her face during the descent and not having to pedal was a boon, and her mood recovered. The sea and some chips were only a sniff away and the idea of hot fluffy potato had her salivating. She fumbled in her bumbag for some gummy bears to keep her energy up.

When they could hear one another again over the rushing air, Charlie moved the conversation away from their respective employment missions.

"Would you consider, Becca, letting me listen to Ally's messages?"

Given how he'd just beasted her up the hill, she was *mostly* considering laughing in his face. However, while she wanted to keep them to herself, she pondered how she'd feel, not remembering Ally's voice.

"Mmm, perhaps," she allowed.

"Pretty please," he said, making her laugh.

"All right, but the chips are on you at the finish line, then."

"Deal."

"It's hard, the forgetting, isn't it?" she said gently.

"You too?"

"For me it's the feel of her company, you know?" She knew that sounded odd. "I have photos, so I remember what she looked like, and I catch her expressions when talking to Valerie, and I can remember her scent when I walk through a perfume department and use the Marc Jacobs *Daisy* tester, but I'm forgetting what it felt like having her around me. Sitting on a sofa watching a romcom, or next to each other in a bar. She gave me so much comfort. She always knew the right thing to say and do." Charlie shook his head in front. "What?"

"You really do have her on a pedestal, don't you?"

"What do you mean?"

"Calm down. I can already hear you getting defensive. She was absolutely the best person I knew. That's why I wanted to spend the rest of my life with her. I adored her, completely and utterly, but Ally had her flaws."

Becca gave a humpf in consternation. "None that *I* knew of."

He chuckled. "*Everyone* has flaws, Becca. Even Ally. You venerate her, back then and now."

Becca was stunned. Ally wasn't flawed, and *she* didn't

idolise people. She just called things as she saw them, and there was nothing to mark Ally down for. "She was perfect."

"Perfect for me," he agreed, "absolutely, but nobody is a perfect person. You know that. Ally had flaws."

"She did not! Other than her singing voice. That was dodgy, but that was from Valerie and you can't fault her enthusiasm."

"BJ, Ally was great. So great in so many ways, but she *did* have flaws. She wasn't a great listener, for a start."

"Rubbish." Becca was astonished. "I talked to her all the time."

"Hearing isn't the same as listening. Unless you were saying what she wanted to hear, she'd bulldoze you with her own plan instead."

"Only because they were *good* plans," Becca insisted, then added, "You're wrong and disloyal."

"It's nothing to do with loyalty. I'd do anything for her if she was here. I just don't see her with the same rose-tinted glasses you do, that's all. I recognised her flaws, and I loved her in spite of them."

Becca wanted to end the conversation there. It *did* feel disloyal to her, not only speaking ill of the dead but speaking ill of his fiancée.

"Take these tasks."

"What about them?"

"She knew we'd do them for her."

"How could she?"

"Because she knew we loved her and she only needed to ask and we'd agree. She picked her timing perfectly: a year on, at the top of Snowdon, knowing we'd be euphoric."

"You make her sound manipulative." Becca didn't like this. She wanted Ally revered, not maligned.

"Wake up, Becca. She was Making it Happen." He tried to do the voice.

"That was a shit impression," Becca snapped, cross at him. "Not that the tasks matter anymore," she said. "This is the last. After today we're done."

That put a stop to his dissing of their friend.

"It is?"

"Yep. All done."

"So what now?"

His question stumped her. "Well. Nothing. I assume all the ashes are gone." The last bottle was in the bumbag, ready to empty on the finish line.

"What do we do from now on?" He sounded lost.

"I guess we get on with our lives and think about her as and when. We'll know we honoured her last wishes, whether she knew we'd do them or not." She said it pointedly, as she wasn't convinced.

A sign distracted her. They were within the Brighton town limits. They were almost there, nearly fifty-four miles done, without killing each other and, checking her watch, in a respectable time. She gave *Regina* a pat; she might have bucked him off once but the purple lady had done them proud.

Becca noticed people out on the pavements watching them – cheering for them. It brought a smile to her face and a tremendous sense of achievement. All that spinning had been worth it. Yes, she might have wanted to pack it all in on the hills, but she'd hunkered down and pushed through, possibly forced on by Charlie and *Regina*, and she hadn't flung herself off the bike, which *had* been an actual option.

"Eyes on the road, BJ!" Charlie shouted from the front, correcting *Regina*'s sudden wobble.

"Am I allowed to wave?" she asked, crossly. "Given this is the only time I'll be doing this, am I at least allowed that?"

He ignored her, and she ignored him, grinning at the bystanders, waving to the kids, like she was the Queen on a bicycle.

The finishing arch came into view and they both naturally sped up, summoning a last spurt of energy, as they sailed along Madeira Drive. Nearing the end, Becca took her hands off the handlebars, manically unzipping her bumbag to pull the blue bottle out. As they crossed the line, the ashes poured from it to cross with them.

Charlie steered them through the crowds, towards the rental drop-off. Coming to a standstill, he dismounted and turned to look at her, a huge grin on his face, the sense of achievement written all over it.

"We did it!"

She beamed up at him, the elation shooting up from her feet to her eyes. They reached for a hug simultaneously, Becca flinging her arms around his waist, as he flung his around her shoulders, and they leaned in, in celebration, but also in utter exhaustion. She parked her cheekbone on his shoulder, and he rested his chin against her helmet. If it wasn't for the bumbag wedged between them, it would have been a perfect fit. Becca closed her eyes, content. Then swiftly opened them. What was she doing? This was Charlie. At lightning speed she unlocked her hands and drew away from him. The look on his face said he was experiencing the exact same thought. Their faces raced to be the reddest.

Panicking, Becca took action and raised her hand. "High five, Lister! Yay us!"

He slapped her hand, mainly missing, but she overlooked it, hoping to shoo the awkwardness away.

He glanced at her other hand which still held the bottle.

"Do we need to...?"

"Oh, no," she gushed, "all taken care of. On the finishing line."

"Great," he said with a nod. Suddenly everything seemed very polite. She half expected him to shake her hand.

"Beccaaaaaaaaaaaaa!" The incoming squeal, though ear-piercing, was welcome. Becca and Charlie both turned to hug Maggie, as if it made their hug just a regular thing. She then waved them together so she could photograph the victorious athletes, but they kept a modest inch apart.

"Do you want to come out with us, Charlie?" Maggie asked. "I've got room for you too."

Charlie didn't look at Becca. Becca didn't know what she wanted him to answer. The exhaustion was making her very confused, obviously.

"Ahh, not this time, Mags. I didn't bring spare kit, and sweaty Lycra won't do."

Again, Becca couldn't sort out her feelings. Was it relief or disappointment, and why was she even confused? She'd been looking forward to a girls' night out.

"The bus to mine goes in five minutes, Becs," Maggie said, "or we'll have to wait for ages."

"I'll drop the tandem off," Charlie offered and Becca gave

Regina a stroke of thanks, "and then I'll head for the station. I've got work to do at home tonight." She wasn't sure he was being completely truthful, but she wasn't going to argue. Perhaps he had some applications to write. She gave him a simple nod.

"Don't forget to pick up your medal," he said, lightly.

Finally, feeling things were on a more even keel now, she looked him in the eyes.

"Thanks for today," she said, genuinely. "And for all the other trips."

He considered it for a moment and said, "Pleasure."

She pulled a face. *Fibber.* And yet…

"It's been quite fun, hasn't it?" she added, not quite ready to walk away.

He see-sawed his head from side to side weighing it up, until she gave him the bug eye.

He conceded a pinched smile. "Can we discount Snowdon?"

"Probably best," she agreed, "but that cup of tea was something else."

That made his smile spread. "Lots of it has been something else."

A wide grin bloomed across Becca's face. "I'll … um … see you around then, I guess."

He held her gaze, as if daring her to set a date, but she didn't and eventually he let her off with "I guess."

"See you then."

"See you." This was painful, but Becca couldn't pull her eyes from him either.

"Becs, the bus…?" Maggie whispered behind her.

Prompted, she gave him a weird little wave which he returned, and then with nothing left to say, he headed for the drop-off.

She stayed put, watching to see if he'd look back.

As his broad back wove into the crowd, her fingertips tapped on her thigh, in some made-up Morse code, calling him to glance at her.

But he didn't. And she didn't know why it bothered her. She still hadn't worked it out as they sat on the bus. In the end she convinced herself this strange feeling was hunger. He hadn't bought her those chips he'd promised. That had to be it...

2017: Spring

I t was a slightly cooler day in Cannes, just eighteen degrees as opposed to the twenties of the previous days, but sunny regardless, with a light northerly breeze and perfectly pleasant for early April. The sun reflected off the ripples on the sea, and pedestrians walking along Boulevard de la Croisette all donned their designer sunglasses as they gazed out over the Mediterranean. Up on the stony hills above the town, the cypress trees stood tall against the blue sky, and the air was humid, whispering hints of summer's heat to come. The restaurants along the palm tree-lined promenade were full with the hubbub of international business deals being brokered in the glamour of the French Riviera.

Charlie, however, was not feeling the glamour.

He'd agreed to come to Cannes for three reasons: he was helping a mate with a staff shortage, he had nothing better to do and he thought he'd be on a jolly. Charlie needed something jolly in his life right now. He'd left Brent's seven months ago and save for a brief maternity cover job, hadn't found anything new. Brent had offered him a decent "redundancy" package, the awkwardness in the office becoming too much, although it wasn't really a choice. The money was buying him some time, but wouldn't last much longer. Growing bored at home, sending out CVs to little response, Charlie jumped at the chance when James, who owned another production company, offered him the reception role at their stand at the MIPTV show. Having heard of the TV programme market, he'd been intrigued to go, not least for the networking opportunities it would surely offer, but primarily because a week in the south of France, bed and board covered, sounded like a welcome shot of vitamin D and drinks.

"OK, Charlie?" James asked, walking up to the reception desk to greet the Finnish programming exec who was his last meeting of the day.

"Seeing daylight wouldn't go amiss," Charlie said.

"Ha!" laughed James. "Takes years and all the monies to get those stands." He ushered his guest to the screening booth to discuss her shopping list and the catalogue of documentaries he had on offer.

Charlie had rather imagined the deals would be done over glasses of champagne on the terraces of the Palais des Festivals, under the cloudless sky, the sea shimmering behind them. And perhaps they were, with the big-boy companies further up in the exhibition centre, but James's stand was a floor below ground, without windows to see any sky, cloudless or otherwise, and the air had been through at least three people before it reached Charlie. For the last five days he'd only seen the delights of Cannes as he'd walked in in the early morning, as the empty pavements were being hosed down, and at high speed as he raced across the boulevard, dodging mopeds, to fulfil panini orders for any of the sales team who hadn't secured a lunch meeting at one of the beachside restaurants. Re-setting the stand each evening for the following morning was his job, so he missed the twilight drinks parties in the gardens of the Majestic hotel opposite the Palais, or at the Carlton or Martinez further along the designer-store-encrusted boulevard, too. He'd crashed a few evening parties, but constantly ended up being targeted by indie producers who'd talk to him right until they realised he wasn't a buyer and then vanish quicker than a wig in a whirlwind.

He only had this evening left and then they'd be packing up and heading home, although now he wished he'd booked to stay a few extra nights to actually enjoy the place. Never again would he mock anyone moaning about going to MIP. His feet were aching, his skin was craving sunlight and no doubt he'd develop a cold from it all the moment he got home.

Casting an eye down his corridor of stands, he caught a flash of red hair. The big curls hanging down her back, the way she moved – proud of her height and her hips – was exactly like Becca.

Fuelled by surprise, curiosity got the better of him. "Becca?" he called.

The woman glanced back.

She took a moment to recognise him. "Charlie?"

It was her, but not quite. Her hair was glossy and groomed, not quite the harried birds-nest it so often was. Her signature cat's-eye lick of eyeliner must be catching men's eyes all over. And her forest green jacquard trouser suit, with a cream camisole under the jacket, looked a million miles from her usual second-hand finds. Her shoes were smart trainers, but matched the suit – someone must have tipped her off to leave the stilettos at home. He'd heard the first-timer saleswomen ruing their schoolgirl error of only packing heels. She carried the MIPTV delegates bag over her shoulder but had made it look coolly scuffed already.

She actually looked pleased to see him. "I didn't clock it

was you," she said, walking back. "The context was all wrong."

"You look… You look…" There was something about her, a glow, a confidence, he couldn't quite explain it, but it needed acknowledging. "Really good." It was lame and not nearly enough. Instinctively, he smoothed his shirt down to look smart, but after a full day in the heat of the basement floor, he wished he'd had a spare.

The compliment made her smile though, so it didn't matter. "Thanks, Charlie." A quizzical expression passed her face, "Do we do compliments?"

"It was accidental," he said.

She liked that. "Phew."

"What are you…? Why are you…?" Eloquence was eluding him, but she'd surprised him on many levels.

"Me? Here?" she asked. He could only nod.

She was clearly delighted he'd asked. "I did the thing. Like you suggested."

His brow furrowed.

"I sat down and wrote something. Just a little thing." Shyness was overcoming her, but then she visibly cast it aside, as if someone had been coaching her to bloody blow her own trumpet because she was worth it. "I wrote a script and sent it in to a new writers' programme the BBC are doing with the Arts Council, and it got selected for development." Something dawned on her. "I meant to call you, to tell you, but it all went mad. I only had a pilot and they needed actual episodes, so, you know, time evaporated. But anyway. They've brought a few of us out for a couple of days for a 'new programming' showcase and some schmoozing." She looked as stunned about it as he did. Faced with his stunnedness, she shrugged. "Mad, right?" She looked like she couldn't believe her luck.

"Well, congratulations," he roused himself to say, but meaning it. "It looks great on you." She looked down at herself, and adjusted a lapel.

"Took me days of trawling the Chelsea charity shops to find this, but as armour goes, it's been a lifesaver." She leaned in and said under her breath, "I've been scared shitless."

"Then you're a true thespian, Becca. You were walking like you completely belong."

That delighted her. Her hazel eyes were wide, their gold flecks sparkling as they gazed at each other, until she suddenly looked between him, the desk and the stand.

"What are you doing here?"

Charlie felt self-conscious. He wasn't wearing a jacket and his shirtsleeves were rolled up. His tie had been ditched after the early afternoon rush when James had done the same.

"I'm helping out. They needed help on reception." He stopped there. He didn't want to tell her he was out of work, but she stood waiting for him to expand.

"I ... um ... took redundancy from Brent's," he said, feeling like his mother was forcing him to explain, "and given I was otherwise unengaged this week, a paid trip to Cannes sounded like a laugh."

Becca looked up at the low ceiling and about the corridor.

"How's that going for you?" She could see it for what it was.

"Yeah, apparently the laugh is going on elsewhere."

Becca delved in her bag and slid something across the glass of the desk to him. "Here. Have some freebies," she said with a conspiratorial smile. A logoed pen and some wrapped sweets lay in front of him. He knew her love for freebies. Her sharing her plunder with him was tantamount to a declaration of ... well, not *love*, of course, this was Becca, but some affection between two people who'd known each other a long time, through thicks and thins.

His stomach growled at the sight of the sweet. It had been a long while since his extortionately priced croque-monsieur. It gave him an idea. "Are you here tonight?"

"Yep. I fly out tomorrow evening."

"The 6 p.m. flight?" She nodded. "Same. Are you booked for dinner? I'd like to hear about the script and everything." Things were looking up for her, and frankly it was about time.

"Well, I haven't anything planned, to be honest – I got hammered last night crashing stand parties with the other new writers. Something more sedate tonight sounds good."

"Bloody hell," said Charlie, "young Becca would be appalled at your sensible stance, although proud of the gatecrashing."

"I know, right? Young Becca would give me the stink eye, but you know, older Becca sees her thirties as being more productive."

From what he could see, older Becca was far better put together, both in attitude and stance. There was something about her he couldn't put his finger on.

"So, dinner?"

Becca checked her watch and asked, "Can I hang around here until you're done?"

"No more schmoozing to do?"

She tilted her head in consideration, then shook it.

"Honestly, I've got so many business cards today, I think I'm spent." The plastic pouch at the end of her lanyard holding her delegate's pass was fat with cards.

All right for some, he thought. His own pouch was decidedly skinny, the only cards in it being his own. But he said nothing. Becca deserved to have some better luck. That his was waning wasn't her fault.

"Take a pew. I'll prep to close the joint as soon as James's meeting's over and then we're outta here."

Watching her take a seat and busy herself with her own paperwork, Charlie couldn't help but think he was pleased to see her. Obviously, he'd have preferred bumping into her at a party outside, with his sunglasses on, in conversation with buyers or commissioners, but for all that, he knew she took him as she found him, wasn't judging him now and so had just made herself the highpoint of the week.

Ten minutes later, Virve the Finn passed him on the way out, closely followed by James, who flung him a quick "Laters." It only took Charlie a few minutes to flip the relevant switches and lock the doors to close the stand.

"Ready?" he asked.

"Yeps. Where to?"

"What do you fancy? There's all sorts here." Like normal, the team had dispersed to dinner meetings, leaving him on his tod.

"Something from Provence, please," she said with a big grin, as she stood, pulled her bag up onto her shoulder and took another look around.

"Can't believe you're here, Charlie. Small world, right?" She was clearly thrilled to be there, making the most of being abroad. It made him feel ungracious for being such a grump about it. Putting a hand on her shoulder, he guided her towards the escalator and the hope of fresh air.

"Did you know this place existed?"

"Cannes? Pretty sure it has a big film festival each year, BJ. I thought, as an actor, you'd have heard of it."

She gave him a light slap to the arm as she stepped onto the escalator, whether for his taking the mick or for the moniker, he didn't know.

"TV markets. Selling programmes like any other commodity."

To be honest he hadn't given it much thought either, until he'd started working for Brent and learned about programme financing: getting investment from channels before you produced something, and then getting the after-sales from channels in other territories once the programme was finished.

"I didn't, and if I did, it was more glamorous than the reality."

"Whaaat?? This is amazing," she said. "You obviously haven't been to the right stands or parties." Now she looked smug.

"Clearly not," he said, then pointed to his lanyard. "Working, remember?"

She shot him an indignant look. "I *have* been working." Then she shimmied, "Working *it*." He rolled his eyes and then looked towards the entrance doors which were appearing at the top of the escalator. He was about to follow Becca off it, but walked into her instead as she'd frozen.

"Beej?" he asked, almost tumbling over her. Thankfully she

reacted and stepped clear, allowing him to flail off the moving steps. "'S'up?"

She stood mesmerised by a poster in front of them, huge and unmissable to everyone using that exit all week. Charlie had given it several long looks the previous evenings. It showed the pale, naked torso of a redheaded woman, face down in brackish water. The woman's skin was milky with a light scattering of faint freckles at her shoulders, around which the wet hair floated in tendrils.

"Fuck," she hissed.

"You all right?" he asked, composing himself from the flailing. Flailing was not a Cannes look. He slammed his Raybans over his eyes, but kept his gaze on the poster.

She pulled him closer by his shirt, and spoke out of the side of her mouth.

"That arse?" She nodded towards it. It was a very fine, nicely rounded bottom, in his opinion. "*My* arse."

"What?"

"I know, right? I do *not* recall agreeing to stills being used for the promo. I'm going to kill Marcia."

The poster was for a police procedural called *The Ophelia Murders*.

She dragged him away, almost clobbering him when he asked her for a selfie next to it.

"When did you shoot that?" he asked as they reached the pavement. He took a good lungful of cleaner air.

"That was the series I'd been filming when I got ill that time." She didn't need to say more. He'd never forget that weekend, and suspected she wouldn't either. Having seen the effect it'd had, Charlie didn't think the swampy water on the poster was Photoshopped in any way.

"It's a good picture of your bum," he offered.

She adjusted her bag strap. "True, but I'm generally selective about who sees it." He drew breath to respond. "Shut up. Those rumours weren't true. Jeez, uni gossip never dies, does it?" She looked about. "I need a drink." Not stopping for any discussion, she propelled him across the street towards the Majestic hotel, pausing outside both Chanel and Prada and forcing him to admire the bumbags which just happened to be in their windows.

"Have you got tickets?" he asked. The front garden of the hotel was cordoned off and brimming with TV execs.

"Stay put," she said, sounding cheeky and bossy simultaneously, and vanished, returning in less than a minute with two glasses of Kir Royale and a wink.

"How?"

"Some of us grew up scavenging. I like to think it's all led to this," she said and clinked his glass before tipping her head back and letting the cool champagne and crème de cassis do its job in the early evening warmth. Then she handed him her glass, and removed her jacket, hanging it over the bag against her leg. With her big Jackie O sunglasses, and her hair down, she looked every bit the star who'd been flown out for promo.

He handed her the glass and told her the truth. "You look like you belong here."

"In the limelight?" she asked gleefully. "I *know*. I think I was made for Cannes. Not my complexion, obviously, I'd look like one of the leathery women in minutes, but the Riviera, in general? I think so. I just need a scarf and a vintage convertible, right?"

He clinked their glasses again in agreement.

"So tell me what got your famous bum in the seat and your fingers on the keyboard?" He noted Becca catching the eye of passing delegates, all of whom were trying to get a squiz at the name on her pass. They would have clocked the BBC logo on it. He stepped closer to her, to ward off any notions of introducing themselves and whisking her away. He'd now realised the key to these drinks dos was having someone striking-looking with you.

She looked about, still not quite believing this was her current reality. If he knew her at all, she'd also be scoping for the hidden camera, sure she was about to be pied in the face, for daring to think she could have this.

"On the train back from Brighton last year, I thought about what you'd said about being funny and writing, and ideas started forming. I made a long list of my shit jobs on my phone and I was off." She stopped and looked rather contrite. "Again, I should have told you."

He waved it away. It was pleasure enough to know he'd coaxed her. It was a small miracle she'd listened to something he'd said.

"Did you call it *It's All About Me!*?"

"I tried. They preferred *Hot Mess*."

He liked that too.

"I wrote it as a one-hour stand-alone, but they said they couldn't place something like that, but what about a series of half hours, at which point I peed my pants both in joy and fear. But the mentor they gave me helped me see it as a sitcom, looking at the reality of being a twenty-something woman and what's hard about trying to adult and what there is to learn. Obviously, the 'what I've learned' has been the hardest bit, because honestly, from this side of thirty, fuck knows, but I appear to have fooled them." She waved her hand around in illustration.

To anyone else it would have sounded self-deprecating, but Charlie knew she meant it.

"You say that, Beej, but you've learned more than most." Definitely more than him. He'd realised recently how aided he'd been in life. This current stint was proving quite tough.

Something about having found each other and a sense of being partners-in-crime meant their drinks disappeared within minutes. He looked towards the party and wondered how he was going to get the next round in. Becca's stomach rumbled.

"Dinner?" he asked. Her smile spread wide.

"Dinner," she agreed.

The twilight was setting in as they walked along the boulevard, the glow from the streetlights reflecting off the water to their left. To the right, on the other side of the street, older locals stood in the shady petanque pitches, vying for victory with the steel balls. He loved the intensity of the game, and their obliviousness to the business folk milling around them, heading back to hotels, before venturing back for the bars. He guided Becca towards Le Suquet, the medieval end of town, overlooked by the Chateau de la Castre up on the hilltop, until they reached the yacht-filled marina of Vieux

Ports, enjoying the view across the bay of Cannes, and all the lights of the town. Now he was glad he'd had evenings to himself; he'd had time to assess the options.

Charlie picked a restaurant on Quai St Pierre, serving traditional dishes from Provence. He'd thought about one of the small restaurants set back off the cobbled Rue Saint-Antoine, but figured on a clear evening the lights on the sea were a view worth having, and luck had a table outside waiting for them. The waiter sat them at adjoining sides, so they could both enjoy the view. Once they would have insisted on having the table between them, but they settled in, shoulder to shoulder, without a thought, immediately ordering two new Kir Royales, as if it was the only acceptable beverage when on the Riviera.

"I think I could live like this," Becca said, sipping hers.

"So much I want on the menu," he said absently, scanning it, trying to focus, wanting it sorted so he could concentrate on her. It had been less than a year since he'd seen her, but she seemed different. Perhaps it was the lack of scowl on her face. He told himself to be fair, she hadn't really scowled at him for some years now, but those early years had made their mark.

Becca slammed her menu shut and placed it on the table. "Bloody hell, that was fast," he said. Then he worried there was nothing that appealed.

"I stop looking after the first thing I see that I'd like. Why confuse things with more choices?"

His stunned expression made her burst out laughing. "Charlie, you look like you've been hit by a revelation. Menus must be a nightmare for you with all those choices. I bet you're twitching to flip a coin to choose between things. Am I right?"

God, she could be annoying. A coin had indeed picked last night's meal.

"No, *actually*, I'm having the ... the bream." He slammed the menu shut, just as she had, hoping to look similarly decisive. "And the fritters to start." He liked a fritter, they were his favourite as a kid. "You can mock the coin, Becca, but sometimes it helps. It cuts through the noise. Using it at uni with girls, *that* was just a flirty game, but it genuinely was all I could do to move me on when I went away to the Americas. Now though, I toss the coin if I have a dilemma, not to make the decision but to *check* it. I ask myself whether I'm disappointed by the coin's result. It's seen me right so far." He felt it was worth saying, he'd didn't see the harm in his coin flipping. "But, as you can see, I'm quite capable of choosing from a menu."

She smirked at his defensiveness. "Well," she concluded, magnanimously, "bream and fritters sounds fab. I'm having the salmon and the seafood."

"You a big seafood fan?" he asked. He'd never had the impression she was adventurous with her food.

"I don't know! But what if I never come somewhere like here again? Got to try, right?"

They clinked to that too, and chatted about the market until the starters came.

"So, no more bucket list tasks," Charlie said, tucking into his ... he didn't quite understand what he'd been served. In his haste to appear decisive, he'd only read as far as fritters, imagining a school-dinners fried splat of something. This was some deep-fried stuffed flower. Becca was marvelling over it, so he pretended it was exactly what he'd expected. Sneaking a look at another table, he discovered how best to dissect and eat it, finding the flavours were incredible. Becca raved about her smoked salmon with pear puree.

"Strange, isn't it?" Becca said, thinking about it. "I think we did her proud in the end."

"Despite the challenges," he added. Acknowledging that some of it hadn't been easy seemed fair.

"Despite the challenges," she concurred. They both reached for their glasses and found there was little in them. They'd been agreeing and clinking to all sorts. Charlie signalled another round to the waiter, giving scant thought to the speed at which they were drinking, on very little food. They were in the South of France, sitting outside, in April, not shivering, and laughing at each other's observations from the show, and frankly it was the best time he'd had in ages. "I think it helped," she said, turning her glass by its stem. "The tasks pushed us through the grieving process. I read a book on it," she added, as if he'd question her view. "You can't hide from grief, it's *in* you. You have to accept it and accommodate it to work through it."

That sounded plausible. He hadn't been able to outrun it on his travels. Things had only improved when he'd included Ally in his moving on, rather than pushing thoughts of her away. "What'll we do to celebrate her now?" he asked. He couldn't imagine doing this solo now.

"I don't know. I guess, we'll remember her birthday from now on? I'd rather that than her death day." He liked her seeing it as a "we" thing.

"That works. Except for the first one, I've got through the birthdays knowing we had a task coming. Like postponing an event for a day with better weather." He didn't know whether that made sense to Becca, but she was nodding as she stared at her glass. That one birthday of Ally's, when he'd been away, had been a horror and he'd handled it with stupid amounts of Peru's best pisco sours and waking up in a stranger's bed. Someone had once told him, "When you're falling, you sometimes just need somewhere soft to land", and he'd been falling hard.

"I get that," said Becca.

"She would have loved this," he said looking about. "She loved dinners out in warm places." He could talk about her with far more ease now, the sadness of her loss being replaced by a gladness of having known her. Time, the tasks and Becca had got him there.

Becca's smile was small. She'd never had the money to take trips to warmer places while Ally was alive, so hadn't been party to that side of her. He didn't want her to be sad, so added, "Your getting here would've thrilled her, Beej."

She kicked him under the table but he covered his yelp well, and drank some more to look composed.

"Tell me about your lead character."

"Well," said Becca, leaning back in her seat, "it's me."

"Well, duh." He rolled his eyes at her. "That was the point."

"True. But I thought it would be a doddle."

"And it wasn't?"

"No, because I was trying to make her the Becca, or *Fliss* as she's called in this, I dream of being – you know, *cool* – and she just came out contrived and wooden on the page. It took me ages to suss I had to dig deep and put myself, my *real* self, flaws and all, on the page." She leaned in and whispered,

"Guess what, Charlie. I have some flaws when I look hard enough."

"Crikey, who knew?" he said.

"So she's this hot mess," Becca carried on, "who's capable, but hasn't had her chance. That's what I want the message to be, that it isn't always you that's failing, it might just be the wrong timing – you know, planets not aligning – but if you don't stick with it, how can you be there when it's your moment to succeed?"

Watching her speak, Charlie saw she was vastly more assured. Possibly this was the pitching patter she'd been giving the last couple of days, but she knew her work, what it meant, and was proud of it. She wasn't playing a role right now. She didn't need to with him, and the fizz would have been sloughing it off already.

"You been chatting to Valerie lately, by any chance?" he asked.

She tilted her head quizzically. "Only for a brief check-in."

"We met up last week," he said, "now I have time on my hands. We played a round of mini-golf. She is a shameless cheat, by the way."

"You lost?"

"Completely whupped. But like I said, she cheats and I am too much of a gentleman to call her on it."

Becca nodded, appreciating his gracious stance.

"She was talking about the universe sending you what you need when you need it."

"Ah, do you think?" she asked, the scepticism written across her face. "I don't think life owes us anything."

"Oh, no, that wasn't what she was saying, and I agree life

doesn't owe us a thing. This was about being aware of opportunities that come your way and taking them. Not passing them up when the universe sends them in your direction. She was saying luck is often simply spotting a moment, and people who see themselves as 'unlucky' have often just been too blinkered or chicken to grab the chances when they come."

"Now, once I might have said that was a bit too woo-woo for me," Becca said, sweeping her hair over her shoulder, "but as I get older, I think she might be right. I'd written my script and happened to be on Twitter coming back from an audition, and saw a tweet. It wasn't an account I followed, just something someone else had retweeted. Totally random. It mentioned the New Writers scheme and from there I went home, polished my script and knew what to do with it. I would've sat on it for ages if I hadn't seen that tweet. I don't think I'd have given it to Marcia."

"Still with her?"

"I've given her notice. Only a week to go." She mimed huge cheers. "Which explains why she didn't inform me about my arse being on display at an international market."

He couldn't help smiling.

"It's not funny."

"Come on. No one can tell it's you, and," he took a breath, because this could go either way, "it actually looks great." It really had. He'd passed it every time he'd left the building, and he'd admired it each time. Of course he hadn't imagined for a moment it was Becca.

"It's objectification," she said, her mouth pulling taut. Then she released it. "OK, fine. Yes, I'll be calling by their stand tomorrow for any spare posters or flyers. I'll keep them for my grandkids. 'Look, Bonnie and Clyde, this is how firm Nana's bum once was ...'"

Charlie's new Kir Royale shot up into his nose. Becca coolly sipped hers as he sorted himself out.

Their empty plates were swapped for two beautifully presented main courses. Her little cannellonis stuffed with seafood looked amazing, as did his fillet of sea bream. He tucked into the accompanying mash straight off, then realised there was truffle oil drizzled across it. Charlie simply didn't have any appreciation of truffle oil, even though every restaurant in London loved the stuff. He wished he'd studied the menu properly.

"How's the divorce?" Becca asked as she had her first taste. He waited until she reopened her eyes again from the moment of pure ecstasy she'd just had, and her moan of "Oh maan, this is lush." Charlie felt he'd been privy to an intimate awakening and felt a deep pleasure at having witnessed it.

"Divorce is over," he said, trying to scrape any visible oil off his food, but gave up. He was a grown-up and should just eat it.

Her head snapped his way. "Over as in finished and done," he clarified, "not cancelled."

She looked ... relieved? He couldn't quite tell, but she hadn't been expecting a reconciliation, clearly.

"It can be straightforward when you don't have kids," he explained, focusing on his meal, steering clear of her eye contact.

"You gave her everything she asked for, right?"

"Couldn't see the point of a fight."

"She had an *affair*, Charlie," Becca pointed out, sounding exasperated.

"Yeah, but what's the point? Ultimately, she didn't want me, so I'd rather walk away." He shifted in his seat. "I don't think I was the husband she was expecting, and as she said, a quick resolution allows us both to move on."

The ensuing silence forced him to meet her gaze. She didn't look impressed.

"How are your wankpuffins?" he countered.

Her sigh was long and deep. "I've managed to steer clear of them."

She didn't seem happy about it.

"That's good, isn't it?"

"Oh, it is," she conceded, "but celibacy's rubbish. I swear I'm not far off regaining my virgin badge. Someone'll need a can opener to get back in there now." Her expression was one of lament. Charlie didn't understand why he was the one blushing.

They both took a drink, but each of them was immersed in their own thoughts on the matter and the clinking was overlooked.

The rest of the meal passed with chitchat, updates on their mutual friends and general laughter between three more rounds. Charlie considered he might be vaguely drunk now, and while the idea of being in the hall tomorrow with a hangover felt grim, the evening was proving too enjoyable to curb. They split the bill, but stepping back out into the street, Charlie wasn't ready to head up the short distance to his hotel yet.

Becca looked about the quayside, the moored yachts

creaking with the waves, the lines slapping lightly against the masts. The little lights on the mast tops made for makeshift fairylights. "Do cabs stop down this way?" she asked.

"They'll be up by the casino." She looked back up the boulevard, considering the walk. The evening had chilled now, and as they stood there side by side, upper arms touching, his instinct was to sling an arm around her to keep her warm as he escorted her. But the mood of the evening gave him another idea. There were many small bars nearby to offer a cosy digestif.

"Want to get a drink and we'll phone for one?" He pointed towards the little cobbled street that was Rue Saint-Antoine. "There's bars up that way."

"It's too nice to go home already, isn't it?" she said, and slid her hand under his elbow. She was swaying slightly, and he clamped his elbow into his side to keep her attached to him.

They ambled towards the bars, and started the climb of the twisting narrow street, Becca regularly pulling him to a stop, to marvel at the menus outside various small restaurants, mumbling about coming back one day.

Just as Charlie spotted the bar he'd had in mind, they heard shouting and cheering coming from further up, and suddenly a horde of noisy revellers came running down the cobbles. Becca flung herself at him to escape being trampled, just as he pulled her into him for protection. The combined momentum made him stumble backwards, until his back met a stone wall.

"Bloody hell," Becca muttered into his collarbone. She looked up at him, as he looked down to check she was unharmed.

Their noses were only a centimetre apart, their eyes fixed

on each other. Without asking, they ascertained the other was fine and yet their hold on one another held tight. Neither Charlie nor Becca seemed to hear the murmurings emanating from the open restaurant fronts, nor the soft music winding down through the alley.

The only sound they could hear was their ragged breathing underpinned by thumping hearts.

Eyes flitted to lips and back in perfect synchronisation, as did the leaning in, which reduced that centimetre to nothing at all.

Still April 5th
Cannes, France

A stillness settled over them as they fractionally drew apart, vaguely comprehending what they were doing, their gazes locked. Charlie slid his hand up to her face, cradling her cheek and tilting his head as his lips met hers once more. Becca released a light sigh as she gravitated into his hand and kissed him anew. She pressed herself closer to him, her chest into his, his hips into hers, their bodies gaining alertness after the unwinding of dinner. A moan reverberated in her throat, captured by his mouth covering hers. It was the sexiest thing he'd ever heard.

Technically, he'd been here before with her, but like a tourist revisiting somewhere they'd come as a child, there was a joyful déjà vu along with newfound wonder. She wasn't coy – not that he'd expected her to be, this was Becca, after all – she gave as good as she got, exploring his tongue with hers. He felt her left hand slide up between them to grab the front of his shirt in a fist as her right hand mirrored his, cupping his jaw. Sinking into their embrace felt to Charlie as if he'd come home from an endless journey, finding a place that fitted. He could have stood like that for the next week, as he held her tighter and let the kiss blossom into something quite the definition of passionate.

The sound of sniggering caused him to open an eye and see a group of passing teens.

His movement caused Becca to draw back, her breath heavy, which pleased him. His own felt the same, ragged and hitched. Her eyes looked bigger in the glow of the street light. Her smile wasn't her widest, nor her most wolfish, but simple and relaxed; she was happy right here, right now, with him. Ignoring the kids, he focused on her flushed face. He knew where he wanted this to go.

"Don't get a cab, Becca," he said, his voice thick. "I'm five minutes up the hill. Stay." She was still gripping his shirt. He took it as a positive. "It's a long cab ride back to Juan-les-Pins," he added, in case she needed practical reasons. Not all delegates got rooms in town.

"An *expensive* cab ride," she agreed, her eyes dancing with what he took as excitement. Given the imminent possibilities, Charlie had no issue being a cost-saving measure.

He felt his heartbeat rise a notch. He drew her back in, their faces close again. "Extortionate."

Her smile pulled to the side, as if she was weighing it up, but her eyes told him he needn't worry, as did his shirt as she stepped backwards and pulled him along with her, away from the wall and up the cobbled hill.

Racing through the connecting streets and over a taxi-infested main road, Charlie thanked his lucky stars for his sense of direction. His mind was fuzzy with drink and kisses, and getting lost with an erection would have been a nightmare.

They didn't speak, laughing instead every time one pulled the other against a wall and he copped a feel or she demanded another kiss. In the delirious frenzy Charlie became clear of one thing: he had no intention of Becca having the sedate night she'd mentioned.

They managed a *"Merci"* to the hotel concierge, who opened the door for them as they barrelled hand-in-hand towards him, a knowing smile on his face. The elevator up to Charlie's floor was a test of strength, to not hit the Stop button and get down to things there and then, as Becca was immediately in front of him, unbuttoning his shirt.

"What if someone's in the hallway," he muttered into her skin, kissing her neck, getting more and more excited by the increasing purr it elicited from her.

"I'm not stopping to chat," she managed, for which he gave her a little nip to her shoulder, escalating her purr to a growl and in response, him from hard to near desperate.

They tumbled out of the elevator into the thankfully deserted corridor, his chest now on display and his shirt not long for his back.

"I need my key," he rasped.

She waved his key-card in his face. Shoplifting *and* pickpocketing skills? *This woman!*

"Room?" She pulled him towards his door as he almost shouted the numbers.

They banged into it, him covering her body against the woodwork, nuzzling her nape as she had a couple of goes to swipe the key-card whilst also leaning aside to expose more neck to him.

The click of the lock made her turn and drink in his face, his bare chest right up against her, their heavy breathing in time. She gave him a deeply wicked smile as he eased his hips harder against hers, and as they finally fell into the room, she moved her mouth to his ear and whispered, "Got a coin, Charlie? Heads, I'm on top first go; tails, it's you."

"Don't need one," he managed on a ragged breath at her earlobe. "It's 'ladies first'."

"Charlie?"

He heard her voice through his dozy haze. They hadn't managed to draw the curtains last night, and he felt the warmth of Mediterranean daylight on them. It felt like a celestial blessing. Perhaps it was. He glanced at the time on the TV opposite the bed, then closed his eyes again. It was still early, he wasn't late yet.

A smile spread across his face as the night replayed itself. Credit where credit was due, he had to congratulate his inner editor, it was an excellent montage ... or if he was lucky, a great trailer. They had time. Becca had places and moves he planned to revisit.

"That shouldn't have happened." Becca's voice was small and dull, nothing like the excited panting and deliciously high gasps of the night before. Was it weird to want a playlist of those sounds and a loop of her shouting his name? *Was it?* A playlist like that would make his training sessions far more enjoyable. But right now, someone needed reassuring.

"It totally *should*. It was amazing." He rolled towards her and laid his hand flat on her bare stomach. He was up for an encore. Literally. She didn't jump away, but she didn't lean into him either, and it caused him to open his eyes.

Becca was staring at the ceiling.

"Becca?" He stretched to kiss the skin on the curve of her shoulder.

"It was wrong."

"There was nothing wrong about it.. It was..." He considered his word choices and went with "*epic*." The merest hint of a smile crossed her profile as she remembered, but she shook it away. He didn't understand. How could she not be revelling in this? He slid his hand lower, but she drew away this time. Not fully away, but as if she was still processing, needing the space. Charlie propped himself up on his elbow to look at her properly. Her face was a mess of confusion. He needed to get in there fast and curb her thoughts.

"Becca, don't rip this apart. This wasn't a one-night thing. We've got something here. You *know* we have. This was like that time in uni, but with all the extras, all the good contextual stuff. It was fireworks with the full trimmings; the sparklers and the wows."

She said nothing.

"Seriously," he brushed some hair, sweated to her forehead, aside, "don't be having regrets about this. Please don't. We've got something." The relaxed Becca from last night, the Becca without all her defences and shoulder chips, wasn't here now, and he wanted her back.

She sat up and from the edge of the bed started looking for something to cover herself. Her back was just like on the poster, but even better for being real and in his room. Charlie knew he should have his eyes firmly on her head, but *man*, it was hard not to let them roam across all of her. He wished all her scattered clothes would suddenly combust, so he could look at her more. She was stunning.

He reached out his hand to touch her, but Becca moved before his fingertips reached her skin. She picked up his shirt and for a second he thought she would put it on. Naked-Girl-in-Your-Shirt was the second-best thing to Naked Girl.

Apparently she wasn't up for that either, as she dropped it again.

He had to get through to her. He'd fallen asleep with her in his arms, thinking how mad this was, considering where they had started, but how right it felt.

"Talk to me. Don't push me away." He moved to sit on the side of the bed. "Tell me what's going on in your head and we can work this out."

She was muttering to herself now as she found her knickers and started searching for her bra, and he could see by the increasing speed of her movements, the jerkiness, she was getting more and more worked up. "Becca!"

"What would she think, Charlie?" She let the words spill out of her. "I am her best friend, and I've slept with her fiancé."

"We'd done that before," he pointed out.

"Don't!" she snapped. "That was before you met her. That was just a … an accidental shag." She didn't know what to call it, but shook it away. "Whatever. This is different. You *belonged* to her. My being with you is disloyal, it's wrong. What would she think?" Her face was a picture of misery. Loyalty was everything to Becca. He knew that.

He gave her a moment to puff out, then said, as reasonably as he could, "She's gone. She isn't here to think anything. Not about us, or what we do. It's not something she'll ever know."

Becca looked up, appalled, from behind the occasional chair in the corner where she was on all fours retrieving her bra, and Charlie suspected he might have said the crassest thing in all history of crassness, although he wasn't sure *why*. He'd loved Ally and his heart broke when she died, but after his immediate free fall, he'd worked hard to re-establish himself, mend his heart and live again. He could remember her, he could miss her, but he couldn't see the value in shaping his life around her. Setting his life in stone for her wouldn't be a life well-lived. Becca didn't hold the same view, it seemed.

"But *I* know, Charlie," she wailed, holding her hand to her chest. "*I* know. It's on my conscience that I've made a move on the man who was going to be her husband."

"I think it was me who made the first move..." he tried, but suspected it was just semantics. He also chose not to mention he'd been someone else's husband since. It wouldn't help.

"What does it say about me? It looks like I was lurking in the wings, coveting her man."

"No, it doesn't." He was doing his very best not to come across as patronising or dismissive, because if he knew her at all, those things would be incendiary. "What it looks like is two people who've known each other for a long time finding each other. Can't you see that?"

He could see it didn't matter. She wasn't listening, having got herself into a full tornado of guilt. She was still finding items of last night's clothes in various places across the room, hastily shoving them into her bag. He had little time.

"You know nothing about Girl Code. I should be blinkered towards you. I shouldn't find you hot or remotely appealing at all, because you are Ally's." Admittedly, his immediate takeaway from that was she found him hot, something which pleased him on many levels, but he fought to stay focused. "But to have acted on it is unforgivable. Our friends would be disgusted." She looked dismayed and raced to the bathroom, where he heard water splashing and the hiss of his deodorant.

"Our friends won't care. They have their own lives to keep

them busy. They'll be happy if we're happy." Shrin and Ollie would revel in it. They adored a love story.

She shot back out of the bathroom, her eyes wide, her mouth pulled in, in consternation. "*Valerie* would be sickened," she said, changing tack. She was on the back foot, but her point about Valerie was valid.

"I think Valerie would side with me on this. Ally isn't coming back, and you and I could be happy together. I know it's only been one night, that this is just a beginning, but we know each other, *really* know each other, so this isn't an impetuous thing. She'd say it was the universe sending us an opportunity. She'd want us to be happy. And so would Ally."

"You don't know women at all, do you?" she exclaimed, throwing her hands in the air, which he thought was a tad dramatic, but let it pass. "It's not about us being happy. It's about us sticking to the rules. You don't lust over your dead best friend's boyfriend. You just don't." *Lusting*, eh? He'd take that too. He gave himself another mental slap to stay on point.

"So women want other women to be unhappy?" That made no sense to him. Most women he knew seemed quite nice. Well, except for Liv, who'd done a nice line in Ice Cold since she'd left.

"No. As long as you stick to the rules, you can be as happy as you like. But *this*," she pointed between them, "isn't sticking to the rules, and I can't have friends pointing out I've done wrong here. Not when it concerns Ally." She zipped up her bag, and then stared at the door, before unzipping it again, having realised she was in fact still naked, and pulled out knickers, bra, top and trousers, all of which she yanked on at depressing speed. "Contrary to popular opinion, I *do* have a conscience and a heart. And mine," her fingers drifted to her chest, her face truly stricken, "tells me I'm guilty. Ally being dead makes no difference at all."

Becca sighed and her tone dropped to something more managed.

"Charlie, you're always happy to be led by the moment, going with the flow, because then you don't need to make decisions. Well, this isn't one of those moments. Us doing this isn't just something to go along with. There are ramifications, and in this case they're too big." She made a swift scan of the room, noticeably avoiding him – or his, for the record, *hot* body – and then headed for the door. "I can't do this."

The door slammed behind her and he was left there, not quite in silence as the hum of morning traffic drifted up from outside, a sign of life going on, while inside, in the sex-messed room, Charlie felt his world had come to a standstill again.

———

Charlie sat in his seat, practising what he was going to say. He'd spent all day on the stand and in the cab to Nice going over it, laying out the logic, role-playing her counter-arguments in his head, finding solutions and answers for all of them.

He hadn't expected her to come and see him, but he knew they were on the same flight home, so he'd planned to talk to her at the gate. Maybe he did go with the flow as she suggested, but perhaps that was him being forward-looking in life, whereas she was fettered to the past in many ways. She might be happier if she tried a forward approach; he just needed to get her to see it and give them a chance.

But she hadn't appeared at the gate either, and here he was in his seat, watching each passenger as they boarded, and she was cutting it bloody fine now.

The woman in the aisle seat next to his stowed her luggage and clearly noted his checking the door, which must have looked, he realised, like a meerkat checking the lie of the land. She sat and smiled as she buckled up.

Charlie checked his watch again. He doubted Becca would be shopping in the terminal, he'd seen the prices. Although, she could be mooning over the bumbags in Versace…

Maybe she just needed time and space to cool off. It was obviously a bit of a shock to her, this thing between them. In a way it was to him too, and yet also *not*. It wasn't one of those "How in hell did this happen?" shocks, more a "Why didn't we spot this before?". They'd been on decent terms for the last few years. He'd actually been looking forward to seeing her last year until she sprang the tandem on him, and even that had turned out well. He'd thought about her most of the way home, the things she'd said, the laughs they'd had despite the cycling. Unless he was mistaken, he believed she'd felt the same, although it would have killed her to admit it. They might rub each other up the wrong way at times, but they rubbed *along* too. They worked. He could see it, even if she couldn't.

Would Ally have minded? He could never know, but she'd told him to be happy. They'd both known she'd meant with another partner, someday. He'd already been through this thought process regarding Liv. Ally'd said his arms were too good not to hold someone else. And she hadn't said, "Just don't let it be anyone I know", or "Except with Becca" or anything like that. Ally was generally pretty specific. His conscience was clear.

Looking again towards the front of the plane, he strained to see her bundle through the cabin door as it closed. But she didn't. Damn. Then, as the crew were closing the luggage bins his phone vibrated with a message.

Took the earlier flight

I can't do this, Charlie

I don't want to talk about it

Let's say it never happened

He sat, stunned. The flight attendant had to ask him twice to switch the phone to flight mode. She'd left. She'd run away. She wasn't even willing to discuss it.

All his arguments were futile, if she wanted to forget the whole thing happened. He wasn't even sure how you could do that. Most of last night was indelibly seared into his brain. When he closed his eyes, he could see stills of them together, and he wasn't willing to expunge them. But she was pretty clear she didn't want this. Or him.

He was used to things being all or nothing with Becca, she wasn't a grey areas kind of girl, but he'd hoped they could at least get to a "let's take it slow" arrangement. He hung his head. She knew he'd respect her request. He wasn't that guy who didn't take no for an answer, who'd decide to wear her down until she finally caved. She knew that. She didn't know how much it hurt him, though. She couldn't see the amazing chance she was passing by, because he felt in his heart that this could have been more than epic.

"Are you OK?" He flung his head back up. The woman in the next seat was looking at him, concerned. He must have appeared broken. Her warm brown eyes were searching his face. "Are you scared of flying?"

"Oh, no," he said, shaking his head. "Just had some crappy news." He thought that covered it quite well.

"Oh, I'm sorry." She seemed genuinely sympathetic. He tucked the phone into his pocket. He didn't need random people seeing him being dumped by text. "First time to MIP?" she asked, pointing to the lanyard he'd forgotten to pocket. She was trying to take his mind off things. How kind. She could so easily have returned to her magazine, having ascertained he wasn't about to throw a hooley and endanger everyone on the flight.

"Ah, yes. I left in a rush to get here," he said, removing the lanyard and pushing out a laugh, to show her he was fine, absolutely fine, no need for concern.

"Good show for you?"

"I was helping a mate. Manning the front desk. Sounds like the company had a good one." James had seemed buoyant as he'd shaken Charlie's hand and sent him off. "And you?" he asked out of politeness. Now she'd started things, there was some etiquette to follow.

"Yeah, not bad," she said, thinking about it first. "It's

exhausting though, running between all the meetings, sitting through a million pitches."

"Oh, you're a buyer. Nice." He definitely thought that would be the better side to be on. "And yes to the exhausting. I've been standing up for a week and now I want to lie down for the next."

"Ha! Yes. I guess I get out and about," she conceded, "but I have to suffer lots of lunches, drinks parties and dinners." She was kidding now, he could see that.

"Ah well, you see, there I have the real luck, having lived on under-done, over-priced paninis." She pulled a sad face. "Bought a lot of programmes then, did you?" He was interested now. Programmes selling was good for the industry, and he'd be knocking on doors next week.

"Mmm," she said with a nod, tucking a lock of her curly brown hair behind her ear, "but I'm more of a commissioner and I didn't quite find the perfect thing."

She was about his age and he was impressed she'd got to this level already. His own career floundering didn't help. He determined to level-up on the job-hunting, starting tomorrow.

As the plane took off, Charlie found he was, in fact, happy to chat. She was funny and observant. It was a two-hour flight, and he didn't fancy reading his book. It was a non-fiction account of a massacre, and he'd had enough slaying for today.

There was something familiar about her, something he couldn't quite put his finger on, both visually and in her ease of conversation. She seemed friendly, so why not immerse himself in chatter to push all thoughts of Becca out of his head? Call it self-preservation or mental health care, call it denial if being harsh, he was simply going with his instinct. After the previous night he was beginning to buy into the whole "The universe sends you what you need" thing, so he plumped for thinking maybe this fellow passenger wasn't someone he should ignore.

"I'm Charlie," he said.

"I'm Alison," she said, stretching out her hand to him. "But call me Ali."

Taking it and shaking it was as easy as breathing. He knew a heaven-sent opportunity when he saw one.

2017: Summer

Tuesday 20th June
North London

I t didn't take long before Becca saw Charlie was right.

Valerie was, just as he'd said, a filthy and brazen cheat. She'd suggested a round of mini-golf after their tea and cake in the park café, and Becca, not having cast off her competitive streak, wanted to score a point against Charlie by not being whupped by the older woman.

At first the play had seemed perfectly honest, although Valerie had been particularly keen to manage the scorecard, and from what Becca could see they were standing pretty even. Then on the seventh hole, where the challenges were getting harder, Becca had taken four attempts to get through the base of the windmill, whereas Valerie had practically dribbled the ball up to it and through, clearly confusing golf with hockey. Becca had stood slack-jawed waiting for Valerie to acknowledge it, but she hadn't and Becca found herself incapable of raising the issue. Charlie would have encountered the same impediment – you just couldn't be mean to Valerie. Her innocent face and childlike glee at being ahead did not allow for invoking international mini-golf regulations.

"Cheer up, Becca," Valerie said, "the next hole might be better for you."

Becca was regretting having agreed to this, but with the bucket list complete, she'd determined to make sure she still saw Valerie around this time of year, though not specifically on the anniversary of Ally's death. That said, the day itself had still made her sad. She'd listened to Ally's voicemails, as she did every year with a large glass of red wine, only this year she'd found herself scrolling to find Charlie's number after. Her thumb had hovered over the dial button. He too must feel something about the day. He understood. She wanted to talk about it, but, given what had happened in Cannes, Becca felt that was closed to her now. She'd switched off her phone and thrown it across to the other end of the sofa, out of temptation's way.

Becca teed off neatly, the ball landing at the edge of the moat in front of the miniature castle that homed the hole. She aimed to chip it over the water, but just as she swung Valerie said loudly, "Mind the squirrel!"

She fluffed the shot. The ball dropped into the moat with a neat plop.

Looking around, there was no squirrel, nor any rustling. Valerie gave her an innocent smile and a "Speedy little buggers, aren't they?"

Becca retrieved her ball and replaced it where it had been, and carried on with the game, suspiciously wary of "squirrels". The ball crossed the moat, Becca blocking out Valerie's noisy shuffling, and stopped a foot from the castle keep and its hole within. It should have been a cinch, but Valerie timed her question of "Have you seen Charlie?" to perfection and Becca's shot missed the doorway, bounced off the wall and rolled back towards the moat, where it teetered on the edge before Valerie's excessive stomping "to get a better look", dropped it over with another mocking plop.

"Oh dear, darling," soothed Valerie, "Charlie had difficulty with this hole too."

As she fished the ball out for the second time, Valerie stuck with the one subject Becca wished to avoid.

"Did you know he went to Cannes this spring? In the South of France? *That* Cannes." Oh yes, Becca was aware. "And the most amazing thing happened."

Oh shit. He wouldn't have told her, would he? A film of sweat instantly appeared on Becca's neck.

"He met a lovely woman..." Valerie prattled on and Becca thought this teasing was most unlike her and slightly cruel, "... a commissioner lady on his plane home, from one of the big channels, and do you know, he pitched her a programme idea – about navigating Central America by coin-toss, just him and a cameraman – right there on the plane, and she loved it. They spent the rest of the flight discussing how it would work as a series and he wrote the proposal when he got back and she commissioned it a week later. Isn't it amazing?" Becca was indeed amazed. And stunned, in a punch-to-the-chest way. The sweat on her neck chilled. Valerie's face, however, shone with delight for him, and Becca couldn't help but forgive her her cheating ways, knowing Valerie was truly thrilled for Charlie. She'd glowed the same way when she'd told her *Hot Mess* had been picked up.

"And that he took the chance," she gushed on. "So unlike him, isn't it? The Charlie we know likes to see what comes, doesn't he? But in this case he grabbed his moment. I'm so proud of him. They're about to start filming in Belize." She stopped to take a breath, but it became a sigh as she said, "He's such a lovely man," and gave Becca an intense look. No doubt she was lamenting Ally not having had a life with him, and not having him as a son-in-law. Becca felt even more awful for what she'd done and focused on the astro-turf.

Along with the guilt, she felt a pang of sadness for not having heard his good news. She was delighted for him; for getting himself a job, having the nuts to pitch his programme, and his idea becoming a reality. But also, just as he'd kicked her to write her script, she'd pushed him to put himself forward, and now she'd have liked the chance to celebrate his success. Only she'd put paid to that, hadn't she?

She'd said she didn't want to talk about it, and then she'd swerved his innocuous messages, even the birthday text he'd sent her. He'd given her her space, quelling all communications after a while, sticking purely to the parameters of being her landlord. That had been an initial worry – he could have evicted her if he'd felt inclined, but she also knew that wasn't his way. He wasn't vindictive. Nor had he turned up on her doorstep. That wasn't his way either, maybe to his detriment sometimes. He was respectful of people's wishes, and had the situation been different she might have been kicking his arse with chants of "Fortune favours the brave", but thankfully, in this case, when she was the object of his affections, he was reverting to his normal passive form. And after all, if he hadn't fought for his marriage, he wasn't likely to fight for her...

The worst thing was, though, while she knew she'd done the right thing regarding them as a couple, she really missed him, right to the bone.

Becca kept her head down, focusing on getting the ball in the hole, blocking out Valerie's series of sighs. She disregarded

Valerie not counting her own air shots or penalty shots, willing the conversation to move on.

"I was hoping you'd both do me a favour, Becca." Valerie rested her putter against her leg and delved in her pocket, pulling out a familiar-shaped purple bottle. Becca looked at it with dismay. "I've got just one bottle of ashes left, and I think it's time to let it go."

"You don't want to keep one?"

Valerie shook her head. "It's for the best."

They'd completed all of Ally's tasks, so this one was for Valerie, which made it impossible to say no.

"Is it a big task?" Becca asked weakly. She couldn't decide whether she wanted it to be or not. A major endeavour could keep them occupied and off the difficult subjects, but it might also throw them together more than was tenable. A simple task, something to complete swiftly with minimal contact, might be a blessing.

"It's to go back to uni and scatter her by your tree." On the face of it, it *was* a simple task, no prepping, training or expenditure required. By her reckoning, it could be over in five minutes; arrive, scatter and goodbye. And then that could be it. For real this time, because in the last months since Cannes, Becca had reached a tit-punching conclusion: that seeing him on a friends basis would be too hard.

She *had* seen him, just the once, since Cannes.

She'd come from a lunch with her BBC mentor and, waiting for her tube, saw him on the opposite platform. His head was down as he perused his phone, but she'd have recognised his frame, his stance, his tousled hair anywhere. She was immediately torn: should she send a spooky "I can seeee yoou" text or hurl herself across the rails to surprise him with a loud "Boo!"? Her instinctive grin dropped as she realised she could do neither. She couldn't joke around with him anymore (legalities of crossing live rails notwithstanding). Calling his name seemed out too, after having blanked his communications. Instead, she stood forlornly staring at him, willing him to sense her and look up. She wanted to see his face properly; she hoped he would send her a smile. And it was at *that* point she'd recognised, to her abject dismay, that aside from missing him, his company, his laugh, his body, she actually *craved* him in a way she could only suspect was love. Since then she'd cried off from nights out with Shrin and Ollie where he might appear, for the simple reason that there was nothing worse in this world, other than your best friend's death, than carrying an impossible love for another.

"Would that be all right? On her birthday?" Valerie prompted.

It *sounded* so simple, yet in reality, this was no mean feat. It would require nerves of steel and a steady resolve not to fling herself at him.

Valerie was sending them back to their roots, back to where it all began, where they were their unsettled and unlikely trinity. Becca understood it, she honestly did; Ally had loved her uni years, and it made perfect sense Valerie would want some of her resting there. But she was asking far more of them than she could know, unaware she was reiterating the very point of their current difficulties. Taking them back to where Ally had been the heart of things was tantamount to a huge STOP sign at the junction.

She gave Valerie a weak smile which the older woman took

as agreement. Becca could only stare at the bottle, feeling guilt and shame rising in her, until they reached her head, which promptly turned hot. She fought hard to curtail her need to blurt out what had happened. Just as she was about to cave, she saw a brief glimpse of worry on Valerie's face as she looked at the bottle.

Becca felt even guiltier now. She'd never really spared a thought for how Valerie felt about Ally steadily vanishing from her. If it was the last time, then the urn on the mantelpiece must be empty.

"Do you mind, Valerie? About the ashes being scattered near and far?"

Valerie fixed her with her lovely blue eyes and a wan smile.

"It's what she wanted, isn't it? It brings me joy, you and Charlie doing the tasks. It keeps her memory alive. When I'm gone, who else will be there to remember?" Becca could only nod. If Valerie could give away what she had left, then Becca could definitely put her feelings aside and carry out the task. It was time to don her big girl's pants and face Charlie. She was sure he'd want to talk about "them" and if that was what he needed, then fair enough. She just hoped it would go better than their "facing things" on the gin bus.

She told herself she could do this, and Valerie need never know the more lurid details of what transpired.

Becca stepped up to the final hole, a labyrinth which required hitting walls at exact angles to bounce the ball onto the next stage. Trigonometry hadn't been her forte at school.

"So, what have you been up to?" she asked, keen to change the subject. Valerie gave her a speedy rundown of her recent activities: the lunch club, art courses and lawn bowls. Valerie's face blossomed to a shade of cerise when she added she was ballroom dancing too. If not for the vivid pinkness, Becca would have simply thought it lovely she'd expanded her social life. But there was unmistakable blushiness and none of those clubs were particularly sources for embarrassment.

"Valerie?" she asked. "Are you being wooed?"

Valerie's hue deepened to flaming, and she got quite fidgety, blustering, "Well, I, well…" before finally settling for a positively coy "Yes."

At last, it was teenage Becca's chance to turn the tables, and with a huge grin she exclaimed "Dish it!", taking the moment to drink from her water bottle as she listened, rapt, to Valerie's news.

"His name is David, he's a widower." Valerie's face glowed as she shared the details, and it made Becca's heart swell. Valerie deserved to have someone in her life, someone to care for her. "He's wonderful on his feet," Valerie said, quite swoony. Becca batted away an image of him in an open shirt, spray-tanned and with a medallion, just as Valerie leaned forward and added, "and he's lots of fun in bed, too." Becca only just managed not to spray her water across the entire ninth hole. There was now a competition for who was most pink-faced.

"That's wonderful," she stammered, more about the relationship than about the sex, but then again she was chuffed for Valerie there too. She might have gone decades without.

"How's the writing?" Valerie asked, her turn to change the subject. The question made Becca positively beam.

"Not bad." Becca checked herself. She was downplaying it again and she shouldn't. She was learning that in the corridors of television you needed to flag your successes. Being humble about your talent in the hope someone higher up would like you more didn't work; they'd just forget you. She was constantly asking herself, would a bloke give the modest response she had, or would they be grabbing the acclaim? She needed to laud her work; it was brilliant and "relevant", as they kept telling her, and it had brought her to a new conclusion that people could take her or leave her, she had something audiences wanted, so she'd be fine. "Actually, it's going really well. The first episodes are getting great reviews and the top secret news is, they want another series."

After Valerie had released her from her immediate hug, they spent the next few minutes discussing her ideas for series two, of which she had plenty. She'd lived through more disastrous auditions, dates and flats than seemed fair for one person, and she wasn't above using all of it. She was barely remembering to change names to protect the not-so-innocent, and herself from lawsuits.

"I'm so proud of you, Becca. I truly am," Valerie said, thrilled. "You've not had it easy, but look at you now. You're a fighter and should be very proud of yourself, too."

Becca's face suddenly felt pinched as her nose and eyes seemed to contract and sting. A lump in her throat made it even more uncomfortable. She couldn't recall anyone saying anything like that to her. Not even Ally had got to be proud of her. It was almost overwhelming as she allowed herself the thought that yeah, she'd weathered some shit, but she was still standing and more to the point, standing tall. Seeing her predicament, Valerie gave a small laugh and pulled Becca in for another hug.

"And now," said Valerie, "you need someone to share it with. Life is far more fun that way." Becca pulled away from her to see Valerie's gleaming eyes. "You deserve someone lovely."

The chink in the dam finally yielded to the pressure. Becca's face twisted before a shuddering sob broke free from her.

"Darling, what is it?" Valerie dragged her back in and rocked her with soothing sounds. Becca threw all dignity to the wind and let herself be completely and utterly babied.

"Have you just broken up with someone?" Valerie ventured.

"Sort of," Becca managed.

"A boyfriend?"

Becca shook her head.

"A married man?" Valerie didn't sound happy. Becca shook her head violently. "Someone else's boyfriend?" Becca was a bit stuck there. It all felt so complicated.

No matter how much she'd tried to square it with herself, to convince herself it was all right, the shadow of guilt always descended on her. And then it festered there, bubbling in her gut, telling her she was a bad person, a disloyal friend and all-round skank.

Valerie had apparently watched something on basic psychology, or perhaps a crime interrogation show, and opted to stay silent until Becca couldn't stand it any longer and fessed up.

"Me and Charlie." Valerie's embrace got ever so slightly tighter but she remained silent, which was excruciating. Again Becca felt compelled to continue. "I was in Cannes too. We got close." Becca really didn't think Valerie should hear the detail.

There were limits to what the mother-of-your-dead-best-friend needed to know about you boffing her almost-son-in-law. Becca could do tact if she had to. Becca extricated herself from the hug, knowing she had to face whatever Valerie threw at her. Actions had consequences, especially the madder ones, and Becca knew to take them on the chin.

She held Valerie's forearms and, looking deep into her eyes, said earnestly, "I'm sorry. These tasks, they've been very emotional. They've sort of brought us closer without us knowing it, and it just happened." Valerie moved to speak, but Becca cut her off, keen to say what she now needed to and hopefully salvage what she could of this relationship. "But I *have* ended it, Valerie. You need to know that. I did it as soon as I got my head together and Charlie's very clear about it. I've minimised all contact with him since. So, once this task is over, then that'll be it, and that's fine." She nodded saying it, hoping it would convince both of them, but the wobble in her voice on *fine* didn't help. "I should never have allowed it to happen, not with Ally's fiancé, and I hope you'll accept my apology." Her lungs were hurting; she was almost out of breath from having unloaded it all, whilst also holding what breath she had left for Valerie's reaction. She'd simply have to accept whatever anger or punishment Valerie meted out.

Despite remaining silent, Valerie's face had been a fast-shifting tide of expressions during Becca's unburdening. And oddly, it had been working in opposite ways to Becca's expectations. When she'd said the tasks had brought them closer, Valerie's eyes had lit up and her smile spread. When she assured her the ... the ... whatever it was was over, Valerie's face had been confused and then dropped as if she'd heard her cat had died. It was all topsy-turvy and Becca wondered whether Valerie's comprehension was delayed, working one answer behind the actual question, like an out-of-synch interview.

"But you're *supposed* to get together with Charlie!" Valerie bemoaned. She cupped Becca's cheek and said, "You're supposed to get together and *stay* together."

Wait, what?

"What do you mean?" It wasn't the first time she'd doubted Valerie's mental faculties.

"It's what the tasks were all about. Making sure you still saw each other, showing you you were a good team, showing you you could be happy together."

Becca felt her world tip on its axis. This was the most surreal thing she'd heard in ages – and she worked in Entertainment, which was generally bonkers.

Becca gave Valerie's upper arm a gentle rub. "Valerie, that makes no sense." She deliberately spoke gently and slowly. "Charlie was her fiancé."

"And you were her best friend," Valerie said.

Ah, she saw. It sounded so simple, and yet. "Life doesn't work that way. Two people having a mutual friend doesn't make them a match. Charlie and I definitely don't match."

Valerie shook her head with a little smile. "Ally was wiser than that. She watched you, she was sure it could work."

Becca still couldn't believe this. "You can't just hand one person over to another. Charlie and I have nothing in common. We certainly didn't back in those days."

"Which she knew," Valerie agreed. "She knew you'd need

to see it in your own way." Delight filled her face, her eyes positively dancing. "And she was right."

Becca shook her head; this was madness. Six years they'd been doing this, and supposedly it was now all some master plan. She slammed on the brakes. "I'm sorry, but no. Things weren't great between Charlie and I in our uni years and that didn't change when she was dying, either."

"Not true," insisted Valerie, but kindly, "she saw you hugging." Valerie was adamant, and weirdly she didn't seem about to tear Becca's head off for it.

"What? No. When?" Becca had made a point of never touching Charlie if she could possibly help it. Hugging would have been a no-no. Unless... A vague foggy memory leaked into her mind. Valerie saw it coming, nodding it along in encouragement.

"That day she told you there was only palliative care left? She left the room to get a bottle of gin for you all to commiserate with and when she came back, Charlie was holding you in a hug."

"We were *devastated*, Valerie." Becca remembered the day, if not particularly the hug, as the world had gone into gloopy slow-motion when Ally had laid "It's terminal now" on them. "We were both in tears. Ally'd had time to process it, but we were both in shock. It was more propping each other up than hugging. There definitely wasn't anything untoward going on."

"Of course there wasn't. Ally knew that. She could see it for what it was. The two of you clung to each other like you had no one else, which in many ways you didn't, but she saw you could care for each other, look after each other *and* love each other."

Becca's chest was still feeling quite empty of breaths. This wasn't how she'd expected this to go at all, but it also had her baffled. "But the bucket list ..."

Valerie suddenly became quite officious. "Completely legitimate, those were all things she would have liked to do." Her expression softened, to something of kindness but also a smidge of pride. "And she knew they were what you needed."

What you needed. The sentence hung in the air around Becca and it bugged her. This was all so surprising, and shocking, and strange. And yet, there was something also niggling in the back of her head saying it was manipulative and underhand too.

Valerie however was positively joyous. "You see she was right, don't you? The two of you should be together."

"But he's Ally's..." was all she could mumble dumbly, her mind whirring inside her head. She wanted to leave. She wanted to be anywhere but here, somewhere quiet where she could process.

"No, darling," Valerie said softly, "they weren't meant to be." Her eyes were sad, but the look on her face said she'd made peace with it. "Ally wanted what's best for you. He's what you want. You have her blessing. Find him, be together." She spoke like this was a done deal, simply because Ally had decreed it.

Becca felt wooden. She supposed she should be jumping for joy, but instead there was a violent mix of emotions going on inside her; one side was shouting she'd needlessly thrown away something potentially brilliant, something she needn't feel ashamed or guilty about, but there was a simmering roar behind that, a roar which was steadily increasing to an angry roil, which had her head aching; it hadn't been real. It was all orchestrated and planned. It hadn't been the real deal, they'd been played, and she'd been right to call a halt to it all along.

On autopilot, she looked towards the park gates.

"I've got to go," she said, her voice void of expression because she would never ever shout at Valerie, and right now she distinctly needed to shout at someone. Loudly and extensively.

Valerie nodded enthusiastically, "That's right, darling. Find him. Tell him how you feel and sort this out." Valerie was almost clapping her hands in glee, obviously imagining some airport "chase and declaration" scene. Becca's version of imminent events was Becca, solo, under her duvet with minimal energy involved.

Pressing her lips tight together, in case she gave air to her thoughts, she simply nodded. Valerie patted her hand. "Goodness, Becca, you're looking quite pale. Don't worry, darling. It's *Charlie*. It'll be fine."

She almost made it to the gate before Valerie stopped her. Becca was desperate to be away. She needed somewhere to think. Somewhere to go over it all, all the tasks, everything they'd done, to see if she could unbraid it all and work out what was Ally, what was them and what was true.

"Haven't you forgotten something?" Valerie said. Becca pulled up. Of course. She spun around and gave Valerie a quick hug.

"Thanks for the coffee and cake." She tried hard for it not to sound robotic.

"Don't be silly," Valerie laughed. "I'm always happy to feed you cake. I meant, you've forgotten this." She held out the glass bottle. Becca didn't want to touch it. Her following performance as she laughed and said, "Doh! What am I like?" was Oscar-worthy.

It was in her bag, out of her hands, within seconds. For the first time ever, Becca didn't want Ally near her.

2017: Autumn

S torm Aileen had been a doozy. Becca remembered it clearly; she'd been huddled on the sofa that night two weeks before, in full-on cocoon-mode with her duvet, trying to concentrate on composing, deleting, composing and deleting the text to Charlie about the final ashes, while Netflix bingeing. She'd seen enough daytime dramas where closure was the endgame to know she needed some for herself. She could complete her commitment to Ally and Valerie and be done. She'd face Charlie, say goodbye and also be done. And that accomplished, she would stop thinking about him all the bleeding time.

Three months on and even after her initial fury, which involved copious amounts of wine and venting, she was still seething at Ally's scheming. She'd had the time to forensically play back every task with Charlie, finding herself smiling at small moments they'd had and then meticulously dissecting each for what she thought Ally was trying to achieve. The end result was the same each time: any good thing they'd experienced now felt shrouded with doubt. It was confusing, because when your mind constantly wandered to a particular face, or to a particular laugh which for some reason meant more to you than any other, remembering it had all been a set-up spoiled everything.

Just like in a suspense film, Storm Aileen had been a portent. Becca's doorbell had rung, and waddling to answer it, still wrapped in her duvet, she found her mother standing outside. Becca faced the dilemma of asking her mother in – a bristling thought – or leaving a fellow human out in a storm. It was a toughie.

"Well?" her mother demanded, as if Becca's parents hadn't brought her up to show proper hospitality, and Becca was inclined to leave her out there, because they definitely hadn't.

The dripping of Stella's raincoat hem showed she'd been out in this for a while, and it occurred to Becca she must really need to see her. Becca turned and waddled back into the flat, but left the door open for her mother to follow.

Ditching the duvet, Becca set the kettle boiling. Thankfully, the place wasn't a mess. Annoyingly, she found cleaning, washing up and ironing helpful with sorting the plot points in her scriptwriting. Why couldn't it have been watching box sets, eating chocolate and long baths? Still, she now had the glory of appearing to have her life together as Stella gave it the once over.

"Nice." It sounded begrudged.

Becca dropped two tea bags in two mugs. She wasn't offering choices tonight. She felt a strong need to stay in control of this, even though the howling winds outside didn't bode well.

She hadn't seen her mother since May, when they'd buried her nan in the most minimal of funerals. Becca had believed it was only men who died in the throes of sex, but apparently not. Wilma had been hit with a colossal heart attack in bed with the Bingo man. Both Becca and Stella had pragmatically agreed – possibly the first time ever, *on anything* – that there were worse ways to go.

Teas made, Becca handed one to her mother and nodded

for her to take a seat on a bar stool. Sharing the sofa would be too cosy, and Becca preferred the breakfast bar between them. Not expecting this to be a long visit, she settled against the kitchen units and gave Stella a "So?" look.

"The solicitor stuff is finished. I signed the papers."

"OK," Becca said. She'd guessed there'd be some inheritance from Wilma, but Stella had been cagey about it. In a fit of altruism, she'd texted asking whether Stella wanted help clearing the place, but got a swift "Not yet" in response, and that was it. Not long ago, Becca would have been desperate enough to ask whether there was any money coming her way, but not now.

Stella was still looking about the place, and while Becca liked her appreciating the things she'd been able to buy recently – plants, new cushions, pointless but cool nick-nacks – her focus was more on Stella looking anywhere but at her. That had always been the case. Becca wondered whether it was yet another reason she wanted to be on screen. She had a deep hunger to be seen.

"I'm moving to Spain," Stella announced.

"Riiight," Becca said. As far as she was aware, Stella had no connection to Spain, but then Stella could have travelled to Timbuktu annually and Becca wouldn't have known. It wasn't like they talked.

"I've had enough of this miserable weather, I'm going to run a bar with a music licence, so I can sing." Heaven help the punters. Becca had not inherited her singing talents from her mother. Which reminded Becca that Stella hadn't yet mentioned her TV success. The first series was up for Best Comedy at the TV-UK Awards.

"OK," Becca said again. Had it been a mate, she would have been raving with excitement or trying to have a sensible chat about the pros and cons, depending on which of her friends had come up with the idea, but with Stella she felt no compulsion to do either. Stella wouldn't give two hoots what she thought. Unlike the singing, Becca's stubborn streak might, she conceded, have come from her mother.

"I fly out tomorrow." Oh, so this was goodbye. She felt vaguely surprised and slightly touched Stella was doing it in person.

Stella rummaged in her handbag, pulled something out and slid it across the countertop.

It was a bundle of keys.

"To Wilma's," Stella said, nodding at them. It looked like there were three sets of every key on the rammed keyring. "Her set, the spare set, my set and you have your set."

Wow. Becca was stunned. Wilma only had the one child so the house would have passed directly to Stella, unless her nan had willed it to the cat just to spite them, which was entirely possible. Becca had thought there might perhaps be some savings, where Stella might give her a token gesture, but the house? OMFG! It was an ugly little place, albeit on the end of a decent street, and hadn't had any modernisation since Wilma bought it, but having lived there, Becca knew exactly what changes she'd make to update it.

She looked at Stella and felt her eyes well up. After so many years of not giving her any attention, or love, she was now giving her a house.

"I … I don't know what to say," Becca began, then started with basics. "Thank you." It felt weird saying that to her mother. She couldn't remember having done so in years. Stella frowned at her. Becca quickly rubbed her eyes, both of them obviously embarrassed by her getting emotional.

"For the keys? Well, how else are you going to get in? The house needs clearing by next Friday, so you can get an estate agent in for pictures and the place on the market the following week. They'll need all the keys when you're done."

Becca's face froze and then her jaw tossed itself towards the floor.

"Is there a problem, Becca-Jayne? You offered to sort the place."

Still stunned, and filling with mortification, Becca could only mumble, "I ... I mean yes, I offered to help ... but I thought..."

Stella stared at her and then twigged. "What, you thought I was giving you the house?" She laughed. "Seriously? I need the money for my bar. You'll have to wait for me to croak before you get yours." Becca didn't hold much hope for her mother's business success; she didn't speak Spanish and had as little ear for languages as she did for music, but right now it was the "Stella croaking" thing she was wishing for. God, she felt so stupid. *Of course* Stella wasn't giving her the house. She felt her face flame and wished for the storm to rip through the flat right that instant.

Stella took a second mouthful of her tea and got off the stool. "Look, I'm not unreasonable, we can split whatever you get for the stuff, so it's up to you whether you can be arsed to eBay it, or just get someone in for the lot. I don't care." No, she really didn't. She never had.

Becca moved towards the door, wanting Stella gone and not

giving a crap whether she was sending a fellow human out into a sixty-miles-an-hour storm. She couldn't help but ask though, "You didn't want to keep the house?"

"What for? I hated living there," her mother said, digging out a B&H.

"Then why'd you send me to live there?" It tore out of her.

Stella sighed. "Fuck sake, not this again." Becca gaped at her, but Stella went on. "Get over it. There's no one like you to hang onto a grievance. You'd be happier if you let things go and brushed the chip off your shoulder."

"And there's no one like you to belittle other people's hurts, Mum. Especially a child's. You are fucking brutal."

Her mum's brow twitched together, then released. "We did what we thought was best." She wasn't trying to soothe Becca, and her defensive approach didn't seem the least bit concerned with what Becca thought. "You just didn't like it," Stella concluded.

"You could have asked me," Becca said, her hands curling into fists and feeling every bit a child again.

Stella rolled her eyes at that, which piqued Becca even more. "You were nine and in a bitchy phase. Although," she gave Becca a quick once-over, "I'm not sure you've ever come out of it. You'd have disagreed with everything we suggested. Your dad and I couldn't stand the sight of each other, there was no money coming in and I was young. You can blame me for everything that's ever gone wrong in your life, Becca-Jayne, suit yourself, but one day when you pop off your high horse, ask yourself what you would have done. You staying with your nan was a sound decision."

But it wasn't about logistics for Becca.

"You didn't *want* me." She put it out there. This was the moment for her mum to deny it, to be horrified this was Becca's perception, to profess her love for her and apologise.

Instead, Stella lit and took a long drag on her cigarette and gave her a hard gaze. "I did what was best for you," she said after taking her sweet time blowing out the smoke.

"Bullshit. It was the best for *you*, being free of me." Becca could feel her heart filling with disappointment, but also with annoyance at herself. None of this was a shocker. She knew Stella wasn't about to surprise her. That would entail having a heart, and she was pretty sure Stella's egg hadn't come with one. "You aren't denying it," Becca added.

With her free hand, Stella opened the door and then braced herself as a gust shot in.

"What difference does it make?" she asked her daughter. "You've already made your mind up about me. But here's the thing: why, then, do you let it affect you so much? Blame me, hate me, whatever. It's on me. So move on and you be you, rather than looking for excuses and not taking responsibility for your own life and happiness."

Becca felt fury rising through her and her mouth opened to unleash it, but her mother's back was already turned and heading away up the path without that goodbye. She was left feeling slapped and reliving the hurt all over again from when she first heard her parents discussing who would, or rather *wouldn't*, take her. But for all the impotent force of it, a small voice in her head was clamouring to be heard; that perhaps it was for the best. Would she really have wanted this woman nurturing her, seeing her through puberty and guiding her to adulthood? For the first time Becca properly understood that she wouldn't, and her waiting for her mother to want her was futile – it would never happen. But more to the point: Becca was here, and doing all right actually, in spite of it. Creasing her face up against the winds, Becca looked out of the door, at the shape of her mother moving further down the street at a brisk pace, certainly not looking back with remorse. Becca drew herself up taller and feeling she'd just learned something, whispered a "Fuck you very much."

Now, two weeks later, in contrasting September sunshine, the memory of Storm Aileen came back to her as she faced the big oak on the university lawn, under the shade of which they had spent so many afternoons. Ally had always sat in the middle holding hands with Charlie, as they leaned against it. The curve of the trunk had meant he wasn't in Becca's eyeline, which had been helpful, but they'd been close enough for conversation, or bickering in their case. So much had changed.

The ancient tree was on its side, a gaping crater cordoned off with hazard tape under the upended root ball. A passing groundsman blamed the storm for having toppled the tree and it was a "bleedin' miracle" the building wasn't hit. She nodded, but without listening, her eyes instead scanning the stricken trunk, the branches and leaves already having been sawn away to reopen a path. It struck her as a metaphor for the three of them.

As the groundsman departed, she stepped closer, estimating where the thing she was looking for might be, wishing hard it wasn't on the underside. The trunk came up to her chest as it lay there, so there'd be no budging it. It had been a decade since she'd last been here, a safe cocoon where they'd learned to adult in a more forgiving environment. The surrounding sounds, of passing students laughing and calling to others, the murmur of the breeze and the birdsong around her, lulled her back into that comfort, as she focused on the rough rivulets of the bark. And there, below an amputated branch, she found it; their initials and the heart they had carved into the wood. So simple then, so complicated now.

Becca climbed up on the trunk. She pulled the purple bottle out of her pocket and sat with it gripped in her hand, not feeling the desire to show it the view as she had with the others. Unable to have it out with Ally, express her fury at her meddling, Becca's only course of punishment was to scatter them without ceremony. She reached to pull out the stopper, scanning the ground for a suitable spot.

"Seriously?" The voice behind her sounded very cross indeed and slightly out of breath from running. "You were going to do this without me? What the hell, Becca?" It cut through her malevolent ponderings, giving her such a shock, she toppled backwards off the trunk, landing on the soft lawn with a thud and an "Ahh fuck".

Charlie stood over her. She took a moment to get her breath back before opening her eyes to look up at him. He wasn't making any effort to pick her up, and that face, even upside down, was like an angry emoji.

"We're supposed to do these together."

"No, that was the tasks," she tried, attempting to get up. "Valerie asked for this as an extra." He still wasn't offering her any help. Well, fair enough. No surprise he was annoyed.

She'd deliberated over the wording of the text about this, but never actually sent anything to tell Charlie what she was planning.

"Bullshit," he snapped. "Imagine my surprise when I called Valerie this morning, and she mentioned us doing this for Ally's birthday."

"*Imagine*," Becca mumbled, on her feet now and brushing herself off. She kept her head down to avoid looking him in the face, unsure she could see it and stay sensible.

She leaned against the tree, arms folded tightly across her chest, then took a deep breath and looked at him, immediately regretting her decision.

Mannnn, she'd missed that face. So badly. She'd even unfolded the photo she had of the three of them on her sideboard, so he was included too, but it wasn't nearly as good as the real thing. His skin was glowing from many weeks in the sun and judging by his toned shape, he hadn't spent them lounging by a pool. Her eyes lingered on the scar on his cheek. *Their* scar...

She noticed his eyes roaming her face too, drinking it in, in the exact same way she was, soaking up the details after their five-month drought. She didn't think she'd changed *that* much, healthier perhaps, having the money to eat better now. As their eyes finally met, she felt her smile twitch at the sides of her mouth, and she believed his was about to do the same, but then he remembered he was cross with her and swiftly abandoned it.

"Why didn't you contact me?"

"Well, I ... um?" She tried different versions, but ultimately they were all fibs, and she didn't fib with Charlie. "I meant to. Truly. I chickened out. I thought this would be too difficult."

He stared at her hard, and she noticed a steeliness to his gaze.

"Well, that's on you." She'd hurt him. It was obvious. But some things in life *did* hurt. She knew all about that.

She didn't appreciate his laying all the blame on her. "Why? Because I was the adult and saw it couldn't work?"

"It could *totally* have worked," he snapped. "But as you insist it can't, I've respected that. You needn't have ignored me completely, though." Yes, well, she *had* done that, she had to admit. Because it was too damn hard to do otherwise and avoiding him had been hard enough. "I can't force you to want me, but I thought we were mates. There's things I wanted to tell you."

"Valerie told me about the commission." That sounded so stingy, but what could she say? "*I know all about your career, I follow you incessantly on Instagram*"?

His mouth was flat. "I'd like to have told you myself."

"It's brilliant though." She wanted to placate him, but it didn't have that effect. They should have been bouncing about in delight. They'd done it, they'd made it happen. But there was no celebration to be had here. Becca felt ashamed for not calling him with congratulations.

There was, however, something he'd said there that she might be able to put right.

"It's not that I don't want you, by the way." Ally's trickery or not, Becca couldn't deny the way she felt towards him. "It just can't *be*."

"Yeah, that's bullshit too," he countered. "You just *won't*. Not the same."

"There's more to it than you know. Things that mean I'm even more right to stop this."

He looked to the sky and laughed mirthlessly.

"What is it you think you've stopped? Me loving you? That's not how that works. Just because you say it can't happen doesn't make it so." He *loved* her. The thought filled her with a warmth she'd not experienced since that night in Cannes. "It's been like when Ally died," he continued, his annoyance building, and while it hurt her to see, she also had a perverse pleasure from it; seeing Charlie get het up about it, about *them*. "I used to 'see' her in places. It drove me mad. Now I see a flash of red hair and think it's you. In a bar, or in a shop or on a passing tube." He'd seen her at the station! She opened her mouth to tell him, but snapped it shut again, because what good would it do? His madness was down to trickery.

"That's not my fault. You don't know the half of it. I'm not the one messing with you."

His eyebrow cocked. "No? How so?"

She hadn't wanted to tell him, because she felt foolish at being duped, and she wanted to spare him that. Better he thought ill of her than his beloved Ally. She hadn't told Shrin, Mags or Tilly for the same reasons. She couldn't talk to Valerie about it either, because Becca wouldn't trash her daughter. But his walking around seeing ghosts again was too much. This was what Ally's meddling caused.

"This is Ally's doing," she stated. He pulled his head back, incredulous. "No, *really*," she insisted. "Look, let's ditch the ashes and I'll explain."

His brow was furrowed at her truculence. Undeterred, Becca unstoppered the bottle and poured the ashes brusquely over the carving in the tree. Charlie watched the ash skitter across the bark, but Becca watched his face, having been starved of it for months.

"There. Now we're done," she said, bitterly.

He considered her warily. "What's going on? Why are you so angry?"

"Because, Charlie, none of this," she waved between their chests, "is real." Even as she said it, it had her confused. Her heart felt his pull, but her brain said not.

"Feels pretty real to me," he said, "though right now I'm plenty pissed off with you."

"Nothing new there," she muttered.

True, he nodded, but without a smile.

"Ally set this all up. The tasks. She had some mad notion we'd be perfect for each other, so she pushed us together. Any feeling we have for each other is down to her scheming."

Charlie looked at her dumbfounded. Well, *exactly*. Becca felt another wave of seething for Ally's audacity.

Watching, she could almost hear the cogs turning as he replayed moments as he tried, tested and double-checked the veracity of what she was saying. He still didn't speak. "Outrageous, isn't it?" she said.

His brow contracted. He was deathly still, save for his eyes which moved steadily between hers. "Seriously?"

Now he was getting it. "I know, right?" she said, nodding.

"But she was *right*," he pointed out plainly. "Admittedly,

I'd never have put money on it, but she clearly saw something we didn't. Why aren't you happy?" He was genuinely baffled.

"What?? Are you not listening?"

"No, I *understand*," he stated. "Sounds totally like her, to be honest, but I don't see the issue. She wanted to show us something neither of us would have seen. And above all else, it means you're absolved of your guilt. She didn't mind the thought of us together." He took a step closer. Becca took a step aside.

"We were *played*. She *messed* with us. You were right about her being manipulative."

"She helped us along," he insisted.

Why was he not getting this? "She meddled!"

He shook his head, stunned. "I don't understand you, Becca," he said. "The thing you were worried about has gone. And now you're finding another reason to stop this. We could be happy."

Becca couldn't find the words.

"I don't care whether Ally had a hand in this," he said. "I don't care. I know how *I* feel. If it means we can be together, I'm *in*."

Becca's jaw dropped and she tried to find a way through her confusion.

"Tell me you don't feel something for me and I'll go."

She couldn't do that. "I do," she said, and she saw a hint of this afternoon's crossness melt from his face, "but I don't believe they're real feelings. For either of us."

"Feels real to *me*. Just be honest. If you don't want me, say it. But don't invent reasons and excuses to not let yourself be happy."

It felt like there was a critique in that and it sounded painfully close to something her mother had said. It made her bristle. "What? Why would I do that? Nobody does that."

"*You* do. You self-sabotage. You think you don't deserve happiness, so when you're faced with it, you run. Or you think it'll be taken away from you, so you demolish it rather than chance the hurt."

"I. Do. Not." She'd never heard anything so ridiculous.

"Then take the risk! Take *me*. Trust Ally on this." He wasn't begging, he wasn't pleading, it was a challenge.

It was the wrong thing to say. It took her head straight back to all the weeks of pulling Ally's plans apart and feeling humiliated. The anger rose back up in her.

"I'm *not* self-sabotaging. Not at all. Of course I deserve happiness. That's nonsense." This felt all too close to the bone. "But let's look at that, shall we?" she snapped. "You once said you only get True Love once in a lifetime. I want that with someone, I *deserve* that, so given you've already had it, it can't be you." The words were spilling from her mouth before she could quite check them.

That steely look was back on his face.

"Another blockade, Becca? You surprise me," he snarked. "I've learned over the years that hearts have vast capacity, and 'one true loves' are a myth."

"Ha! Got it right with Liv, did you?" she scoffed and a flicker of something crossed his face. He held his ground, though.

"I made a mistake," he said. "I thought I was moving on and in hindsight it was too soon, and perhaps it was too fast, but I learned from it, what I want from life, and again I moved forward. I *want* to love again, I want to share my life with someone. Unlike *some*, I won't let my past scupper my future happiness."

"Well, your mistake has repercussions," she flung back, ignoring his barb. It was a bratty response, but this wasn't going how she'd imagined. He was viewing her valid resentments as petty excuses.

"Is being apart really making you happier? It makes me flipping miserable."

She ignored the question. The last months hadn't been a bundle of laughs. "You've been swept up in another of Ally's plans, which is just your way, always happy to go along the easiest path."

He barked a bitter laugh at her.

"You are not, and have never been, the easy path. Bringing Ally back from the dead would be easier." He closed his eyes and calmed himself. "Becca, you and I have always been straight with each other. I am asking you to be with me. You deserve to be happy and I want to be part of that. We'll take it slow if that's what you need. But if you say I'm mistaken, that you don't want me, then I'll go, and I won't try you on it again."

Becca felt a drop in her stomach. This was so messed up. *Fucking Ally…*

Slowly, she stretched out her hand to him.

He looked at it, a twitch of hope at his mouth.

Then she unfurled her fingers, revealing the bottle.

"Take it," she said. "Ally's interfering has twisted our friendship to something fake."

"No," he said, his face setting to again, "Ally's faith in us couldn't overcome your self-doubts. This is on *you*. You've passed up one of the universe's opportunities."

"Maybe our planets weren't supposed to align," she said, disliking the notion she'd screwed up, or, for that matter, snubbed the universe.

He rolled his eyes crossly at her. "They *did* align. In Cannes. That was us. Nothing to do with Ally."

"Cannes was booze and holiday madness," she said, but the words felt like poison on her tongue. Cannes was one of her best memories.

He moved to say something, then chose not to bother. He took the bottle, disappointment clear on his face.

"You don't want it with the others?" he asked, tersely.

"I don't want *anything* of hers," she said angrily, watching him give up. Yes, it was at *her* behest, but it still hurt and it was all Ally's fault. "I'll be moving out of the flat, too," she suddenly added. "I need to move on." She waved at the ground. "We're done." She meant far more than just the ashes.

Sadness darkened his face. "She doesn't deserve this. She wanted something good for us."

"She *does* deserve this, because she was controlling and manipulative. Just took me a while to see it."

He shook his head, resigned. It nearly broke her. Turning to go, it looked like he was leaving without a goodbye.

But he swung back.

"Send me her voicemails. The ones you'd saved."

Becca's mouth pulled in.

"Um … no."

Irritation flashed in his eyes. "Why? You obviously don't

want them. I *do*. Let me have them." He thought she was playing games.

"I can't," she said slowly, feeling a shift in her righteous footing. "I deleted them."

His eyes narrowed. "What?"

Becca drew herself up tall. They'd been hers, and she had the right to do what she wanted with them.

"I'm angry with her and I've deleted them. I don't want to hear her voice again."

His face was turning very red. "But *I* do. You *knew*!"

"I was *angry*," she reiterated, but felt her high ground crumble.

"How could you do that? To *me*?" His hiss became a shout. "You knew I wanted to hear them. I thought they were safe, and you'd share them when we'd got through this … this bollocks." Her eyes widened. She'd never seen him like this. It was the explosion she'd hoped for earlier, but instead it was directed at her. He was still going. "And how could you do that to Ally? *Deleting* her. You are bloody vicious."

He turned this way and then that, so livid he couldn't decide where to go.

"You know, this is you all over," he raged. "So fucking melodramatic! Everything has to be about you. Ally tried to do something good, something to last beyond her, something to make the two people she cared most about happy, but oh no, in your crazy, self-obsessed head it's all to mess with you, to let you down, just like your parents let you down, and the Yank and the wankpuffin let you down, and presumably anyone you ever dare to let in will let you down. It's always all about you!" Becca stood stunned. "You've been doing it since she died, tallying Ally's death up as another way of life kicking you in the nuts. You know what that makes you?" He took a step closer and spelled it out. "The *worst* best friend ever."

He might as well have slapped her. She understood he was hurt, but the things he'd just said were despicable.

"How fucking dare you!" she stumbled out, then regained her indignation. "I was the best*est* friend. I've being doing her fucking tasks for years, celebrating her memory, and for what? So she could have a final laugh. How controlling can you bloody get? It's our *lives*. And how dare you suggest I've used her death for personal benefit. I do NOT always make things about me!" Jeez, that stung. She wasn't having it. "If we're looking at poor friends, look in a mirror, Charlie. You used her death as an excuse to go on a bloody holiday!"

"That was not a holiday! Fuck sake. I couldn't bear to be in my home. Every single thing in my life linked with Ally. Everything I touched, saw or heard brought me back to her being gone, and it was driving me mad. I *had* to get away."

"Wouldn't we all?" she interjected, sourly. It had always bugged her how he'd been able to do that.

"I am sorry I was *privileged* enough to be able to do that while you weren't, but it changes nothing. It *wasn't* a jolly. The first seven months, I was an absolute mess. I couldn't move without a coin to tell me in which direction. Have you any idea what that's like? And you were right, I went to the most dangerous places, because I didn't care whether I'd be alive the next morning. But finally, I started to rebuild myself, because I kept moving, because I *needed* to. I needed to look to the future to be happy again, and right now I'm sure it was the healthier way to go than sitting festering in a woe-is-me life, like you!"

"Don't you come at my life!" she said defensively. "I *couldn't* go running off like you. I grieved properly rather than running."

"Who are you? The grief police? You do not get to decide how other people grieve!" he scolded. "We're entitled to mourn as we need and to rebuild ourselves. Ally lives in my heart, but in my past. I haven't *forgotten* her. You hold it against me that I can move on, but I'm not apologising for it, not to you, not to anyone."

"And you did that pretty bloody quick, didn't you, the moving on." She was still reeling from him calling her the worst best friend. She was a bloody *beacon* of best friending. "You replaced her so fast, her ashes were probably still warm. Take a bow, Charlie, the worst fiancé prize goes to you." She was vaguely aware that clusters of students were stopping to watch them, but she didn't care.

"I already said that was a mistake. And I wasn't the worst fiancé. I loved Ally one hundred per cent and I still loved her even when I loved Liv. Because guess what, a heart makes room. It isn't a one-in-one-out deal – not that you'd know, as you've never let yourself love anyone, in case they let you down."

Dammit. How was he back onto this?

"You *didn't* love her one hundred per cent," she swerved. "You picked at her flaws. I *only* saw the good in her. *I* loved her one hundred per cent. I loved her more than you."

"I loved her *in spite* of her flaws. I was a realist about her, whereas you never saw her for who she really was. I loved the whole package, not just the shiny bits."

"The fact you could pick non-shiny bits in her makes you disloyal!"

"Bollocks. I was in love, not *blind*! And besides, you're now seeing her flaws and you're hating her for them, so who's the better friend now? You can't forgive her for what she's done. What a shit friend you really turned out to be. I might have moved on with my life, but at least I can remember Ally healthily and face my life with positivity rather than festering in your persistent needy aggrieved state. I don't think you loved her more than me. You'll never truly know love because your heart is so guarded and you're too cowardly to unlock it."

Becca felt like she'd been punched. And then kicked for good measure. It hurt drawing breath. Did he really feel that way about her?

The stabbing words had their way.

"And I'd be right, wouldn't I?" she said, icily. The fury and pain raced through her veins, making her shake. She wanted to hurt him back.

He looked confused.

"In what way?"

"I'd be right to protect my heart. I'm right in telling you no."

"And why's that?" he asked, not sure where she was going, but his anger not subsiding.

"Because you never stay, do you?" she said, pointedly. "You ran after the funeral—"

"I explained that—" he started, but she didn't stop.

"You never put up any fight for Liv, you just walked away—"

"Liv didn't want—"

"There's every chance you might have left Ally, given that you picked all these flaws in her."

"I said I loved her *in spite*—" He was getting angrier and angrier, but she couldn't stop.

"So really I have no assurance you'd stay with me, Charlie." It was crystal clear to her now. "As you seem convinced I'm so worried someone will let me down, why on earth would I ever risk my heart with *you*? That coin of yours, it's just a facade for how fickle you are. You'll literally turn on a dime. Women want a man who's determined and dependable, and that," she took a step closer, "will *never* be you. You'll always be a passive disappointment, and who wants that? Not me." Becca looked him plainly in the face, using all her years of drama training to hold it, in case he saw the hurt inside her.

She'd said more than enough, but she was beyond measure and reason now, so carried on. "You know, maybe Ally would have got bored of you, like Liv did." It was a nasty thing to say, but she couldn't stop herself. "Perhaps after a few years she'd have wanted a man who knew his own mind, who didn't need steering. She couldn't have thought too much of you, given she sent you in *my* direction, a woman you didn't like and didn't get on with. Who does that to the man she loves? Got to question whether she really loved you at all…"

She'd gone too far. She knew it, but she wanted to make him feel the same way she felt inside.

His face was thunderous. "I *know* Ally loved me. And I loved her, and until today I thought I loved *you*. You say I'm passive, but I might just not be the relentless egotist you are – in everyone's face, at any opportunity. And how would you even see it, being as self-absorbed as you are? And here's the thing, Becca: *I* see you. I properly see you, I have for years, and while people seeing you is what you crave, it's *you* that needs to take a long hard look at yourself. Ally would be devastated by this."

"I don't give a shit what she'd think." Her rage had her close to tears now.

"Liar." The fury in his eyes was almost unbearable, but she forced herself to hold his glare. He'd said awful things to her. He deserved the same.

"I don't give a fuck what you think either. Like I said, I don't want anything of hers. Including you."

They stared at each other, the vitriol crackling between them. He exhaled, bridling his anger, and she thought, hoped, it was the prelude to an unreserved retraction and apology.

"Fuck. You. Becca," he said, his voice no longer raised. And as he left her, Ally's bottle in his white-knuckled fist, Becca felt a dread that it could really be for the last time.

2017: Winter

Monday 13th November
North London

Charlie looked about the near-empty flat. The old dining table and four chairs, sofa and bar stools were still there, and the armchair and double bed in the bedroom, but everything else was gone. And yet the place was still full, with memories and small reminders of times he'd had here.

The keys lay on the breakfast bar; he'd picked them up from the doormat. Charlie scratched the back of his neck as he surveyed the place. She'd left it spotless, everything cleaned and polished. Altogether better than the last time he'd been there. That had been quite something else, and yet his memories of that weekend were some of the strongest, despite his having lived there too for years. Those memories, of him and Ally, were like faded photos in an old album now.

Somewhere in the last two years – and the lack of scuffing suggested recently – Becca had repainted the entire flat in a calm jasmine white. Everything looked bigger, fresher, new. In fact, it was only his memories and the remaining furniture that placed Ally there at all. Plus the four bottles left in the window, casting their near rainbow across the wooden floor.

A note lay on the table for him now, a simple polite thank you for giving her a beautiful home when she'd needed one. He didn't think he'd expected more. *Hoped* perhaps, but she was the most unbudgable woman he'd ever met, and he wasn't sure she even knew how to apologise, even if she was so inclined. Recalling their row still stung. They'd both said some vicious things. He recognised his own culpability there;

he had some apologies to make too. But she brought out the anger in him like no one else. Or rather he didn't *quell* it with her like he did with others. Why was that?

Looking about the kitchen, he remembered various occasions before Ally's diagnosis, where rows had been brewing, due to another revamp of the flat without consultation, undiscussed holidays being booked, or the big one where she'd blanket-bombed his CV to news stations without his knowledge. It was well meant, she'd insisted she was just trying to make it happen for him, but she'd always had a way of pushing, over-stepping and taking control when it wasn't asked for or even appropriate. He'd been so angry some of those times, but he'd always backed down, unwilling to disturb the peace. There were times, now Becca had sent his thoughts that way, when he wondered whether living like that with Ally would have been sustainable in the long run. Considering Ally was dead, he'd chosen to put those thoughts aside. What did it matter? What she'd done hadn't shocked him. The flat, his career, his and Becca's happiness, Ally would have seen it all as a project. Whether Becca would ever forgive her for it, who knew?

He reread the note. There was nothing there to say they were anything other than acquaintances now. Nearly two months had passed and all he'd heard from her was an official notice email for the flat, and a second, a few days ago, to confirm she'd left. No doubt she was still seething from their slanging match – it had taken him weeks to calm down and start unpicking it, but Becca bore her grudges as raw scars, so he wasn't holding his breath there. She'd yet to forgive him for that review, so there was a queue.

The doorbell rang. The letting agent stood on the doorstep.

"Mister Lister?" she asked, and then laughed, "That rhymes!"

"It does," he agreed amiably. "Call me Charlie, though."

"I'm Serena," she said, shaking his hand. "This is such a lovely street and the flat's kerb appeal is perfect." He had to give Becca her due there as well; she'd kept the small hedge and narrow flower bed running along the path beautifully. Therein lay the real thank you. It felt like she'd cleaned and groomed the place to express her gratitude not just to him, but to the house itself, for giving her sanctuary these last years.

"I'm sorry," he said, "I can't offer you a cup of coffee or anything." The flat was empty of anything like that.

"That's fine," she said with an easy laugh. "I'll need both hands for my note-taking." She looked about and then back to him.

"Smart move with the neutral colours. Is the flat part of your portfolio, Charlie?"

"Ha!" Being seen as a property mogul tickled him. This resulted from life's events, not an entrepreneurial plan. "No. I'm a TV producer." That normally impressed people, and Serena was no different. She asked whether she would have seen any of his programmes and he mentioned a couple of Brent's shows, then briefly raved about *Travels by Chance*. He didn't mention he was the presenter. He was still getting used to seeing his face on the screen.

As Serena moved around the room, ticking items on her iPad and taking pictures for her notes, he suspected it wasn't just the flat being assessed. Those were definitely side glances from Serena, and she kept flicking her long brown hair over her shoulder.

"Why are you letting it?" she asked. "It's lovely. Great light, good space, perfect for a young couple."

It was as much a fishing expedition as a professional question.

"My tenant left," he said, mildly.

She nodded, but hadn't got the answer she was looking for.

"And you don't want to live here yourself? It makes a nice bachelor pad or a pre-family home for two." Yep, definitely fishing. It both amused and pleased him. It didn't hurt to find he still had some appeal, even if it wasn't enough for Becca. His wounded heart welcomed the caress.

He *had* considered moving back. Liv's flat had been useful for working at Brent's, but that was irrelevant now. But moving into a space he'd once lived in with Ally and wouldn't have with Becca felt like a backward move. And Charlie didn't really do that. In all his coin-flipping years, the options had always taken him forwards. Scanning the blank-canvas walls, he considered it again and instinctively knew this would be someone else's fresh start.

He gave Serena a break. "No, I'm single. I lived here once, but it's a closed chapter now."

Though Serena busied herself checking the cupboards, he thought he could see a smile on her face as he watched her from the breakfast bar.

"Can you show me the rest?" she asked. He guided her through the bathroom and the bedroom, then out through its French doors to the courtyard. He'd deliberately set the meeting for noon, the light being best then. The sun was compliant today, the sky blue and the air crisp. The courtyard looked glorious. Becca had made this space her own. Neither he nor Ally had been gardeners, and he hadn't expected Becca to be, but here she was, still surprising him. The courtyard had only held a bench and a barbeque when he'd left. She'd bought pots to line the walls, with pretty plants now climbing the bricks: winter-blooming clematis and jasmines adorning the space with little white flowers. Everything was pruned perfectly, all the dead leaves cleared, and he imagined in summer the entire courtyard would be full of delicate scents and colours. He felt a pang in his chest that he'd spent no time out there with her, experiencing this side of her or this space with her, which was hers alone. This had been a labour of love.

"I bet it's gorgeous in summer," said Serena. He could only agree, but said little as he sought to push his thoughts of Becca aside.

He'd been so angry that day. The things she'd said, savage things he knew not to be true but aimed purely to hurt him. His seething had subsided over the weeks, but that was easier when you recognised what pushed other people's buttons, wasn't it? He still meant most of what he'd said, he just wasn't proud of the delivery. Charlie felt the shame creep up his neck.

"Perfect for drinks with close friends," Serena said, prodding him out of his thinking.

He nodded towards the door. "Take the time and any pics you need. I'll be back inside," he said, mustering a smile. It was far harder being out there, experiencing a side of Becca he'd never seen, than being back in any of the rooms. If he'd needed a firmer sign to not move back, then he'd just got it.

He retook his seat on the barstool and turned Becca's note in his hand.

Maybe it was time for him to move on, too. What if he was to leave his current place as well and find somewhere which was completely his, without memories of his pasts that hadn't worked out? The idea gave him a boost inside, telling him it was a sound decision. He *could* make decisions, he just had to get his arse in gear and act on them. Ideas were filling his head now; Shrin and Ollie had moved to Chiswick. There was a rowing club there too. Now he had his own company, he could work from anywhere. Maybe he'd look for somewhere out that way. Charlie felt his mood lifting with each new idea.

"This'll be easy to let," Serena said, breezing back into the room, interrupting his planning. She glanced at the paper he was turning in his hands. She was curious, but polite enough not to ask. She didn't mind giving him another once-over though, but that was fine. Again his ego enjoyed the attention.

"Serena? Are you busy this afternoon?" he asked. Her eyebrows rose, followed by the sides of her mouth. "I've got another property I'd like to show you. It might be better to sell than let, but I'd appreciate your opinion." She was positively beaming now. He suspected it wasn't purely down to potential business.

"Let's stop for a coffee on the way," she said, her eyes firmly on his.

Unless he was very much mistaken, he was being asked out. Charlie had always appreciated a confident woman.

Looking about, Charlie considered there were many ways to move on and Becca had made her position clear. She didn't want him, and his feelings weren't completely shatterproof. He might be one of life's optimists, but there was no "see you soon" in that note.

He didn't need to flip a coin on this.

He returned her smile. "Sounds good."

It only occurred to him as he turned the key in the door and followed her up the path away from the flat and its memories, that he'd spent most of his adult life moving on from something.

Wednesday 13th December
TV-UK Awards, The Hilton, Park Lane, London

Charlie never felt completely comfortable in a tux, but he took heart in women insisting all men looked better in one. Alison had passed him tickets to the TV-UK awards, a commissioners' perk she couldn't use due to a family event. Next year he was hoping they might nominate his programme for something like this. It would be enormously helpful for the business. Becca said he didn't like making decisions, and while that might still be true in some areas of his life, the company wasn't one of them. It was his, *completely* his, and if he fucked up it would be his funeral, and that was fine.

The auditorium was packed, with gown- and tux-laden industry professionals, from either side of the camera. Of course the stars were right down the front for the cameras and Charlie sat in possibly the furthest corner, at the back. He didn't mind. It had allowed him a little kip through the Best Reality and Best Soap categories.

He felt the body in the next seat lean in.

"You're practically snoring, Charlie."

Ollie was loving this. He'd tried to play it cool when Charlie had mentioned the tickets, but it hadn't lasted long. Shrinidhi was away on business again and Ollie was thrilled to tux-up and lad about with Charlie, like a pair of James Bonds. The look on his face as he gazed around the auditorium was like a toddler's in Hamleys. His eyes were sparkly with excitement and as they announced each award winner, he clapped and cheered wildly. Watching his best friend, Charlie admonished himself for being such a grouch. Ollie was absolutely doing this in the right spirit. If Charlie ever won something, he'd want someone clapping like that for him. He upped both his alertness and clapping game, which earned him a "Now you're getting it!" as Ollie stood up and whooped for the Best Daytime award.

The next category was Best Comedy where Becca's *Hot Mess* was nominated. She was up against some well-established competition, but her show had been going down a storm, hitting the mark with her target audience and garnering praise everywhere. Charlie crossed his fingers. Yes, so he wasn't just here for the networking, much as he'd told himself so.

"And the winner is … *Hot Mess!*" the host announced, and the room erupted with applause, most of which Charlie thought might have been coming from himself and Ollie.

He watched, rapt, as a small team of bodies bounced onto the stage, a scarlet figure leading them. He was too far away to get a proper view, but the side screen suddenly provided an enormous image of her face and mass of red curls. Wow. She looked both amazed and amazing.

"She won!!" Ollie hollered, cack-handedly trying to clap at the same time as filming it on his phone. "Shrin's going to blub when she sees this."

Charlie said nothing, keeping his eyes fixed on Becca at the microphone.

"I'd like to thank TV-UK for this." She took a proper look at her award. It was a brass old-style television attached to a wooden block and widely considered the ugliest gong in the industry. Nevertheless, Becca beheld it like a mother gazing at her firstborn, blind to its unattractiveness. "And to the team who've made my sad life into entertainment for you lot." The audience laughed and Becca's beaming rose a notch. Charlie knew she was loving this moment, not just the winning, but the glory of it. She'd always been a glory hound, and she wouldn't have slapped him for saying so. Watching her now filled him with an enormous sense of pride, but underpinned with a sadness he didn't want to name. He pushed it aside. Right now he only wanted to be over the moon for her.

A more serious look settled on her face. "An old and dear friend once hounded me to Make Things Happen. But I didn't quite know how. I would try, shaping my life around auditions, over-preparing or gatecrashing the ones I clearly wasn't right for, hoping I might highlight the error of their casting plans," the audience laughed again, plenty of them having been there, done that, "but I kept bashing my head against the wall, getting frustrated at not catching a break.

"I was trying to make things happen, but in a way which was very reliant on others. Later, another friend…" she paused, "a *dearer* friend, showed me how. He suggested I stop waiting for people to pick me. He told me to write my own roles, to decide my own future. So I'd like to thank him too." Charlie felt his face turn scarlet, touched that right now in all this hubbub he was in her thoughts. She'd referred to Ally as a friend, so that had to mean there was some climb-down. And she'd referred to him as even dearer than Ally. He couldn't think of a higher accolade from Becca.

The host said something to her. Her time was up. Charlie wondered whether she'd go willingly or need dragging from the stage. It could go either way. In the end, she behaved.

Holding her award higher for all to see, she leaned further in to the microphone and said, "This is for the capable girls out there who just can't catch a break. Listen to your dearest friends, even when you think they're wrong. At least listen, then face your fear, take the risk and make your own future. Thank you."

As the audience applauded and Ollie whistled, Charlie stood still, his mind tumbling over her words. She'd said to *take the risk*. He'd said those words to her. He couldn't help wondering, his heart pounding in his chest in time with the clapping, whether by any chance she might just have listened to him and had second thoughts about *them*?

Ollie propelled them towards the after-show bar, charging Charlie with hunting Becca down while he sorted the drinks.

The bar was full of younger celebs, the older ones, having been through this song and dance before, now heading for home and more comfortable shoes. Charlie was thankful for being tall, as he scoped the buzzing throng of heads, before bee-lining for the far corner where a shot of red stood out from the crowd.

Approaching, he had a couple of seconds to watch her. She was alone, her team huddled in chat behind her while she gazed at her award, her *T-Vuk* as it was unlovingly called, which she clutched in one hand, a glass of champagne in the other.

The gown, now he could see it, was long, single-strapped and shone. Standing tall and assured, she looked like a scarlet-sheathed statuette. If she'd found *that* in a charity shop, then he'd never take the piss again.

The juxtaposition of Hollywood sleek dress and big tumbling curls was *hot*. There was no other word for it.

Charlie found himself quite breathless, before pulling himself together to say, "I wasn't sure it was you without the bumbag," making her jump as he bumped her out of her reverie.

As she met his eye, his heart soared as her smile stretched to fill her face, like it once had not long ago in a narrow street in Cannes. His mind suddenly conjured all the images that night had brought with it, and there he was, breathing funny again. The smile faltered, just for a fraction, before she regained it. He hadn't been the only one who'd been hurt, then. She might give a fuck what he thought, after all.

"Charlie!" Was she surprised to see him? She'd mentioned him in the speech, but he was there by default. "Ollie said you were coming." It gave him confidence, but things felt very polite between them. They were in the acquaintance zone. It wasn't what he wanted. If nothing else, he wanted them back on friends grounds. Despite everything, he'd missed her. He wanted her back in his life.

She gave him a quick look up and down, the approval showing on her face. He *loved* this tux.

Spurred into action, he leaned in and gave her a chaste kiss to the cheek. "Congratulations, Becca. Well deserved."

"Isn't it bloody amazing?" she asked, totally and unequivocally stoked. "Paraphrasing Sally Fields, they *like* me!" she said, genuinely astounded. She placed the T-Vuk next to her on a little drinks shelf, giving it a tender little stroke as she did so, before smoothing down her gown. A small scarlet clutch bag lay next to it.

"A tenner says there's gummy bears in there," he said, giving it a nod. Small talk, the language of strangers and tentative reconciliations, seemed the best approach.

She cocked her head to one side, her lips pursed. "Dammit. How well you know me."

She was acting. He sensed it. She'd been prepared to see him, but her wary eyes said she was far less cocky about this than she was portraying. She was worried he'd hurt her again. It pulled at him, an ache that she thought he would, but a tiny delight that he *could*, that what he thought mattered to her.

"Other than ecstatic and the queen of bloody everything, how are you?" he asked. He needed to know whether he was reading too much into her speech.

"Good," she said with a nod, but like she was being interviewed. But then she seemed to remember this was him. "I moved into my nan's old house. Ugliest house on the street, but I'm renovating it."

"That's great," he said, wondering where she got the energy. The recommission was obviously providing the cash.

As if reading his thoughts, she leaned in and said conspiratorially, "I conned my mother into selling it to Harridan Productions. She's clueless it's me. She thought it was clever cutting out the estate agents' fees, but I got a bargain because she was too lazy to do the market research. I'll renovate, sell it, and sign off that part of my life with a tidy profit. Winner, right?"

The triumphant look on her face, definitely genuine now, was almost brighter than her glow at winning the T-Vuk.

"Winning on all levels, Becca." He couldn't think how to ask whether she was winning in her personal life too. "And the new series?" They were conversing like old friends who hadn't recently shredded each other, and not for the first time they pointedly ignored the elephant in the room.

"Filming starts on the third of Jan. Can't wait. We're shooting in Ally's church, by strange coincidence."

That *was* strange. His eyebrows agreed.

Her mouth pulled up to one side. "Or maybe that's how I wrote it. It was a while ago, before things got messed up." Her eyes dropped for a moment before she diverted the conversation. "What about you?" she asked. "Chance Productions. You passed up Tosser Productions, then?"

"After some deliberation, yes," he said. This was all stuff they should have been celebrating in the last year. "It's good. Show's in the can and planning the next one. They want to roll it out to different continents."

"That's brilliant, Charlie!" She genuinely appeared delighted for him. He was quite made up about it himself. His bank manager had been pretty chuffed too.

He glanced towards the bar. It was heaving, but Ollie would pitch up soon. There were things he needed to say, things to make better and speeches to address.

"Becca, look," he started, "about September."

She fixed her eyes on her award and he got the impression it was simply anything rather than him. He waited. Eventually her eyes found their way back to his.

"Is that why you're here?" she asked, quietly. Despite the gown and the hair and the winner's glow, she suddenly appeared vulnerable. "Was there more you had to throw at me?" She was doing her best to sound blasé about it.

"No," he said, gently. "I came because I wanted to be here when you won" – he'd never been in any doubt – "and like you at my wedding, I came in Ally's place, too." He saw her tense, but ploughed on. "She would have been so proud of you."

Becca didn't know which way to look, anywhere but at him again, so chose instead to neck the rest of her champagne. Her silence told him Ally was still off the table, but at least she hadn't walked away.

He touched her wrist. "I'm sorry, Becca," he said. "September was..." he didn't quite know how to describe it, "out of control? Both of us, I think." He suddenly wished he'd rehearsed something. "I said some things that weren't fair."

Now she looked at him directly, her eyes glistening.

"I don't understand how someone who insisted they loved me could say things like that to me." Her hurt was palpable.

"Who else is there to do it, Becs? Home truths. Straight talk. That's what we *do*. And you gave as good as you got."

Her face pinked up. Her eyes dipped to her glass, its emptiness dismaying her, and then they scrutinised the floor as she worked herself up to something. Finally she looked up at him.

"I wanted to hurt you back," she said, then took a deep, steadying breath and said, "I'm s—"

"Queeeeeeeeen Beccaaaaaaaaaa!" The booming made all the nearby conversations halt. Charlie's heart sagged as he watched Becca being swept up into one of Ollie's world-beating bear hugs. "Shrin's calling you tomorrow, when she's stopped her joyful sobbing." Ollie was bouncing up and down, and Becca, still clamped in his embrace, had no choice but to follow.

Charlie looked about and located Ollie's bottle of champagne and three glasses on the table behind them. He poured himself a glass and downed it.

Eventually Ollie released her, and she took a moment to regain her breath and smooth her gown. Ollie busied himself informing a group of nearby strangers that he'd known "*Hot Mess* Becca White" since uni. Charlie and Becca held each other's gaze, beaming broadly for Ollie's sake, but another conversation passing between them. Unless he'd been mistaken, she might have been about to apologise. He'd never heard an apology from her before.

"You were amazing up there," Ollie told her, grabbing the bottle and pouring her a glass.

"Thanks, Ols," she said, accepting the new one, and immediately taking a sip. Charlie wondered whether her throat was as dry as his.

"Charlie slept through the whole thing, actually snoring, until you were up." She gave Charlie the pleased look Ollie wanted. "It's definitely more exciting when it's your mate winning."

It was even more exciting when it was *more* than a mate winning. Ollie had no idea. Charlie was glad he hadn't told him about Cannes. This would have been all the more awkward.

Ollie pulled his camera out and took a selfie with Becca, sending it to Shrin, all within a matter of seconds. Everything seemed to have sped up, Charlie's intimate bubble of conversation with Becca long gone.

"Your turn, Charlie. You, Queen B and the gong." Ollie was wafting Charlie into frame and the two of them could only oblige. It felt strange. He sensed she felt the same. "Arm around her shoulders!" Ollie directed. "Smile." Charlie tried to make this feel totally natural and fine, only, aside from that chaste kiss, this was the closest he'd been to her – outside of his head – for months. The touch of her bare shoulder had memories sparking. Her hand came to rest on his side, her arm around his back. Even through his tux and shirt, his skin became hyper-alert.

He felt her lean into him, ever so slightly, but more than she needed to. Doing the same came naturally. She didn't pull away. Charlie felt his heart up its beat.

Ollie admired his work and waved the phone at them. "Great shot, kids." Charlie wanted it. Mural size. "Wait 'til Serena sees this, mate," Ollie gushed. "You and a celeb. Want me to airdrop it, so you can send it to her?"

Ahhhh shit.

Becca froze. Charlie felt his entire insides clench, as he now wished he'd told Ollie everything about Cannes – or not invited him.

Her hand dropped away and the warmth of her body at his side vanished.

The expression on Becca's face was shark-like. "Oooh, interesting. Who's Serena, Ollie?"

Ollie didn't know what he was walking into. She was an actor, after all, and all he saw was an old friend touting for gossip. He never stood a chance.

And so Charlie could only stand and watch, sweating and dismayed, as Ollie dished all the details about him having a new girlfriend, one he'd gained while letting the flat, and wasn't it fabulous he'd found someone again after Liv? Charlie eyed Ollie's bow tie, sizing it as a garrotte.

"Fabulous," Becca agreed, stepping fully aside, her hand reaching for her clutch. That show-time smile was back on her face, although to everyone else in the room it was simply the "English Julia Roberts" smile the nation now knew and loved. She checked her watch and gave them both an apologetic head tilt.

"Guys, I know this is very luvvie-knobby, but I've got to go. The team booked a dinner in case commiserations were required, so I have to…" She waved weakly towards the doors. Her eyes drifted to Charlie and then quickly away. Charlie glanced at her team behind her, all settled in for the duration. "So wonderful you've found someone new, Charlie," she said and gave his arm a feeble squeeze. He didn't even warrant a kiss now. "But then," she continued, her voice light, "you've always been good at moving on."

He felt his jaw set tight. Her eyes were steely. He'd lost this completely. He wasn't rolling over, though. "And you were always so good at pushing people away," he countered and saw her breath catch at the blow.

For once, she didn't retaliate.

He stood lamely and watched as Ollie got a full hug, after which she fumbled quickly for her T-Vuk, before heading into the throng of people and away.

So much for making things better.

Monday 25th December
Park Town, Oxford

"And it's so lovely to have Christmas with you, Esther," Serena said, clearly meaning every word.

Charlie had always thought it a winning scenario to have your girlfriend get on with your mother. You heard so many nightmare stories, and yet as Serena and Esther moved around the kitchen, he could tell they were birds of a feather. They agreed on everything, found the same things funny, spoke to him in the same way, and both spoke *about* him as if he couldn't hear them even though he was in the same room. Thinking about it as he sat at the table, the aftermath of the Christmas dinner in front of him, he recognised Ally and Esther had done the same, and Liv had too. Maybe it wasn't coincidence?

It dawned on Charlie, like a slap to the chops: he had a *type*, and that type, to his distress, was his mother. He physically shuddered. That couldn't be right, could it? Shunning the post-Christmas dinner film, he watched them more closely and wondered why this hadn't occurred to him before. Becca though? She was definitely unlike his mother. She didn't fuss around him, for starters. She didn't take the decisions off him like the others did. Quite the opposite. She didn't speak to him like he was a teen or a bewildered bloke who knew nothing of home-life logistics. He hadn't really minded when he was younger; he had been a bona fide teen once after all, and in his twenties, home-making had been Ally's domain and he'd not wanted to argue about paint or scatter cushions. Liv had already had her place so he'd just slotted his stuff into the spaces she'd given him, and after Liv, well, home had just become the place where his bed, telly and fridge lived. So perhaps they had a point, but why wasn't he finding it so funny?

"Christmas is all about family, isn't it," Serena went on, "and we knew it would be a great idea, didn't we, Charlie?" It wasn't really a question, as she immediately steered onto asking his mum about the secret of her Christmas cake (*all* the brandy, and then some). Serena was the one who'd suggested Christmas with his mother. They'd only been together four weeks then. How did you say, "It's too early for that," without hurting feelings? Besides, Christmas alone with his mother and Arthur, whom she insisted on referring to as her companion, like she was a dowager countess and had advertised for him in *The Lady*, would have been excruciating. Charlie recognised his motivations were shallow and selfish and denied himself a Quality Street as punishment.

It had been two long days, and he was looking forward to leaving that evening. He picked up the discarded napkins, cracker parts and paper crowns from the abandoned table, ditching them into the bin bag they'd handed him. He paused to launch the plastic cracker frog, which landed on Arthur's stomach as he snoozed on the settee in his food coma. Charlie had a chilling premonition of this being him in thirty years' time. *Feck.*

"And what's the New Year bringing you, Serena?" his mother asked.

"You know," Serena immediately said, "I think 2018 is going to be great."

"Go on," his mother encouraged as she washed the dishes and Serena dried. They'd shooed him out as if he were some wildebeest who would demolish the crockery.

"Well, work-wise, I'm up for a promotion. I just won the regional lettings awards again this year. That's a free holiday. I was thinking Charlie and I could go to Cancun."

"Lovely," gushed Esther.

"I know, right? Two weeks of cocktails around a pool. Bliss." Charlie was going to have to have words there. He'd done the sunlounger thing on his honeymoon, and he simply wasn't built for it.

"Then on a personal front," Serena went on, "the lease is up on my flat in April, so if things are still on with Charlie – and why wouldn't they be, because he's so lovely, Esther – you've done such a good job there – it stands to reason that I move in with him."

Charlie walked into the kitchen just as she dropped the last of her plans. She didn't seem remotely worried by his having overheard. Instead, she cupped his cheek as he passed. "Sounds good, doesn't it? I'd have dinner on the table for you every night and you wouldn't have trek to my place all the time." He gave her a wink which he thought was non-committal and she took as acceptance. Moving past her, getting a full waft of the perfume he'd bought her for Christmas, Charlie busied himself taking the rubbish out to the wheelie bin, taking his time despite the drizzle.

"Look at you, you're all wet, you wally," Serena laughed as he returned, and tried to dry his damp hair with the wet tea towel. "Your mum invited us to stay for another night," she added as he headed for the lounge. "I said we'd love to. That's fine, isn't it?" He wasn't sure she was asking. She certainly hadn't told his mother she'd ask him first. It irked him.

Charlie paused at the door. Both Serena and his mother were looking at him expectantly when he turned around. He'd told his mother he could only stay until that evening. Asking Serena, to have another shot at getting her way, was typical. But both women's faces were really hopeful, so he felt the guilt creeping up his chest.

"There, see," said Esther, delighted, "I knew it'd be fine. He just needed you to suggest it, Serena. Boys don't want to listen to their mothers!" She laughed and Serena joined her, but blew him a kiss.

"Actually," said Charlie, pushing the guilt right back down, "I can't. Like I'd told you Mum, I have rowing tomorrow at 6 a.m."

Serena's face dropped. "But it's Boxing Day."

"Yep. That's why it's the Boxing Day Row. Club tradition. Can't miss it."

"At 6 a.m.?" He didn't get the impression she'd be there to cheer him on.

"That's the tradition." *Tradition* might have been over-egging it, and it wasn't as formal an event as he was making it sound, but it *had* happened over the last years, Ollie seeing it as penance for the Christmas indulgence. It was his turn to bring the Bloody Marys they started with.

"Oh." Serena looked disgruntled, but then remembered she was standing next to her prospective mother-in-law and plastered an accepting look on her face. Esther had no qualms about looking disgruntled next to a prospective daughter-in-law, but Charlie was used to that. She'd pouted her way through his childhood, but it wasn't working today, and he amiably ignored the cooler shoulder he got until it was finally, and thankfully, time to push off.

"Try not to get my bag too wet," Serena called from the porch as he packed the car in the continuing rain.

"Shall I come and stand with an umbrella, Charlie?" His mother called from next to her. Yeah, he definitely didn't need that.

"No, it's fine," he responded, glancing at the two women. Standing there, they held a similar stance, overseeing his work, looking so similar bar the thirty years' difference; it gave him another chill. What was he doing? His mind went straight back to his having a type. Ducking his head back under the boot lid, rearranging the many tote bags they apparently needed for the two nights, Charlie tried to convince himself it wasn't true. He'd been with a wide range of women in his time, although most of them fleetingly, so he really didn't know most of their "types". But the ones he'd settled with, and he could see it now, were definitely a type.

Slamming the lid, he decided no, he definitely didn't go looking for someone like his mother. That would be weird, at the very least. He heard a voice in his head and he pushed it away, because he didn't particularly want to hear what Becca had to say, thank you. Only, he knew the voice was right; he wasn't picking a type, he was *defaulting* to type, and that was different because one was active and the other wasn't. He didn't need her to be there to tell him what it was, he could hear her calling him passive, in his head. He'd planned to move on, and he hadn't. He'd just reverted to form. Well, not anymore.

Walking back towards the house, Charlie felt the cogs click into place in his head. It was almost New Year. He needed a new start, one where he steered things, for better or worse, one where he felt he'd given things his best shot. This approach was proving successful in his work, so why couldn't it work in his personal life too?

"You'll come again soon?" Esther asked, clinging to Serena. "You're always welcome, even without Charlie. He only comes at Christmas and my birthday," she said, shooting him a disappointed look. He was used to those, so ignored it.

"Bye then, Mum," he said cheerily. "Say bye to Arthur." No one had bothered to wake him up.

As the car pulled onto the motorway, the Christmas rain hurling itself at the windscreen, Charlie couldn't think of a worse place to do what he was about to do. Conflict in a fast-moving, confined space at Christmas was the Venn diagram of hell, but there was nothing else for it.

"Here's the thing, Serena…"

2018

Wednesday 3rd January
St Raphael's Church, North London

F ive minutes earlier, St Raphael's had been milling with people: crew doing their jobs, extras trying not to fidget or appear starstruck. Now, with lunch break having been called, the place was deserted and silent. Becca sat in a pew, beholding it all, still amazed they were filming another series and *here* of all places. She hadn't imagined herself coming back to this church ever, not unless Valerie had died. But when she'd written the scene, she'd had this church in her mind's eye, and then she'd hunted down the location scout. He'd loved it – or else he'd known what was good for him – and so here they were, shooting the scene in Ally's church, and Becca faced it all again.

She'd worried she might fall apart walking in, but instead she'd experienced a sense of calm. And now, while her fellow actors were in the catering bus, she'd taken a moment to stay and remember. She could envisage the shaft of light through the stained glass casting down over Ally's coffin. It was the thing she remembered most about that day; she'd been thinking that if there was a God – and she'd had strong doubts – then She'd be in those glorious shafts, and Ally being bathed in that glory was absolutely right. The rest of the day was both a blur and a distant memory. The mardy vicar, the dodgy organ playing, Charlie getting upset. Thinking of him gave her a pang. His crumbling had almost broken her. Reading for him had been instinctive.

"Can I get you a tea, Miss White?" the young runner asked

her. She almost said yes, just because someone was deeming her too important to walk the few steps to the tea urn. *My*, how things had changed. People were sending *her* scripts now, which amazed her.

"No thanks, Cici, I'll only need a wee mid-scene." She was wearing a voluminous salmon-pink bridesmaid dress, due to her character moonlighting as a professional bridesmaid in this episode. It would be a nightmare in the narrow toilet cubicle. She wore a thick parka coat and Ugg boots too. The costume's satin ballet slippers on the freezing stone floor were for filming only. The runner grinned and scuttled off.

She carefully leaned her head to the side, so as not to disturb her flower crown, letting the pew end prop her up. She'd been in this position before, albeit minus the flower crown. That day she'd been grieving and wondering how she'd go on. Today, she was revelling in how far she'd come. Knowing she had employment for another spate of time and money coming in was an enormous help to life. It calmed that struggling-to-keep-her-head-above-water feeling she'd lived with for years.

The pew behind her creaked. She braced herself. Most likely it was an extra wanting a chat about career progression. But when the inevitable "Hi" came it was a voice she knew. A voice she regularly heard in her head.

"Charlie?" She spun in her seat. And there he was, right there, wrapped up in his peacoat and a teal-striped scarf. His dark hair was recently cut, his face filled with a smile. He looked like hot buttered toast to her Charlie-starved eyes.

"Happy New Year," he said, sitting relaxed in his pew, an open packet of gummy bears in his hand.

"Happy New Year to you too," she replied, conflicted on whether to gaze at his face or the bears. He popped one in his mouth.

He didn't offer her one. It felt like a dare. She refused to beg.

"How did you get in here?" There was security on the perimeter of the church grounds.

"You mean Bob?" he scoffed, casting a glance back towards the door. "You're a BBC2 comedy, not a Hollywood blockbuster. Got past him easily."

"He recognised you from the telly, right?" she said with a *tsk*. "Some people are shameless in using their fame."

"No, actually. I told him I was from your proctologist's office, coming to collect a sample." He held up a white paper carrier bag, which had presumably held the Haribo packet. "Told him you'd been known to shit yourself inside out, so best keep on top of things. He waved me straight in. He clearly knows who the star of the show is," he said, feigning awe.

Any normal person would have been mortified, but Becca had had her bum on Cannes billboards, so brushed it off. And as he said, the guy knew who the star was, so.

Meanwhile, she had no idea what Charlie and his gummy bears were doing there. This was as out of the blue as seeing him in Cannes, and that had taken the most unexpected of turns.

"Did you come for confession?" she asked. "It's not that kind of church."

"What makes you think I have anything to confess?" he asked. She liked the smirk on his face. She liked his face, full stop.

"You must have something to atone for. I know you of old," she pointed out.

"No more than you," he said, his eyebrow cocked. "And I did my atoning at the awards."

Yes, she supposed he had. Well, he'd apologised. Hearing him say he was sorry had been more healing than she'd imagined it would be. And she'd imagined it *a lot* after their fight.

He was watching her face, waiting for her to say something, or just enjoying seeing her, she wasn't sure, but he seemed calm enough.

"Aren't you supposed to be far away? Flipping coins around the Philippines or something?"

The pride was obvious in his eyes, but he shook his head. "I came to see you." He popped another bear in his mouth. Her stomach growled. Traitor...

The space between them was full of so many feelings. There was a familiarity that came with seeing old friends, but also a tentativeness of recent enemies, unsure which way this would go, neither of them wanting to spark things off.

She was on the back foot. He'd surprised her, and she didn't know why he was there, but she couldn't deny she was pleased to see him. Naturally, she schooled her face not to show it.

Her eyes drifted to the sweet packet.

"Oh, I'm sorry," he exclaimed, "would you like one?", as if it had never occurred to him they were her favourites.

He offered the packet. She studied the olive branch. If she accepted this now, bygones would need to be bygones.

Becca had always been weak in the face of Haribo. She

picked out a single bear and put it in her mouth. He watched all of it.

"So, um, what's going on, Charlie?"

It was a fair question. He might have texted to see if she wanted to go for a coffee or something. That would have given her the choice to say no… Oh. Right. She saw.

Becca scratched the pew with her thumbnail as she gazed at him. Young Charlie had been decent looking, but not her type. Too pretty. Young Charlie was a far blanker canvas, tinged only with a hint of shell-shock from his family life. He'd been perfect for Ally, who loved to fill in the blanks, whether by encouragement or her own design. Looking at him now, she could barely see *that* Charlie. This was a man, broader for having carried more of life's experience, good and bad; wiser, she was sure, given the lines on his face. Her eyes fell on his scar. It gave him the smallest hint of badass. She was ridiculously fond of it. It was something about him that was theirs, a feature in a story which only contained the two of them. The tips of her fingers twitched as she felt the urge to get up on her knees, reach over and touch it, but she remembered herself and slid them under her thighs.

"I've brought you a present." He rummaged in the bag and laid a wrapped gift, about the size of a box of chocolates, onto the top of her pew. She eyed it with suspicion and also a whopping great dollop of greed. She *loved* presents. She didn't touch it though, choosing instead to knot her fingers now for safety.

"My birthday's in April." This was January and she'd seen him only three weeks ago at the awards. Now *that* had been a hard night: travelling home in a cab, wanting to stop for comfort chips, but being unable to stand in a chippie queue in vintage Valentino and not being ballsy enough to ask the cabbie to queue for her. Moreover, she'd been fighting the urge to punch herself in the face for not having said what she'd wanted to say to Charlie, and simultaneously cheering herself that she hadn't, because now there was a Serena on the scene, and wouldn't that have been awful to have vommed her heart out, only for him to say, "Sorry love, too late"? (But nicer than that, as Charlie would always be nice about it.)

"Well then," Charlie said, unabashed. "I'm early." With his index finger he flicked the gift and she caught it as it dropped off the edge. "Happy early birthday," he said.

The paper was shredded within seconds to reveal a deep picture frame. Mounted within it was a square of bark. The weathered heart and three initials were clear on it.

"How?" she breathed, running a fingertip across the glass above the carvings.

"I went back and cut this bit off. I wanted us to have it. I'd like *you* to have it."

She looked up at him. He prompted her: "Forgive her, Becca."

Becca's gaze swung up towards the nave and the sun shafts. She'd done a lot of thinking since moving out of the flat and over Christmas. She'd been alone and renovating. Demolishing and rebuilding her nan's home had felt like examining and reconstructing her lifetime. Working by herself most of the time allowed for many hours of contemplation and reflection on certain things certain people might have shouted at her.

"She *hurt* me, Charlie," she whispered. "I felt she was messing with me."

"Ally was *always* meddling," Charlie said. "Generally they were good plans, which was part of what made her brilliant, but not always, and perhaps it's better to recognise it?" He ducked his head to catch her eyes.

"She's becoming more and more of a distant memory," Becca said.

"Same," he answered, "but let her just be a good, well-meaning one, then."

Becca was feeling quite teary looking at the framed bark.

"You were right about how I saw her," Becca said. "I needed her to be perfect. When you've grown up without love and someone picks you up, you want them to be the best of the best. You want their choice to see the good in you to be infallible. If I'd acknowledged she had flaws, I would have doubted her wisdom in loving me. Does that make sense?"

"It does." He offered her a gummy bear for solace.

"She was my best friend," Becca went on, taking two. "She would never have hurt me deliberately. I know that."

The past months sat between them, and they needed addressing.

"I'm sorry, Charlie, about the things I said. At the tree. They were ... out of control, as you said. I wasn't at my best and I said some awful things." She felt better for having said it, she'd wanted to at the awards, but she'd been interrupted and then thrown by her jealous feelings about Serena. She'd had plenty of time to think about *that* over Christmas, too.

Charlie suddenly slumped in his seat, as if he'd been shot.

"You all right?" she asked, alarmed, and looked around for help.

"It's a miracle!!" he shouted, throwing his arms up to the ceiling in praise, his voice reverberating around the church. "Becca-Jayne White has issued an apology."

"Shush!" she scolded, "I *can* apologise." She *must* have apologised before in the past. Not often, granted, but it must have happened. "You just haven't warranted any."

He placed his hand flat on his heart. "Thank you, BJ." His grin said he'd been waiting ages to call her that. Her arm jabbed out to punch him but he was just far enough away, and he ignored it. "You've no idea how much that means to me." She didn't think he was completely taking the piss.

"It's a new year," Becca said. "New Starts and all that. And here we are," she checked her watch, "five minutes in each other's company and we haven't had a fight, so how about we start afresh? We should be friends, Charlie." She meant it whole-heartedly, because she'd missed him. Even when she was angry with him, she missed him, and that was a mad situation to be in.

"That would be a good new start," he agreed. Something like amusement danced in his eyes, but she didn't quite get it. She still didn't know why he was there. "We said some horrific things to each other though, didn't we?"

They really had and recalling it made her face flush.

"You know, for someone who hides from the merest whiff of conflict, you don't have any issue fighting with *me*."

"Most conversations with you feel like a fight," he conceded. Then pointing a bear at her before eating it, added, "I think you get off on it."

382

"Maybe it's *you*? You rile me," she said, and leaning over the backrest, grabbed a bear from the packet. "*And* you don't give a shit whether you hurt my feelings."

"Ha! Right back at you." It was all very amiable.

"We fight all the time," she said, sadly.

"Not all the time."

"We bring out the worst in each other." It really did make her sad.

"We bring out the *truth* in each other." It didn't seem to make *him* sad.

"You're wrong."

"You're stubborn."

"Because I'm right."

"Rarely, and not this time, White," he said, clearly assured, and scoffed another bear to show he was unswayed on this.

Charlie tilted his head to the side.

"Some of it was out of control, but there *were* home truths in there. It's what we *do*, Becca, and I like it."

"Really?"

He leaned closer. "There's no one to serve up my faults like you do, and I can always choose to ignore them. You *can* be ignored, you know. But they make me think and address my actions, and they push me on."

"Is that what I should have been doing with your mean stuff?"

"I don't intend it to be mean. But who else is going to do that for you? The straight talk? Someone has to, and I'd rather it was me, because someone has to risk upsetting you, to get you to love your own skin."

She felt her eyes sting again. He did know her, unlike

anyone else. And maybe – just maybe – she couldn't think of anyone she'd rather be at her lowest ebbs with.

"I'm sorry about the voicemails, too," she said. "I'm sorry I didn't send them to you. You deserved to hear them."

He exhaled and looked her in the eyes. "Man, I was so angry about those. And the stupid thing was, I knew you'd regret it in time. It was such a self-hurting thing to do."

Yes, so, on reflection, she had cut off her nose to spite her face. It hadn't been one of her finest decisions, and yet...

"Having apologised for not sending them to you, I actually think letting them go was right. Maybe not quite as it played out, but I needed to move on. I don't need to hear her critiquing a *Homes Under the Hammer* makeover, nor what time she'll be in, in case I want to drop over. Leaving the flat was the same. I think if I truly want to work out who I am without her, I need to do it without the reminders. Like you did, I suppose. She'll always be in my heart, but I don't need her as a crutch anymore."

He nodded. "I get that. Once I'd calmed down, I wondered whether hearing her voice would've benefited me. It wouldn't have brought her back."

"Now *that* would be awkward, what with Selina," she quipped, before filtering it properly.

"Serena."

"Exactly."

Becca smiled, making sure it reached her eyes as she was professionally trained, but she didn't mean it. Briefly, she wondered whether Serena was like Ally and Liv, and then she wondered how honest he was being this time regarding his past.

"Where does Serena think you are today?"

He shrugged. "Not her business."

Becca raised a stern eyebrow at him. He raised his eyebrow right back. "I ended it."

Her eyes widened. Because it was over, or that *he'd* done it, she didn't know. "When?"

"Christmas."

Becca whistled through her teeth. "Harsh, Lister."

"Just *after* Christmas. We'd done presents," he clarified. "I'm not a monster."

"Well, um," she fumbled, somewhat thrown, "singledom clearly suits you." He did seem happy.

"Not really," he said. "It's boring."

"So why ditch her?" she asked. "Was she more boring than being single?" Becca hoped yes.

"She was a nice enough woman, but she wasn't what I want."

A sudden thought occurred to her. "Please don't be here to ask my advice on your love life. I'm no authority on such things and, as we both know, I'm prone to misjudgments and fuck-ups."

Charlie tilted his head, his expression inscrutable. She took a breath. "Look, I know I push people away. I see that now."

He settled back in the pew, one arm along its top.

"Perhaps, given the parenting I've had," she explained, "I don't feel happiness will come my way, and given the job I have, where being not-picked is common practice, who wouldn't go a bit doolally trying to pre-empt the hurt?"

"Sounds reasonable," he agreed and rewarded her with a gummy bear. "Recognising it has to be a start? I know I'm prone to seeking the easy life because of my childhood. What was it you called me? A passive sloth?"

Oh, God. That had been unfair.

"OK, I didn't mean the sloth bit. You've always been a hard worker."

He waved it away. "'S'fine. Women think sloths are adorable. It's the passive I'm working on. When you've been forced to pick between your parents as a kid, over and over, you instinctively learn to avoid conflict, to do as you're told, or find the least damaging path. Do you know what I mean?"

She did, in so far as it was the opposite to her experience. She'd forced conflict, refused to do as she was told and wreaked havoc simply to get some reaction from her parents, to signal they gave a crap. Which they hadn't.

"But here's the thing, Becs: once you spot it, you can choose whether that's who you want to be."

Well, that sounded reasonable too.

"I've thought about what you said," she said, "about being lovable. I see now there *are* people who love me. Ally did, Valerie does, you did, my audience does, so, in theory, I could allow both myself and someone else to."

"Stop."

She looked alarmed.

"This is the bit where I tell you why I'm here and where you listen, Becca," he said, popping a gummy bear into her mouth to keep it occupied, then put the packet aside and leaned forward, elbows on thighs, hands together, fingers threaded. "I've things to say, about a decision I've made, and then at the end you'll say, '*Best decision in the history of all decisions, Charlie, you are clearly a decision-making god.*'"

The laugh bubbled out of her. His impression of her was as ridiculous as the notion she would ever utter such words.

He shot her a strict look, and she composed herself. She was enjoying bossy Charlie.

"The thing with Serena was, she wasn't *you*." She just caught the bear from shooting down her throat. Her eyes bulging didn't deter him. "I *miss* you. I miss you making me laugh. I miss the joy in your face when you make me laugh. It makes me feel a million dollars, that it matters to you. I miss the sting in your tail, I miss when you're kind even though you don't want to be. You give me a tonne of crap and it challenges me, and it entertains me. You make me work hard for things which inevitably are the better things I would have missed otherwise. We bicker and we laugh together like no other couple I know. And when we argue, I don't feel like the sky's about to fall in on me. I don't want to hurt your feelings, Becs, not ever, but I always want to be honest with you. I can speak my mind with you, and perhaps early on that was because we were at loggerheads, but now, we've grown into being straight-talkers together, and it's something I value beyond measure.

"I miss you kicking my arse to do things and refusing to do them for me. Life *is* easier when others sort things, but bloody hell, it's stifling," he continued. "After our fight, I thought I should move myself on, rather than addressing things. Ally's death broke the man I thought I was, but after my initial free-fall I started thinking about the man she'd want me to be, and I tried to become him. When Liv crossed my path I thought I was already there, that it was my 'true self' who'd attracted her. Only, turns out I'd defaulted to old Charlie. Sometimes I'd know I wasn't being the true me. Because I'd always been able to be the true me with *you*. And with Serena, it took me a moment to spot I'd done it *again*. I saw what the future would look like in that guise and I didn't want it. I don't want to be a Charlie who has things decided for him. I like the Charlie I am in my business, who calls some shots and collaborates on others."

He drew himself up.

"The thing is Becca, *you're* the one who makes me *that* Charlie, the man I want to be. *You* do that. So, I'm here, to fight for you, for *us*, to say I've decided we should be together. Chances, *big chances*, are we'll be happy. These last years have shown us we *can* be. So, I choose you, Becca, I *pick* you, and you can kick and scream all you like, that's my decision."

It was remarkable. He was clear and concise and utterly determined. It stunned her.

"That thing about true love only happening once in a lifetime?" he added. "I think that's bollocks now. I'm not the same Charlie I was when I met Ally, or when I said that. Are you the same Becca you were back then?"

"Shit no," she said. "*That* Becca had a very poor taste in men. Present company excepted," she hastily added.

"Exactly. So I was thinking, that *this* Charlie's true love," he placed his hand on his chest, "would be very different from Ally – older, wiser, and kicks my butt to make my decisions. Some days I feel I've lived more than one lifetime, so, couldn't we be right for each other this time around?

"I'm not prepared to give you up. I *love* you, and *that's* the reason you should say, 'Charlie, you're so right, let's do this.'" He stopped, his speech ending, his chest rising and falling quickly from the rush of it all.

Becca, ever so slightly weepy in response to it all, could only say, "Why do you make me sound like Miss Piggy?" His impression was consistently rubbish.

He rolled his eyes and then she simply watched as he climbed over the pew onto hers and cupped her cheek.

"'*Let's do this,*' you'll say," he repeated, ditching the impression this time.

This was Charlie fighting. He knew what to say and how to say it (and he knew to bring her presents).

"You really think...?" They'd been enemies, then mates, then lovers, then enemies again, then apparently mates again, so perhaps...

He nodded slowly, his eyes fixed on hers. "Yes, I really think."

"And you will not be budged?"

"Never again." He was determined now and she'd known *for years* she could depend on him.

She'd thought about him so much in the last months. Every time anything good had happened, she'd wanted to share it with him. He was top of her phone favourites list, just so she could fool herself he was still her friend and cheering for her. Why, when he was here of his own accord, being direct and reasonable, considered and ever so slightly bossy, would she have any hesitation about this? This was wonderful.

But he took her pause of wonder as doubt.

Retrieving something from his pocket, he placed it in her hand.

"I don't need this anymore, but perhaps you do, so use it. Let the universe show you. It's completely on my side."

She raised an eyebrow at him. And then looked at the coin in her palm.

He wasn't cowed at all. He appeared ever so slightly smug. She liked it.

"Check it. Toss the coin. Heads, it's us; tails, we walk away. If you're disappointed by the outcome, there's your answer."

Feeling far warmer than the glacial church warranted, she considered the coin. The look he was giving her was decisive and confident and frankly, *cocky*. It suited him. It was a blend of Charlie when he'd lived next door, but with added purpose and self-determination.

She flipped it. Heads. It definitely wasn't disappointment she felt.

"Double check," he said, nodding back to the coin. He seemed utterly unworried, yet it could go very wrong.

"You really think you've got the universe on your side, don't you?"

"I have total confidence in my decision," he said. "I just need you to see it."

She tossed the coin again in defiance, almost wanting to prove him wrong and wipe the smugness off his face, but mentally crossing her fingers she wouldn't.

Heads. Charlie wasn't even looking at the coin, just at her face. He seemed so relaxed and content. The contentment appeared to be from simply being with her, and it was thrilling.

"Third time lucky," he said and gave her a wink. Cheeky bugger.

"We've already done best of three, why chance it?"

He leaned forward.

"Trust me," he whispered, and it did funny things to her in her knickers.

She tossed the coin and, befuddled by the knickers thing, missed catching it. It fell at his feet. She scrambled down to pick it up. Heads. She looked up, to find herself a centimetre from his face. His smile was infectious.

"Bloody hell, you *do* have the universe on your side," she breathed.

"And you're not disappointed?" he asked, pulling her up to him in the pew.

Her eyes flitted between his.

"Not one bit," she said and kissed him. Softly, as if testing the deal, scarcely believing this was really happening. He pulled her up onto his lap. She wrapped her arms around his neck, still clutching the coin as they kissed again and again, deeper and longer each time. He trailed some kisses down her neck and, remembering where there were, Becca opened an eye to check for the crew, but they were still alone. She gave the lucky coin a quick glance. Hurrah for heads! She turned it over in her fingers.

"Er, Charlie?"

"Becs?" he murmured into her skin, his hands holding her sides tight. She had sensations flooding back, reminding her of Cannes, but forced herself to park them for a second.

She pulled back to see his face, faintly aware her flower crown was askew. Then she held the coin between their eyes.

"The universe is on our side?"

His smile quirked. "Of course it is," he said with a slow nod. "Fate, right?"

"Of course it is," she agreed, turning it the other way. "Fixed, right?" There was no tails.

He didn't appear remotely contrite.

"You already chose," she said.

"I did. I decided. *Us* was the only acceptable outcome."

She leaned her forehead against his. "Best decision in the history of *all* decisions, Charlie," she whispered.

"... *and* I am clearly a decision-making god..." he prompted, but "Mmhmm," was all she'd commit to, as she kissed his scar and enjoyed the growl it elicited.

"Heads, I make the best decisions ever," he tried again.

"Heads, we've created a decision-making monster," she countered with a laugh.

"Heads, I'm the best lover you've ever had." He pulled her in even closer and she wondered whether there was still any lunchtime left to spend in her trailer.

"Heads, you're the least humble man I know."

"Heads, you are the most beautiful, stubborn, beguiling woman *I* know." Hmm, yes, she'd take that.

"Heads, your reviews are excellent now, but used to be poor."

"Jesus, let it go." He looked towards the altar and its cross, "Sorry." Returning to her, he gave her her own trademark bug-eye. "Heads, it was an awful play."

"Heads, I was the best thing in it."

"That we can agree on. Heads, you should kiss me now."

Becca sighed with contentment. "Heads, I love you," she said and did just that.

2020

Early March
North London

Valerie watched David from the lounge with a smile. He was a lovely man. He was funny, kind and energetic. He made her happy again. And right now he was outside planting a rose for her in the centre of the garden.

She watched as he hefted the coclibee with its peachy flowers into the hole he'd dug, appreciating his broad back and bare arms. She appreciated the rest of him too. *No*, she wasn't too old for smutty thoughts. He'd recently moved in and it was wonderful to have someone around the house with her again. She hadn't realised how much she'd missed it: the low noise of another person pottering, the sound of another breath at the breakfast table, the warmth of her hand in another as they watched television in the evenings.

She ran her fingers over the top of Ally's urn as she watched him work. They needed to get this done before Charlie and Becca arrived. She lifted the lid just enough to peek at the ashes. It was still full to the brim. Her lovely Ally. Ten years had passed and Valerie still thought of her every day. She'd been such a joy. Always smiling. Always fixing things, though not always orthodox in her methods. Valerie *knew* that. Her little girl had taken charge of things very early on. Like mother, like daughter. Valerie didn't always follow the rules either. But Ally had been right with Charlie and Becca, hadn't she? She'd known there was a chance for those two. A chance in a million, many would have said – Valerie chuckled at that – but like Ally said, there was *always* that one.

She almost missed the tasks, to hear how it had gone, to smile at her end of the phone connection as Becca ranted or Charlie grumped. She didn't miss making up the ash bottles; cutting into her hoover bag, sifting the dust then mixing it with bone-meal from the potting shed and funnelling it all into the bottle which would invariably topple, causing a mess. Letting Ally go had been unbearable back then, but time had passed and now it felt right. Lowering the lid again, Valerie lifted the urn down and carried it to the open French doors. David sent her a cheeky wink. She'd scatter the ashes properly now, under the rose, so Ally could bask in the sun.

Acknowledgments

Sooo, lockdown is an interesting time to write a book! That low level hum of worry that sits constantly at your ear. Having your extended family in other countries, so you can't just pop in to check on them or see them at milestone events. It isn't always easy to find the funny in things, when the world doesn't seem a very funny place. So it is safe to say the process was long and often frustrating.

However, I had so many lovely people cheering me on (or kicking my lockdown-enlarged bottom, in some cases) all of whom I'd like to thank;

First and foremost is Charlotte Ledger for the wonderful first spark for the story and for reading it at its worst, telling me when scenes were 'too gross for romance', and yet still consistently loving it. You are The Loveliest of Loveliests and the best editor a girl could wish for.

Lydia Mason for the excellent and game-changing insights. Hope you like the grenade.

Lucy Bennett for all your cover work and patiently putting up with my 'little tweak' suggestions.

The wider OMC team for your work: Bethan, Emma, Sara, Zoe, Emily, Lana, and everyone on the credits roll. Please do read the credits roll – a book takes so many brilliant hands to arrive in yours.

My early readers, Suki, Yotti, Signe, Federica, Ailsa, for your encouraging feedbacks.

The cheersquads: The Book Campers, The Wordracers, the BXP Team, Chick Lit and Prosecco & ChickLitChatHQ FB groups, and my gorgeous Pilates coven.

Linda Barnes for your soothing words and amazing skills, which helped my head to settle and the words to form again.

Mark Stay and Mark Desvaux of The Bestseller Experiment for, well, so many things: Your podcast for a start and the wisdom, knowledge, and joy it brings; for the BXP Team community; And during the writing of this book, your 200 word Challenge, which got my Arse In The Chair™, fingers on the keys, and eventually the words on the page. Any aspiring authors out there should make this podcast part of your writing life.

Covid-19 and its various lockdowns made research tricky. I had planned to walk Snowdon (I have been up, but as a train-passenger person) but lockdown said 'No'. Instead, thank you to Terry Dolman and Huw Roberts for advice on the path and thanks to James McKinven and Jules for their 2015 YouTube walk up the Rydd-Ddu path, which I followed intently with my notepad.

Thank you, The Internet, in general, especially Wikipedia.

Thanks to Krister and Ian for their Physics and Statistics

help respectively. Obviously my job is to make stuff up, but I like it to have some sense behind it :) There are a couple places I have taken some Artistic License, but I'm not telling you where.

Also a big Twitter thank you to David Blanchflower, Sara Smith, and Daniel Aubrey for coming to my emergency aid on constellations.

Thank you, lovely readers, for the reading.

Thanks even more to those of you who now leave me a review, because they help SO much. Even a very short one. Even if you didn't buy the book yourself or borrowed it at the library.

(Additional thanks to those who follow me on BookBub, and the socials. And have I mentioned I have a newsletter? Sign up at pernillehughes.com and get a free short story.)

Thank you and so much love to my kids for their patience and food-foraging skills.

Thank you and all the kisses to Ian.

Don't miss *Punch-Drunk Love*, another enchanting romantic novel by Pernille Hughes...

Tiffanie Trent is not having a great week. Gavin, her boyfriend, has dumped her unceremoniously on their tenth anniversary, leaving her heartbroken and homeless. Frank Black, the owner of Blackie's boxing gym and where Tiff has been book-keeper for the last decade, has dropped dead. He's not having a great week either.

And if that wasn't enough, Mike 'The Assassin' Fellner, boxer of international fame and Tiff's first love, is back in town and more gorgeous than ever. Tiff can't seem to go anywhere without bumping into his biceps.

When she discovers Blackie has left her the gym, Tiff, with her saggy trackies and supermarket trainers, is certain she'll fail. Can Tiff step up and roll with the punches, or will she be down and out at the first round?

You will also love *Probably the Best Kiss in the World,* a fabulously feel-good romcom that will make you laugh till you cry…

Jen Attison likes her life Just So.
But being fished out of a canal in Copenhagen by her knickers is definitely NOT on her to do list.

From cinnamon swirls to a spontaneous night of laughter and fireworks, Jen's city break with the girls takes a turn for the unexpected because of her gorgeous mystery rescuer.

Back home, Jen faces a choice. A surprise proposal from her boyfriend – 'boring' Robert has offered Jen the safety net she always thought she wanted.

But with the memories of her Danish adventure proving hard to forget, maybe it's time for Jen to stop listening to her head and start following her heart…

YOUR NUMBER ONE STOP

ONE MORE CHAPTER

FOR PAGETURNING BOOKS

The author and One More Chapter would like to thank everyone who contributed to the publication of this story...

Analytics
Emma Harvey
Connor Hayes
Maria Osa

Audio
Charlotte Brown

Contracts
Olivia Bignold-Jordan
Florence Shepherd

Design
Lucy Bennett
Fiona Greenway
Holly Macdonald
Liane Payne
Dean Russell
Caroline Young

Digital Sales
Hannah Lismore
Fliss Porter
Georgina Ugen
Kelly Webster

Editorial
Simon Fox
Charlotte Ledger
Lydia Mason
Bethan Morgan
Jennie Rothwell
Tony Russell
Kimberley Young

Harper360
Emily Gerbner
Jean Marie Kelly
Juliette Pasquini
emma sullivan

HarperCollins Canada
Peter Borcsok

International Sales
Hannah Avery
Alice Gomer
Phillipa Walker

Marketing & Publicity
Emma Petfield
Sara Roberts
Helena Towers

Operations
Melissa Okusanya
Hannah Stamp

Production
Denis Manson
Simon Moore
Sophie Waeland

Rights
Lana Beckwith
Samuel Birkett
Aliona Ladus
Agnes Rigou
Zoe Shine

Aisling Smyth
Emily Yolland

The HarperCollins Distribution Team

The HarperCollins Finance & Royalties Team

The HarperCollins Legal Team

The HarperCollins Technology Team

Trade Marketing
Ben Hurd

UK Sales
Yazmeen Akhtar
Laura Carpenter
Isabel Coburn
Jay Cochrane
Sarah Munro
Gemma Rayner
Erin White
Leah Woods

And every other essential link in the chain from delivery drivers to booksellers to librarians and beyond!

ONE MORE CHAPTER

One More Chapter is an
award-winning global
division of HarperCollins.

Subscribe to our newsletter to get our
latest eBook deals and stay up to date
with all our new releases!

signup.harpercollins.co.uk/
join/signup-omc

Meet the team at
www.onemorechapter.com

Follow us!
@OneMoreChapter_
@OneMoreChapter
@onemorechapterhc

Do you write unputdownable fiction?
We love to hear from new voices.
Find out how to submit your novel at
www.onemorechapter.com/submissions